HIGH HEATHERTON

JUDITH THOMSON

Copyright © 2016 Judith Thomson

The moral right of the author has been asserted.

Matador
9 Priory Business Park,
Wistow Road, Kibworth Beauchamp,
Leicestershire. LE8 0RX
Tel: 0116 279 2299
Email: books@troubador.co.uk
Web: www.troubador.co.uk/matador
Twitter: @matadorbooks

ISBN 978 1785891 281

British Library Cataloguing in Publication Data.
A catalogue record for this book is available from the British Library.

Printed and bound in the UK by TJ International, Padstow, Cornwall
Typeset in 11pt Bembo by Troubador Publishing Ltd, Leicester, UK

Matador is an imprint of Troubador Publishing Ltd

MIX
Paper from
responsible sources
FSC
www.fsc.org   FSC® C013056

1681

1801

PROLOGUE

❦

The Pont Neuf was teeming with people, as usual. An alchemist was selling his wares, but Thomas' attention was drawn not to him, or to the juggler performing his act, but to a press of people clamouring excitedly around the mounted statue of King Louis' grandfather, Henri 1V.

He pushed his way through, staying well clear of the policeman who always stood beneath the statue. Sixteen year old Thomas had not always been an honest citizen and he could never get close to an officer of the law without experiencing the familiar cold knot in his stomach. Today, however, even the policeman looked amiable and when Thomas managed to hear the news which was on everyone's lips he was as happy as all the rest. Probably happier.

He took off across the bridge at a run, dodging the crowds, towards the Tour Saint Jacques. Thomas was a Londoner by birth, but he had come to know Paris almost as well as his home city and in a short while he had reached the fashionable Marais quarter and the house of his master, Lord Philip Devalle, an Englishman away serving in the French army.

Without even pausing to catch his breath, he darted up the steps and burst through the front door.

"Strasbourg has been taken, my Lady!"

Philip's wife, Theresa, rushed downstairs to meet him, closely followed by her maid, Bet. "Are you certain?"

"Of course. I heard it on the Pont Neuf," Thomas said matter-of-factly.

That was good enough for Theresa, who knew that he usually got to hear the latest gossip on the streets before ever any formal announcements were made at Court.

Bet had her own reasons to celebrate Thomas' news. Not only would her master be returning home but his Welsh servant, Morgan, would be with him, and Morgan was the man she hoped to marry, if he ever got around to asking her!

"Were there many casualties?" Bet asked Thomas worriedly.

"Not at all," Thomas reassured her. "The word is that they surrendered without a fight!"

Philip glanced round at the crowd, who were cheering as King Louis was driven through Strasbourg in a coach drawn by eight grey horses.

"If the citizens were this keen to be French they only had to say so," he remarked to Morgan, over the sound of the bells that rang from every steeple. "We need never have come at all!"

Philip's troop was lining the route and, as their Colonel, he was with them, riding Ferrion, his great black stallion. He was a handsome man, tall and blonde with bright blue eyes, and he cut an elegant figure in his uniform.

Morgan, by contrast, was small and stocky, with a swarthy complexion and wild black hair, which only partly concealed the fact that he was missing half of his right ear. He looked unimpressed, both with the sight of the royal family parading themselves triumphantly before their new subjects and the salvos that were being fired from nearly three hundred cannon to greet them.

"You'd think, from all this fuss, that we'd won the place in a battle," he muttered.

Philip laughed at that. "Are you complaining? It was the easiest occupation we've ever had!"

That was true. The French army, some twenty thousand strong, had blockaded the city and it had yielded without a shot being fired. Their victory had been so easy, in fact, and the city so strategically important to France, that Philip suspected there had been some bribery involved, but he did not much care. What he did care about was that, this year, he was likely to be back in Paris with Theresa before the winter set in.

The golden coach drew level with them and Philip could see Louis and the Queen inside, together with the Dauphin and Dauphine and Louis' flamboyant brother, Monsieur, with his wife. Monsieur caught sight of him and blew him a kiss.

Louis acknowledged him too. It was only a brief nod before the procession passed by, but from the King of France it was significant and Philip was pleased. He had great respect for Louis, more than he had for his own monarch, King Charles.

The city certainly seemed to be welcoming its new ruler but, even so, Philip was watchful. In England, during the time he been involved with the Earl of Shaftesbury and the Whig party, he had learned a great deal about the behaviour of crowds. Above all he had learned never to underestimate the power of what the Whigs called the 'Mobile Vulgus', for he had seen them rioting and looting when Shaftesbury's agents had roused them against the Papists. The memories of that time were not good ones for him. He had been called upon to do things of which he was not particularly proud but he had needed money badly then and Shaftesbury had been generous.

Three years ago he had left the Earl to return to the French army and the life suited him well enough, at least until such time as he could claim what he regarded as his rightful inheritance.

Morgan was watching the crowd too, but he cared little for the safety of the King of France. Morgan's concern was solely for his master, as always. They had met in Holland some years before, during a real campaign, fighting for France against the Dutch troops led by William of Orange. Morgan had saved Philip's life upon the battlefield when he had been unhorsed and was in danger of being trampled to death. The Welshman had been by Philip's side ever since and he had become more of a friend than a servant to him.

The coach passed by without incident and two young girls ran up to Philip, each clutching a flower. Giggling at their boldness, they held the rather wilted blooms up to him and he accepted their simple gifts with a smile, doffing his plumed hat to them.

He followed with his men behind the coach and some of the citizens cheered for him too and shouted out his name, for he had become well known to them during the three weeks since the occupation.

Philip liked that, but he might not have liked it quite so much if he could have looked inside the royal coach and seen the King's expression when he heard the sound.

Louis did not take kindly to sharing his moment of glory with anyone. Even his own brother, Monsieur, had reason to know that for, unlikely as it seemed to look at him now, he too had been a military hero once. He had won a great victory for France five years before at the Battle of Cassel, when his troops had defeated the Dutch forces of William of Orange, and he had been acclaimed by the people as a hero. Monsieur had never been given another command.

The following morning Louis attended a Te Deum in Strasbourg Cathedral. It had been a Protestant place of worship before but all that was to change now, just as Strasbourg's status as a free city had changed. Four days later, leaving Vauban and his engineers behind to fortify his new city, Louis left, taking the rest of the army with him.

Philip and Morgan were going home.

ONE

∽

The Duke of Monmouth and his friend, Giles Fairfield, rode into the courtyard of Lord Shaftesbury's London home, in Aldersgate Street.

Monmouth was in fine spirits. "Did you see how many called out to me in the streets today, Giles?"

Giles nodded but made no reply. It was one thing, he felt, for the people to raise their hats and their voices as the bastard son of King Charles rode by but quite another to expect them to raise their swords and pistols to put that bastard son on the throne after his father's death.

Monmouth was obviously too elated at the warmth of the Londoners' reception to notice Giles' silence. "Why do you suppose Lord Shaftesbury sent for me?" he said, taking Giles' arm as they went into the house.

"Perhaps he has a suggestion to put to you."

"Dear Shaftesbury, does he not work tirelessly to advance my interests?"

"Tirelessly," Giles said, for so he did, although only a person as naïve as Monmouth would have believed that Shaftesbury acted with no thought for his own interests too! "Don't let him talk you into doing anything rash."

Giles knew Monmouth to be a fine commander, for he had served under the Duke when they had fought against the Covenanters at Bothwell Brig, but Giles also knew that Monmouth was no match for the wily Shaftesbury.

Monmouth just laughed. He was far too easily persuaded of his own importance and had always been flattered by Shaftesbury's attentions. He believed the Earl to be infallible and, at times, believed himself to be so too. Both were dangerous mistakes to make, as Giles had sense enough to realise.

Shaftesbury greeted Monmouth warmly. He was even cordial to Giles on this occasion, and Giles wondered why. He knew that Shaftesbury had never really liked him, even though his sister, Theresa, had once been the Earl's mistress.

"Affairs go well for us, I trust," Monmouth said.

"Not as well as I might have hoped." Even for such a seasoned campaigner as Shaftesbury the prospects were hardly encouraging. During the last few years he had seen the Whig parliament he had worked so hard to have elected dismissed by King Charles and now there was talk that the King might allow his Catholic brother, the Duke of York, to return from his exile in Scotland, even though folk feared the prospect of having a Catholic as the successor to the throne. It was a fear which Shaftesbury had always exploited, but he could not do it alone, especially now that he was suffering so much from the stomach abscess that had plagued him for years. "I will be frank, your Grace, we are no longer heroes to the people or damnation to our enemies."

"But we discovered a Catholic plot against my father's life," Monmouth pointed out, aggrieved.

Shaftesbury shrugged his thin shoulders. "The Popish Plot is all forgotten now."

"Then discover another," Monmouth said, with a simplicity which made Giles roll up his eyes to heaven.

Giles knew that, to the Duke, the indomitable Shaftesbury seemed like a Court magician. The instant that one trick had been performed another would appear out of the secret cabinet he kept inside his clever head.

"Have you heard from Theresa lately, Giles?" Shaftesbury asked him.

He appeared to be changing the subject, but Giles knew better. Theresa was married to Philip Devalle and he could guess at what might be coming next. "She wrote to tell me that Philip has returned to Paris."

"I thought perhaps you might like to travel to France to visit him before he goes off upon his next campaign."

"To congratulate him on France's acquisition of Strasbourg?" Giles said blandly.

Shaftesbury glared at him. "Never mind that," he snapped. "What I want you to do is to persuade him to come back to England and work for me again."

"You parted on bad terms," Giles reminded him, although he supposed Shaftesbury would have conveniently forgotten that. He knew that Philip suspected the Earl of trying to have him killed, although he would never be able to prove it.

Shaftesbury ignored Giles' remark entirely. "If Monmouth's cause is ever to prosper again we need a man who can persuade others where their destiny lies. A man with courage and a silver tongue, and the ability to make men follow him through God knows what. We need Philip Devalle."

Monmouth cried out delightedly at that.

Unlike Monmouth, Giles was not responsive to every suggestion the Earl made. "What inducement could you possibly hope to offer him that would persuade him to abandon his army career, my Lord?"

Shaftesbury smiled craftily. "I shall offer him the one thing he wants most in this world. I shall offer him High Heatherton."

High Heatherton was Philip's family estate but his older brother, who had inherited it, was suffering from the malady of the mind which had affected several generations of the Devalles. Before he left for France Philip had committed his brother, Henry, to Bedlam and lodged his own claim to the property with the courts, but these things took time and Giles guessed his brother-in-law would be growing impatient by now.

3

"Can you get it for him?" Giles wondered.

"Of course I can. I still have influence you know," Shaftesbury said irritably. "Tell him that if he agrees to come back and assist us then I pledge he will be the master of High Heatherton within six months."

"But will he risk everything he has achieved in France for my sake?" Monmouth said anxiously.

"Philip has always been a gambler," Shaftesbury reminded him, "and he is your friend, don't forget."

Philip and Monmouth had been friends since Philip first came to Court, when they were both thirteen years of age, but Giles very much doubted that his shrewd brother-in-law would consider returning just for Monmouth.

Monmouth, on the other hand, obviously did not doubt for a moment that he would. "Please go to Paris, Giles," he begged.

"Give my regards to your sister when you see her," Shaftesbury added.

Giles wondered if this was another part of his plan. Shaftesbury had been their neighbour in Dorset and he had taken Theresa to London with him and found her a place at Court. It had actually been Shaftesbury who had arranged for Theresa to wed Philip in order that he might provide her with a title, but, against all odds, they had fallen in love and she had left him and gone to France with her husband. The Earl had predicted the marriage would not last and he would soon get her back, but he had been wrong.

Shaftesbury could not order him to go, and Monmouth would never have done so, but Giles had no income of his own and he existed mainly upon the goodwill of his friends and whatever he could wring from his indulgent female admirers. There were quite a few of those, for Giles had a pleasing face and women found him attractive, with his auburn hair and pale skin, but even with the tokens of love that he occasionally received from them he was in no position to risk displeasing either of the men in front of him. He looked at Monmouth, who was watching him expectantly, and at Shaftesbury, cold and calculating, a desperate man prepared to go to any lengths to obtain the power he craved.

Giles sighed. He felt instinctively that if he went to France he would be setting in motion matters that were best left alone but he knew what he had to do

"Very well," he said heavily. "I will go to Paris."

TWO

❧

"You're looking prosperous," Philip told Giles, noting the jewelled rings upon his fingers and the gold bracelet on his wrist.

"Tokens of appreciation. If women find pleasure in rewarding me for the happiness I give them why should I refuse?" Giles said. "There's not one of them who cannot well afford it."

"Really, Giles!" Theresa looked a little shocked, but Philip only laughed. "It's good to know you're still the same mercenary little bastard you always were!"

He had been Giles' patron once and had introduced him at Court, instructing him in all the skills and refinements necessary to one who hoped to make his way in society. Giles was a credit to him, for he had learned his lessons well. He had a self-assuredness that belied his twenty years and, from his manners and his graceful bearing, no-one would have guessed that he was only the son of a lowly Dorset squire.

Theresa was delighted to see her brother again, even if she did think that his moral code left something to be desired. They had always been good friends when they were children, although they were very different. Theresa, older by two years had always been the idealistic one, quick-tempered and impulsive, and quite unable to hide her feelings about anything or anyone. Giles was quieter and more calculating. He rarely allowed his anger to show and usually got his own way because he knew exactly how to manipulate people. Philip knew this only too well but, even so, he had always enjoyed his brother-in-law's company. Giles could be the best of companions when he chose, and he had been able to deny him very little when Giles had been his protégé. It did not surprise Philip in the least that women fussed around him and wanted to buy him presents, or that he accepted them!

Physically Giles and Theresa were similar. Theresa was slight of build, like her brother, although her hair was a more vivid shade of red than his, and they both had the same grey, slightly slanting eyes, but, whilst Giles' looked seriously on the world, Theresa's sparkled with good humour. She was not truly a beauty and her figure was far too slender to be fashionable, but Philip had come to love her very much in the four years they had been together and he knew she loved him too, not for his looks or for his title but for himself. That he had found a rare thing, having lived for most of his life at Court surrounded by beautiful, ambitious women.

"So why are you here?" Philip wondered when Theresa had left them alone.

"Does there have to be a reason?"

"Yes, of course there does." With Giles there was always a reason. "I can't believe you have torn yourself away from your admirers simply for the pleasure of seeing your sister and me again?"

"Not entirely," Giles confessed. "Shaftesbury asked me to come. He wants you back."

"Does he indeed!" Philip was not unduly surprised. He was up to date with all the news from England and it did not sound promising for the Whigs. "And he has sent you to persuade me?"

"It's little to me what you decide to do, but I have to say that Monmouth's Cause grows weaker every day. He needs your help."

"I feel sorry for Monmouth," Philip admitted, "but it is too late. I have not the slightest intention of going back to pick up the pieces other folk have scattered, and why should I?"

"Shaftesbury can get you High Heatherton."

"I doubt that. The fate of Heatherton rests with the Court of Common Pleas."

"Are you aware that George Jeffreys is now its judge?"

Philip pulled a wry face at that. Judge Jeffreys had advanced through his favour with the Duke of York and made no secret of his dislike for anyone who had ever been connected with Shaftesbury. "In that case I shall likely be dead and buried before it is granted to me."

"Not if you accept Lord Shaftesbury's offer. He still wields great power in the city and he pledges you his help, in return for your own."

"Shaftesbury's promises bind him for just as long as he has need of a person and then they are forgotten as swiftly as a man can blink," Philip said, unimpressed. "Even if I still had a mind to help Monmouth, which I don't, I could not abandon all I have here on such a flimsy proposition. I'm sorry, Giles, I would be a great fool to hazard everything upon Shaftesbury's whim and Monmouth's fading dream."

"It was your dream once," Giles reminded him.

"That was a long while ago," Philip said firmly. "Monmouth has no chance, I know that now."

Philip had always known it really, yet it had been difficult to resist Shaftesbury's enthusiasm for the bold design. It might still be difficult, even considering how badly Shaftesbury had treated him, but Philip was a soldier now, with obligations to the French Army.

Giles shrugged. "Never mind. At least this has given me the opportunity of seeing you again before you take off upon your next glorious campaign. Whilst I am here I was thinking perhaps you could introduce me to Monsieur."

"Be careful of him," Philip warned. "He's nowhere near as harmless as he seems and he has a weakness for good-looking young men. There's no telling what you'll need to do if you hope to earn a 'token of appreciation' from him!"

Giles laughed at his fears. "I'll take my chances. It may be I have need of an influential friend in France if matters should go awry for me in England."

"Giles, I beg you not to get drawn too deeply into Monmouth's Cause," Philip said, suddenly serious.

"I won't," Giles promised, "but Charles can't live forever. Neither you nor I will prosper when York comes to power."

That was the truth. Philip had made some powerful enemies amongst the Duke of York's Catholic supporters, including Charles' mistress, Louise de Quéroualle, and both he and Giles had already suffered on account of her. She had once tried to coerce Giles into betraying Philip and he was lucky to have escaped from her clutches with his life. Philip had fared even worse. He had received a wound at the hands of her agents and had been thrown, close to death, in the Bastille. He had spent six months there before Louis had heard of his plight and had him freed, and another year suffering agonies from the effects of his injuries. Philip's hatred of her knew no bounds.

Giles stayed a month in Paris and he spent a lot of that time with Thomas. Thomas had originally been his servant before Giles had gone to join Monmouth's forces at Bothwell Brig and, despite the differences in their birth and upbringing, the two had struck up a friendship from the very first. Thomas had shown both loyalty and courage when he had helped Giles on the night he had been taken by Louise, and from that day on a bond had been established between them which would last their whole lives.

Philip did present him to Monsieur, much against his better judgment. Philip liked Monsieur, and even felt a little sorry for him at times, but he was under no illusions as to his character. Monsieur, handsome and frivolous though he was, could be spiteful if crossed. He was devoted to Philip, despite the fact that he had always known Philip would never become one of his tame admirers. Even so, Monsieur had helped him a great deal by advancing his interests at his brother's Court, and Philip would always be grateful to him for that.

He had still not been recalled to action by the time Giles was preparing to return home to England.

"You won't change your mind about coming with me?" Giles asked as they said goodbye.

Philip shook his head, "I'm sorry, Giles. I'm certain Louis will be sending for me any day now." In fact Philip found he was looking forward to being back in the army. Much as he had enjoyed his time at home in Paris he was not a person who could be idle for very long.

Theresa kissed her brother goodbye and then frowned as she noticed the diamond brooch that Giles was wearing. "Wherever did you get that?"

"From Monsieur," Giles said, laughing as he caught their expressions. "Don't worry! It is a token of his undying friendship, nothing more!"

༄

Philip was not summoned to Versailles until late spring.

The Chateau had changed considerably since he had first visited it over ten years ago, when Louis had turned his father's simple hunting lodge into a retreat where he could hold entertainments and escape the pressures of state.

Philip had only been in his early twenties then and he had found it a magical place, but now he spent as little time there as possible.

Louis was moving everything away from Paris and making Versailles the very centre of his government, in place of the Louvre. In order to do this the chateau had needed to undergo extensive additions and improvements. Louis had insisted on retaining the original house and the architect, Le Vau, had added wings on either side and a storey above it, so that the little lodge was now completely encased in the new building.

To Philip's mind the work seemed to have been going on forever.

"Another reason to be glad about leaving the Court," he muttered to himself as he stepped over the obstacles in the long gallery, which had been started four years before to connect the north and south apartments. Now it was blocked with the scaffolding belonging to the painter Le Brun, who was responsible for the paintings that decorated the ceiling. They depicted scenes from Louis' reign, in particular the military triumphs.

Louis greeted him warmly. "What do you think of my gallery?" he demanded. "Are Le Brun's paintings not magnificent?"

"Indeed they are, your Majesty," Philip said dutifully.

"Those victories for France's glory would never have been possible but for such bold soldiers as yourself, Philip," Louis said.

"Thank you, your Majesty. I have always considered it an honour to serve you and my mother's country."

"And you have served us both well," Louis assured him. "However, I have decided that the time has come for you to retire from active service."

Philip stared at him, stunned. It was the very last thing he had expected.

"Have I displeased your Majesty in some way?"

"Indeed not," Louis said emphatically, "but I fear I may have driven you too hard."

Philip had served in the army almost continually since he had returned to France, even through the winter months the previous year, when many other troops had been recalled to Paris. Notwithstanding this, he knew it was unlikely that Louis would relieve him of his duties for that reason alone, and he said as much.

Louis sighed. "Very well, I will be frank. There has been some resentment amongst the French officers and it has been suggested that I may have heaped too many laurels on you."

Although Philip was half-French he knew he was regarded by some as a foreigner, but he had some good friends amongst his fellow officers and felt he had earned their respect. He doubted very much that it was they who had caused Louis to make his decision, but he could guess who had. Louvois, the Minister of War, had never liked him. The one thing Louis feared most in others was ambition and he guessed that a suggestion from Louvois might have persuaded the King that it was dangerous to allow him to advance too far.

He was angry at the injustice of the situation, but he could not show it, any more than he could argue with the King of France. No-one did that, not even Monsieur. "What happens to me now?" he wondered.

"I thought to find you a position here at Court," Louis told him.

Philip said nothing, though he could ill-conceal his horror. Although he had been a courtier from an early age, Philip was no longer one by disposition and he certainly had no wish to fritter away his days at Versailles, which he considered to be no more than a tribute to Louis' vanity. To do so meant complete renouncement of all personal liberties, including even the right to think for yourself, whilst to dabble in politics was the greatest folly for a nobleman if he hoped to live in any kind of favour.

The interview was over and Philip walked thoughtfully back through the gallery. Picking his way around the scaffolding he could not resist a wry smile as he noticed a painting representing Louis' victory over the Dutch a decade before. Philip had played a part in that himself and he thought how well he was being rewarded now for his contribution to France's glory!

He returned to the quarters that had been allotted to him and Theresa. Despite the grandeur of the chateau, the accommodation available to all except the Princes of the Blood was worse that those in the old-fashioned palace of Whitehall, in London. Philip regarded the small room with distaste although, according to Bet, who believed in having her opinions heard, the servants were infinitely worse off. They lived in little more than caves, overcrowded and with no air and hardly any light.

He was not the only person to feel discontented with his quarters. The corridors and staircases that ran behind the rooms were already being appropriated by some and turned into tiny suites of private apartments. The better off amongst the courtiers were purchasing houses in the town that was rapidly springing up around the chateau, but Philip was not rich. He had no private income, in fact he had no income at all now that he was no longer serving in Louis' army, and the only way he could buy a property at Versailles would be to sell his house in Paris. That idea did not even bear thinking about.

Philip stood at the window and looked out onto the brick wall opposite, its monotony broken only by a drainpipe. He thought how impossible it would be for him to live here all the time, no matter what appointment Louis offered him.

He had received very little by way of education and was lamentably ignorant of anything outside the scope of what could be learned in the army or at Court, but he had a lively mind and a rebellious streak. Much as he admired King Louis, both as a monarch and a man, the prospect of spending the rest of his life attending on him was unbearable.

Theresa rushed in a few moments later, flushed with excitement. "Oh, Philip, everything here is so beautiful. Wait until you see what has been done to the gardens since we last came."

Extensive gardens were being created behind the chateau, although not without some difficulty. Trees had needed to be transplanted from the forests of Compiègne and water piped from the Seine to create ponds and fountains, whilst Louis' gardener, Le Nôtre, was turning the flat, uninteresting wasteland into flowerbeds and groves graced with marble statues.

At any other time Philip would have laughed at her enthusiasm, but the very last thing he wanted now was to hear her extolling the virtues of the place he feared would shortly seem like a prison to him.

The smile died on Theresa's lips as she saw his expression. "Philip, what's wrong?"

"Louis has taken away my army," he said bleakly.

She frowned. "What do you mean, taken it away?"

"Just that. I have been relieved of my command."

"But you're a hero," she cried indignantly.

"Precisely the problem, sweetheart! Apparently I have done a little too well – for a foreigner."

Theresa shook her head disbelievingly. "Louis would never do that to you."

"And yet he did. The only mystery is why I am so surprised at it."

He threw himself disconsolately down upon the bed. Theresa joined him, laying her head upon his shoulder and he held her close. He knew she would be staunch beside him, no matter what he did, and that thought was a comfort. "What happens to you now?" she wondered, after a few minutes.

"Now? Oh, I am to remain at Court, dancing attendance upon him like all the other useless bastards in this palace," he said bitterly. "Oh, Tess, what are we to do? I can't waste my years away watching Louis when he eats and passing him his stockings when he dresses in the morning. If such was the limit of my ambition I could have made myself more agreeable to King Charles."

Theresa could not resist a smile at that. "You are a man of many talents, my darling, but I doubt even you could have managed that!"

"Well alright, I probably couldn't have done," he admitted, "but no-one, not even the King of France, is going to tell me how to spend my life." He got up, filled with sudden decision, and pulled her to her feet. "Come on."

"Where are we going?"

"Back to Paris. I can't think straight inside this blasted building site."

"You're considering Shaftesbury's offer now," she guessed, as the coach took them out of the cobbled courtyard and through the ornate, gilded gates of the chateau.

"I might, if it gets me Heatherton."

"But, Philip, only think of what you'll have to do for Shaftesbury if you work for him again."

"Probably nothing worse than I have done already. Anyway, it wasn't all bad," he reminded her. "Don't forget that one of the things I had to do for him was marry you!"

"I don't recall your being too pleased about that at the time," she reminded him archly.

Philip kissed her. "My darling, there are many things I have regretted doing in my life but believe me when I say that marrying you is not one of them!"

THREE

∝

"Philip, you are the most wonderful sight," Shaftesbury said.

"Delighted you approve of me, my Lord!"

"How could I do otherwise? You're looking well."

He sounded envious, and Philip could well see why. The Earl looked far from well, in fact Philip had never seen him look so frail.

"To serve in Louis' glorious campaigns does tend to keep one fit!" he said dryly.

"And are you ready to work for me again, now that you have rested from Monmouth's Cause for so long?"

"Rested?" Philip gave him a wry look. "I have worked harder these last three years than I've ever worked in my life. I have been shot at, soaked and parched. I've slept upon the stony ground and in the snow. I have endured to ride for days, to walk for miles, to lie in dirty trenches and to stand in holes up to my waist in mud. On top of that I've had the responsibility of those I commanded. If this is resting I had better start work right away before I grow fat and lazy!"

Shaftesbury laughed. "You don't change, Philip."

Philip sat down, carefully arranging the folds of his coat. "I trust I have not made a diabolical channel crossing merely to afford you some amusement, my Lord."

"I have work for you," Shaftesbury said, "although I doubted you would come."

"I might not have done had I still been on active service," Philip confessed, "but Louis has decided he can win his wars without me now."

"Then his loss is my gain. How did Theresa feel about leaving Paris?"

Philip glanced at him. Shaftesbury's face was expressionless but he could easily guess what was running through the Earl's crafty mind. "Theresa is happy to be wherever I am," he said stiffly.

"I meant nothing by the remark," the Earl assured him. "It would not do for there to be any hostility between us. I need to be able to trust you."

"Speaking of trust, it seems to me that I should be the one to be wary after the way you treated me," Philip said.

"How can you say so?" Shaftesbury protested. "Did I not have my own surgeon, John Locke, perform the delicate operation that saved your life?"

"It very nearly ended my life," Philip said, "and probably would have done if Morgan had not watched Locke closely."

"Why ever would I have wanted you dead?"

"Why? Because you had seen fit to dismiss me, after I had tainted my honour and ruined my health in your service, and you feared I might be troublesome."

Philip had been in constant pain then from the old injury inflicted by Louise's agents. Doctor Locke had, indeed, successfully removed a piece of rib that had broken off inside him, but Theresa had been warned, just in time, that Shaftesbury had ordered the surgeon to make sure he died on the operating table.

Shaftesbury's face betrayed nothing. "If you truly believe me capable of that why are you here?"

"You know damn well – for Heatherton."

"Is that all?" Shaftesbury sounded disappointed.

"Well I haven't come back for Monmouth."

"At least admit that the prospect of working for me again intrigues you," Shaftesbury persisted.

"I admit nothing," Philip said. "Get me High Heatherton and I will serve you once more in whatever capacity I can. Do you still have influence?"

"Of course I have. Do you think a lifetime in office brings no reward?" Shaftesbury said, a little testily. "I'll get you your country estate, though what you will do with it is beyond me."

"I intend to live on it, naturally. If you must know I am sick and tired of working for my living, whether for you or King Louis. I want the kind of life that's mine by right of birth. I was born a gentleman and I fully intend to live like one."

"I shall see to it that your case is heard quickly and that it is fairly dealt with," Shaftesbury pledged. "Here's my hand upon it. Now let's forget the past and work together for the future of the country."

"Agreed." Even though Philip knew the Earl was given to making extravagant promises he took his hand to seal the pact between them. "Now tell me why you wanted me back."

"The situation is worse than it has ever been now that York has returned from exile," Shaftesbury told him frankly.

"How could that happen, for goodness sake?"

"Through Portsmouth's meddling."

"That bitch!" Louise de Quéroualle was the Duchess of Portsmouth. "I might have known she'd have a hand in it somewhere, but since when have she and York been such good friends?"

"Since she's been trying to raise some money for a trip to take the waters at Bourbon. She's spent all hers on improving her lodgings at Whitehall and she tried to raise a loan on her pension. When she found she couldn't use that as security, she wanted to exchange it for some of York's income from the Post Office. He said he could only do that from London and in the end Charles gave way to her to keep the peace, as he always does."

"Incredible!" Philip shook his head in wonderment. "Charles must be addled in the head to risk alienating every Protestant in the land for no better reason than to enable his Catholic mistress to take the waters!"

"Quite. Anyway since his uncle has returned from Scotland Monmouth has been ostracized at Court, even by his father. If something is not done, and quickly, his opportunity will be forever lost."

"Surely he has other friends besides me to help him."

"He has great faith in you," Shaftesbury pointed out.

"Which means he is to be persuaded to something," Philip guessed.

"Precisely so."

"Precisely what?"

"Can't you guess? An early insurrection."

"Whilst his father is still alive?" Philip was surprised, for that had never been Monmouth's plan.

"Look at me, Philip, I'm a sick man," Shaftesbury said. "Does it seem likely I'll outlive King Charles?"

"No, but then it never did," Philip said, for Charles was younger than Shaftesbury and far more robust. "You planned this all along, didn't you?"

Shaftesbury smiled. "We understand each other, you and I."

"Understand you I may, agree with you I do not," Philip said firmly. "I would go up against the Duke of York for Monmouth but I never said that I would fight King Charles."

"Charles has hated you since you joined forces with me," Shaftesbury reminded him.

"Maybe so, but he is still the King. You may have helped execute his father but I will play no part in regicide."

Philip was aware that Shaftesbury had been both Royalist and Parliamentarian during the Civil War, changing sides whenever he saw advantage.

"But I am not suggesting we should kill Charles," Shaftesbury argued.

"And do you think he will stand by and see us take his kingdom and give it to his bastard son?" Philip said scornfully.

"He once said he would sooner see Monmouth hanged than sat upon the throne!"

"I recall that, but supposing only York was killed. What do you think of that?"

"I think you're mad," Philip said. "Who would I have to help me if I did agree to take part in this?"

"Lord Russell and Lord Grey, as well as Sir Thomas Armstrong and Ferguson, the Scottish preacher."

"And with those four you imagine I can engineer an insurrection of this magnitude?" Philip said, unimpressed.

"What's wrong with them?"

"I'll tell you. Russell is too cautious, Grey is too devious and Armstrong is too headstrong, whilst Ferguson is a pamphleteer who delights in plotting for the sake of plotting." Philip had good reason to dislike pamphleteers, for in the past he had been the target of a Tory scandal sheet. "Not a helpful one amongst them for my purposes."

"Then what about the Earl of Argyle?"

Philip had heard that Argyle, who had been imprisoned in Edinburgh Castle by the Duke of York, had managed to escape to Holland.

"Is he back in London?"

"Yes, and eager for revenge. He has promised to gather up his forces and rally for us."

Philip knew that Shaftesbury had never been one to miss the chance of gaining influential allies but, with or without Argyle, he had no intention of plotting to kill the King's brother.

However, there was no need for Shaftesbury to know that.

Philip looked at him. The Earl was emaciated and his face was deeply etched with lines of nagging pain, caused by the suppurating abscess in his stomach. Philip calculated that six months – a year at most – would finish him. High Heatherton should be his long before then and he would not be forced play any part in Shaftesbury's preposterous scheme.

"Very well. I'll try."

"You will dispose of York and lead Monmouth into rebellion against his father?" Shaftesbury cried.

"If that is what you want."

Shaftesbury was gripped by a sudden wave of agony. Philip turned away, for he knew the Earl would never want his pity.

"Is there nothing more that can be done for you, my Lord?" he asked when the spasm had passed.

"Nothing," Shaftesbury panted. "I care not what I suffer just so long as I can live to see Charles toppled from his throne."

Philip prepared to leave so that the Earl could rest. "Speaking of Charles, he's sent for me." He had received word from Whitehall almost as soon as he arrived back in London.

Shaftesbury frowned. "Tread carefully, Philip."

Philip tipped his hat to him as he left. "I'm always careful! It's good to be working with you again, my Lord," he added, for he knew that was what the Earl had longed to hear him say.

King Charles was dignified and stately, every inch a monarch but with none of the showiness of his French cousin. To Philip he would never be other than a second-rate version of King Louis.

Against all predictions, the once frivolous young cavalier had turned into a clever statesman. Shaftesbury often underestimated him, but Philip never had.

"I little thought to see you home so soon, my Lord," he said, when Philip had bowed to him with the flourish that was so fashionable at Versailles, and which he knew irritated Charles immensely.

"I've stayed away for nearly three years, your Majesty."

"But you have done well in France, by all accounts. What brings you back?"

Philip smiled. "I was homesick."

"More like you've quarrelled with my cousin," Charles reckoned.

"The Sun King does not quarrel with his subjects, Sire. He demands complete and absolute obedience."

"That is not your style at all, is it? I still see the spirit in your eyes."

"I would be of little use to your Majesty without it," Philip said smoothly.

"You are of little use to me in any case, unless you've much altered," Charles retorted. "Through your association with Lord Shaftesbury and his Whigs you were partly responsible for the deaths of many innocent Catholics. You even had the temerity to involve my wife in your accusations."

"I cannot speak for Lord Shaftesbury, Sire, but for myself I have never had anything but the deepest respect and admiration for Her Majesty the Queen," Philip said.

He meant it. He had always felt extremely sorry for the King's Portuguese wife. Queen Catherine had made few friends at Court and Charles flaunted his mistresses in front of her.

"You certainly always treated her with the greatest consideration," Charles allowed, "and yet you permitted your wife, who was one of the Queen's own ladies, to aid those who wanted to bring about her downfall."

"I would respectfully remind your Majesty that Theresa was not my wife at that time and, in addition, I assure you she was most unwilling to do anything to hurt the Queen."

Theresa had been answerable to Shaftesbury in those days. Philip had married her, at the Earl's insistence, after the incident had brought about her disgrace and caused her to lose her position at Court.

"I know full well who was responsible for it," Charles said heavily, "nevertheless I cannot forgive her actions and she is not welcome at Whitehall."

"Do I take it that I will also be unwelcome?" Philip said.

Philip's birth entitled him to a place at Court but he wanted to be certain of where he stood.

"I have never forbidden you to attend upon me, but I warn you, Philip Devalle, I shall not let you lead another plot against my brother."

"Is that what your Majesty thinks I am here to do?" Philip said, in an injured tone.

"By God I wish I knew, but if you have returned to plague me once again then remember that Lord Shaftesbury will not always be able to protect you," Charles warned.

Philip flicked an imaginary piece of fluff from his velvet cuff, a little affectation of his. "I trust I shall not need Lord Shaftesbury's protection, since I intend to conduct myself within the limits of the law."

"Are you attempting to convince me that you are a reformed character?" Charles asked sceptically.

"Oh, but I am!"

"Then why are you here?"

"My brother, Henry, has been committed as insane and I wish to claim High Heatherton," Philip said.

Charles still looked suspicious. "Is that all of it?"

"That's all. I have had a petition registered with the Court of Common Pleas since I left England. I am hoping that, in view of Henry's incompetence, it will be but a matter of formality unless, of course, your Majesty decides to oppose my claim."

"Indeed not. I can see no reason in the world why you shouldn't have it," Charles said. "It may well keep you out of mischief, or at least out of London. I suppose you're hoping for the earldom too."

Charles had mentioned the possibility of giving him an earldom once before, when he was hoping to entice Philip into betraying Shaftesbury. Philip had refused that time but this title would be different, for it was his family's earldom and he felt it should be his.

"I had hoped I might be so fortunate, your Majesty."

"There would be a price," Charles said, "and if you do not care to pay that price then, so far as I'm concerned, your brother's earldom can stay locked up in the madhouse with him until he dies. What I require, Philip, is your loyalty."

Philip had been a loyal subject once, until he learned of a secret treaty Charles had made with France, a treaty which had agreed that England be converted to the Catholic faith in exchange for French aid. Charles had never been able to honour his part of the bargain, for English feelings still ran far too high against the Papists since the Popish Plot, but his perfidy had lost him the lofty position he had once held in Philip's eyes, and he would never regain it.

"Am I forbidden the company of the Duke of Monmouth?" he asked Charles cautiously.

"My son associates with whom he pleases. It is of no consequence to me, until such time as those who count themselves his friends advise him on a course of action which can only end in disaster and disgrace."

That message was plain enough.

Charles indicated that he might withdraw. "Oh, by the by," he added, as an afterthought, "don't bother trying to seek out your friend Titus Oates in the palace. I had him removed from his lodgings here last September."

Philip winced to hear Oates described as his friend. Oates had been the main witness Shaftesbury had employed to implicate Papists during the Plot and it had been one of Philip's, often unpleasant, tasks to see that he behaved and gave the evidence he was told to give. Philip was under no misconceptions as to the nature of the man, or the morality of what they were doing, but he had been in no position to object. Both he and Theresa had been dependent upon the Earl at the time, indeed it was through helping to give credibility to one of Oates' fantastic claims that Theresa had lost her place at the Queen's side.

"I did hear that Oates had left Whitehall," he said, hoping Charles would drop the subject.

It was vain hope.

"And did you also hear how your band of perjured witnesses turned upon one another, like the base animals they are, accusing each other of heaven knows what?" Charles continued remorselessly.

Philip hadn't heard about that, but it did not surprise him, knowing the type of men the Earl had employed.

Charles laughed, obviously enjoying his discomfiture. "Their true light showed plain enough then and made honest folk wonder how they could have been duped for so long."

Philip knew that Charles himself had never for a moment believed in the probity of the witnesses who had condemned so many Papists to a traitor's death, but then neither had he been prepared to take any action to stop them. It was put about that when Charles took the throne he had vowed he would never go upon his travels again and Shaftesbury had gambled that he would not risk his crown by interfering with anything which did not directly concern him or his family. The gamble had paid off.

In Philip's view that made Charles scarcely more honourable than anyone else with regard to the Plot.

He managed to excuse himself at last and drove to the house he had rented in Cheapside, mulling over the proposal Shaftesbury had made to him. It was a pretty desperate one, made by a desperate and determined man who knew he had not long left to accomplish his ambitions, but Philip felt himself able to cope with him and Monmouth too, and even, if needs be, with the King himself.

A loud cheer from the street chased away his thoughts. Philip's flamboyant carriage was easily recognisable. It was painted in shiny black, with a gold, domed roof, and his initials were emblazoned in gold leaf upon the doors and embroidered upon the black livery of his negro coachmen, Jonathon and Ned, who he had brought back with him from France. The vehicle had been in storage whilst he had been away but now, pulled by a freshly purchased pair of jet black horses, it was as magnificent as it had ever been, and just as conspicuous.

Philip had always been popular with the people. Even the scandal sheet had not damaged his reputation, for he was regarded as a Protestant champion. His association with Lord Shaftesbury and the Whigs had done him no harm either and he had always played his part well, appearing prominently with the other members of the famous Green Ribbon Club, and allowing the Londoners to gawp at him as often as they liked.

It was good to know that they had not forgotten him. He knew he would need all of their support if he was to succeed this time!

FOUR

⁀

Morgan somewhat grudgingly admitted Philip's tailor, Monsieur Robertin, and his apprentice, who was carrying a coat in lustrous burgundy satin.

Since Philip had returned to London the dapper little Frenchman had been regularly leaving his shop in Paternoster Row to 'pay his call'. It was a rare day that Philip did not make it worth his while.

There were very few things which gave him true pleasure, but beautiful clothes had always been one of his passions and he never tired of acquiring or wearing them.

He was still trying on the coat when a second visitor arrived. This time it was the Duke of Buckingham.

Philip was always pleased to receive Buckingham, who had once been his patron at Court. They were still good friends and Philip was genuinely fond of him. The amiable Duke had helped him out of many a scrape in the past and Philip, for his part, had stood by Buckingham through his frequent unsuccessful business ventures and his even more frequent scandals.

"Well, what do you think?" Philip said, showing him the cuffs, which were embroidered in gold and edged with no less than three layers of gold lace.

"Quite superb, dear boy."

"You are a fine craftsman," Philip told Robertin. "How much?"

"Eight pounds, my Lord."

"And you are a great thief besides! Eight pounds? Why, for that I would expect to have a waistcoat and a pair of breeches too."

"But not of this quality, my Lord. See the delicacy of the embroidery? With my own hands I have worked this for you because nothing but the very best can suffice to enhance the form of one so exquisite, so graceful, so…"

"Yes, yes, I know that you can flatter," Philip interrupted him, "but I am not such a rich man as you seem to think."

"But your Lordship does have impeccable taste."

"And expensive taste too, it seems! Ah well, what would go with it? A waistcoat in cream, perhaps, with matching breeches?"

"Perfect, perfect," Robertin cried, clapping his hands together.

"And some embroidery on the waistcoat, please. Not too much, I don't want to appear ostentatious!"

"Heaven forbid," Morgan muttered, glaring at Monsieur Robertin's apprentice, who had the temerity to attempt to remove Philip's new coat.

"What do you know about such things?" Philip said, turning so that Morgan could take the coat instead. "How much for a hat, Monsieur Robertin?"

"One pound and a gold hat-band another pound, my Lord."

"Then that is absolutely all of it. You have some patterns for me?"

Philip studied the swatches in the book before holding out a sample of lilac brocade to Buckingham. "That might look pretty, don't you think, made up with some pink?"

The Duke nodded approvingly.

"I will have bows upon the sleeves, like Monsieur wears," Philip instructed Robertin, "and pleated at the back with two vents, pink lapels and cuffs, with some silver trim. Now away, before you tempt me further."

"You are spending too much," Morgan grumbled, when

Robertin and his apprentice had packed away their wares and he had shown them out.

"Nonsense! Would you send me out in rags?"

In answer Morgan silently indicated Philip's closet, which was filled with the clothes he had brought from France.

Philip shrugged. "I'm bored with most of those. If it will keep you quiet you may take your pick of any that you especially like."

"Most gracious of you, I am sure," Morgan said sourly.

Philip had known he was on safe ground, for he was a good head taller than Morgan and much slimmer. Besides that, the brawny Welshman, with his wild, black hair and weathered face, would have looked as ludicrous in Philip's clothes as a raven with a peacock's tail!

"Never mind. Regard it as an investment," Philip said. "I am sure the money is as safe upon my back as it would be on loan to Charles' exchequer."

"Is he right about your spending?" Buckingham asked when Morgan had gone.

"I'm afraid he is," Philip admitted. In the old days Buckingham had settled all of his accounts and later, when he worked for Shaftesbury, he had always managed to wring money from the Earl. Now he was, in truth, finding it quite difficult to make ends meet, but Philip had always lived extravagantly and he felt he had to keep up appearances. "Practically every sou I had left of my army pay went into paying our passage back here and renting this place. I still have to provide for the upkeep of my Paris house too, and I can't let that go. I may need to return to France one day."

"I guess you'll always be Louis' man at heart," Buckingham said. "Or will you?"

Philip gave him a sidelong glance, surprised by the question. "Louis is still the man I most admire, but that is not to say I want to spend my life adorning his palace."

"What is it you do want?"

"All I care about now is Heatherton," Philip told him. "When I have that I shall be happy to leave London and move to Sussex."

"Surely not! The people love you here. You can't abandon them."

"I dare say they will learn to love me at High Heatherton as well!

"What use are country hobs to you? This city is your home and the Londoners your people."

Philip said nothing, but leaned upon the mantelshelf and eyed the Duke curiously. He guessed there was a reason for the direction in which Buckingham had steered the conversation and he was waiting for him to continue.

"I simply would not wish to see you make a great mistake," Buckingham said, by way of explanation. "You are not a farmer, you're a politician."

"That I'm not," Philip said decidedly. "*You* are a politician, George. I'm a soldier."

"Then why did you leave the army?"

"You know damn well why! What exactly is all this about?"

"If you must know I am glad you're free of Louis, and I'm not the only one. When the Duke of York becomes king then you know as well as I that Louis will support him in everything he does and all the power will be in Catholic hands. Would you like to see that happen?"

"I don't quite see how we can stop it happening," Philip said frankly. "York is Charles' legal heir, after all."

"There is one who could take the throne from him," Buckingham reminded him.

"Monmouth?" Philip asked wickedly.

"Don't be contrary, Philip," Buckingham said with a sigh. "You know perfectly well to whom I am referring."

Philip did know. Buckingham had long favoured William of Orange, who was, at least, a legal claimant to the throne, since he was married to York's daughter, Mary.

"He has about as much chance as the Duke of Monmouth," Philip said dismissively.

"You're wrong. Too few will rise for Monmouth, without someone like you to lead them."

"And that is why you are interested in the following I have in London?" Philip said. "You're afraid that I will work against you."

"Certain people are, including William himself."

Philip laughed at that. "I can't believe he fears me." The only time he had seen William was during the Dutch Wars, when their forces had met upon opposing sides of the battlefield.

"Don't be so modest. Your reputation has spread further than you think. He has always made it clear that he would sooner have you for a friend than for an enemy."

"He could solve that problem by simply having me killed," Philip pointed out.

"He'd sooner use you, if you'd let him. In fact he is prepared to buy your friendship at a price you cannot fail to find agreeable."

Philip stared at him. "Surely he must know that everything I've done has been for Monmouth."

"Everything you've done has been for Shaftesbury," Buckingham corrected him. "Only Monmouth thinks you schemed for him."

"But you are asking me to go against all that I have worked for since I first joined with Shaftesbury."

"If you mean Monmouth's so-called Cause, then you know better than any that the Cause is dead," Buckingham said. "It died the first time that a victim of our Popish Plot escaped the hangman, and neither you nor I nor Shaftesbury can resurrect it. Every day more Whigs turn Tory, and no amount of money buys them back again. Your name is tainted by association with them. Join with Halifax and I," Buckingham pleaded. "Do it now, before it is too late."

"George, it is already too late. I have given Shaftesbury my word and, whilst I will admit to you that I have no intention of seeing this thing through to the bitter end, I have to make a show of it or I shall never get High Heatherton. Shaftesbury will see to that."

"Shaftesbury will never even know," Buckingham said. "William will not make a move whilst Charles lives, but he will pay well to be kept informed of what is happening here. He fears there is already some French intervention, and you could use your contacts in France to discover it."

"So I am to betray not only Monmouth but King Louis as well? Preposterous!"

"And what do you suppose will happen to your precious Heatherton when York does come to power?" Buckingham said. "You have been his enemy for too long, and he's vindictive. He will find a way to strip you of everything you own. You'll perish under his rule. Think on that."

Philip had thought on it, long and hard. He had once hoped that the King of France might ensure that he was safe from York's spite but he couldn't be sure, not now he had gone against Louis' wishes.

However, an idea was forming in his head.

"What would William have me do after Charles is dead?" he said.

"Why, raise an army for him. You can help him defeat York the way you know best, with military might, and afterwards you would be powerful and secure."

It was becoming more tempting.

"Give me time to think, George."

Buckingham smiled. "Take all the time you want, dear boy."

Directly he had gone Philip sent for Morgan, for he rarely made a move without consulting him.

"Do you trust the Orangeman?" Morgan said, when Philip had related the conversation to him.

"I trust no man in this world except for you," Philip said truthfully, "but I am interested to see in which direction the

Protestant wind will blow. I have seen a way in which I cannot lose, no matter whether it is Monmouth, William or York on the throne."

Morgan nodded. Evidently he saw it too. "You mean to work for both Monmouth and the Orangeman's interests and at same time sell information to the French," he guessed.

"Why not? A gambler I may be but I have no wish to hazard Heatherton upon such an uncertain thing as the Succession. This way I can ingratiate myself with Louis again, for I may need him to protect my interests here if York does come to power."

"It is a dangerous game you're planning to play," Morgan warned him.

"I've played dangerous games before." Apart from any other consideration, Philip needed the money.

"What of Monmouth?" Morgan asked.

That was the thing that bothered Philip the most, for he regarded himself as a man of honour and the thought of working against his friend's interests troubled him. "When the time comes I will do all I can to dissuade him from rebellion," he promised. "Either way, I will abandon Monmouth's Cause as soon as High Heatherton becomes mine, but in the meantime I need to convince Shaftesbury of my good intentions."

Morgan muttered something in his native tongue, which Philip assumed to be his opinion of the Earl.

"It will all be worth it one day, Morgan. Believe me you cannot dislike the man any more than I do. By the way, it might be better if you make no mention to your mistress of Buckingham's visit, or of what I am proposing to do. She's gone to the 'Change with Bet this morning so I don't see why she should need to know anything about it. I have a feeling she would not approve!"

Morgan's expression made it plain that he didn't exactly approve either.

"Since I must be seen to be working in Monmouth's interests I'm going to address a meeting of the Green Ribbon Club tonight," Philip told him. "That should please Shaftesbury."

"I think I should accompany you," Morgan said.

"Really, Morgan! I am quite capable of looking after myself."

"I know how capable you are, my Lord, but London is a very wicked city."

Philip laughed. "And I, Morgan, am a very wicked man!

Theresa and Bet were enjoying themselves in the New Exchange, at Cornhill. The 'Change, as it was popularly called, was the place to buy laces, ribbons, combs, in fact every item essential to anyone who wished to be fashionably dressed, and Theresa did not intend to be outdone in that respect by her elegant husband!

They had made their purchases and were about to return to the carriage when Theresa spotted a flower seller's stall in the street outside. She selected a bunch of roses and buried her face in their fragrant blooms.

"Oh, Bet, you don't know how much I miss walking in a garden filled with flowers, especially now the summer is here. Won't it be wonderful when we live at Heatherton? I'm going to have a rose arbour, like the one we had at home when I was a girl." Theresa had spent her childhood in Dorset and at times she still missed the beauty and the clean air of the countryside.

Bet shrugged. She was a Londoner, born and bred, and would, Theresa knew, prefer to stay there, given a choice. She took the flowers from her mistress whilst Theresa paid for them. "Herbs will be more use than roses! I shall plant a physic garden, finer than the King's."

Bet was skilled at healing. She believed in the old remedies and, although her concoctions were often not for the fastidious, they were usually effective.

"Always the practical one," Theresa laughed.

"Why, if it isn't Lady Devalle. How fortuitous that I should find you here."

The laughter died on Theresa's lips as she turned to see who had addressed her and found herself looking at Louise de Quéroualle, the Duchess of Portsmouth.

"Madam Carwell." Bet fairly spat the words out. Madam Carwell was the derisive name given to Louise by the Londoners, who had difficulty pronouncing her French surname. Bet could pronounce it perfectly well but chose not to.

Louise outranked Theresa, and she knew she ought to make an effort to be polite, but it was hard when the woman had caused Philip so much suffering in the past. "Good day to you, your Grace," she said stiffly.

Bet, moving to stand protectively at her side, did not need to bother with social niceties. Duchess or not, she glared at Louise with open hatred.

"I've been longing to have a chat with you since you returned," Louise said, "but of course you're not welcome at Court are you? Not since your little escapade which put the Queen in jeopardy. No matter, I've run into you now. Perhaps you'd like to join me in my carriage?"

She pointed to the vehicle, which was stopped beside theirs. Theresa guessed that it was catching sight of the distinctive Devalle carriage which had caused the Duchess to stop and seek her out.

Even without Bet's warning touch on her arm, there was no way Theresa would have accepted the invitation.

"I think not, your Grace. We were just about to leave."

"Very well. What I have to say can just as well be said here." Louise smiled, but without warmth. "If you have any regard for your husband I suggest the pair of you return to France while you still can. I wield more power than you can possibly imagine and I will not let anyone, especially him, help Monmouth to succeed his father to the throne."

Theresa's grey eyes narrowed. "I wonder why that means so much to you. Don't tell me that your only concern is protecting the interests of the Duke of York!"

"What other reason would I have," Louise demanded.

"Why the same one you had when you approached my brother three years ago," Theresa said. "You offered Giles the chance to betray my husband and, by doing so, discredit Monmouth's Cause because you sought to put your own son on the throne after the King's death."

"What if I did?" Louise snapped. "He is just as much the bastard son of the King as Monmouth, born of a Welsh whore! Why should my son not reign after Charles' death?"

"Because the people would never let him," Theresa said frankly. Louise was far from popular, being both a Catholic and a foreigner. People feared her influence on Charles and they insulted her quite openly on the streets. "Fortunately Giles was too high-principled to accept your offer to betray his friends."

Louise snorted at that. "High-principled? Your brother? Half the women at Court are paying him for his favours! If he'd listened to me he would be rich now in his own right, but he chose your wretched husband over me."

"Is that why you had him set upon, as you had Philip set upon in France?" Theresa demanded.

"I advise you against making rash accusations against your betters," Louise said haughtily. "I'm a lady, remember, not a country strumpet, like you."

"You, madam, are an evil slut!" Theresa could no longer restrain her feelings. Trembling with fury, she grabbed the pail of water standing beside the flower seller's stall and hurled it at Louise's feet.

The water splashed up, soaking Louise through to her petticoats and staining her silk skirt. "You will suffer for that, Theresa Devalle," she hissed, gathering up her wet skirts as she stalked off back to her carriage, "and sooner than you think."

FIVE

∽

The gentlemen of the Green Ribbon Club met less frequently than in days gone by and took less part in affairs since the Whig government had been ousted the previous year. Nevertheless an impressive number had returned to their old haunt, above the King's Head Tavern, in order to hear Philip speak.

Amongst them were Lord Essex and Lord Russell, standing a little apart from the rest as though not wishing to be associated with such fiery republicans as Major Wildman and Algernon Sydney. Monmouth and Giles were there, talking with Lord Grey and Sir Thomas Armstrong, and also Ferguson the pamphleteer, deep in conversation with Lord Howard.

Philip allowed himself a moment of misgiving as he prepared to make his entrance. This was a powerful mixture of people, and he knew he would have to handle them very carefully. He had made a bargain with Shaftesbury, however, and he knew he had to keep it if he was to be sure of acquiring High Heatherton.

After some thought he had invited Titus Oates to accompany him. He did not intend Titus to play any part in the proceedings that night, but he thought it no bad thing to take him along, as a reminder of what had once been achieved from small beginnings.

"Are you ready for this?" Philip asked him.

"I am, my Lord,"

"Then let us go in."

Titus was no longer enjoying royal favour, or the royal purse, but he was none the less arrogant for that as he surveyed the assembled company, amidst much rustling of the parson's silks he always wore, in keeping with his claim to be a Doctor of Divinity.

"Of all things," Armstrong cried. "Philip has resurrected Titus Oates!"

"Well one thing's for certain," Grey said, a little too loudly, "he doesn't't improve with keeping!"

Titus had many peculiarities. To begin with his chin was so very long that his mouth seemed to be almost in the centre of his strangely purple face, and a wart grew above one of his small, sunken eyes. He walked with an ungainly gait, for he had one leg shorter than the other and his whole appearance was rendered even more laughable by his pathetic attempts to emulate Philip, who was his idol. None had laughed at Titus Oates, however, when he screamed accusations from the witness box, and Philip had figured that the sight of him would still chill the blood of those who could vividly recall the Popish Plot.

He was right, a quick glance around at his audience showed that, and he was more than satisfied with the effect of their entry.

He fixed his eyes on Grey. "You find it easy, do you, to scoff at Doctor Oates, without whose courage we would never have become the people's heroes?"

"I meant no harm, I'm sure," Grey muttered.

Philip knew that Grey had never been a match for him. "I hope not," he said, "else it signifies to me that memories are not quite so sharp as wits, for he, at risk of his own life, was prepared to condemn any Papist, be they priest or lord, if we commanded him. Even today, thanks to his diligence, there remain Catholic prisoners in the Tower, although I understand Stafford was beheaded in my absence."

"We can manage some things without you then, Philip," Armstrong joked.

Philip bore the laughter that followed the remark good-naturedly. "Minor matters, maybe, but nothing of any real consequence, such as the establishing of a Protestant heir to the throne. I have not called you here to reminisce, my friends, but to remind you of how much can be achieved from how little. The Popish Plot began from nothing and, thanks to Shaftesbury's leadership, my organisation and the competence of Titus Oates and others we recruited as witnesses, it grew to such proportions that there was not a Papist in the land who did not go about in fear of his life."

"They were glorious days for us," Sydney said. "Every man here can remember the bonfires we lit to celebrate each Papist downfall, but what would you have, my Lord, another Popish Plot?"

Philip shuddered inwardly at the thought, for he had detested some of the distasteful tasks he had been forced to perform for Shaftesbury during those 'glorious days'. "No, Sydney, for that was but a part of the Earl's plan. It served its purpose but now I think the time is right to organise a bolder plot, one which ends in victory, complete and absolute, and with the Duke of Monmouth on the throne of England."

"And who do you propose shall lead this mighty plot?" Lord Howard said sneeringly. "You?"

Philip had never liked Howard. He turned to face him. "Would you object to that?"

"Yes. You are in no position now to give us orders, Devalle. There is no denying what you did but things have changed here since you went away to seek your glory elsewhere." Howard's voice was brimming with resentment. "Shaftesbury is a broken man, and I believe you to be nothing but an opportunist."

Philip thought, wryly, how near to the truth that was, but he had no need to defend himself, for there were immediate murmurings of disagreement to be heard. Old Major Wildman, one of his most ardent supporters, thumped hard upon a table top to show his disgust at Howard's remark and others followed suit.

Titus could be heard over all the commotion. He had cultivated an excessively affected drawl, for reasons best known to himself, and he had a voice which sounded at times more like the bray of a donkey. Even worse, he tended to speak with the same forcefulness as he had used when he was an Anabaptist minister ranting at his flock.

"My Lords, I really must protest. Lord Devalle is a man of integrity, an upright citizen and a noble inspiration to us all."

"Be silent," Philip ordered him, a little ungratefully under the circumstances. "You made a fine witness for the prosecution but I will conduct my own defence."

"Why, you are not on trial before us here," Monmouth cried.

"Am I not?" Philip looked about him. He could read hostility written plainly upon a few faces. "You, Howard, say that Lord Shaftesbury is a broken man, yet he has persuaded Argyle to gather up his forces and await our word. That is your broken man, my Lord."

Monmouth applauded wildly at that, and was soon joined by others in the room.

Philip waited until they quietened down before continuing.

"He intends our own troops to be marching with Argyle's a year from now."

"As soon as that?" It was Lord Russell who had spoken this time. "But Philip, nothing is prepared."

Philip was ready for that. "Then we must work the harder. In the meantime I suggest our Duke shows himself to the people once again."

"There is nothing I would like better, but my father has forbidden me to go upon another tour," Monmouth said sadly.

"But has the King forbidden you to take a holiday?" Philip said. "Perhaps to Wallasey in September for the races?"

"No, indeed not. That would be alright." Monmouth sounded delighted. "Shall you come with me?"

Philip shook his head regretfully. "Alas, your Grace, it would be my greatest pleasure, but it seems there are those here who reckon me to be less than beneficial to your Cause."

"Surely not!" Monmouth got to his feet and turned around to face the company. "Who can doubt the worth of one who did so much for me, regardless of the perils in which he placed himself? Gentlemen, is there one man in our number so forgetful, so presumptuous that he would not choose Lord Devalle to be his leader?"

Philip smiled. Monmouth had played right into his hands, as he had known he would.

He protested all the same. "I beg you to consider carefully, your Grace. There may be another better qualified to lead your followers. "Lord Grey, perhaps?"

"Good Lord, no," Grey said hastily. "I will appoint you gladly."

"Or the Earl of Essex?" Philip suggested.

Essex held up his hand. "No, Philip, I'll not be the leader, though it seems we need one, for the Cause has fallen sadly into disarray."

"Then as things have changed so much since I went to France," Philip looked directly at Howard, his voice growing colder, "a better man might be Lord Howard of Escrick."

Howard swallowed as he faced him. It was an open challenge Philip had offered him and the only way to save his face before the others was to answer it, but Philip knew he was a coward and would never dare defy him.

"Let him get on with it," Howard muttered, averting his gaze. "I shall follow him if all the others do."

"I'll follow him," Algernon Sydney said, holding up his glass. "Lord Devalle!"

The cry was taken up from all sides until nothing could be heard but Philip's name, as his health was drunk by one and all.

He winked at Giles as he waited for the room to quieten down once more. "Gentlemen, in the face of such tumultuous and unexpected appreciation, what can I say but that I shall be honoured to lead this glorious campaign? I will discuss a plan with you after Monmouth and I return from Cheshire."

The meeting broke up then and Monmouth embraced him warmly." My dearest friend, I knew my trust in you was not misplaced. I can practically hear the crowds proclaiming me their king already! How soon are we to leave?"

"The races are in the second week of September," Philip said, feeling a little guilty. "I suggest that we depart at the beginning of the month."

He pressed some money into Oates' hand and slipped from the room to wait for Giles, who he knew would follow him.

"So, what did you think?" Philip asked.

"About what, your theatricals?" Giles said. "You were quite superb, as ever."

"Why, thank you, Giles, but, as you very well know, I really meant what did you think to my proposal."

"Oh that! I was simply wondering why you are advising Monmouth to make a tour of Cheshire when you know full well it will bring his father's wrath down upon him."

"So much the better if it does," Philip said. "I want him to be forced to take a stand."

"It's much too soon. Lord Russell says..."

"Never mind Russell! With Argyle and those we can incite in Cheshire and the West, Monmouth can rise within a year, just as I said."

"With you beside him?" Giles asked cynically.

"What do you take me for?"

"I am no longer certain, to be frank," Giles said. "I thought you cared about Monmouth."

"I do care," Philip admitted, "but it will all come to nothing, for Lord Shaftesbury hardly looks as though he has a year left to live."

"And what about the dangers you are exposed to in the

meantime?" Giles said. "I can't believe your estate is worth so much to you. I thought you hated it."

"I hate the memory of the miserable years I spent there," Philip said, "but Heatherton is my estate by right. I have been forced to undertake some distasteful tasks since my father died and left me penniless, but High Heatherton can provide the wherewithal for me to live exactly as I choose, servant to none. Damn it, Giles, I've reached an age when I would like to please myself."

Giles snorted at that. He had no prospect of inheriting a rich estate and, as Philip knew, he would always have to make his own way in the world. "I can't agree with this."

"But it was you who persuaded me to take up with Shaftesbury again."

"I did no such thing. I merely delivered the Earl's message, and I wish now I had never done so," Giles said with feeling.

"Even so, I trust I will have your support."

"By that I suppose you mean me to accompany you and Monmouth to Cheshire."

"That is what I had in mind," Philip said. "Actually it might be fun. Shaftesbury could lend us two of his racehorses."

"You intend us to compete?"

"Why not? The people love to see us at play. What do you say?"

Giles still looked far from happy. "I wish I could be surer that you knew what you were doing. What is this marvellous plan you spoke about anyway?"

"I'll tell you later."

"Why not tell me now?"

"Because I haven't thought of it yet," Philip said patiently. "I had to give them something or they would have never followed me. Don't worry," he said, seeing Giles' expression, "I'll come up with such a notion as will fill them with dreams of glory!"

"And suppose you don't?" Giles was a practical soul.

"For heaven's sake! If you do not trust my motives you should at least trust my ingenuity. Shall you come to Cheshire?"

"I'll come," Giles said. "I'll even race, if it will please you. You will have my absolute support in all you do, but only on the understanding that you will abandon this madness directly Heatherton becomes yours."

"I promise."

"It may not be so easy when the time comes," Giles warned.

"Nonsense! I can finish my involvement any time I choose."

"You always have the damnedest way of being blind to problems you don't wish to see," Giles said despairingly, "but let us say no more about it now. Are you dining with Monmouth and me at Chatelaine's tonight?"

"No. You go without me," Philip said. "It's been a busy day. I think I'll just go home."

The truth was that he had quite a lot to think about, following his conversation with Buckingham, and he rather fancied a walk on his own to clarify his thoughts.

Giles looked doubtful. "Is it wise for you to go about alone? Theresa told me that Portsmouth has been making threats."

"Wise or not, it's what I intend to do tonight. Don't lecture me," Philip begged, seeing the beginnings of a frown on Giles' face. "I can't tread warily all my life for fear of that bitch."

It was just starting to get dark when Philip stepped out into the street. He saw a link boy, standing with his lantern at the corner of Chancery Lane and gave the boy directions, tossing him a coin. He was quite glad of the illumination, for in summer houses were not obliged to show a light and there was no moon that night.

Fleet Street was eerily quiet at that late hour and Philip was deep in thought as they as they headed towards Ludgate Hill. It had rained earlier in the day and he stumbled on the cobbles, which were still damp. The jolt focused his mind sharply back to the present. They were about to pass the church of St. Dunstan's and although he could see no-one save his link boy, some six paces ahead, Philip suddenly knew all was not well.

It was a chilling sensation and, as a soldier, he had learned never to disregard his instincts. He stopped and listened. There was nothing untoward and yet the feeling remained with him, almost a sixth sense.

Philip was alert now and anticipating trouble as they drew level with the church. He decided to see better what might be lurking in the shadows and he was about to call out to the boy to bring over his lantern when he heard faint footsteps behind him.

He swung round. Six masked figures materialised from the blackness and barred his way.

The link boy saw them too and must have realised what was afoot. He fled, dropping the lantern in his haste and leaving them in darkness, save for its glow as it sputtered in the gutter.

"Who would have thought he would be so easy to take?"

The man might have been wearing a mask but Philip had no trouble in recognising the slight French accent of Louis Duras, the Earl of Feversham, once a friend of Monmouth but now an ally of the Duchess of Portsmouth.

"You haven't taken me yet, Feversham."

The Frenchman laughed and, as if it were a signal, six swords were simultaneously drawn.

Philip reacted swiftly. He leapt to the side and drew his own sword, at the same time releasing his cloak from his shoulders.

As his attackers advanced he swirled the cloak with his left hand, tangling two of their swords in it, whilst he lunged with his own sword at a third man and caught him squarely in the chest. This one went down with barely a sound, and Philip knew at a glance that he would be no more trouble.

"The bastard's killed my man."

Philip knew that voice too. It belonged to Lord Bentham, and Philip guessed that his other assailants were probably servants of the two noblemen.

Bentham, Feversham and the remaining servant were on him in a flash and he warded them off, scything the air with his sword. Holding them back as best he could, he drew a dagger from his belt with his left hand, but the first two men, having retrieved their swords from his cloak, were advancing too, and now looked more than ready to fight.

Bentham brought his sword down on him but Philip was quick and dodged the blow, managing, as he did so, to plunge his knife into another servant's belly.

Now that he had dropped his guard Feversham and his henchmen attacked as one and, as Bentham joined them, Philip was driven back against the church wall.

He fought furiously but he soon sensed the futility of his efforts as he began to tire against the force of four men. He managed to strike Bentham on the arm and heard his weapon clatter to the ground, accompanied by a cry of pain. The next second Philip cried out himself as a sharp blade came at him from the right, by mischance piercing the site of the old injury upon his side. It was not a deep cut but the scar tissue was thin.

Feversham, quick to take advantage of Philip momentary weakness, knocked the sword from his hand. With three blades now pointing at his chest Philip knew it was all over, and he cursed his own folly in not heeding Giles' and Morgan's advice.

He was no coward, however, and with death mere inches away his eyes met Feversham's unwaveringly. They had not always been enemies. The dandified earl was, more than anything, a courtier and they had often enjoyed each other's company in the past.

"Well, Feversham, for I know it is you," he panted, "you have me at your mercy, so kill me now and get it over with."

"That's all very fine, but those are not my orders," Feversham said quietly. "Seize him," he ordered the two surviving lackeys, "and hold on to him tightly, for he is stronger than he looks."

Slowly, and almost reluctantly, he drew out a small stiletto.

Philip viewed it in horror. "What are you planning to do?" he asked, fearing that he already knew.

Bentham, who had been tying a handkerchief around his arm to staunch the bleeding, laughed harshly. "You like to follow fashion, Devalle. Did you not know that nose-slitting is in vogue this season?"

Philip felt sick as the Frenchman raised the knife. This was different altogether. Men whose noses had been slit to the bone were horribly disfigured forever and ridiculed as freaks. "In God's name, Feversham, kill me. Anything but this."

"Lady Portsmouth said to tell you that it was to cure you of your vanity," Bentham continued remorselessly.

"I can't do it." Feversham handed the knife to Bentham. "You may take the credit for ruining his looks. I want no more to do with it."

Philip swallowed. He knew he could expect no quarter from Bentham. The knife drew closer until he felt its cold touch on his skin.

Suddenly Feversham pulled Bentham's arm away. "Stop! Someone comes."

A shot rang out.

One of the servants holding Philip's arms dropped to the ground, dead.

Philip shook off the other with ease and the man bolted for cover, but he was too slow. A second bullet broke the silence of the night and he went down, the back of his head a gory mess.

Giles ran out from the shadows, throwing down his spent pistols and drawing his sword, but Feversham and Bentham had slipped swiftly away into the night.

Philip leaned against the wall and took a deep breath.

"Giles! You were always a fine shot."

"Are you hurt?" Giles asked, as Philip gingerly undid his waistcoat, revealing his bloodstained shirt.

"Not as badly as I might have been," Philip said, shuddering at the thought. "What the devil are you doing here? I thought you had gone with Monmouth."

"I decided to follow you instead. If you must know I was worried about you," Giles admitted crossly, as he picked up his pistols. "I met with your link boy, who was scared out of his wits. He told me you'd been set upon."

"I'm very pleased you did come after me. That was a close thing." Philip retrieved his sword and cloak and they left the scene quickly before any came to investigate the shots.

"Who were they?" Giles said.

"Only footpads."

"Don't try my patience, Philip," Giles warned. "I've had quite enough of your inventions for one night. Who attacked you?"

"Feversham and Bentham," Philip said, a little sheepishly, "though they were masked and I could never prove a thing against them."

"What shall you do?"

"Bentham is a dead man," Philip said grimly. "You may depend on that. Feversham will be trickier. He is too prominent a person and any misfortune that befell him would throw suspicion upon Monmouth's supporters, but I will find a way to remind him that it is a bad idea to cross me."

"Yes, I'm sure you will! And have you learned anything by what happened tonight?" Giles asked him.

Philip smiled. "That you worry about me?"

Giles gave a fair imitation of one of Morgan's heavy sighs. "What I meant was that you are being closely observed. You must be on your guard at all times if you are determined on this mad scheme of yours."

"Yes, Giles," Philip said meekly, amused that he was being lectured by his young brother-in-law. "I promise that in the future I shall never leave home without you, Thomas or Morgan by my side!"

SIX

A mile from Nantwich the Duke of Monmouth climbed out of his coach to ride the last part of the journey on horseback, as had become his custom when entering a town.

He rode alone. At a distance before him were a small band of noblemen, which included Sir Thomas Armstrong and Lord Macclesfield, with his son, Lord Brandon, all resplendent in plumes and colourful costumes. Behind them rode their servants and tenants, about a hundred men, all finely turned out and armed.

Philip rode at the head of the whole procession with Giles at his side.

The church bells were ringing out in Monmouth's honour and Philip had to draw nearer to his brother-in-law to be heard above their clamour. He pointed out a small boy, who stood in the crowd with his mother. Behind the boy's ears and under his chin were seeping sores.

"Look over there, Giles, what do you see?"

Giles looked. "That's scrofula. What of it?"

"King's Evil!"

"You're not suggesting Monmouth should touch him?"

Traditionally a king's touch could cure the complaint.

"Why not?" Philip asked. "Let him have his little bit of glory."

Giles shrugged and glanced back at the boy. "I don't suppose it can worsen him."

"Of course not. Hold the child whilst I bring Monmouth over."

Giles wheeled his horse around. "I thought, somehow, that I would get that job!"

He dismounted before the boy, who cowered away from him. Giles was wearing his captain's uniform and must have seemed formidable to the child at such close quarters.

"May I see your son?" Giles said to the woman, whose skirts the child held tightly.

"Yes, Captain. He has the Evil, see?"

Giles inspected the boy's swellings, which were discharging a white, curdled matter, and he nodded. "That he has. The Duke will touch him for you."

The woman fell to her knees in awe as Monmouth approached. He reached out his hand and stroked the boy's ulcerated neck. "God bless you, child."

"A good idea of mine, I reckon," Philip said to Giles as the townspeople shouted their approval.

Giles gave him a sidelong glance. "I'm not sure Monmouth's father would agree with you!"

That night they stayed at an inn just outside the town, where they talked over the events of the day. Monmouth seemed unhappy, despite the success of the Progress, and Philip guessed he was missing his mistress, Henrietta Wentworth. He was very much in love with her and Philip suspected that, at times, dreams of a life of blissful peace with Henrietta almost surpassed his desire to sit upon the throne of England.

Shaftesbury had never encouraged him to dream.

When the Earl reminded him of the duty he had to his supporters Monmouth had always set aside his romantic visions and accepted that he must sacrifice his own happiness for the good of the country, for he was very conscious of his responsibilities. Shaftesbury would not always be around, however, and Philip hoped that, without him, he would be able to persuade the Duke to follow his heart.

He glanced around. All of the company was familiar to him,

save one. Sitting at the other end of the table was a quiet man called Shakerley. No-one knew too much about Peter Shakerley. He always seemed to be studying everyone, and Philip had a strong suspicion he was now trying to listen to the conversation Thomas Armstrong was having with Lord Brandon further down the table.

"Who are you watching?" Giles said, looking up from his dinner.

Giles had a good appetite, like his sister. On this occasion he had already enjoyed a dish of anchovies, some prawns, a portion of neat's tongue and a chunk of cheese. He was finishing with a plate of stewed fruits.

"Shakerley. There's something strange about him."

Giles wiped his spoon and replaced it in his pocket. "Maybe he's a spy."

"That's just what I was thinking."

"We ought to tell the others."

Philip looked at Macclesfield and at the stolid figures of Sir Willoughby Aston and Sir Henry Booth, who were drinking with him. I don't believe we should, or we'll never get them to Wallasey."

"Then what are you going to do?"

"Nothing," Philip said. "I suspected Charles would place one in our midst, for you know he reckons that these northern counties are full of Whigs and malcontents. I think he is looking for an excuse to have Monmouth arrested."

"They should still be warned," Giles said. "What if Charles has anyone else arrested with Monmouth?"

"Well he won't," Philip said confidently. "He will seize Monmouth as a warning, that is all, and pardon him, as he always does. If he takes any others into custody with him he will either have to pardon them too, which would look bad, or prosecute them for a crime for which his son goes free, which would look worse. Don't worry, Giles. Everything is under control."

The Wallasey races were a welcome break for everyone. Philip and Giles each won a race, to the delight of the crowd, but the most important event, the twelve stone plate, was won by Monmouth himself.

There was wild rejoicing in the town that night and Philip saw to it that bonfires were lit in several streets to celebrate. Even though a few were extinguished by those who did not support the Duke, most burned throughout the night.

The following day they travelled on to Liverpool, where Monmouth played bowls and ran footraces with the locals. All seemed to be going well until they left the city.

There was a sudden disturbance amongst the crowd that lined the route and a man pushed forward, shouting abuse at the Duke.

Philip cursed. The fellow did not appear to be armed, but he could not take the chance. He rode directly into the assailant's path and blocked his way.

The ground was slippery, churned up by those who had come to watch the procession, and the man fell, right under Ferrion's hooves. The horse reared and it took all Philip's skill to stay in the saddle and to urge him back without trampling the prostrate figure into the mud.

The crowd gasped, for it seemed certain he would be crushed, but he managed to scramble up, unhurt.

The spectators enthusiastically applauded Philip's display of horsemanship but the incident had soured the day. It was the first open hostility they had met with.

They encountered no further problems, at least not until they reached Stafford.

Mr. Phipps, a mercer in the town, was entertaining Monmouth, Philip and Giles when their meal was interrupted by Phipps' servant, who whispered urgently in his master's ear.

The mercer looked at them in alarm. "Gentlemen, it would appear that a Sergeant-at-Arms has called upon us and demands that we admit him. What should I do?"

"What can you do?" Philip asked him, taking charge of the situation, for Monmouth had turned quite pale and seemed incapable of speech. "Since he obviously knows the Duke is here you may as well admit him."

Sergeant Ramsey entered and bowed before Monmouth. "Your Grace, I have been instructed to arrest you in the name of the King, and to deliver this warrant into your hands."

"Oh dear! I fear my father is angry with me again," Monmouth said in a resigned voice, as he took the warrant.

Philip watched him coolly, that is until Ramsey turned to him.

"I am to arrest you too, my Lord."

That took him totally by surprise.

"All is under control," Giles muttered. "Huh!"

Monmouth was reading his warrant.

"Whereas his Majesty has received information that James, Duke of Monmouth, Orkney and Buccleugh, has lately appeared in several parts of this Kingdom with great numbers of people, in a riotous and unlawful manner, to the disturbance of the public peace, and to the terror of His Majesty's good subjects." Monmouth turned to Philip despairingly. "This is unjust. However am I to defend myself?"

But Philip had problems of his own.

Giles had taken the warrant from his hand and was reading it out loud. "That upon the 12th of September, in the town of Liverpool, you did willfully and maliciously attempt to murder a man who had given you no provocation." He looked at Philip in horror.

Philip, on the contrary, felt rather relieved. He could not believe that Charles was seriously intending to press the charge, for he would know that there were plenty of witnesses who would give evidence on his behalf as to the true nature of the incident. He guessed that Shakerley had sent back a report from Liverpool and that Charles, seeing no way in which he could touch him for merely accompanying Monmouth to the races, had seized upon any excuse to arrest him.

"It's nothing much to worry over," he said.

"Nothing much?" Giles repeated. "You will be returned to London under guard accused of attempted murder, and that is nothing much?"

"I'll never be accused of it in court. The Sergeant knows it quite as well as me, eh Ramsey?"

Ramsey scowled. "I only know that I am to arrest you, my Lord," he said stiffly.

Philip smiled. "You might as well arrest my horse too, since he was party to the crime of which I am accused."

"You will be lucky if the brute isn't shot."

The smile left Philip's face. He grabbed Ramsey by the collar. "What do you mean by that?"

"Let go of me. I am an officer of the law," Ramsey gasped choking.

"What have you done to my horse, Ramsey," Philip demanded, letting go of him.

Ramsey staggered backwards, coughing. "My men are examining him now."

"You idiot! He'll kill them!"

Philip pushed past him and ran out to the stables, followed closely by Giles and Monmouth. Before they were even in the yard they heard a furious whinny and then a man's scream.

Inside the stall three soldiers were desperately trying to avoid Ferrion's flailing hooves and a fourth was staggering to his feet, blood streaming from a gash upon his head. The horse was attacking them like a thing possessed, his teeth bared and his nostrils snorting steam.

Philip needed to act, and swiftly. He seized the soldiers one by one and hurled them unceremoniously out into the stable yard. As soon as he approached Ferrion a remarkable change came over the magnificent black stallion.

Philip spoke his name in a low voice and Ferrion immediately came to him, shaking his noble head. Philip walked him out of the stable, his hand upon the horse's neck, speaking softly to him all the while until he quietened.

Ramsey looked relieved. "You certainly have a way with him, my Lord. Are you not afraid that he may one day turn on you?"

"Of course not. I trained him myself and, if he's properly handled, he's as docile as a lamb."

Even as he spoke the dark muzzle nudged his face as though for reassurance. Ferrion was an Andalusian cross, with the long curling mane and tail so characteristic of the breed, although at seventeen hands he was much taller than was usual for a Spanish horse. Philip had acquired him in Holland during the Dutch Wars and loved the horse, though none could really control him save himself and, curiously enough, young Thomas, who was the only other person who dared to ride him.

"He's a killer," Ramsey reckoned.

"He's a war horse, strong and fiery. Your clods angered him."

Ramsey looked about to say more, but Philip glared at him and he turned his attention to Monmouth instead.

"Your Grace, will you submit yourself into my custody?"

Monmouth sighed. "I might as well."

"What of you, Lord Devalle?"

Philip shrugged. "Do what you like with me, Ramsey. You'll be a laughing stock in London when folk learn of this."

From Ramsey's expression it seemed as though he feared Philip may be right. "Then if you are ready, gentlemen, we should be leaving."

"I would have a word with Captain Fairfield first," Philip said firmly, drawing Giles aside. "Ride post haste to London and have Shaftesbury obtain a writ of Habeas Corpus for Monmouth," he instructed him. "It will reflect badly on the King that he has seized his own son without sufficient evidence to do so."

"What if he has evidence?" Giles said.

"He hasn't," Philip said confidently. "He's arresting him because he is afraid of what may happen if he doesn't. This will all look well for us, I promise. I suppose you'd better ask Shaftesbury to obtain a writ for me as well," he added, with a wry smile. "I won't be too much use to him in the Tower!"

❧

Shaftesbury took the news of the arrests philosophically. "How did the tour go?" he asked Giles as he handed him the two writs of Habeas Corpus, signed by Judge Raymond.

"Better than we could have hoped," Giles said. "The people cried 'a Monmouth and no York', wherever we went."

"Then we can rise," Shaftesbury said exultantly. "It is time."

"Monmouth does not think so, my Lord," Giles told him. "He still says it is too soon."

"Too soon? Too Soon?" Shaftesbury looked exasperated. "The Duke of Monmouth is an unfortunate man, Giles. Three times now he has had the chance to use his popularity to seize power; once in Scotland, when he was a general, once in the West and now in Cheshire, and each time he has neglected to make use of his opportunities. I wonder sometimes how Philip still has patience with him. How did they behave on their arrests, by the by?"

"Monmouth made no protest whatsoever."

"And Philip?"

"Philip?" Giles smiled as he recalled the scene at the stables. "Oh, Philip took it very calmly!"

❧

"What is to happen to my nephew?" The Duke of York demanded of Charles.

"I have forbidden him to appear at Court for a while and sent him to live at Moor Park with his wife and children," Charles said.

York looked at his brother incredulously. "He is to suffer no punishment?"

"He says he does not even know of what he is accused."

"And what about entering Chester with seven hundred horse and those about him crying out against me?"

"He swears he had not intended to disturb the peace," Charles said. "He was released on bail of £20,000 and summoned to be of good behaviour and to appear before the King's Bench upon the first day of next term."

York snorted in disgust. "I can't believe he has managed to charm you again. Why did you even have him arrested if you were going to forgive him, as you always do?"

In answer to his question Charles handed him a letter he had received from one of his many agents. "This is why. It reports that some gentlemen from Cheshire and Shropshire, under the pretext of attending the Wallasey races, held a meeting in the Forest of Delamere and there pledged their loyalty to me, swearing to combat any disturbances caused by Monmouth's friends. I feared I would have another Civil War on my hands if I did not act swiftly. The pity of it is that my son is not to blame," he said, as York read the letter. "He is weak and easily led by those much cleverer than himself, such as Philip Devalle."

"Yet he, too, has been freed," York said acidly.

"The Earl of Shaftesbury is as well conversant with the law as any lawyer, and he would make a mockery of the case against Devalle. What has he done, after all, but attend a horse race with some friends? There is no crime in that. It is my son the people turned out to see. If I arrested all those who rode with him I would have a rising on my hands before the week was out."

"What about the charge of attempted murder?"

"I never expected to hold him on that," Charles admitted.

"It was intended as a warning, one which I hope he will heed. I intend to see to it that he does not have Shaftesbury to protect him for much longer."

"What are you going to do?"

"Nothing yet, but the Sheriff's elections are next month and this time I am in no doubt that the Whigs will lose. Then at last I will have justice in my own hands, with my own men in the courts and the Earl will be at my mercy. I don't believe he could endure another visit to the Tower, do you?"

"I think it would kill him," York said.

Charles black eyes gleamed. "Yes. So do I!"

"But what if Devalle is hatching another plot?" York persisted.

"Let him. Whatever he is planning will come to nothing," Charles said confidently. "Philip has too much sense to fight me on his own."

York was less sure of that. What he could be sure of, however, was that if anyone in the world knew what Philip Devalle was planning it was Devalle's wife.

"Don't push him too far," Charles warned, as though reading his thoughts. "Whatever he does my son will defend him and get himself into trouble."

York did not reply. As it happened he had his own reasons for wanting to question Theresa Devalle, reasons which had nothing whatever to do with any business involving the Duke of Monmouth!

SEVEN

∽

Cheapside was crowded. It had rained heavily earlier in the day and, now that the sun had come out, it seemed as though every Londoner was out and about.

Theresa, a basket on her arm, was among them, picking her way over the slippery cobbles and trying to avoid the stinking mud that coursed along the centre of the street.

She stopped before a vendor with a tray of apples around his neck and bought some for a pie. All around her street sellers were shouting out their wares.

"White-hearted cabbages," called a country maiden, pushing a cart loaded with vegetables.

"Fine herrings, eight a groat," cried a fishwife.

"Any brass pots, iron pots, frying pans to mend?"

"Buy a mousetrap, a mousetrap?"

"A tormenter for your fleas?"

"What d'ye lack, mistress?" an apprentice, standing before his shop, bawled at her.

Theresa passed through, unconcerned by the crush or the noise, for she had grown accustomed to it since they had moved to the little house around the corner. It was a very different life to the one they had lived in Paris, but Theresa did not mind that in the least. It had been her own idea to save money by not engaging any new household staff and, since Bet, Morgan and Thomas had more than enough to do, Theresa, brought up in a large, country family, did not consider it demeaning for her

59

to lend a hand by sometimes shopping for food and cooking meals.

Two milkmaids came along the street and she stepped aside to let them pass. The rattling of their pails obscured the sound of iron wheels rumbling over the damp cobbles. Theresa did not hear the carriage and was not aware it had stopped just behind her.

A strong arm grabbed her around the waist. She struggled and cried out, but no-one turned to look as her own cry mingled with the voices all around her. She dropped her basket, the apples rolling across the street as she felt herself being lifted bodily into the coach.

Theresa kicked out at her attacker but he held her down easily, for she was slim and light.

"Be still," a coarse voice rasped in her ear, "and you will not be hurt."

She managed to bite the hand that held her down and she heard the man curse. The next second her head jerked back as he fetched her a vicious slap across the face.

"I said be still, you bitch!"

The world began to spin around her and she could struggle no more.

Philip returned home to find Morgan, Bet and Thomas frantic with worry. When Theresa had not returned from her errands Thomas had gone out to look for her, only to find that she appeared to have vanished without a trace. He had just returned from questioning some of the tradesmen in the street but, although the apple seller remembered serving her, none of the others could recall one person amongst the many that were out and about that day.

Philip listened, stunned. He was well aware of the risks he was taking and he had dismissed them carelessly, as he always did. It had never once occurred to him that he was putting the woman he loved in danger by his actions.

"She must have been taken," he said, feeling sick at the thought. "Thomas, go and fetch Giles. Bet, stay here in case she returns or there is news. Morgan, you and I are going hunting in St. James' Park."

"May I ask what we are hunting?" Morgan said as they set off in Philip's carriage.

"Certainly. The Earl of Feversham. It's my guess that Louise is behind this."

Philip knew Feversham liked to take a constitutional, when his duties as Lord Chamberlain to Queen Catherine would permit. Knowing how keen Feversham was to ingratiate himself with Charles, Philip guessed that he would time this to suit the King's regular stroll in the Privy Garden. Charles went there every day at the same time to adjust his watch at the sundial and he was always happy to converse with any of the courtiers who cared to keep him company.

Philip and Morgan positioned themselves by the little physic garden, from which the King culled herbs for the laboratory he'd made beneath his closet. They did not have long to wait.

Philip smiled as the royal party came into view. Feversham was close by Charles' side. "Here comes our quarry, Morgan!"

Feversham saw him and stiffened. They had not come face to face since the night of Philip's attack and he guessed that Feversham would have excused himself from the company if it had been remotely possible, but it was not.

Charles stopped and looked at him. If he was surprised to see him he was obviously not about to show it. He nodded to him as though they were the best of friends. "Philip! It is not often we see you here."

As well as Feversham, Charles was accompanied that morning by Sir William Temple and Sidney Godolphin. Temple, being strongly for the King and the Court party, had never been friendly with Philip and he eyed him now with frank suspicion, but Godolphin spoke to him. He was a clever financier who never took sides, caring only that the Treasury work was properly done, no matter who was in power at the time.

Philip indicated the flourishing patch of herbs. "I see your Majesty still pursues your experiments."

"Indeed I do. I am progressing every day." Science, Philip knew, was one of Charles' passions. "Perhaps you would care to see my laboratory one day, if you are interested."

Philip had no more love of science than he had of anything else vaguely academic, but he attempted to look pleased, since Charles was making an effort to be civil to him. "I should be honoured, your Majesty."

The walk continued towards St. James' Park. Charles had planted the park with flowers and walks of trees, and filled it with unusual animals. Guinea goats and antelope roamed there amongst Arabian sheep and Charles bred all manner of wildfowl on the canal that he had employed his disbanded soldiers to dig.

Philip joined the others, insuring that he was never more than a pace or two from Feversham, whilst Morgan walked a few steps behind the Earl. They crossed the Mall and were approaching the canal before he had an opportunity to take him on one side.

He put an arm around Feversham's shoulders, as though they were engaged in an intimate conversation.

The Frenchman laughed nervously. "I'm actually rather pleased to see you here today, Philip."

"I'm sure you are!"

"No, I mean it, for there is a slight misunderstanding that we should discuss."

"There is no misunderstanding, you two-faced evil bastard! If you and your friends had not been interrupted on the night you ambushed me I would never have been able to show my face here, or anywhere else, again."

Philip had lapsed into the Frenchman's native tongue, for he was aware that Godolphin was still beside them. It was easy to forget he was there, for he was an unobtrusive man, never in the way and never out of it, but that did not suit Philip's purposes today.

"What are you going to do?" Feversham asked uneasily, as Philip steered him away from the others over towards the trees.

"What do you think?"

"I think you might be going to kill me."

"Kill the nephew of my old commander, General Turenne?" Philip said. "I don't believe I could do that. I am not altogether certain, mind."

Feversham swallowed. "Don't jest with me."

"Feversham, I rarely jest. I have very little humour; Morgan has even less."

Feversham looked round. Morgan was just behind them still, his knife now in his hand.

"You would never kill me here!"

"I wouldn't. Morgan might."

To convince him of the fact Morgan held the sharp blade so close to Feversham's back that the point pierced his coat.

The Frenchman sucked his breath in sharply. "You're trying to frighten me and you're succeeding. Stop this game, I beg you."

"I'll stop it when I'm ready. I have not forgotten that you refused to injure me and for that I am prepared to spare your life," Philip told him, "but there will be a condition."

"Anything. You have me at your mercy," Feversham said. He was hardly in a position to argue, for they were between the trees that bordered the canal now, out of sight of the others.

"I want to know who has Theresa."

Feversham stared at him. "I don't know what you mean."

"She was abducted off the street this morning. I want to know where Portsmouth is holding her."

"I know nothing about it." Feversham flinched as Morgan's

knife scratched a line across his skin. "I'm telling you the truth. You cannot kill me on account of something I do not know."

Philip cursed, for he felt inclined to believe him. Feversham looked totally bemused and he doubted that the Frenchman was that good an actor, particularly with a knife at his back. He indicated that Morgan was to let him go.

"You've finished with me?" Feversham asked, breathing a sigh of relief.

"Not yet. You're going to help us find her."

"And I would gladly do so, Philip, but I don't believe that Lady Portsmouth had a hand in this."

"She has a hand in everything," Philip said.

"But not in kidnapping your wife, I'm certain. The Duke of York, though, is a different matter."

"York?" Philip raised an eyebrow. It had never occurred to him that it might be York. What would he want with her?"

"Probably to discover what Lady Portsmouth is up to. York has spies following her everywhere, for he doesn't trust her."

"I don't blame him, but what has that to do with Tess?"

"I understand she and Theresa had an altercation at the 'Change. He probably wants to know what it was about."

"You see, Feversham, you're being useful to me after all." Philip spoke lightly but he was even more worried now than he had been before. York was as ruthless as Portsmouth and if Theresa was caught between the two he knew she could be in very serious trouble indeed. "As a well-informed courtier, into all the dirty little secrets of Whitehall, where would you imagine he might be holding her?"

"No," Feversham said, shaking his head. "I have already told you more than I should."

Philip reached out and grabbed him by the cravat. "That was not a request, you understand, Feversham. I want an answer to my question."

He twisted the cravat tighter until Feversham's eyes began to water as he gulped for breath.

Philip released him suddenly and watched as he coughed and retched. "Answer me!"

"York owns an old grain warehouse by the Thames near Rotherhithe," Feversham gasped. "Certain people have been taken there for questioning in the past. That is all I know."

"Let's hope, for your sake, it is enough." Philip took his arm and began to walk briskly.

"Where are you taking me now?"

"Back to my carriage, whilst Morgan walks behind us, like the good servant he is, lest we be set upon by footpads, as I was not so long ago."

"But I have told you everything I can," Feversham protested.

"Now all I have to do is prevent you from running to the Duke of York or Lady Portsmouth."

"You intend to keep me prisoner?" Feversham cried. "That's unjust."

Philip nodded sympathetically. "Yes, I know."

It was dark when Thomas led Philip, Giles and Morgan down to the edge of the Thames, beneath Strand Bridge.

Feversham had been left at the house, locked in a room and in Bet's charge. Philip knew there was no chance of him managing to persuade the maid to release him until they returned.

Despite the lateness of the hour a few watermen could still be seen sitting upon the benches on either side of the steps, awaiting customers.

Thomas looked about until he spied the one he sought, a giant of a man, his muscles bulging under the short-necked doublet that he wore, the uniform of King Charles' 'nursery of seamen'.

"Next oars," the man cried hopefully. He grinned as Thomas pulled back the hood of his cloak. "Why, if it ain't young Thomas, and done up like a bloody gentleman!"

Thomas flushed. "Hush! If you hold your tongue and do not show me up you can make yourself some money."

"Show you up, you cheeky little blighter? Me who knew you when you had no shoes upon your feet and all ten of your fingers?" Thomas had lost the little finger of his left hand years ago when he was trying to steal a lady's purse and she had slammed her carriage door shut on his hand! The huge man slapped him on the back with a friendly clout that nearly put him in the water. "Who's that with you, then, his Lordship?" he joked.

"Yes." Now it was Thomas' turn to smile as the waterman's jovial laughter tailed away.

"So it is, by God!" He nodded in Philip's direction. "Good evening, Lord Devalle. What is it I can do for you?"

It was scarcely the deference usually accorded to his rank but Philip knew that for one of the watermen, who prided themselves upon their insolence to high and low alike, it was considerable.

"Let us discuss, instead, what I can do for you," Philip said. "I can put five gold pieces in your hand if you take us to Rotherhithe and keep your great mouth shut about it."

The waterman bellowed loudly at that and beckoned them to his craft, laying out some damp cushions for his passengers to sit on and wiping, with the sleeve of his sweaty shirt, the board on which they were to lean. Then he pointed to his lips. "Sealed!"

Philip winked at Thomas. "They had better be or Thomas bears the brunt of my displeasure."

"I beg your Lordship not to lay a hand on him, for he's a good boy, and his uncle won't let you down."

"Uncle?" Philip asked, turning to Thomas.

Thomas shrugged. "I don't believe he is, but I have always called him so."

"And should he ever need protection I'm as good as any family he could have," the waterman insisted.

"Should Thomas ever need protection I am all the family he will need," Philip said possessively, and he saw Thomas glow with pride.

They started off at a fine, fast pace, for the night current was swift and a fresh breeze helped them on their way. There were few other craft upon the water so late, which was fortunate, for the watermen loved to indulge in coarse exchanges with all and sundry that they passed and Philip had no wish to be conspicuous on this occasion.

Thomas stretched a worn cloth over the hoops fixed across the stern as they approached the arches of London Bridge, and their oarsman rested as the little boat was pulled down into the foam. The river roared about them as they were sucked almost into one of the great piles which protected the stonework and then, suddenly, they shot free.

Many passengers, nervous of these rapids, disembarked at the Old Swan, just before the bridge, and rejoined their boat upon the other side but none of Philip's party were unnerved, whilst their boatman laughed gleefully.

"Last flood-tide I caught a haddock in my hands at this very spot, as it lay there blinded by the rushing water," he bragged.

The cover had been of hardly any use at all and they were all soaked, exactly as they had expected to be, but they shook out their wet cloaks without complaint. They had other things upon their minds.

The boat travelled on past Wapping and nearly to Rotherhithe before Philip motioned the boatman to slow. Ahead of them, looming large and black against the pale, moon-flecked clouds, stood an old warehouse.

There was no sign of life, save for the faintest glow which

emanated from one window, as though a single candle burned within. It was sufficient indication, nonetheless, for that dim light shone like a beacon in the darkness.

"That has to be the place," Philip said. "Move in as quietly as you can."

Keeping very close to the bank, the boatman approached the building cautiously, but there was no-one to be seen outside.

"Evidently they are not expecting visitors," Philip said. "This might be easier than I anticipated. Put up ashore just here, please," he told their oarsman, "and take your money."

The boatman pulled in and he pocketed his payment eagerly as his passengers disembarked. Philip was the last to leave the boat and he passed a large sack to Morgan as he did so.

"Stow that in the bushes, Morgan. We may need it later."

He knew that they were all wondering about the contents of the sack but he was keeping it a secret for the moment.

The waterman put his filthy, brawny hand on Philip's shoulder. "May good fortune shine upon your venture, Lord Devalle."

Philip smiled. "You don't even know what I am about, man! How can you wish me fortune?"

"Yet I do, sir, so do all of us, whatever you are at. The people of this city love you."

"God alone knows why," Giles muttered, to no-one in particular.

They crouched down until the boat was out of sight. It seemed that no-one had spotted their arrival so they scrambled up the bank, obscured by the thickness of the undergrowth.

Closer to the warehouse they could see that a second, even paler, light also burned upon the upper floor.

"That's where they are keeping her," Philip guessed. "The other room, I'll warrant, is a guard room. Morgan, you and I will seek them out and stop any who try to leave whilst you, Giles, locate Theresa and bring her down."

"What shall I do, my Lord?" Thomas asked him.

A coach stood empty in the court yard and there was a stable nearby. "You hitch up a team to that coach, Thomas, and be ready with it, but for God's sake keep the horses quiet, or we may all be dead men."

Thomas sped off quickly and silently toward the stables whilst Philip moved toward the warehouse with Giles and Morgan beside him.

"Now there's a curious thing," he murmured as they drew near.

The door was open.

"A trap?" Giles suggested.

Philip did not answer for a moment. He looked about him. From this vantage point above the river he saw something they had not noticed from the bank – a small rowing boat, tied up and half-hidden amongst the rushes.

"I don't believe it is a trap," he said. "More likely we are not the only visitors to this place tonight."

They edged forward cautiously until they reached the open door. It was dark inside the warehouse, and with a fusty smell, reminiscent of the grain it had once housed. As Philip's eyes grew accustomed to the blackness he saw a shape against the wall. It was the body of a man.

"I thought it strange that York's men had not posted a guard, and I'll wager here he is." He examined the corpse. "His throat has been cut, and not long ago, I'd say. This mission, my friends, just became more complicated!"

EIGHT

Theresa looked down from her window but could see nothing save the black river swirling far below her. She had not been harmed since being brought to the warehouse that morning but a guard was posted outside her room and she could think of no way out of her predicament.

She had managed to learn that she was being held prisoner by the Duke of York, but for what purpose she had no idea and nor did she know what was going to happen to her.

She tensed, hearing a sudden noise in the corridor outside. A moment later the door was thrown open.

Theresa saw two men, their faces half-hidden by the hoods of their cloaks. Before the door closed behind them she glimpsed the prostrate body of her guard, and she knew these were not York's men.

"What do you want?" she said suspiciously.

"We've come to rescue you, Lady Devalle."

Theresa frowned. "Who sent you? My husband?"

Neither man replied and she drew back, more frightened than at any time during her captivity. There was something very sinister about these two.

"Don't touch me," she cried, as one moved closer to her. "I refuse to go with you."

"You have no choice," he said tersely.

"You're not here on Philip's behalf," she guessed.

"What does it matter? Would you rather wait here for York to come?"

"I think I would. At least I know the Duke of York for what he is, but who is your employer? The Duchess of Portsmouth?"

The man threw back his hood and laughed. Theresa recognised Lord Bentham and her worst fears were confirmed. Not only was he one of Louise's creatures but he was the very monster who had tried to maim Philip.

"Why should Portsmouth have me rescued?"

"If you must know she's afraid you might tell York a bit more about her intentions than she wishes him to learn."

"A fine mess I am in," Theresa muttered. "I'm caught between the two of them."

"When you have powerful friends you must expect to make powerful enemies, my Lady."

"Speaking of powerful friends, Lord Shaftesbury would reward you well for my safe return," Theresa said, none too hopefully.

"If I had all his fortune it would not protect me from the wrath of Lady Portsmouth if I fail her twice. Your confounded husband escaped me, but you won't," Bentham said determinedly.

"You couldn't take my husband, so now you think you will have better luck with me?" Theresa tossed her head defiantly. "It is noble work you do for her, Bentham, kidnapping women!"

"You talk too much. Gag her," he told his assistant.

Theresa struggled but a handkerchief was soon tied across her lips so tightly that it cut the corners of her mouth.

"The easiest way with her is through the window," Bentham said. "Tie her up and, if you can't keep her still, then kill her. It makes little difference, since York will be blamed for her death." He looked down at the river and then turned back to Theresa. "Now, Lady Devalle, my servant waits somewhere below in a boat. If you are lucky he will pluck you from the water. If you are not then you will drown. Unlike York, the Duchess cares not whether you're delivered to her alive or dead."

Theresa felt the panic rise within her as they tied not only

71

her hands but her feet as well. She certainly did not relish the prospect of being dropped from the window into the Thames, hobbled in that fashion and left to the mercy of any servant belonging to Lord Bentham.

She was quite incapable of struggling now. It was as much as she could do to even breathe, for the gag was nearly choking her. Theresa felt her end had come.

She had always vowed that when it did she would be brave, but it wasn't easy. She heard the window being opened and looked about her fearfully. Her eyes widened as she saw the handle of the door begin to turn.

While Bentham lifted her, the other man leaned out from the casement to make sure no-one was in sight below.

With lightning speed Giles burst in through the door and dived for the fellow's feet. Before the man could even cry out Giles had seized him by the ankles and tipped him through the open window.

There was a sickening crack. Directly below the window was not water but a stone jetty.

Bentham dropped Theresa on the floor and turned upon Giles, drawing his sword. Before he could free it from its scabbard Giles had pulled the pistol from his belt and smacked him hard across the side of his head with it. Bentham slumped to the floor, insensible, with blood trickling down his face from a cut on his temple.

"Well, well, who would have thought I would have to rescue my big sister from a scrape like this?" Giles said, smiling as he untied her feet and hands and, finally, her gag.

Theresa touched the raw place where the cloth had cut her mouth. "I'm certainly glad to see you, Giles."

"I bet you are!" Giles looked out of the window and saw the body of the man he had dispatched through it. "If they planned to throw you down there I don't believe you would have fared too well. Even if you had landed in the water, Morgan's knife has already dispatched the boatman who, I presume, was intended to pull you out!"

"Morgan's here too?"

"Yes, he's with Philip. Thomas is downstairs readying the horses. How many guards are there?"

"Eight, I think."

"One is dead outside your door and one downstairs. We have to leave without delay before the others discover they have intruders." Giles looked down at the still-dazed Bentham uncertainly. He couldn't bring himself to commit the cold-blooded murder of an unconscious man, no matter what Bentham had tried to do to Philip. "I think I'll leave him for Philip's vengeance," he decided, tying Bentham's hands with the rope that had been used to bind Theresa. "Now follow me."

"Not through that window, Giles, I beg you."

"Indeed not! We'll use the stairs, but we shall have to risk passing the guardroom. Stay close."

As they edged their way in the darkness along the corridor and toward the stairs it was as though they were once more childhood companions upon some wild adventure in the New Forest, near their home. Theresa gripped Giles' hand and it was a comforting sensation, for she knew she could depend upon him.

Suddenly the guardroom door opened just ahead of them. One of the guards came out, carrying a candle, and they pressed back to the wall as tightly as they could. The flame flickered in the draughty corridor but it would still give out enough light for him to spot them, and there was nowhere they could hide from him. Theresa held her breath as he approached. It needed but the faintest sound for every guard to be alerted.

Giles' lean fingers tightened on the hilt of his sword as the guard drew level with them. Theresa saw the man's eyes dart towards them. His mouth began to open and then a horrible expression crossed his face.

She managed to stop herself crying out as he fell to the floor at her feet. A knife, Morgan's own silent messenger of death, was protruding from his shoulder blades.

Philip and the Welshman were at the top of the stairs.

Philip breathed a silent prayer of thanks when he saw she was unhurt. He pulled her to him, holding her briefly while Morgan retrieved his knife. No-one spoke until they were safely past the guard room door and on the stairs. The staircase was old and made of wood, so they walked close to edge of the steps, testing each tread before putting their full weight upon them in case they creaked.

"Did you dispose of her guard?" he asked Giles, when they were halfway down and out of earshot.

"I had no need. Lord Bentham had already done it for me."

Philip stopped where he was. "Bentham is here?"

"Yes, I knocked him unconscious and tied him up."

The memory of Bentham holding a knife up to his face, intent on disfiguring him, was still painfully fresh to Philip. "Then I shall finally have my revenge," he said grimly.

He started back up the stairs. Morgan made to follow him but Philip stopped him. "Not this time, my friend. You and Giles are responsible for Theresa. See her safely to the coach then get the hell out of here, all of you."

"But what about you?" Theresa protested.

"I'll find my own way home."

He left quickly, before she could argue. This was something he knew he had to do.

Thomas had the horses hitched to the coach and was standing ready with them. His happiness at seeing the others turned to concern when he realised that his master was not with them.

"He's gone back to deal with Bentham," Morgan told him. "We're to go without him."

"But we can't leave him here alone," Thomas cried.

"Those were his orders. Whether you obey them is up to you." Morgan's eyes met those of the worried Thomas.

Thomas nodded, understanding. Without another word he disappeared soundlessly inside the warehouse.

It was then they heard footsteps coming down the stairs.

Two guards came out into the courtyard. Thomas had slipped by them unnoticed but they spotted Theresa, Giles and Morgan straight away.

Giles pushed Theresa into the coach and he and Morgan ran to meet them side by side, Giles with his sword ready in his hand and the Welshman brandishing his knife.

Philip heard the sound of the fight below. He knew the three remaining guards must have heard it too and would be out in a second. He cursed as he realised that, alone, he might not be able to deal with them.

A silent shape materialised beside him.

Philip reacted quickly. Before the unknown person could make any sound Philip clamped a hand over his mouth and forced his head back. With his other hand behind the fellow's neck Philip had him in an iron grip and pulled him tight against his own body.

"Thomas!" He released his hold. "I might have killed you. What the devil are you doing here?"

"I thought, no matter what you said, you might need help, my Lord."

"Well perhaps I do at that! Find something heavy we can push against this door. If we can keep them in here then the coach will stand a chance of getting away."

Even as he spoke the door opened. The guards, realising there was trouble outside, would have rushed out but Philip put his booted foot in the first man's stomach and he staggered back into the others. They were quickly in the doorway again, but it was narrow and no more than one could tackle Philip at a time.

Using the point of his sword he forced the first guard back again and managed to close the door as Thomas, straining every muscle, heaved at a heavy table he had found in an adjoining room.

"Excellent! Leaning with all his weight upon the door, Philip helped him shove the table in place. "Now to find Bentham, but we must move quickly." The door was already creaking as the guards commenced kicking it and hammering with the butts of their muskets. "We may need more time than this old timber will allow us."

⁌

Downstairs in the courtyard the two guards were dead, but Morgan's expression was solemn as he lifted Giles bodily into the coach beside Theresa. "He's passed out," he told her. "He took a cut to his face."

Theresa gasped and held her brother's limp body in her arms. She blanched as Morgan pulled aside Giles' auburn hair.

The moon was retreating behind the clouds but before its pale light vanished she saw only too plainly the full extent of his injury. The left side of Giles' face had been sliced open from his temple to his jaw.

"Oh, dear God! Look what they did to him." Sobbing, she tried in vain to staunch the bleeding with her handkerchief. "Hurry, Morgan, we must get him back to Bet. She'll know what to do."

Morgan closed the coach door and climbed up into the driving seat. He gently urged the horses on without so much as a backward glance towards the warehouse where his beloved master was. No matter where his heart might be he knew well enough where, on this occasion, his duty lay.

⁌

Philip heard the coach leaving and breathed a sigh of relief. He followed the thin strip of light that showed around a door further down the corridor and entered the room cautiously. Bentham was lying where Giles had left him, with his hands tied. Thomas, following closely, locked the door behind them.

Bentham was still dazed but he attempted to get to his feet when he saw who it was.

Philip kicked him back down.

"Aren't you going to give him a fair chance?" Thomas asked as Philip drew his sword.

"Exactly the same as he would have given me the last time we met, Thomas."

Bentham shuffled away as best he could on his backside. "I would never really have scarred you, Devalle, I do swear it."

"You're a lying bastard!"

Philip advanced upon him slowly and deliberately, enjoying Bentham's anguish. When he had him cornered he brought his sword down on him. Bentham cried out, anticipating that he had driven the weapon into him but Philip laughed, for he had only cut the rope which tied his hands.

Bentham staggered to his feet. "Mercy, Devalle."

Even as he said it Bentham tried to draw his own sword, but he was too slow. Philip's blade pierced his ribcage and penetrated his lung.

"Would you say that was giving him a fair chance?" Philip asked Thomas as Bentham writhed upon the floor, gasping his last feeble breaths, blood frothing from his mouth.

Thomas regarded Bentham without a qualm, for violent death was commonplace to one who had been brought up with thieves and cut-throats. "I'd say that was fair, my Lord. Now we really should be leaving if we are to escape from here with our own lives."

They heard the guardroom door splinter and the sound of footsteps in the corridor. The guards were now putting their full force against the door that Thomas had just locked.

Philip looked at Thomas and was reminded of the situation in which he had placed the youth. His thirst for revenge had clouded his reason and now he had risked Thomas' life as well as his own.

"I'm going to get you out of this, I swear it, Thomas."

He did not quite know how. The only exits from the room were the door, which the guards would soon come bursting through, or the window. He opened that and saw the river below them. A desperate idea formed in his head.

"Can you swim, Thomas?"

"A bit, my Lord,"

"What is 'a bit'?"

"Not very much," Thomas admitted.

"Then you will have to trust me. Take off your shoes and coat and get rid of every heavy object you are carrying."

Thomas did so and Philip likewise, although he looked regretfully at his sword, which was a favourite one. He threw it down into the water and then climbed onto the window sill.

"There is no time to lose. This door will not hold out much longer. Jump directly you see me in the water and, for God's sake, jump wide. There is a jetty just beneath us."

Thomas had turned pale. "I don't know if I can do it, my Lord."

"You must. They will kill you if they find you here. You are a brave boy, Thomas. You can do it."

The door of their room was straining at its hinges as Philip leapt into the dark water.

He hurtled down and then an icy coldness was around him and he sank. His feet touched on the muddy bottom and, struggling and kicking with all his might, he forced his body upwards until he felt the night air upon his face.

"Jump, Thomas, now!" he cried out.

Thomas jumped.

He hit the water a few yards away from Philip and sank like a stone. For an agonising moment Philip could not see him, but then he came to the surface, thrashing about and coughing. His strength was nearly failing but Philip managed to grasp him firmly by the shoulders. He was safe.

"Stay absolutely still," Philip said into his ear, "and do not make a sound. They are looking for us."

The three guards, with muskets in their hands, were in the room and leaning out of the window. Thomas gulped air as quietly as he could.

One of them held out a lantern.

"Down!" Philip, still holding Thomas firmly, pulled him beneath the water as the light skimmed over them.

When they surfaced again the guards had abandoned the search.

"They must have assumed we drowned." Philip towed Thomas to safety and they lay upon the bank for several minutes, getting their breath back.

"Is there any mortal thing you can't do?" Thomas asked him at length.

Philip laughed. "I cannot think of anything!"

"You are a marvel, that you are, my Lord."

"You may not think so highly of me when we've walked to Cheapside without shoes, dripping wet and cold."

"But there's a boat." Thomas pointed to Bentham's rowboat, moored close by. "If we used that we could get all the way to Paul's Wharf and then we'd be nearly home. I wonder, can you row, my Lord?"

"I don't believe I can," Philip said in surprise.

"Then you will have to trust my oarsmanship," Thomas said, sounding pleased.

"I will, and gladly. Wait, though, everything is very quiet. Aren't they even going to look for us?"

They both listened. There was no sound, save for the river slapping against its banks.

"It seems a shame to sneak away like this," Philip said.

"Especially since there are men in there who will have discovered Bentham's body."

"What are you proposing to do now?" Thomas said despairingly.

"Have a little fun, that's all. Can you remember where we landed?"

Thomas pointed to a flat-topped rock. "It was near that."

Philip, moving low to the ground, made for the rock and was quickly back, carrying the sack he had insisted on bringing with him on the boat. He drew a tinder box out of it first and then showed Thomas what else the sack contained.

"What are they?" Thomas said. "Bottles?"

"Grenadoes. Titus got them from his brother, Constant. I persuaded him to part with them today, for I felt they may be useful."

Constant Oates was a Southwark glazier but as Thomas turned a bottle over in his hands he found it to be full of holes. "What is that stuff inside?"

"Gunpowder and wildfire, I am told. He made them during the Popish Plot when he feared he would have to defend himself against Catholics seeking retribution when his brother was testifying against them."

"But what exactly do they do, my Lord?"

"Let's find out, shall we?"

Philip held the flame from the tinder box to a cloth that protruded from the neck of one of the bottles. When it had well and truly caught alight he hurled it, managing to get it through a downstairs window of the warehouse.

There was the sound of breaking glass as the window shattered and then silence.

Philip looked at Thomas and shrugged.

A moment later there was a huge explosion.

Thomas threw himself at Philip and they hid their faces as pieces of glass blew outward. When they looked at the warehouse again the room was totally engulfed in flames.

"They work! Good old Titus," Thomas cheered, as Philip disentangled him from his wet hair. "Here, let me try."

He copied Philip's action and hurled one at the door, which was soon blown right off its hinges as the bottle exploded and a sheet of flame shot upwards, setting the timber walls alights.

"Well, I'll be damned! They're as good as cannon balls," Philip said delightedly, for he had not expected anything nearly so spectacular.

They lit all the bottles they had left and threw them until there was no part of the warehouse untouched by fire.

"Come, Thomas," Philip shouted, over the noise of crackling flames and crashing wooden beams. "I believe our work here is done."

He untied the rowboat and fell into it wearily.

"I was a help to you, wasn't I?" Thomas said, taking up the oars.

Philip regarded him with real affection. He had first made his acquaintance when Thomas had taken refuge in their house. He was running from the law at the time, after stealing a purse, and Theresa, Bet and even Morgan took pity on him and begged Philip to let him stay.

Much against his better judgment, Philip had agreed to take the scruffy young urchin into his service, but in the four years since that day Thomas had never given him the least cause to regret his decision and now Philip would not have been without him for the world.

"You were invaluable, my little friend."

Thomas beamed with pride at the praise. "I've learned a lot from you today, my Lord."

"I've been taught a lesson too," Philip said, seriously. "It is that my life is not my own to throw away on some vengeful whim, not whilst I have loyal followers like you who would risk themselves to save me."

He lay back with a sigh. He was exhausted and it was pleasant just to close his eyes as the tips of Thomas' oars dipped in a regular rhythm through the water.

Thomas glanced back as they rounded the bend at Wapping and gave a low whistle. "Did we do all that, my Lord?"

Philip opened his eyes and looked with him at the blazing mass, whose reflection was turning the Thames to the colour of sunset.

"Yes, Thomas, I'm rather afraid we did!"

Philip's elation died quickly when they finally arrived home and he learned of Giles' misfortune.

Bet had done the best for him that she could, cleaning his wound and applying the salve she prepared every spring from primroses. Afterwards she had given him a syrup, which she distilled from poppy heads, to ease the pain and he was sleeping.

Philip was filled with remorse as he stood by Giles' bedside looking at his bandaged face. He would be scarred for life, the handsome face, that he had always said was his only fortune, ruined forever. Philip was vain enough to know how devastating that would be, especially since he had come so close to losing his own looks when he had been at the mercy of Bentham's knife.

Bentham was dead now and Theresa was safe. He had won this day, but at what cost?

Theresa came in and stood beside him. "It wasn't your fault," she said quietly.

"Of course it was. Thanks to my ambition, Giles is injured and you might have been killed." He shuddered at the thought. "What was I thinking, Tess? How could I put you both in such danger?"

She slipped her hand into his. "You did what you felt you had to do."

"Without thought for those I love, as usual," he said wretchedly. He could recall sitting by Morgan's bedside after the Welshman's ear had been bitten off by a dog, a vicious dog Philip had refused to get rid of because it had once belonged to a dear friend of his who had died. Morgan had never blamed him for his disfigurement, but he knew Giles would, and rightly so.

He turned away from Giles' bedside and led her from the room. "This has prompted me to make a decision I should have made long ago. I was a fool to think that I could tread such a perilous path without risk to the people who mean most to me in the world. I want you to go back to France."

"You mean on my own?" she said uncertainly. "You won't be coming with me?"

He shook his head. "I can't. I have gone too far down this road to retreat, not with Heatherton so nearly in my grasp. If I return with you to France now it will all have been for nothing, but I do want you to go back. You will be safe there, Louis will see to it."

Theresa opened her mouth to protest, but he put a finger to her lips. "No, hear me out. I love you, Tess, you are my life. Without you I have nothing and no reason to carry on." He kissed her and tasted the salty tears that had started down her cheeks. "Call this, if you will, an act of selfishness, but I cannot lose you, and I will not. So do as you are damn well told, for once!"

Theresa smiled through her tears. "Yes, Philip," she said meekly.

NINE

❧

Philip's watchful eyes missed none who were admitted to the house of the wine merchant, Thomas Sheppard, in Abchurch Street.

Tonight it was essential that nobody was present save those he had personally invited. Monmouth was there, of course, talking to Sir Thomas Armstrong and Lord Russell, and there were some others he knew he could rely upon to support him, including Major Wildman and Algernon Sydney. There were a few he was less sure about but had needed to invite, such as Lord Howard and Ferguson, the Scottish pamphleteer, and Lord Grey, who arrived last and came over to join him.

"It's a strange assortment you've gathered here tonight, Philip," he said, looking about him. "Not the kind of men with whom you should take liberties."

"I assure you that is not my intent," Philip said coldly.

He had never been too fond of Grey but he could not have justified excluding him since Grey had become such a close friend of Monmouth.

"I don't see Giles here," Grey said.

Giles had not appeared in public since his injury but, even if he had been willing to attend, Philip would not have let him come to this meeting. After what had happened he was convinced that the more he distanced his family from his plans the better. He missed having Giles by his side all the same. Theresa had been

84

gone for a fortnight now and he was feeling very much alone without the pair of them.

"Is it true that he was set upon and disfigured?" Grey persisted, when Philip did not answer.

"It was an accident," Philip said firmly, for that was the tale they were putting about.

"Something else I've been meaning to ask you, Philip," Grey said, smirking. "Was what happened in Cheshire all part of your splendid plan? It was original, I must say, to get both Monmouth and yourself arrested as you did. Not to mention vulgar!"

Philip was not about to allow himself to be baited by the likes of Grey. "Vulgar! I will remind you of saying that, when they eventually arrest you for debauching Lord Berkeley's fifteen year old daughter!"

"Is it true that Shaftesbury has been taken ill since the elections?" Grey asked, changing the subject hurriedly. "There is even talk of him planning to flee to Holland."

"There is always talk," Philip said dismissively.

The recent Sheriffs' elections had been disastrous for the Whigs, just as Charles had predicted, but the Earl, although beset by pain and disillusionment, had relinquished none of his ambitions. Philip still needed to prove himself if he was to gain his reward from Shaftesbury before it was too late, particularly if the Earl was truly intending to leave the country. That was the very reason he had decided he had better hold another meeting.

He called the gathering to order and took his place at the head of the long table, with Monmouth beside him. There were seventeen of them altogether around the table. When the others were seated, Sheppard placed a glass of sherry before each of them.

Philip took a substantial swig of the wine to calm his nerves. He was about to take the biggest gamble he had ever contemplated and he hoped he had correctly judged the mood of his audience tonight, as well as his own ability to control them in the future.

He took a deep breath and began. "Each of you is here tonight by invitation, and each of you has been selected with great care, for the future of our country may depend on you. There are those present, and I must number myself amongst them, who support the Duke of Monmouth and would see him on the throne of England, but there are others here who, I know, favour a republic. Though we each work toward different ends, one difficulty besets us all. King Charles is adamant that his Catholic brother will succeed him, despite the people's hatred of the Papists. I venture to suggest that either of these alternatives must be infinitely preferable to this."

There was a murmur of agreement and Philip waited a moment before continuing.

"During my time in the French army I was trained to recognise my objective and attain it by using advantages of both terrain and men. I have also learned that if another fights the same enemy, then it will often be advantageous for the two sides to unite and defeat him with their joint resources, even if their own differences may need to be resolved at a later date. To fight amongst ourselves will only serve to diminish what chance we have and, therefore, I propose that we join forces and take action now."

"What action do you have in mind, my Lord?" Major Wildman said.

Philip braced himself for what he was about to say.

"The Duke of York must be prevented, by whatever means we can, from taking the throne and, since King Charles will undoubtedly oppose us, he will need to be removed from his position."

Philip knew that the words he was speaking were treason. He glanced around. To his relief there were no shocked faces at the table, indeed most were nodding in agreement.

Monmouth was the first to speak. "We shall not kill my father, Philip. Tell them that."

"How else do you suppose you will ever get the throne?" Wildman asked him sneeringly.

"If that is the only way it can be mine then I say here and now I do not want it. My father is to be unharmed," Monmouth insisted.

Wildman, when he was a Leveler, had been the mouthpiece of the common soldiers and was not a man easily subdued. He ignored Monmouth and turned to Philip. "Then, my Lord, you have no chance of success, and we would be mad to follow you."

Philip was prepared for this. "Then follow me no longer, Major. The door is there. I beg you take your leave."

"I shall not," Wildman said stubbornly. "I wish to fight the Duke of York, the same as you."

"Do you wish to fight me too?" Philip asked quietly. "If you do then I warn you I shall be a troublesome opponent."

Wildman hesitated. He might be headstrong but Philip knew he was no fool. "I'll not be counted as your enemy, my Lord."

"Then listen to what I say. The King is to be captured, that is all, and every care is to be taken of him."

"You have to swear it will be so," Monmouth insisted, "or I shall not help you, not one jot."

Philip gave Wildman a long look. "Well, Major, shall you heed me now? If we expect the Duke's support we must agree to his terms."

Wildman's eyes met his. "I shall be guided by you in the matter, my Lord," he said, with a readiness that Philip feared Monmouth would suspect, but evidently he did not.

"How will we prevent William of Orange taking the throne in his wife's name once we have removed the King from power and assassinated York?" Algernon Sydney said.

"Possibly by putting Princess Mary's younger sister on it."

"Princess Anne?" Robert West, a fervent republican, cried. "How will that benefit us?"

"It will gain us time, West," Philip said patiently. "She should be easy enough to control until such time as we decide what's to be done, and William is less likely to take action straightaway if we have placed upon the throne one whose claim cannot be legally disputed. Whilst Princess Anne is not the next in line she is legitimate and does have rights which cannot be ignored. The people will then judge our motives well, for we can insist that we have been forced to take such steps to ensure that that we do not have a Catholic king."

"Catholic or Protestant, it's all as bad to me," West said, for as well as being a republican he also admitted to being an atheist, "but I accept what you say."

"Thank you, West. Do any others have doubts before I reveal my plan?"

Philip was glad to see that, if any had, they were keeping them to themselves. Since the meeting was intended merely as a token show to impress Lord Shaftesbury, he wanted to get it over with as swiftly and as seamlessly as he could.

"Then we are all agreed that we shall join forces and, together, seize the King and York?"

All indicated that they were.

"But how shall we do it?" Armstrong said. "They are surrounded by people all the time, even in St. James Park. It will be near impossible to even take the Duke, much less the King."

"On the contrary, it will be easy, and we will take them both together, but not in London," Philip said.

"Where then?"

In answer Philip picked up the roll of paper he had placed on the table next to him and spread it out before them.

"Some of you will be acquainted with Richard Rumbold. For the benefit of those who are not, 'Hannibal Rumbold' was a guard at the old King's execution. Now all of you, study this map I have prepared."

Philip was rather proud of his map. It might not have been up to the standard of those drawn by a mapmaker, but it was clear and neat, with areas well-defined.

"Rumbold's house is here." He indicated it upon the map. "The Rye House. Here is Bishop's Stortford and here, as you can plainly see, is Newmarket."

"The races," Armstrong cried. "You mean to seize them when they are on their way to the races?"

"Actually no. I mean to seize them on their way back. On their return to London they invariably leave the road here, at Bishop's Stortford, and go on via Hoddesdon. The Rye House, as I've tried to show, is situated on a narrow piece of road and from its tower one gains a fine, commanding view of all the roads around it. As the coach approaches from the north, it is necessary to cross this narrow causeway." Philip traced with his fingernail the route the royal coach would have to take. "There is a toll gate leading to a yard and then to this small meadow. Another gate, here, leads directly into this narrow lane. There is a ditch, here, in which armed men could wait.

If an obstruction, say a cart of hay, should block the road at this point and the coach was forced to halt then the men positioned in the ditch could shoot the King's postilion.

Rumbold, with some horsemen, can leave Rye House during the confusion that would follow and they could engage the guards. The Duke of York could then be killed and King Charles taken prisoner."

"Philip, you are a genius," Lord Russell declared. "The plan is so simple and yet I do not see how it can fail."

Philip, relieved to have got that over with, acknowledged the praise that was starting to come from all sides.

West and quite a few others even declared that they wished to be amongst the number which rode out to fight the royal guards.

"After York is dead, what then?" Russell said.

"Then we have to seize Whitehall," Philip said matter-of-factly. "I thought that yourself, together with the Earl of Essex, Grey and Monmouth might do that."

Russell vouched for himself and so did all the others.

"What of the people, though, will they support us?" Monmouth wondered. "John Trenchard writes to me that the west is ready to rise at any time, and there are many who say they will stand for me in the north, but how many can we count on here, in London?"

"Shaftesbury reckons ten thousand," Philip told him.

"Lord Shaftesbury's 'brisk boys'?" Russell asked. "I fear we can depend on them no more."

"Not so, my Lord." Robert Ferguson, known as the Sworded Preacher, stood up to speak. "There are here, in this city, twenty gentlemen, each of whom can bring in hundreds at my word."

Philip fought back a stab of irritation. It was not in his interest to dispute Ferguson's claim to be able to raise an army in the streets, but he considered the lean, stooping Scotsman to be nothing more than a mischief-maker, like all pamphleteers. He had deemed it necessary to include him amongst the plotters, but that did not mean he had to like the man!

"I hope you are right, Ferguson. Now, my friends, I believe this meeting can be concluded."

"Before we go, there is one other thing that I would ask." This time it was Lord Howard who had spoken. "You have told us all what you expect of us, but not when we are to put your plan into action."

"Why, when Charles and York attend the spring race meeting," Philip said smoothly.

"But that is not until March. They will be travelling to Newmarket before that, for the autumn meeting," Howard pointed out.

Since Philip was not proposing to continue with the plan

after Heatherton had come into his possession the very last thing he wanted was an early date for its execution!

"We shall never have all the arrangements made before then."

"It seems to me that the longer we wait the more risk we run of the discovery of our intentions," Howard persisted.

"Since only those inside this room know of what we plot I would say that the risk is not a great one. We will lose much more by rushing in before our plans are properly laid." Philip glanced over at Russell. What say you, Lord Russell?"

"I say there is too much at stake for us to fail in our attempt. The lives of all here in this room may well be forfeit if we do. I would suggest that March is soon enough."

Philip smiled. Russell always counselled caution. "So would I, my Lord. It is settled then. Goodnight gentlemen."

Morgan was waiting for him in the coach outside, indeed the Welshman insisted on accompanying him everywhere lately.

"How do you think you're going to satisfy both Monmouth and Wildman?" Morgan asked when Philip told him how the meeting had gone.

"Obviously I can't, therefore I will propose two separate plots," Philip explained. "The Wildman faction may plan to spill Charles' blood if they wish, whilst Monmouth and Lord Russell can pursue their more fastidious ideals."

Morgan looked sceptical. "Even you can't manage that, to have them think they're working for different ends."

"What does it matter? Nothing is going to come of this," Philip reminded him.

"But what if it does? Have you considered that? You may have lit a fire you cannot dowse," Morgan warned him.

"You worry too much."

"And you," Morgan muttered, "don't worry half enough."

"A message just arrived from Lord Shaftesbury, my Lord," Thomas told Philip. Answering the door was one of his duties now that Bet had gone to France with her mistress.

Philip read the note. "He says he wants me to attend upon him right away. This could be good news, Thomas."

"Do you think he's got you High Heatherton?" Thomas cried excitedly.

"Perhaps he has."

Philip hardly dared hope. He had been waiting so long for this.

When he arrived at Shaftesbury's house, however, his heart sank. The Earl's face was grim and he did not at all look like the bearer of glad tidings.

"What's happened?" Philip asked him.

"The King is after me. Ferguson has discovered that there will soon be a warrant out for my arrest."

That came as no surprise to Philip. He had half-expected it ever since the Whigs had lost London. "On what charge?"

"It hardly matters, for whatever the charge I can expect no justice in the city now." Since the Tory sheriffs had been elected Shaftesbury could no longer control the law. "I cannot face prison again, Philip. I would die there."

"You could go into hiding," Philip suggested.

"Not forever. I must flee the country now, before it is too late."

Philip had never known the Earl consider such a thing before, not even in the darkest of days. "You could stay and fight," he said, his dream of gaining High Heatherton fading by the minute. "You have in the past and you have won."

"Not this time," Shaftesbury said bleakly. "The fight is over, Philip. Ferguson is going to help me get to Amsterdam. Prince William has no jurisdiction there and I've a friend that I can stay with for a while."

Philip sighed. He had come so close, this time, to getting what he wanted most in the world. "The game is up then?"

"It would seem so. I am going tonight. Colonel Walcot is coming with me and so is Ferguson."

That, at least, was welcome news. Philip had sensed he would have trouble with the Scotsman.

"There remains but one thing left for me to do," Shaftesbury continued.

"And what is that?"

"Can't you guess?" The Earl opened a drawer and took out a document bearing the seal of the courts. "The last reward you will ever earn from me."

"Heatherton?" Philip hardly dared hope that, at last, High Heatherton was his.

"Yes, your precious Heatherton." Shaftesbury held it out to him and Philip seized it eagerly. "To save you the trouble of reading it I can tell you that it says the estate is henceforth yours and that it will pass to your issue. Should you die without heirs then it will belong entirely to Theresa, even if your brother still lives. That is what you wanted, I believe."

Philip scanned the long-awaited piece of paper all the same, and the first thing he noticed was the date.

"You've had this for a month, you bastard! Why didn't you tell me?"

"To be honest I didn't entirely trust you."

"That's rich coming from you," Philip said indignantly.

"We've had our rifts," Shaftesbury allowed, "but let us part friends, for we owe each other much. I have trained you to my ways and made you what you are today. God help me, you are all my work."

"Am I supposed to thank you for that?" Philip was still nettled at the length of time the Earl had waited before giving him the document, especially since, if he had only known of it, he would not have needed to hold the risky meeting at Abchurch Street the week before!

Shaftesbury smiled at his tone. "You have more than repaid

me for my trouble. But for your effort and your ingenuity the Cause of Monmouth would still be a wistful dream, locked in the hearts of those who have not your ability or courage. It is I who should thank you, and I do so sincerely."

Philip was surprised by Shaftesbury's words for he had been more often berated by him in the past than paid compliments. He took the frail hand Shaftesbury offered him. "May fortune go with you, my Lord. I shall never forget you and we do part as friends for, when all is said and done, I probably owe you more than I owe any other man. I only wish it could have ended differently, for your sake."

"It has not ended, Philip. You could still help the Duke of Monmouth on to victory."

"Without you? Who would hold us all together?"

"You, Philip. You must take my place."

"Oh no." Philip shook his head. "It is not for such as I to govern England, and that is what it means. You know better than any how incapable Monmouth would be to rule."

"You must not desert him," Shaftesbury said. "He needs you."

"I'll watch over him, I promise that." Philip meant it. He intended to do all he could to dissuade his friend from any rash actions.

"From Sussex?" Shaftesbury said. "It's too far away. You must stay here where you belong."

"Give me a little time just for myself. I've earned it," Philip reckoned. "I have worked and schemed and fought for enough years and now I want no master but my own whim. I shall do exactly as I please, like other men born to my rank. I've been degraded by my poverty for too long."

"I disagree. You've been uplifted by it," Shaftesbury said. "Had you been rich all these years then the qualities which have helped you to survive might never have been discovered. Go to High Heatherton, if you must, and fool yourself that all you want from life is there. I only wish I could be here when you discover differently!"

TEN

~

Philip persuaded Giles to accompany him when he paid his first visit to High Heatherton. Giles had hardly shown himself since the night of Theresa's kidnap. The wound had healed cleanly, thanks to Bet's care, but for the rest of his days he would bear a dreadful scar. Philip knew that Giles felt his life was blighted and already he sensed a subtle change in his brother-in-law's nature, a bitterness which he feared would worsen as the years went on.

Even so, Philip enjoyed his company along the way, for he had always found Giles to be a most engaging companion. The journey to Sussex was not unpleasant, despite the bitter winter weather, and they made good time, for the roads were hard and frosty. They only stopped twice, first at Epsom for a meal and then to pass the night at Horsham, a small town on the outskirts of St. Leonard's Forest. In the morning, with their destination only a few hours away, Giles questioned him about High Heatherton and his family.

Philip rarely mentioned any aspect of his life before going to Court. His childhood had not been a happy one, for his mother had died when he was a baby and his brother had terrorized him from an early age. Not allowed friends outside of the estate, for fear the world should learn the severity of Henry's condition, Philip's only friend had been John Bone, a labourer's son. Philip had learned, alongside John, to swim and wrestle, and had become adept at all the other rough pursuits which had developed the strength that so surprised his enemies. These were some of the things which Philip never spoke about, but not because he was ashamed of them. He wondered whether John would still be there. He hoped so.

"One of my ancestors, Roger De Valle, came over with the Conqueror," he told Giles. "He was given the land when William rewarded his Norman friends for their services. The earldom was bestowed much later by Henry V11, in gratitude for the part my family played at Bosworth, and it was the first Earl who built the present house. It must have been immense at one time, for it housed a ridiculous number of people, more than a hundred and fifty, I believe."

Giles whistled at that. "All dependants?"

"Yes, though not all of the serving classes. Squire's sons, like you, would have held positions there. It was considered quite an honour," he said, smiling as he saw Giles' expression of disgust, "particularly if you became a steward or comptroller. You would have your own men serving you and they, in turn, might have their servants."

"Your family must have been extremely rich," Giles said.

"They were, in those days. They even kept a private army, whilst most families only paid retainers to attend them in emergencies or to make a show. There was a London home as well, as large as Clarendon House and twice a year the entire contents of High Heatherton would move there, with every servant and all the furniture, the carpets and the hangings, even the cooking pans and beds. Now Morgan complains bitterly when he has to pack two trunks of clothes for me! To think they should have enjoyed all that and yet I live in poverty."

"Hardly poverty," Giles corrected him. "You have pleaded penury for as long as I have known you and yet you have always lived the life to which you were born."

That much was true but Philip had no income now save the little he was receiving from France and Holland in exchange for passing both of them information about the plans of the other. Giles was as ignorant of this as was Theresa, for Philip knew he would be just as disapproving as his sister.

"Our circumstances changed when my great, great grandfather fell foul of Queen Elizabeth," he continued. "By her reign most families had disbanded all their private forces, offering their services to the Crown instead, but not him. He must openly defy the Queen and even a madman, which he was, by all accounts, could have foreseen the consequences."

"She withdrew the friendship of the Crown?"

"Would that she had! I might still own the London house. Instead she took to visiting us for three weeks each year, upon her annual progress. Have you any notion of how expensive it can be to accommodate one's sovereign, especially when they bring with them a household as large as your own? For the duration of her visit the woman took over every room and held her Court at our expense. She needed to be royally entertained, her servants fed and housed. Five years of that and we were nearly ruined. It must have been quite the subtlest way to keep control of rebellious lords!

The London residence was demolished and the land sold off to pay our debts. Half of Heatherton was pulled down when it could not be repaired and our army was disbanded. Luckily a Stuart king was next upon the throne and our fortunes improved somewhat."

Whilst Philip talked the country had been changing. They had left St. Leonard's Forest far behind them and, on the other side of the River Adur, they could see across the downs towards the woods of Bramber and the boundaries of the Heatherton estate.

"I wonder what I'm going to find there," Philip said, for he doubted that what he was about to see would bear much resemblance to the grand estate he had left twenty years before. "I little thought that I should one day be returning as the master of High Heatherton, or even that I'd want to return at all."

When they had gone a little further he tapped upon the panel that divided them from Jonathon and Ned. "Slow down, we are nearly there."

Upon one side of the lane were fields, vast untended acres without crops. No cows lay in the meadows and no sheep grazed upon the hills behind.

The barren sight was not encouraging.

"Those are my fields," he explained to Giles, "and here, on our right, begins the boundary of the house."

A flint wall ran by the side of the lane and at right angles to it, stretching as far as they could see. They drove for nearly two miles more before a cluster of farm cottages came into view upon one side of the lane and a pair of gates upon the other. The lane ahead continued on into thick woodland.

"Those woods are all mine too," Philip told Giles. "In fact they are the true wealth of Heatherton. We send the timber to the boat builders at Shoreham, or at least," he added, "we did."

Philip looked up at the gateway, rusting but still fine, with the Devalle arms born proudly by the two rampant lions on the stone pillars. "Go through," he instructed his blackamoor coachmen.

Giles touched his arm. "Your estate workers have come to welcome us...I think."

A few families had come out of their cottages and were watching them. One of the men was carrying a pitchfork and no-one looked very welcoming.

"They seem about to attack us," Philip said, more surprised than alarmed.

"What are you going to do?" Giles' hand was already on the pistol at his belt.

"Not shoot them certainly! I think, in any case, it is Jonathon and Ned who are attracting most of their curiosity."

Philip guessed that the labourers and their families had probably never seen a Negro, for the sight of two of them seem to have them stupefied. They stared and pointed disbelieving fingers until one man, standing a full head taller than the rest, stepped forward.

"What do you think you're doing, black man?"

Philip smiled. He recognised that voice.

Jonathon, who had climbed down from the seat, looked at him coolly. A man could not serve Philip for as many years as he and Ned had done without being used to encountering trouble. "I would say that I was opening these gates, and if you gawp at me a little longer you will see me do it."

"I wouldn't be so sure of that."

"Talk to him, Giles," Philip said, "but do not tell him who I am yet. I'm interested in what he has to say."

Giles opened the door and got out. "We are here to visit the house."

"By whose authority?"

"Whose do we need?"

"Mine to begin with," the man said.

"Why should we need yours?"

"Because I am in charge here until the owner returns, and you're not him."

Philip noticed that some of the others were looking warily at Giles. The wind had blown the hair away from his face, revealing his scarred cheek, which made him look quite fearsome to strangers, but Philip knew it was John Bone who was speaking and guessed he would not be easily unnerved. What Philip did not know, however, was how pleased John would be to see him after all these years. He had, after all, turned his back on the estate and the plight of those who had been subjected to his brother's whims and rages.

"The owner, would it be Lord Southwick?" Giles was asking.

"No, sir. He's locked up, for he's insane. The one we wait

for is his brother. He's a good man, and he'll put things right for us, but until he comes then none shall pass through these gates whilst I am here."

Philip had heard enough. He stepped down beside Giles. "You always were a tiresome, noisy fellow, John Bone!"

"By God, it's him!" John cried. "It is Lord Philip. He's come back to us."

The rest of them looked at Philip in amazement. Some of those who remembered him came forward hesitantly, but John seized his hand with a roughness that caused Giles to wince, although Philip stood his ground.

"You're prettier than you ever were, Lord Philip, and that's the truth."

An old man, nearly as tall as John, pushed forward.

"Forgive this lummox of a son of mine, my Lord. He never learned his proper manners. Welcome back amongst the people who love you."

He went down upon one knee but Philip gently raised him up. "It's good to see you, Sam, but what has happened here? Where are your crops, your animals?"

"Your brother, the Earl, took everything, my Lord, and gave us nothing back. He slaughtered all our livestock, sold our corn and did not even give us seed to put back in the ground. We would have starved if it were not for the goodness of our neighbours."

"But there is a fortune in those woods beyond, just waiting to be felled," Philip said.

"He wouldn't let us touch it," Sam explained. "We have sent no wood to Shoreham in the six years since your father died."

"But why?"

"Because he had the Devalle sickness." A harsh voice sounded loudly above the others.

Philip recognised that voice too and turned toward the man who had spoken. "I don't have it, Searle," he said quietly.

"So you say. Your family has been cursed with the sickness for as long as this estate has been here and I say you're no better than the rest, for all your fancy clothes."

John leapt at Searle and with one brawny hand lifted him into the air and brought him crashing down upon his back, where he lay, dazed, on the frosty ground. "Any other man who dares to show disrespect toward his Lordship gets the same," he warned.

Philip looked at him with amusement, "I never thought to see you be my champion, John. Do you think I have grown so delicate I am no longer capable of dealing with the likes of Dick Searle?"

John grinned. "No, for I learned long ago not to be taken in by the way you look!" He dragged Searle to his feet and shoved him back into the crowd. "Go home now, all of you," he told them.

They moved away, though some looked surly.

"They don't seem all that pleased to see me," Philip said ruefully.

"I'm sure they'll accept you in good time, Lord Philip."

"Accept me?" Philip had never considered that they might not accept him. "Surely they have no choice. I am their master, am I not?"

"They lived in fear of your brother for too long, Lord Philip. It is only my father and myself who have persuaded any of them to wait for you. Without them you'd have nothing here, and well they know it."

"But these are their homes," Philip said. "Where would they go?"

"Where all the others went – upon the road to find new livings and new masters. There is labouring to be done on other big estates or harvest work, and they must feed their families."

Philip looked at him. "Why didn't you go with them, John?"

"Because of you," John said simply. "I knew you would come back and I knew, too, that you'd be a man worth waiting for."

Philip was touched by his loyalty. "Thank you, John."

"So who is this John Bone?" Giles asked, after he and Philip had returned to the coach and were driving up to the house.

"John was my boyhood companion," Philip told him. "His father, Sam, taught me how to fight, not with a sword but with my bare hands, and it is a talent I have blessed many times."

Giles looked shocked. "I can't believe you used to tussle like a farmer's boy!"

Philip knew that Giles, spoilt and petted by his mother and protected from harm, would never really understand his own lonely childhood.

They drove through the gate and along a curved path, leading through a neglected orchard of apple, pear and plum trees. Another, smaller, gateway lay ahead of them and, behind that, was a long drive, which passed through what had once been the formal gardens. These had been left so long untended that Philip barely recognised them as the neat and ordered flowerbeds he recalled. Now the grass grew high around the tangled patches of weeds.

John had already warned him that a fire had destroyed part of the house but, even so, he was not prepared for the sight which met his eyes as they neared the building.

Of its two fine wings only one remained intact. The other wing had been gutted. Its tower still stood bravely, but there were empty holes where once had been windows and most of the slates were gone from the roof, leaving gaping places for the wind and weather to do their worst. Even the little ornamental turrets that had once enhanced the gables were broken, their jagged outlines standing out grotesquely against the dark, November clouds.

Philip stared in horror at the smoke-stained shell.

They turned into a circular, weed-covered drive and he

alighted from the coach beside the studded door, which still bore the marks of Roundhead musket balls.

"High Heatherton survived over two hundred years of glorious history and Henry nearly managed to destroy it in six," he said bitterly.

Giles was silent; indeed there was not much he could have said.

Philip sighed as he considered the cruel irony of his situation. "I bound myself once again to Shaftesbury, risked my neck rallying support for Monmouth and sent my wife away, and for what, Giles? For this ruin?"

"You could sell it," Giles suggested.

"And what of John and those others who met us at the gate? They are my responsibility and they expect me to help them."

"How can you?"

Philip did not know. All he knew was that he was the master of High Heatherton now, and he would have to find a way.

"Last year was a most unfortunate one for me," Titus Oates complained, "and it looks as though this one will turn out to be no better."

Philip rested his legs upon a footstool and studied his high-heeled shoes. He still sported some of the fashions of Versailles which, to his mind, were more stylish than those of Whitehall.

"Come and tell me all your troubles, Titus, though I can no longer promise to put them right the way I used to do when I had access to Shaftesbury's money!"

"I was jailed for slander for one thing," Titus said. "Fortunately I still had some friends who were prepared to lay down bail for me, so I remained there but a short time, but still, the shame of it! That I, once called the Saviour of the Nation, should be brought so low."

"I wouldn't worry about it overmuch. A few years ago I spent some time under lock and key myself, in the Bastille," Philip reminded him.

"It's not the same for you. You're titled, so you can never lose your dignity. It is more than I should have to bear." Titus put his hand to his heart. "I who have dedicated myself to the salvation of the English people from evil Papists, with no reward except an easy conscience."

Philip laughed, for he had seen this touching act before. "No reward? You once had apartments in Whitehall and a pension from the King."

"I haven't got them now."

"More fool you!"

"I thought you were going to listen sympathetically," Titus said, sounding aggrieved. "You don't know the half of my troubles yet, for I was arrested once again in April because I was in debt for board and lodgings, though they bailed me out once more, and then, on Restoration Day, the people burnt an effigy of me at Covent Garden."

Philip nodded absently. His thoughts had drifted fifty miles away, to Heatherton. Since he'd returned from Sussex he had found that he could think of little else for very long. Giles called it his obsession.

Titus rambled on, happily unaware that most of what he said went unheard.

"You see what straits I'm in?" he finished.

Philip looked at him blankly. "What?"

"Have you been listening?"

"Yes, of course I have. You said you needed money," Philip guessed. "I can only wonder what you've done with all you had."

"I spent it. Surely I'm entitled to some luxuries. You spend yours lavishly enough. What about your clothes?"

"My clothes," Philip mused. "What do you suppose they would be worth?"

"Hundreds of pounds, I would imagine," Titus said, enviously eyeing the outfit Philip was wearing. It was the lilac brocade that Monsieur Robertin had made up perfectly to order. "But I could not allow you to make such a sacrifice on my behalf."

Philip smiled at that. "On yours? I was thinking about myself actually. I need money too, a large amount."

"What do you want money for?"

"My house. I've asked the Duke of Buckingham if I can borrow ten thousand pounds from him."

Titus whistled. "That is quite a sum. What did he say?"

"That he would give it thought and answer me today. I dare say I'll win him round. I always have before."

But later, when he called on Buckingham, Philip felt less hopeful. The Duke's face was grave.

"I have turned the matter over in my mind, Philip, as I promised, but, after due consideration, I'm afraid my answer will not please you. I have decided not to lend you the money."

Philip was bitterly disappointed. Despite the vast amounts that Buckingham had squandered, he was still the richest friend that Philip had. "May I ask why?"

"It is simply not a practical proposition. I agree with Giles, that you should sell High Heatherton."

"It's my house, not Giles', and I shall make my own decision," Philip said crossly.

"Yes, of course you will," Buckingham soothed, "but from what he says it's badly damaged."

"It can still be restored," Philip said, "and so it will be, even if it takes every penny I ever earn and all my life to do it."

"But why?"

"Why? Because it is my family home, of course."

"You've no affection for your family," Buckingham said. "This is just a whim of yours and I am certain it will prove a costly error."

"Why should you care? I will pay you back."

"Whether you do or not, I hate to see you waste your life on such a project," Buckingham told him frankly. "Philip, my dear Philip, you are what you are, a creature of the city, of the Court. You don't belong at Heatherton any more for you have lived too long amongst us here. London is your home now."

"Why does everyone presume to know me better than I know myself?" Philip muttered, recalling Shaftesbury's parting remark. "I thought in you, at least, I had a friend."

"It is because I am your friend that I will not aid you," Buckingham told him.

"But you have spent vast amounts on gifts for me in the past, and without the slightest quibble," Philip cried in exasperation.

"And I would do so again. If it were anything else for which you wanted such a sum I would give it to you gladly. Buy some racehorses, a yacht, invest it in the Colonies, but I'll not aid you in this folly."

"Folly?" Philip could hardly believe what he was hearing. "I'm trying to do a decent thing, to help the families who depend upon me. I'd have thought you would encourage me, not scoff at my endeavours."

"It is out of character for you," Buckingham said. "You have not the makings of a philanthropist, so don't delude yourself."

Philip struggled to keep his temper, for he knew there was little to be gained by losing it. "They need me, and I need them. Don't you see that I must restore High Heatherton or I have nothing, and then it will all have been in vain?"

"You have whatever the estate is worth and, with all the land you now own, that must still be quite a considerable amount. Do as Giles suggests," Buckingham advised. "Sell it. Buy yourself a decent house in town and spend the rest upon some nonsense you enjoy. There's more to life than gloomy country houses. God knows I spend as little time as possible in mine! As for your pathetic bunch of peasants, who have let your house rot and your fields lie uncultivated, tell them to look to the Parish for their charity and not to you. I'm sorry, Philip, you'll not move me, not this time."

Philip realised there was no point in arguing further. He knew the Duke well enough to recognise that he was adamant.

"It is of no consequence," he said airily. "I dare say I shall find another who has sufficient sympathy to advance me the sum I need."

"I rather doubt you will," Buckingham said softly. "Any who like you enough to lend it to you will try, as I have done, to change your mind."

ELEVEN

⁓

Shaftesbury died in January. Philip was not surprised when the news reached him from Holland but, despite everything that had passed between them, he did feel a pang of regret for the passing of the once powerful man who had been such a huge influence on his life.

It seemed to Philip that since his own interest in the plot had waned Monmouth's, perversely, had grown more vigorous and Shaftesbury's death seemed to strengthen, rather than weaken, his determination to carry it out. Urged on even by his gentle mistress, Henrietta, Monmouth seemed fired with new enthusiasm, almost as if he sought to prove that he was not the mere tool of Lord Shaftesbury but a leader in his own right.

Philip had always liked Monmouth but he had never rated his intelligence very highly. Whilst there was a good deal of superstition in Philip's nature, Monmouth's fascination with the occult and his almost fanatical belief in the power of magical charms had often caused Philip to doubt the Duke had any wit at all!

Nothing he could say would dissuade Monmouth now from his intention of participating in the Rye House Plot, as it had become known amongst the conspirators.

"Monmouth talks of going on another progress," Giles told Philip, as they sat drinking in the Nonsuch Tavern, an alehouse run by Major Wildman.

"So I've heard."

"He has been invited to stay with Richard Holmes in

Chichester and then to hunt with Lord Grey. I trust you won't be going with him this time."

"I might accompany him as far as Chichester."

"Then you're a bloody fool," Giles said. "If Charles has you arrested now you won't have Shaftesbury to help you."

"I'll be careful, I promise."

"Don't talk to me of promises! You promised, not so long ago, to abandon all this nonsense when Heatherton became yours. You have it now, for what it's worth."

Philip smiled. "Why, Giles, I do believe you're vexed with me!"

"I have good reason to be vexed. It's bad enough that the others are proposing to carry out this plan of yours. The trouble with you is that you never consider the consequences of your actions."

Philip knew that Giles was right. He had been responsible for Theresa's kidnap, and he felt he was responsible for the scar that had marred Giles' handsome face.

"It might have been better if I had never come back to England at all," he admitted quietly, "particularly for you and Tess."

"That was not my meaning," Giles said, in a softer tone, "anyway, if anyone is to blame for your return I suppose it's me, since I'm the one Shaftesbury sent to France to persuade you to come home. I'm just concerned, that's all. You once said you could finish your involvement in this plot any time you chose."

"I did say that."

"Then do it now," Giles urged, "before it is too late."

"It's not that easy, I'm afraid."

"Nonsense! You can usually find a way to do the things you want."

"But, Giles, it is my own plot the others are following, a plot I concocted when I wanted to impress Lord Shaftesbury. I never truly thought they would be mad enough to carry out the blasted thing! If I desert them now what will they think? Either that I've lost my nerve or, more likely, that I've set the whole thing up as a trap. One of them will kill me certainly, and who could blame them? I would do the same thing in their place."

"You surely don't propose to go through with it?" Giles looked appalled.

"Of course not. I am hoping to persuade Monmouth to abandon the idea himself. That is why I need to stay near him. Besides, Chichester is close to Heatherton and there is something I must take to John Bone."

"What's that?"

"Something he will like; five hundred pounds."

"Five hundred?" Giles cried. "I thought you could not borrow any money."

"I couldn't. I have sold a few things."

"What things?"

"Nothing important," Philip said dismissively, although that was not quite the truth. He had needed to sell most of his clothes and a great deal of his jewellery to raise such a large sum. "As you said, Giles, I can usually find a way to do the things I want!

The visit to Chichester was far more successful than Philip had wanted it to be. There was a procession and a large gathering of people to see Monmouth at the old Market Cross, where link boys paraded with their torches lit. True, the Bishop spoke out against him in the Cathedral but Monmouth was not discouraged by that.

It was no more than twenty miles from Chichester to Heatherton and Philip was glad of the excuse to escape from it all. Monmouth's progress had turned into a travelling spectacle, and he wanted to play no part in it.

Thomas went with him to Heatherton. Giles chose to remain in London this time, but he had lent Thomas his little

Arab stallion, Scarlet, and Philip was pleased to find that young Thomas was a good enough rider for them to be a match for him and Ferrion. They both enjoyed the ride through Arundel and along the quiet country lanes in the watery February sunshine.

John Bone came out to greet them as they stopped before the gates.

"I'd like a word with you alone," Philip said, "then I want you to bring the others up to the house."

"They grow discontented, I'm afraid, Lord Philip," John warned as they walked the horses up the long straight avenue that ran through the tangled remains of the formal gardens. "They don't believe that you are really going to help them."

"I'll help them," Philip said, "although it might not be on quite the scale I'd hoped. I am not a wealthy man, John. Everything was left to my brother and God alone knows what he did with it all. I have worked hard for my living since my father died, although I don't expect anyone to believe that."

"I believe you," John assured him, "but if you haven't any money then however are you going to be able to put right all this damage?" He pointed to the mansion.

"I never said I hadn't any, only that I did not have enough." Philip took the leather bag that was fastened to his saddle and handed it to John. "Here. There will be some more as soon as I can manage it."

John's eyes grew large as he looked inside the bag. "We can do a lot with that much money."

"I fear you'll find it won't go far, but spend it wisely. You'll need some seed for sowing and some livestock; new equipment too, I shouldn't wonder. My servant, Morgan, was once a farmer and he will accompany me when I next come down. He understands these things much better than I, so you and he can then decide what is to be done, but for the moment you must take all the responsibility yourself."

"You put much trust in me, Lord Philip," John said proudly.

"You'll not cheat me. Tell the others nothing yet, save that I wish to talk to them."

"Are they not to know what you have given me?"

"Not yet. I shall not buy their loyalty, John, but earn it if I can."

"And if you can't?"

"I have faced soldiers, kings and rioting Londoners," Philip said testily. "Do you really imagine this will be my most exacting audience?"

John grinned. "I'm sure you'll handle them!"

Thomas had disappeared whilst the two men talked and Philip went to look for him. He found him busying himself in the stables. He had unsaddled Ferrion and Scarlet and found some fairly clean straw to spread upon the floor and, by the time Philip arrived, he was scrubbing out the water trough.

"There will need to be some money spent in here, my Lord."

Philip looked up to where patches of sky showed through the roof and feared that Thomas was right. The stables, like everywhere else, were in need of repair.

"Perhaps we could convert the kennels." he indicated the adjoining building, which had once housed packs of hunting hounds.

Thomas looked doubtful. "It will be cramped with all three horses."

"Three?" Philip had already made a decision regarding the magnificent matching pair of black trace-horses which drew his elegant London carriage. "The blacks may not be coming with us," he said gently.

"You mean to sell them?" Thomas cried.

"Sacrifices must be made. What use would such dainty creatures be out here? I shall have more need of sturdy working horses."

"Even so, I would be sad to see them go, my Lord."

"And so would I, but when I sold a pair once before they paid our fares to France. The sale of these would pay for the repair of the stables and feed Ferrion for a year."

Thomas looked upset. What if I repaired the stables all myself? Would you consider keeping them then?"

"I'll think about it," Philip promised, for he knew how much Thomas loved the horses. "Come and see the inside of the house."

The city-bred Thomas had never been in a country house before. When he saw the huge, two-storeyed hall, with its gigantic iron chandelier with places for two hundred candles, he whistled in amazement.

"You were brought up here, my Lord, amongst all this?"

"Why yes. I am the son of an earl, don't forget," Philip pointed out. In fact his childhood here had been such an unhappy one that the only room which had ever meant anything at all to him was the one which had belonged to his late mother and had contained all her things. Although he had no memory of her, that room had been his sanctuary during his young life and he had been relieved when he discovered that Henry had not despoiled it.

Thomas darted this way and that, looking into rooms and exclaiming at everything he saw. Some chambers were still furnished, after a fashion, but others were completely bare, where the contents had been sold or else destroyed during one of Henry's rages. The whole place was icy cold and smelled of damp.   Thomas suddenly let out a shriek of fear.

"What is it?" Philip called. "What have you found?"

"I don't know." Thomas stood with his back firmly pressed against a door, as though bent on keeping whatever was in there from getting out, but Philip remembered the room and smiled.

"There is nothing in there that can harm you, at least not by itself! That is the armoury and in here are stored the weapons used by the private armies we raised in the past to support the Crown." Philip led him in and showed him the Fleur de Lys carved in the centre of a halberd. "This one dates from the reign of King Henry VlIl."

Thomas looked embarrassed when he discovered that what had scared him was only a suit of armour, and he delved deeper into the long, narrow room. They were still engrossed in the rusty old weaponry when they heard voices and they immerged to see families timidly entering the Great Hall.

Although they had lived their lives within High Heatherton's boundaries, Philip guessed that most of them had never been inside the house. The old custom of inviting every labourer on the estate into the Hall to dine with their lord on feast days had been long discontinued by Philip's father, on account of Henry's unpredictable behaviour.

Now they stood staring round them, obviously as awestruck as Thomas had been. They stared at Thomas as well and Philip beckoned him to his side.

"They are a ragged lot," Thomas whispered to him.

"They are indeed. They look a little hostile too."

"More like they're scared to death of you, my Lord."

"Perhaps, but I still think we have some trouble-makers here. No matter, I shall win them over."

Philip paraded slowly before them a few times to let them all have a proper look at him. Whatever else his faults might be in their eyes, he knew that his looks could not fail to impress them.

When he thought they had seen enough he stopped suddenly and turned to them.

"My friends, and I call you that because I sincerely hope that is what you will become, you are aware that High Heatherton came into my possession only a short time ago. Until then I had not set foot inside this property for more than twenty years and I had no notion of the sorry state of things. If you reckon that I should have made myself acquainted with how matters stood then you are right and I am very wrong. The only defence I can offer for my negligence is to appeal to those of sufficient age to remember how I spent my childhood here. They, perhaps, can understand why I never came to visit with my brother."

Looking at their faces he could see that many did remember, and he guessed that those who did not must have heard the stories of Henry's brutal treatment of his younger brother.

"We know why you didn't come before," ventured one, a little bolder than the rest, "but now you are here are you going to go away again?"

"Aye, back to London, I expect." said another. "Entertaining dukes and earls whilst our wives and children starve."

There was a rumble of agreement and Philip held up his hand for silence. "I have some pressing business which I must return to London to finish and then it is my intention to devote my time exclusively to Heatherton."

"This business, is it more pressing than your duty here?"

Philip looked at the last man who had spoken. It was Dick Searle, who John had felled for his impertinence on Philip's last visit. Small and shifty-eyed, Searle had never been a friend of his when they were boys. He had been loud-mouthed and belligerent, and always jealous of John Bone.

"My duty? You are as impudent as ever, Searle. I tolerate that from no-one?" Philip subjected him to a withering glare. "You will not question what I do if you intend to benefit from my generosity."

"We've seen no evidence yet of your generosity," Searle sneered.

"Have you brought us money?" asked another.

"Are you going to help us?"

"Of course he's not," Searle said. "I say we should sell whatever's left in the house and live as paupers no longer."

One or two murmured their assent and even began to move menacingly toward Philip. Both John and Thomas started to his assistance but Philip shook his head, for he was not afraid of them.

"You will do no such thing. Get back!"

Philip was used to giving orders, and to having them obeyed. There was an authority in his voice which evidently none, even Searle, felt inclined to challenge.

"This house and everything in it is mine," he told them, "and so it will remain. You can air your grievances when the time comes and each one will be listed in the proper manner and dealt with as I see fit. Now hear me out. Firstly there is something you should know about me. Contrary to all you may suppose, I am not a rich man."

"Then how are you going to help us?" several voices cried out in dismay.

"Ask rather how you are going to help yourselves," Philip returned sharply. "You turn to me for money as I once turned to the Earl, my father. Do you imagine I have lived on Henry's generosity these last few years? No, I have not. Instead I have employed my talents as best I could, and that is what you, too, must do. It is of no use to beg to me for money which I do not have. You must resume your farming, for crops can grow in the fields again, sheep can graze once more upon the downs and cows be milked. You need to work together, share you gains, for this time there will not be any madman to rob you of them. I'll restore High Heatherton and turn this wilderness into the rich estate it used to be, but firstly we must cut the timber."

"And when we have cut it you will take your money and be off again," Searle reckoned.

"Dear God!" Philip cried in frustration. "Is it not enough that my inheritance should be a dilapidated house and barren lands? Must I also have as my dependants folk who are capable of no emotion save resentment and no words save accusations? You demand I house you, feed you, care for you; what do you offer me?"

"What can we offer you?" cried one. "Only ourselves."

"And a sullen, peevish bunch you are!" Philip had decided

that the time had come to show them who was the master. "I would fare badly on the deal I think. John Bone is the only man of spirit amongst you."

"What do you expect?" Searle's voice could be heard again. "Your brother bled us dry."

"And what is it that you expect, Dick Searle? That I shall spend the rest of my days making amends to you for Henry's failings? I have suffered quite enough on account of him, for I still bear the marks of his spite. All I offer you is the chance to help yourselves, to change from whining beggars back to proud men who can hold their heads high in the knowledge that they support their families with their own toil, not the charity of their lord."

His audience looked taken aback. They had obviously not expected him to turn upon them.

"You have a very poor opinion of me, that is clear," Philip continued, in a gentler tone, for he had learned the winning arts. "I suppose I cannot blame you. I have not lived a life of any particular virtue, nor will I pledge I shall do so in the future." He smiled at them disarmingly. "What I do pledge is that I will not desert High Heatherton, even though I've been advised to do so. Whether or not I am proved right depends on all of you." He made an eloquent gesture which embraced them all and then his smile faded and he glared at them. "Or, to be more precise, it depends on whether or not you are capable of crawling out of the morass of self-pity in which you are wallowing.

I want your labour, and I want it willingly. In return I offer myself as your defender. I will provide for every man in sickness and for every man's dependants when he dies. I will uphold your rights, protect your property and render unto each of you the income that he earns."

John looked unable to restrain himself any longer. "That sounds right honourable to me," he called out. "I stand for Lord Philip!"

"And I," cried nearly a hundred voices more, whilst even Searle could apparently find no argument with Philip's terms.

"Listen, all of you," Philip ordered, when they had quietened down. "I am used to commanding troops upon the battlefield. I expected complete obedience from them and I demand the same of you. We fight not foes but poverty here, and it will prove as difficult an enemy I am sure. I never asked my soldiers to attempt anything I was not prepared to do myself and I say the same to you. I'll work beside you when I return, as hard as you and for as long, but I am the master. You will not forget that, any of you, and I shall not tolerate rebels or dissenters. Those who follow me will ultimately share in my rewards, I promise that, though it may be a little while before we harvest all the fruits of our endeavours. Who is with me?"

"All of us," cried John, and this time the rest shouted with one accord that they were with him.

"Shall you bring any with you to help us?" John asked, when the cries had died down.

"Very few, I'm afraid, John. My household is small, but I have young Thomas here. He tends to my horses but he will turn his hand to anything. You will discover him to be a willing worker."

John guffawed loudly. "Willing he may be, though how much use is something else. There's nothing to the boy!"

Thomas drew himself up angrily. "You'll find that I am strong and not afraid of work."

"What work could we give him, lads? If you were country born you'd have some muscles on those arms, like my own boy here."

"You'll find that I can fight, though." Thomas squared up to Bone's son, who was about his own age but far more solidly built.

"That he can," Philip smiled, "and he has, for me. You must not tease him, John, for he is a good boy and much tougher than he looks." He put his arm around Thomas' shoulders. "I value him, in fact he is indispensable to me."

Thomas looked smug.

John laughed. "I meant no harm. You know that."

"I know it," Philip said. "Thomas, do not mind his taunting. He would do the same to me when we were boys, but I could always equal him in a contest."

"That's true, Lord Philip," John agreed, "but you haven't grown too much since then."

"I dare say I am still a match for you. Your father taught me very well." Philip sought out Sam Bone in the crowd and saluted him.

"You never are! I'd beat you now for certain."

Philip looked him up and down. "I don't believe you would. You were always heavier than me, but you were slow. I'll warrant you still are."

"Is that a challenge?" John cried in delight.

"If you like. We'll make a match of it when I return."

Those watching cheered his nerve. It was obvious that few would have taken on the huge John Bone.

"Lord Philip! Sam pushed his way through. "I beg you not to let this son of mine persuade you into this. It's not right, not now. You are no longer boys, you are our master, and you, John, if you have respect for me, your father, you'll not lay a finger on his Lordship."

"Who are you protecting, Sam?" Philip asked him, amused. "Your son or me?"

There was no way now a fight could be prevented and Thomas groaned. "He will murder you, my Lord," he said as they went to saddle up the horses.

"Not he, for he lumbers like an ox. Don't worry."

Thomas shook his head despairingly. "I dread to think what Morgan is going to say about this!"

"I think now would be a good time for you to visit your family in Dorset," Philip told Giles, the week before the March race meeting at Newmarket.

"And why would I do that?" Giles hardly ever went home. He preferred to be reminded as rarely as possible of his humble beginnings.

"Because it would be best. You need not stay there long, just until the King returns from the races."

Giles regarded him steadily. "Then you do expect him to return?"

"Charles will return and the Duke of York with him," Philip assured him. "Nothing will happen to either of them. I have the matter in hand."

"So you say, but you still haven't told me what you are proposing to do."

"Nor do I intend to tell you," Philip said firmly. "I don't want you involved in this at all, and I certainly don't want you anywhere near Monmouth or the others for the next few days. If anything should go wrong, not that I expect it will," he added hastily, seeing Giles' expression, "but if it should then the more you are distanced from events the better."

"What about Monmouth?" Giles asked. "He is still your friend, and mine. Would he not see this as a betrayal if he knew the truth?"

"What would you have of me, Giles? Monmouth's Cause is doomed since Shaftesbury died. You know it as well as me."

"But Monmouth doesn't't seem to know it."

"Then he should. He is surrounded now by self-seekers like Grey who will lead him to disaster. I beg you, Giles, do not get involved with them."

"That's very fine advice indeed to come from you! You have been involved in plotting and scheming ever since I've known you and now *you* preach caution to *me*?"

"I've reformed!"

Giles gave him a sidelong glance. "I doubt that. Are you sure there is nothing I can do to help with whatever you are planning?"

Philip shook his head. "Not this time, Giles."

Giles sighed. "Very well. I just hope you know what you are doing."

"Yes," Philip said quietly, "so do I."

TWELVE

∾

In the early hours of the morning three figures, swathed in thick cloaks, urged their horses through the dark, damp streets of London.

Philip rode Ferrion and Thomas was on Scarlet, whilst Morgan was mounted on a sturdy little cob that Philip had borrowed from the Duke of Buckingham. The sound of their horses' hooves upon the cobbles was muffled by the chilling river mist, which hung around them like fragments of a veil as they headed out of the city and through Waltham Forest to the Cambridge road.

It took them two days to travel to Newmarket, where they found the town in a state of excitement, as it always was on the occasions when it played host to the King. People from as far away as Cambridge or Bury crowded in, hoping to catch a glimpse of him when he watched the races or strode over the heath, which he did every morning.

Charles could still walk ten miles with ease, and never missed a horse race or a cock fight, but he had begun to feel his years and was in bed most nights by nine o'clock. The town still continued to celebrate his presence after that, however, and Philip figured that, with the streets being so crowded, the arrival of three more horsemen would go unnoticed amidst the comings and goings of horses, carriages and carts.

"There are the stables." He indicated a building visible on the outskirts of town. It had been quite a few years since he had accompanied King Charles to the races at Newmarket but he remembered the place well enough.

Morgan looked at the clouds scurrying across the sky. "It's a good night for what we have to do. The wind is strong."

Philip nodded. "But we are early yet. The streets are far too full." He looked toward an alehouse. "We will pass an hour in there."

The landlord of the Wheatsheaf Tavern regarded them with only mild interest as he served them, for the place was packed. Philip had pulled his hat down low across his eyes, for he did not want to risk being recognised, and he turned his face away as Morgan ordered three tankards of ale for them.

When the landlord had brought them their drinks and left them alone, Thomas opened the pouch that hung from his belt and took out a piece of sacking and then a small pot, which he held against the candle burning on their table. When the pot was warmed he wrapped it quickly in the sacking and put it back inside his pouch.

Philip and Morgan exchanged questioning looks.

"Tallow," Thomas explained. "To grease the bolts and hinges."

"Good boy! I would never have thought of that," Philip said.

"I know my old trade," Thomas told them with some pride. He had been schooled in thievery by the most audacious rogues in London's criminal district of Alsatia when he was little more than a child.

Philip glanced at his two servants. Morgan was as impassive as himself and Thomas, despite his youth, had the composure of one trained early into the ways of stealth and cunning.

"You realise neither of you have to do this," he said quietly.

"Yes, my Lord," both answered.

"I would never order you to risk your lives in order to repair the damage I have done."

Thomas gave him a cheeky grin. "You need a professional on this job, my Lord. You're a soldier, not a felon!"

"I think what he's trying to say is that we don't trust you to do it without us," Morgan said gruffly.

Philip smiled. As usual they were staunch beside him, no matter what he did. "My two most loyal friends," he said fondly. "I think if I rode through the gates of hell you would insist on accompanying me!"

Before the hour was up the crowds had begun to dwindle.

Philip threw some coins upon the table. "Come, the time is now."

His plan was simple. They would start a fire at the stables, which, with luck, would cause the races to be cancelled and the King and Duke to leave Newmarket earlier than intended. The Rye House conspirators would not have time to be in position ready to intercept the royal coach and Philip's plot would have to be abandoned.

What could possibly go wrong?

They rode past the first stable as far as the adjoining field, which was used by the grooms when they exercised the horses in the morning. It was nearing midnight now and the road was quiet, for most of the outgoing traffic had already left.

They removed their hats and cloaks and stowed them in their saddle-bags. Thomas then climbed onto Scarlet's back and, shielded by the figures of the other two, mounted the top of the gate. Soundlessly he leapt down upon the other side.

Pulling out his pot of tallow, which was still soft, Thomas carefully greased the bolt that held that held the gate. It slid silently across.

Waiting until the road was clear, Philip and Morgan pushed the gates open and entered with the horses, which they tethered to a tree in the far corner of the field.

Whilst he waited for them Thomas had greased the hinges and latch of the gate to the stable yard. The wind was strong, as Morgan had said, and the creaking of the trees made more noise than the gate as Thomas opened it.

As they crossed the dimly lit yard the racehorses in the stable stirred, for they were nervous and sensed that something was afoot.

The greater part of the yard was covered with earth, well trampled by horses' hooves, but cobbles paved the area around the building. Thomas greased the moving parts of the upper and lower sections of the door to the stables while Philip and Morgan crossed the yard to the barn, from where they carried out armfuls of straw. This they spread down in the centre of the paving to make a path wide enough to lead the horses through.

When all was prepared to Philip's satisfaction he slipped inside the stable and looked about him. There were twelve horses in the stalls and the one nearest to him, seeing a person he did not recognise, snorted, backing noisily into the side of his stall.

Philip gently held out his hand and whispered some words in the horse's ear. The animal quietened and even nuzzled against him as he listened for any sound coming from the upper storey. It was reached by a staircase built against the wall and he had wondered if any of the grooms might still be up there, but he could hear nothing but the wind, which was whistling around at that height and rattling the windows in their frames.

Morgan stood watch by the door, his knife ready in his hand, as Philip and Thomas slipped bridles over the necks of the first two horses and led them slowly from their stalls.

It was a slow process. Philip calculated that the first trip had taken nearly four minutes to complete and there were ten more horses to escort. Although it appeared that the grooms in charge of them had already gone to their beds there were more stables in the immediate vicinity and, despite the lateness of the hour, it was conceivable that there may be other grooms still about. If they were spotted he knew it would be extremely difficult to explain what they were doing there!

All went well until they came to the final pair. Thomas led his out first but, as Philip unlatched the door of the last stall, the one remaining horse realised it was alone and took fright. Before Philip could stop it the nervous beast reared up, whinnying loudly, his flailing hooves hitting the side of the wooden stall.

Thomas had returned and together they managed to get the panic-stricken animal from its stall.

"Take it and bring our horses," Philip ordered him. "Fast!"

He took a tinder box and an oiled rag from his pocket. He set the cloth alight and then hurled it into the furthest corner of the building. The straw caught straight away and the wooden stalls soon began to smoke as the flames started. Satisfied that it would burn, Philip turned to go.

It was then he saw a figure outlined in the smoke rising up the staircase. There had been a groom upstairs after all, and from the way in which he was staggering Philip guessed he had been roused from a drunken stupor by the frightened horse.

"Murder! Murder!"

Philip cursed under his breath. It had never been his intention to hurt anyone but the man needed to be silenced, and swiftly.

Fortunately Morgan had seen him too, and Morgan never hesitated if Philip was in any kind of danger.

He hurled his knife with deadly precision.

The groom dropped where he stood and Morgan raced up the stairs to retrieve the knife.

The fire was burning well now, a little too well. The hayloft had caught alight and the flames were spreading up to the ceiling. Philip looked up impatiently as Morgan pulled the blade from the dead man's chest.

"Move!" he shouted. "Leave the damned knife!"

Even as Morgan thrust it into his belt Philip saw the danger through a drift of smoke. A beam above the landing had started smouldering and the joint was weakening. Before he could shout a warning, part of the beam crashed down.

It struck Morgan squarely on the head, pitching him forward. He fell from the top of the stairs to the floor and lay quite still.

Blood was running from a gash on his head and his right leg was twisted in an unnatural way around the bottom post.

Philip rushed to his side, for the flames had already nearly reached to the staircase. Even as he knelt to raise him he saw his own coat catch alight. He tugged it off, though not before some of his long hair had been singed, and then, with a supreme effort, he lifted the stocky Welshman in his arms.

The heat by now was overpowering and the weight of Morgan almost more than he could manage, but Philip had an iron will and, at times, he could drive himself beyond the normal limits of endurance. He reached the door only seconds before the flames and, coughing, staggered out into the cool night air.

Thomas, waiting with the horses, looked silently at Morgan.

Philip heaved him across Ferrion's back and hung onto the horse for support, for the heat and activity had left him dazed.

"Lead on!" he told Thomas. "I'll be behind you."

Thomas hesitated.

"I said lead on," Philip snapped, shaking his head to clear it, "or shall you disobey me too?"

Thomas needed no more telling. Holding the cob's reins, he rode Scarlet through the gates and out onto the road to Cambridge. Philip swung himself into the saddle behind Morgan and followed swiftly, before anyone saw that the stable was on fire. They rode about a mile before Philip noticed a small barn, set back a few yards from the road and housing a plough and other farming implements.

He lifted Morgan from Ferrion's back and carried him inside whilst Thomas tethered the horses behind the barn, well out of sight of the nearby farmhouse. Philip was kneeling by Morgan's side when he returned.

"Is he dead?" Thomas asked in a strangled voice.

Philip shook his head. "No, thank God, though he barely breathes." Morgan's skin was cold and clammy to the touch and his breaths were so shallow as to be almost imperceptible. "His leg is broken. It must be attended to without delay or he may never walk properly again."

Philip did not add 'if he lives', although that thought was in his mind. He tore a strip from the bottom of his shirt and gave it to Thomas. "Here, bind his head."

It was not easy to work in the confines of the barn, for it was dark save for the light of the moon and even that was occasionally obliterated by the clouds. Thomas dabbed at the deep cut from which the blood still ran profusely, soaking Morgan's clothes and hair. They had no water so he could not bathe it but he bound the wound tightly.

Philip meanwhile, had found a hazel tree close by. He took Morgan's knife and trimmed some of the thin branches to use as splints and then tore some more strips off his shirt.

"Have you done this before?" Thomas asked as Philip ran his hand along the leg, which had been broken just below the knee.

"Never, but I have seen it done upon the battlefield, with the poor wretches screaming out in agony." He gripped Morgan's ankle. "At least we can be thankful he does not know what I am doing to him. Hold him tightly around the waist, for I am going to pull hard against you."

He put his foot firmly in Morgan's groin and tugged sharply. The ugly lump, which had been protruding from his leg, disappeared.

"I've done it! I should have been a bloody surgeon." Philip held the strips of cloth between his teeth, taking them one by one as he needed them to pad the splints and tie them round. When he had finished the leg was held quite straight.

He pushed his hair out of his eyes and looked toward the town. A red glow lit the sky and, even from that distance, it was plain the fire was spreading fast in the high winds that were whipping across the flat heath land.

He shuddered. "Half the town's alight, by the look of it. I'd not bargained on that, but at least we can be sure the races will be cancelled now. The Rye House Plot is foiled and we'd have ridden away into the night and perfectly escaped discovery. Now we may be caught, and for a damned knife. Oh, Morgan," Philip looked sadly at him, "I would sooner have killed ten kings than have you taken from me."

Thomas was plainly upset too and Philip knew he must take action right away if he was to get himself and his faithful servants to safety.

"We must get Morgan away from here, but not upon a horse," he said. "I need a vehicle."

"From the farm?" Thomas suggested.

Philip looked toward the farmhouse. There were lamps burning in one of the windows and a dog was already warning an unheeding master of their presence. "I think not. I'd do better to return to Newmarket."

"That will be dangerous, my Lord."

"On the contrary, I shall pass unobserved for I should think the town will be in uproar." He ruffled the youth's spiky hair. "Stay alert."

Before Thomas could say anything more Philip slipped out of the barn and was soon running back along the road they had just ridden.

He kept well to the side, for carts loaded with possessions were already heading out of the town. As he neared it he could see flames leaping high into the sky, carried from one thatched roof to another. He regretted causing the conflagration but his only concern now was for Morgan. He moved swiftly and was soon mingling with the panicking crowds until, outside the open door of a house not yet touched by the blaze, he saw an unattended cart.

Philip pulled a face at the sight of the poor old animal between its shafts but the vehicle was large enough for his purposes and he guessed he would get no better chance.

He pressed himself against the wall of the opposite building as a thick-set man, a little older than himself, ran from the house with a full sack in his arms. He threw it onto the cart and ran back inside the house. Philip seized his opportunity and darted across the street. He jumped into the driver's seat and took up the reins but, despite the speed of his reactions, he had not been quick enough.

"Thief!"

The man ran out, shouting, and wrenched the reins from his hands. Philip swore and put his boot into the fellow's chest, shoving him backwards so that he landed on the ground but before he could reach the reins again the man was back on his feet. He gripped Philip's leg and attempted to pull him from the seat.

Philip managed to lean back far enough the grasp the bundle from the cart and he hurled it at the man's head. This time he did succeed in grabbing the reins before his assailant could be upon him and he started the cart moving but he had reckoned without the courage which desperation was giving to its owner, who hurled himself upon the back of the vehicle. Even as they started down the street he tackled Philip again.

"For God's sake, man, let me have it," Philip cried out in frustration, holding him back with one arm whilst, with the other, he attempted to drive the horse on.

"Never," the fellow panted, struggling free. "I'll die first."

"For a blasted cart? Don't be an idiot. I will pay you for it if you like, but I must have it."

For a moment it did seem as if the cart's owner would relent but the crashing of burning timbers nearby must have reminded him of his own dire need for the vehicle.

"No. Who are you anyway? One of the King's party?"

The words sealed his fate. Even as the man said them it occurred to Philip that he could not afford to be merciful to someone who had seen him at such close quarters. He let go of the reins and pulled out Morgan's knife, which was still in his belt. "So be it."

A knife was not Philip's weapon of choice but there was neither the time nor space to use another. With his left forearm he smashed the man's head back and plunged the blade into his lung.

His victim's eyes opened eyes wide as bright red blood gurgled from his mouth.

Philip had not wanted to do it but he was past caring about anything but Morgan now. He heaved him from the cart and headed out of town, slapping the whip against the horse's rump.

Thomas saw him coming and ran to take the horse's head. "You did well, my Lord."

"Not really. I had to kill the owner for it, stupid bastard. They may not have found him yet in all that confusion but it can't be long before they do and then the constable will be after us."

As he talked Philip half-dragged, half-carried the still unconscious Morgan from the barn and hoisted him, with difficulty, into the vehicle, with Thomas guiding the splinted leg.

"Can you drive the wretched thing?" Philip asked him.

"Yes, my Lord."

"Then start. I'll bring the horses."

Riding Ferrion and leading the other two, he set off behind Thomas, who drove at as fast a pace as the old carthorse could endure.

Cambridge was in nearly as much of an uproar as Newmarket had been, for the Vice-Chancellor of the University, on hearing of the fire, had ordered the bells of Great St. Mary's to be rung.

Fortunately they passed through without attracting any undue attention, for there were many carts upon the roads that night, driven by refugees from Newmarket.

Safely out and heading towards St. Albans, Philip sought about to find a place where they could spend the night. The horses were exhausted and both he and Thomas felt they'd had enough. There were no buildings of any description as far as he could see, but there was a clump of trees and they pulled the vehicle off the road and led the horses into it. The cartwheels left no tracks, for the ground was hard and fairly dry. Having satisfied themselves that nothing could be seen from the road, Philip and Thomas made the four horses as comfortable as possible for the night.

Thomas stretched out on the ground, having nowhere better to sleep, and he wrapped his cloak around him. His upbringing had accustomed him to hardship and to suffering cold and he made no complaint but he did not look sorry when Philip, searching the sacks which had been left in the cart, discovered two blankets. He tossed one to Thomas and the other he folded double and tucked around Morgan.

He felt for the faint, fast heartbeat, looking intently into Morgan's face and almost willing him to live through the night.

Glancing up he became aware of Thomas' dark, solemn eyes watching him.

"Is Morgan going to die, my Lord?"

"I don't know. I only know he must not die." Philip climbed down from the cart and came to sit beside him. "You should be sleeping, for tomorrow may be a difficult day."

"I'm not the least bit sleepy, my Lord."

"Nor am I." Philip lay down with him and looked up at the sky. "Oh, Thomas, may your conscience never trouble you the way mine troubles me tonight."

"You always blame yourself for everything." Thomas moved nearer and spread the blanket over them both, for Philp no longer even had a coat beneath his cloak. "It can't always be your fault."

"Can't it? What about yourself?" Philip said. "Twice now I have led you into dreadful danger."

"What do I care about danger when I have the bravest man who ever lived right here beside me?" Thomas said staunchly.

Philip smiled, in spite of everything. "Dear God! Shall I never cure you of this hero worship?"

"No, never. I would give my life for you, my Lord."

"You are much too young to think of dying," Philip said, touched by his devotion. "Don't talk any more now. You'll sleep soon enough."

Thomas was, indeed, soon asleep and Philip was lost once more in the darkness of his own thoughts.

THIRTEEN

∞

When they awoke there was a heavy dew upon the grass and both were stiff with cold.

Philip immediately checked the motionless figure in the cart.

"He still breathes," he said, relieved, "but we cannot let him spend another night out in the open. Let's ready the horses and get going."

"How long will it take to get to London with the cart?" Thomas said.

"I don't believe we can risk returning to London, not with Morgan as he is. We are certain to be seen and questions will be asked. I think we should make for Heatherton."

"How far is that?"

"Perhaps five days from here."

"Five days?" Thomas, who had saddled Ferrion, Scarlet and the cob, was looking on as Philip eased the carthorse back between the shafts. "I doubt that old nag can take it."

As he fixed the harness Philip's sharp eyes spotted some soldiers coming down the road in the pale, dawn light. Their uniforms were unmistakable. They were the King's Own Lifeguards.

"Get back," he hissed.

There were six of them silhouetted against the pinkish grey of the sky.

"Are they looking for you, my Lord?" Thomas said.

"It's possible, although I doubt my crime was the only one

reported last night. The King must have dispatched his own guard to keep order."

The soldiers separated, taking off in different directions like so many spokes of a wheel. One headed their way.

Philip drew out his pistol.

The soldier skirted round the trees. There were no tracks visible and he seemed about to leave. Even as he turned around, the old carthorse, which was neither so well-trained nor as trusting as the others, let out a fear-filled whinny.

Philip and Thomas froze. It was too late. The soldier had heard the sound. He dismounted and approached them purposefully.

Suddenly he darted back. Leaping into his saddle he started off toward the hill where he had left the others, shouting for them to join him.

"He saw us!" Thomas cried.

"Blast!" Philip looked down at the heavy cart. "We'll not outrun them, not with Morgan."

"But we can't leave him, my Lord."

"Did you think I would?" He rested the pistol on the crook of his left arm.

Thomas gasped. "You're going to kill a soldier?"

"Hopefully not, but I need to disable him before he can tell the others what he saw." Philip sighted carefully. "I'll only get one chance for he is almost out of range already. We could do with Giles here now. He has a better aim than I."

Nonetheless it was a good shot. The soldier fell heavily from his horse and lay motionless on the ground, a dark patch of blood clearly visible on the sleeve of his scarlet coat.

"Bravo!" Thomas cried in admiration.

"That is only half the job. Cheer me when I've finished it." Philip mounted Ferrion. "I shall try to lead them off. If I should not return then you must get Morgan to Heatherton as best you can." He looked down at the Welshman. "Poor old friend. Another trouble I have got you into. He is in your charge, Thomas. Take every care of him."

"You can rely on me, my Lord."

"I know it." Philip took his silver watch from his pocket and handed it to him. "Wait one hour for me, certainly no more. I will try to catch you up along the way."

Two of the soldiers were lifting their injured comrade into the saddle and Philip was pleased to see that, from the way he was slumped over his mount, he appeared to be unconscious and therefore incapable of describing what he had seen. The other three were already riding towards them.

Philip set off at a furious pace, joining the road a hundred yards ahead of the soldiers. He glanced over his shoulder and made sure that all three were following him and then veered off the road again.

A shot rang out. The leading man had fired his pistol but Ferrion, trained as he was for war, did not falter for an instant and they headed out over the fields, closely followed by the Life Guards, their red sashes billowing out behind them.

The next hour went by slowly for Thomas. He occasionally cast an anxious eye over Morgan, hoping against hope to see him stir or hear him speak, but the Welshman did not move and made no sound.

"Don't die on me, please, Morgan," he begged. "His Lordship would never forgive me."

There was no sign of any more soldiers, indeed the road was strangely quiet, the only traffic being a coach and four travelling in great haste from Cambridge. Bearing news of the fire, no doubt, thought Thomas, watching it out of sight.

As the last few minutes of the hour ticked away he forced himself to think of both his master's and his own predicament.

He knew he must seriously consider that Philip might have been taken, or even shot. As he tied Scarlet and the cob to the back of the vehicle and led the carthorse to the road he wondered how he'd fare alone. Thomas had not the slightest notion of how to get to Sussex and, although Philip had left him his watch, he had neglected to give him any money!

Before climbing into the driving seat he had the forethought to cover Morgan over completely with the blankets.

He encountered only one person all morning, a horseman bound for Newmarket, who nodded to him as they passed without appearing to pay him any particular attention. Encouraged by this, Thomas drove quite confidently past the few farmhouses along the road.

He stopped a little way from one and sniffed the air.

"Newly baked bread!"

As the sweet aroma wafted to him Thomas was reminded that he'd not eaten since the afternoon of the previous day. During the time had been a member of the Devalle household he had become accustomed to more regular victuals!

"Well I've no money," he told the three horses who, it occurred to him, must be hungry too, "so I guess I'll have to ply my old trade, if I can still remember how."

There were woods nearby and, investigating them, he discovered a little copse, not too far in. It had been recently cut so it was an easy matter to secrete his cart and animals in there. He found an empty sack in the cart and, having made a final check on Morgan, he tucked the sack into his belt and crept through the undergrowth until he reached the farmyard wall.

Scaling it nimbly, he peeped over the top and surveyed the layout of the yard. The kitchen lay directly opposite him and he could see the fresh loaves cooling on the windowsill. On the table behind them there was a large cheese, the sight of which made Thomas' mouth water. He determined to get that as well.

A young girl of about his own age came from the cowshed

carrying a pail of milk. When she had disappeared into the dairy Thomas leapt down lightly from the wall and darted into the shed. A nearly full churn of milk stood by the door. Thomas tucked it out of sight behind some bales of straw stacked in the yard and put an empty churn in its place.

Beyond the cowshed was a stable and it was to there he next went. The only occupant, an ageing plough horse, looked interestedly at him as he struggled with a bag of bran.

Thomas talked all the while to the horse, making the sounds he had heard his master make to the racehorses the night before. That seemed to reassure the animal, just as it had the highly strung horses at Newmarket. He dragged the bag to the stable door but, hearing voices, he left it there and dived behind the straw himself, alongside the churn.

It was the little milkmaid talking to a plump woman who, from the looks of her, was her mother. Thomas peered out at them from his hiding place and pulled a face. He did not relish the prospect of a clout from one of her brawny arms should she discover him! He heard her tell the girl to hurry with the butter making and then be away to the fields to take her father and her brothers their lunch. He guessed that lunch was to be the bread and cheese, so he knew he would not have long to make his move.

The girl went back to her work and Thomas watched in dismay as the farmer's wife took up a broom and commenced to sweep the stone steps outside the kitchen door. He heard the girl's churn-staff moving faster in the butter churn. He had counted only eight cows in the shed and he was afraid she could not be much longer with only that small amount of milk to churn.

He looked about him for something to distract the girl's mother.

Across the other side of the yard he could see a store house containing the barrels of pickles and jars of preserves that

that good woman had put by. An earthenware pot, balancing precariously upon another, caught his eye. He sought about him for a stone and, finding one of a good size and shape, he raised himself sufficiently to take aim.

His accuracy at hurling a rock was a skill of which Thomas was justifiably very proud, for he had practised it to perfection. He hit the base of the pot with sufficient force to dislodge it and the pot crashed to the ground, disgorging its contents upon the flagstone floor.

The farmer's wife shrieked and ran inside the store, chasing out a cat that had been innocently sleeping in the corner!

Quick as lightening, Thomas dashed inside the kitchen and shoved the whole cheese inside his sack. The larder door stood open and, inside, he could see a ham hanging from a hook in the ceiling. He reached in and grabbed that too and then made for the bread upon the window sill.

Before he reached it he heard the heavy tread of the farmer's wife returning and he dodged beneath the sill.

She finished the steps and started sweeping along the path around the house, banging her broom noisily against the wall, so Thomas could always guess where she was. When he judged her to be a safe distance away he tucked a loaf of bread into his sack and climbed through the window. He looked around and then let himself down, landing soundlessly.

There was no sign of either the wife or her daughter so he sped across the yard and threw the sack straight over the wall. He ran back to fetch the milk and, sitting astride the top of the wall, he reached down to grab the handle of the churn and then lifted it over.

He saw the wife come out of the shed, her daughter close behind her, and he quickly dropped down into the woods on the other side of the wall.

The churn had been awkward but the sack of bran was heavy, far too heavy for him to lift. He knew he should leave it and make good his escape with what he had, yet he could not. The horses needed it and he could not rely upon the opportunity to get more.

He listened and blessed his luck as both women passed by without noticing anything was amiss.

As they went into the kitchen he dodged back over the wall for the last time. His eyes lit on a rope hanging from a nail upon the wall, just above his head. With the aid of a rake left leaning against the cowshed he succeeded in unhooking it. He tied the rope securely around the neck of the bag and then, safely back upon the woodland side of the wall, he pulled with all his might.

The bag dragged across the yard until it came to rest against the base of the wall. Just then he heard the farmer's wife cry out as she realised they had been robbed.

Thomas made a final effort. The bag slowly rose to the top of the wall and tumbled over, almost landing on him.

He left it where it lay, smiling as he picked up the churn and shouldered the sack of food. "So, Thomas," he said to himself, "you still make a pretty good thief!"

He approached the coppice quietly, so as not to alarm the horses. It was fortunate that he did for, as he got nearer, he saw a man bending over the cart.

Thomas stopped quite still, the beating of his heart sounding loud to him in the stillness of the wood. The stranger was carrying a flintlock and, from the look of him, Thomas guessed he was a poacher.

He was starting to lift up the covers in the bottom of the cart and Thomas held his breath, but the poacher suddenly jumped back. A low muttering could plainly be heard coming from the cart and Thomas realised it must be Morgan who was speaking, although the words were unintelligible.

The sound had obviously unnerved the poacher, who let go of the blanket and shot off through the trees as though the demons of hell were after him.

Thomas breathed again.

He pulled the covers back when he got to the cart. Morgan was silent now and had not moved.

Thomas guessed that whatever he had been saying must have been in Welsh. "You knew just when to speak," he told him. "You may well have saved our lives."

He dipped his hand into the churn and, raising Morgan's head, poured some milk into his mouth. Morgan choked a bit but he seemed to swallow most of it and Thomas repeated the exercise several more times before settling him down again.

He drank a little himself and broke off some cheese and bread. He devoured that ravenously, ramming it into his mouth in a way he knew would have disgusted his fastidious master!

He next dragged the bag of bran over and held up a little in his cupped hands before each horse.

"We must be on our way now, as swiftly as we can," he told them.

But the old carthorse was slow. Even though they made no more stops they had covered barely twenty miles before the evening came. Thomas remembered that Philip had said Morgan must not spend another night outside; in fact he did not relish the idea of doing so himself, although he knew they would not make it to St. Albans before dark.

By five o'clock the fields had emptied and, as they ambled by at a pace growing ever slower, Thomas spied a roomy barn which he reckoned would easily take the horses and the cart as well. He knew that if he took advantage of its shelter he would need to be away before the farm workers came back in the morning but he trusted the dawn light would disturb him in good time.

The barn was perfect. On the one side was stacked the farmer's winter store of grain and on the other fresh, sweet straw. He was able to drive the cart right in and shut the door behind them.

After he had seen to the horses and given Morgan a little

more of the milk he feasted on some bread and ham before throwing himself down in the straw. After the previous night, spent upon the cold, hard ground, the straw felt as luxurious as a feather bed. Although thoughts of his master's whereabouts were troubling him, Thomas was exhausted and sleep came readily enough.

❦

Philip was heading for St. Albans too, but from the opposite direction.

Despite Ferrion's fleetness and his own ingenuity, he'd had the devil's own job to lose the soldiers. They had run him near to Hertford before he could be sure they were truly off his trail and both horse and rider were in a sorry state.

"Alright, my beauty." Philip leaned down and patted his horse's neck. "You've had enough, I know. You've run your heart out and you've earned your rest. It is sufficient that I've probably killed Morgan; I'll not finish you as well."

They were on the outskirts of the town and, easing back his pace, Philip went on until he saw a stable.

He lead the weary animal in. "I want one night's quarters for my horse and feed him well, please. Good hay, mind, not oat straw."

The ostler looked a little apprehensive when he saw the stallion. Exhausted though he was, Ferrion snorted as the man approached.

"I'll take care of him myself," Philip said, for he wanted the job done properly and he doubted if Ferrion would even let the ostler touch him.

Inside the stall he removed the horse's tack and rubbed him gently with a towel, wiping the splashes of mud from his legs and then cleaning out his hooves. The ostler watched them curiously. Philip thought he was probably wondering how such a disreputable-looking rider had come to own such a fine horse!

When Ferrion had been settled to his satisfaction Philip walked down in the direction of the inn the ostler had recommended to him. He no longer feared discovery, for he thought it unlikely that the soldiers would double back and find him in the town, and he promised himself a drink, a wash and a night in a soft bed before he went back in search of Thomas.

He was limping slightly as he entered the inn, for the old scar on his side was aching, as it often did after exceptional exertion. Notwithstanding that, and his dirty and dishevelled state, the serving wench's eyes widened in delight as she caught sight of him.

He removed his hat and ran his fingers through his tangled hair. "A bottle of wine, please."

"I shall fetch the very best," the girl said eagerly.

He smiled at her. "So I should hope!"

She bobbed a curtsey and sped away, to return shortly with a bottle and two glasses, one of which she filled and set before him.

Philip took a drink and set it down distastefully. The wine was raw and tasted bitter to his refined palate.

"Is it not to your liking?" she said anxiously. "We have no better."

"Then it will suffice." He looked at the other glass, which she still held. The last thing he felt like was company, but he guessed he was going to get it anyway. "Did you want to join me?"

The girl accepted the drink eagerly. "I don't mind if I do. Have you come far?" she asked, perching herself upon his table.

"I've been riding since first light," he said evasively.

"Then you must be hungry."

Philip thought back to when he last ate a proper meal. More than a day ago, and he had ridden hard since then.

"Yes, I suppose I am. What do you have?"

"There is a pullet ready-roasted in the kitchen," she offered.

"Is that all?"

"We do but simple fare here, sir, though it is plain you're used to something better."

"You think so?" Philip raised an eyebrow, looking at his mud-splattered boots and filthy breeches. "I would have thought I was the least genteel customer that you have had today!"

"Don't you believe it, sir! I think you're most impressive," she said frankly. "Shall you have the pullet?"

"Bring it if you please, and bring another bottle of wine."

He downed a second glass as if it were water whilst she rushed to do his bidding.

The pullet soon arrived, steaming hot in gravy, and some dark bread, which he declined.

"Are you from London?" she asked, watching him intently as he delicately stripped the flesh from the bird's bones.

Philip nodded, realising, when he began to eat, that he was hungrier than he'd thought.

"Have you ever seen the King?"

"Lots of times."

"And do you know any of the lords and ladies?" she said excitedly.

"A few."

"What about the Duke of Buckingham, I've heard he's very grand, and the King's son, Monmouth, is he as dashing as they say?"

"He certainly is," Philip said blandly, wishing she would leave him alone, but her next words brought him up sharply.

"I don't suppose you would know Lord Devalle?"

Philip concentrated fiercely on his meal. "Why?"

"Why? Every girl dreams of meeting him," she sighed.

"They do?"

"Of course. He is reckoned to be the handsomest man in all England. Do you think he is?"

Philip wondered for a moment whether she was sporting with him, having guessed who he was, but when he searched her face he could find nothing but ingenuousness written there. "I think it very likely," he said solemnly.

"Handsomer even than you?"

Philip rubbed a hand across his unshaven face. "Yes, much!"

"I can't believe that." The girl looked at him saucily. "I don't know when I have ever seen a better-looking man than you, sir, pardon me for being forward."

"You are pardoned." He refilled his glass and hers as well. "I've stabled my horse along the road and seek a bed for the night. Would there be one here?"

"No, I'm sorry, sir. There is a fair in town now and the inn is full. We don't have any rooms left, unless you want to share mine." She giggled coyly at her own boldness.

Philip pushed his plate aside and really looked at her for the first time. No more than twenty years of age, he guessed, she had a fresh complexion and dark brown curly hair. Youthfully rounded without being plump, she had a body few could find fault with, for the breasts which showed above her bodice looked firm and her waist was good whilst her face, by any ordinary standards, was pretty. Philip did not have ordinary standards, however, and he groaned inwardly at the price he was going to have to pay for his bed that night.

"What is your name?" he said, taking her work-roughened hand in his.

"Audrey, sir."

"You need not call me 'sir'. My name is Thomas," he told her, selecting the first name to come into his head, for Thomas had been very much on his mind all day. "So you find me handsome, do you, Audrey?"

"Oh yes, Thomas, I find you very handsome," she said breathlessly.

"And you would like me in your bed tonight?"

"I meant it as a jest but...," Audrey gazed into his eyes, as though spell bound, "...but yes, I would."

"Then you shall have me, sweetheart. What time do you finish here?"

"I'm finished now, it's after ten o'clock."

"Then take me to your room."

Audrey looked for the landlord, who sat with his cronies paying her no mind at all. "Come, quickly."

Philip picked up what remained of his wine and followed her through the door and up a dingy flight of stairs into an attic. By the light of the lamp she carried he saw a bed which looked clean, though covered with coarse linen, and he longed to sink himself into its inviting softness but he knew he had yet to earn his night's rest!

Resignedly he kissed her, not too fiercely for he guessed that Audrey's previous experiences had been with the slow and fumbling country boys who came to town to sport with a pretty wench.

Even so she trembled in his arms and when he let her go she stared at him as though stupefied.

"You are something very special, Thomas."

"I would be even more special if you could bring me up a pitcher of water and some soap," he suggested.

Audrey laughed. "You don't need to wash for me. I don't mind a bit of dirt upon a man."

"Sweetheart," Philip said patiently, "I am absolutely filthy and I assure you I am more delightful than ever when I'm clean! Besides, I must reek of horse sweat."

"You do have a strange smell," she said, "Although it isn't that. You smell of smoke. Have you been in a fire?" As she spoke she pointed to an open sore upon one of his hands. "I'd say you had, for that looks like a burn to me. You've even singed some of your lovely curls. Let me get you some salve for that hand."

"No!" Philip shook his head, recalling Bet's many and repulsive remedies for his ills. "All I want you to fetch me is some water." He kissed her once again. "Please."

"I'll fetch you anything you want," Audrey promised, looking back as she left as though she could not bear him out of her sight. "I'll not be long."

When the door had closed behind her Philip, fighting back the weariness which threatened to engulf him, ventured a glance at his reflection in the small mirror propped up on Audrey's table. He rather wished he hadn't.

"So she has never seen a better-looking man than me?" He chewed off a broken fingernail. "The poor bitch!"

FOURTEEN

∽

Thomas woke early, feeling refreshed. The day was bright and dry and, after breakfasting upon some ham and the last of the bread, he felt fit and able to cope with whatever the day might bring.

Morgan seemed to be breathing a little easier and Thomas gave him the remaining drops of milk. "Perhaps you'll recover today," he said hopefully, "and perhaps the master will return to us."

Thomas had not properly considered what he would do if Philip did not return and Morgan never did recover. He put such thoughts determinedly from his mind. "I shall get you to High Heatherton somehow," he promised Morgan, "even if I don't know where it is."

He led the horses from the barn and fed them and was on the road again by six o'clock, heading for St. Albans,

He was almost cheerful as the old horse plodded along through the deserted countryside that fine morning. The sun climbed over the Chiltern Hills, which rose to his right behind the neat, hedged fields and Thomas felt that he would have good luck that day.

He had been travelling but two hours before he changed his mind.

The cart lurched with such violence that he was almost thrown from the driver's seat. He reined the horse in quickly and scrambled into the back to look at Morgan. Although the jolt had moved him he appeared to be in no worse state than he had been before.

Thomas climbed down and grimaced as he looked at the front wheel of the cart. The bolt which was driven through the end of the axle had been sheared off completely, leaving the nave of the wheel hanging on to the timber by a prayer.

A prayer was the last thing in Thomas' mind as he surveyed the full extent of the damage. In fact he treated the waiting horses to a flood of obscenities, most of which he'd learned in his early years and none of which he would ever have dared to utter in his master's presence, but it relieved his feelings!

He pulled off the road, easing the cart as gently as he could over the ruts and, miraculously, the wheel stayed on, although he dared not go too far. He turned the horses loose for fear they should move the cart, for if the wheel did come off he would never have been able to repair the vehicle unaided.

"And I thought this was going to be my lucky day," he muttered as he pondered on what to do.

Scarlet nuzzled Thomas' ear, as though he understood his disappointment, and the gesture cheered him, for Thomas never stayed dispirited for very long.

He threw his arms around Scarlet's neck. "I'll get us going again, you'll see, but how long it will take I do not know."

It took him the best part of an hour. There was a wood nearby but he had no tools save the small knife he always carried, and with this he managed to cut off a thin branch, which he shaped into a peg the size of the bolt hole. He drove it in firmly with a stone but, even though it seemed secure, he knew it could not last for long.

If he had to replace it again there was no telling in what surroundings he might next be forced to stop, or how quickly he would need to be on his way, so he cut several more to the same pattern.

There was a little brook not too far away and, whilst he

painstakingly whittled the wooden pegs with his knife, he let the horses drink from it and graze upon the sparse grass around them.

He had just thrown the last completed peg into the cart when a pheasant flew out of the woods, squawking loudly.

Scarlet and the tired carthorse barely stirred but the cob, younger and more skittish, whinnied and reared up, startled.

"Oh God, he's going to bolt!"

Thomas reacted quickly but he was still too late. The frightened animal turned and made off into the woods.

Stopping only to tie Scarlet and the carthorse to a tree, Thomas sped off in the same direction but, although he searched and called, the cob had disappeared without a trace. For as long as he dared leave the others Thomas followed what little trail the horse had left until, drawn deeper and deeper into the wood, he began to wonder whether he would even find his own way out. Giving up the search he sadly turned about and tried to retrace his steps.

It was not easy. Thomas was a creature of the city. He could find his way around the London alleys with ease but this dense wood was a mystery to him, for each tree looked almost the same.

Fighting back the panic that was rising in him, he sat down and calmly thought out the solution to his predicament. Since he could not see his way out because of the trees he reasoned he must try to see above them. Feeling better already, he selected a tall oak and scaled it easily, for Thomas was as agile as a cat. He needed to climb only halfway before he saw the direction he would have to take. Making a swift descent, he set off confidently and was soon within a few yards of the cart.

Before he had quite emerged from the wood he heard the sound of horse's hooves, coming from the direction of St. Albans.

He willed the rider to go past but he stopped beside the cart, just as Thomas had feared he would.

"You are all I need right now," Thomas muttered. He was

just about at the end of his patience, for he felt the fates had truly joined against him that day.

The rider had dismounted and was approaching the vehicle. Thomas could not see him clearly through the trees but he caught a glimpse of a brown shag coat, such as a farmer or a country tradesman might wear.

Thomas had left his pistol in the pocket of his coat, and he'd removed that whilst he worked upon the wheel. He still had his knife, though, and he knew he must somehow manage to stop this fellow from discovering Morgan.

"Step away from the cart! I have a loaded pistol in my hand," he lied. "On your way, whoever you might be."

The next thing he heard was the sound of applause.

"Oh, that does it!" Thomas strode furiously out of the wood brandishing his knife.

And stopped suddenly when he saw who it was.

Thomas could have been forgiven for not recognising him. Philip's hair was much shorter and he was wearing a suit of black shalloon and a plain linen shirt beneath the rough, shag coat.

"I apologise for my appearance" he said, smiling at the shocked look on Thomas' face. "I must look dreadful!"

"I don't care how you look! I'm just so glad you're here, my Lord." Thomas impulsively hugged him.

"Better put that knife away then, before you do me some irreparable damage," Philip said, laughing at his enthusiastic welcome. "Can you even use the thing?"

"A little. Morgan taught me. He is still alive, my Lord. He's even drunk a little milk and talked a bit, although I couldn't understand him."

Philip scrutinised the Welshman closely. "Yes, I think his colour is improving."

"Did you have much trouble losing the soldiers?" Thomas asked him.

"Nothing Ferrion and I couldn't handle," Philip said dismissively, "but how have you fared. Why did you stop here?"

"We almost lost a wheel." Thomas pointed to the replacement peg. "I fixed it though, see?" he said proudly.

"So you did. Wherever did you learn to do that?"

"From Jonathon and Ned. They show me lots of useful things. I have some food left, if you're hungry. There is some ham and cheese, although I've finished up the bread."

"No, thank you, I have eaten. But I never left you any money," Philip recalled. "How did you get food?"

"Oh, I stole it," Thomas admitted blithely.

"Seems to me you've managed rather well," Philip said. "I'm pleased with you."

Thomas sighed. "You may not be so pleased with me when you know all."

"I don't understand," Philip said, frowning. "Your spirit is evidently undaunted and your brain is as nimble as your fingers. Why should I be anything but pleased with you?"

"I've lost the cob," Thomas blurted out.

Philip looked around. He had not noticed before that the cob was missing. "So I see. How did that happen?"

"It was entirely due to my stupidity, my Lord. I did not tether him whilst I mended the wheel. He took fright and ran into the woods. I looked for him, I truly did. I had just given him up when you arrived."

"So that is where you were," Philip said. "I guessed it must be something quite important if you had left Morgan here alone."

"And there's another thing," Thomas cried wretchedly. "If it had not been you, then all may well have been discovered. You trusted me, my Lord, and I have failed you."

"Yes, indeed you have," Philip said solemnly. "You have

transported Morgan safely all these miles and found him shelter for the night, if I am not mistaken. On top of that you have acquired food and repaired a cart. All in all a pretty sorry show for one of your years and experience!"

Thomas hung his head. "Even though you're making fun of me I know you're angry."

"I am not, I swear it." Philip put his hand on Thomas' shoulder. "I think you have done wonderfully well."

"But I have lost a horse that is not even ours."

"It was a most unfortunate accident," Philip said, "but we must not lose sight of our main purpose, which is to get Morgan and ourselves to safety. If you believe the wheel will hold then I suggest we move without delay."

"And leave the cob? He may starve to death."

"A fine, strong horse like that? He will be taken in by someone, mark my words. He is a friendly little animal and he'll seek company before too long."

"Whatever will the Duke of Buckingham say?" Thomas said gloomily.

"I'll pay him for the horse and tell him we want to keep him. That way he need never know. Now, shall you move this cart or do you fear your handiwork will not stand up to the test?"

"That wheel will hold," Thomas said.

And so it did.

Thomas cast a last glance over his shoulder in case the cob came trotting from the wood, but there was no sign of him. Sadly he cracked the whip on the side of the cart, which made the old horse lumber just a little bit faster.

"How did you know I'd found us shelter for the night?" he wondered.

Philip leaned down from his saddle and picked a wisp of straw out of Thomas' hair. "You look as though you spent the night in a barn."

Thomas grinned. "In fact I did, and a comfortable night it

was too! What about yourself? Where did you get a change of clothes, and how the devil do you manage to stay so clean?"

"As it happens I spent the night in a woman's bed. Only a serving wench," Philip added, seeing Thomas' envious expression.

"Why is it you that gets the luck, my Lord?"

"You call that luck? I would have sooner spent the night with you and Morgan."

"In that case," Thomas retorted, "I shall take the wench next time and you can sleep in the barn!"

"If it is any consolation I did use your name," Philip remembered.

Thomas shook his head. "It isn't. Where did you get the clothes?"

"Audrey stole them from the landlord. She is one of your own kind! When she saw my burnt hair and the old scars on my back she got it into her head that I must have been beaten in prison and had started a fire in order to escape. The notion appealed to her romantic little head so much that I had not the heart to disillusion her!

"She never guessed who you really were then?"

"Hardly!" Philip started laughing and Thomas looked at him quizzically.

"Did you know that every woman dreams of meeting me, Thomas, and that I am reckoned to be the handsomest man in England?"

"Who told you that, my Lord?"

"Why, she did."

Thomas laughed as well. "I wonder what she'd say if she ever found out!"

They skirted around the town of St. Albans, for Philip did not want to risk running into Audrey, and headed south.

"Where do we make for next, my Lord?" Thomas asked him. "If we should be separated again I want to know where I'm going."

"I think we should head for Hampton Court," Philip said. "It is only about fifty miles from there to Heatherton."

He made it sound an easy distance but as they watched the carthorse plodding ever slower they both knew he would never make it.

"We shall kill him, shan't we?" Thomas said, patting the horse's bony rump.

"I fear we shall. The poor old thing is almost finished now. Since neither Ferrion nor Scarlet would go between the shafts we have to either acquire another horse or…" Philip brightened as an idea occurred to him "…or we could go to Ham House, if we can get as far as Richmond. What do you say to the prospect of a comfortable bed tonight as the guest of the Duchess of Lauderdale?"

"Would she take us in?"

"She might. She's always liked me. Unless I'm much mistaken she'll be glad of the company, for I hear she leads a lonely life since her husband died last August. From Ham I could go on to London and fetch the coach."

Thomas looked dubious. "But to call uninvited, and like this! Supposing she throws you out?"

"Of all the notions! Do not underestimate your master's charms, young Thomas!" Philip winked at him. "I am, apparently, irresistible to women!"

Philip's clothes proved to be far from a disadvantage for their journey that day. The little party attracted few looks from the workers in the fields, or from fellow travellers. One of these, more curious than the rest and eager to pass the time of day, seemed to believe perfectly in Philip's story that they were on their way to Richmond market to sell the little Arab stallion tied behind the cart.

They stopped only once, to rest the horses for an hour, but it was still quite late before they reached the River Thames. The old horse somehow found the strength to walk the last few miles and at nearly ten o'clock they turned into the long, wooded drive of Ham House.

"I hope she's not in bed," Thomas said.

"I hope she's at home. I've just recalled she often goes to take the waters at Tunbridge Wells."

"You tell me this now?" Thomas groaned, stretching his aching back. Although Philip had taken a turn upon the cart it had been Thomas who had driven most of the way. "I think that, sooner than go another step, I would sleep here, beneath the trees.

Philip rang the bell by the iron gates and a footman appeared at the door of the house. He held up a lantern, although the light could not have carried as far as the gates.

"Who is it calls on us at dead of night?" he cried timidly.

"Dear God! How I hate provincial servants," Philip muttered. "Bring your lamp a little closer and you will see us," he called out.

The footman approached the gates, his lantern flickering in the night breeze. "Well, who are you?" He looked suspiciously at the cart. "What do you want here?"

Philip totally ignored his questions. "Is her Grace at home?"

"She is."

"Then would you kindly tell her that she has a visitor."

The footman evidently thought he had better do as he was bid. The Duchess of Lauderdale had many important friends and he probably thought it would not do to offend one of them.

He led the way up the drive, which curved around a circular lawn, which had a reclining statue in the middle. It reminded Philip of Heatherton's drive in its grander days. When they reached the door and the footman could see Philip better he looked even more doubtful. All the same he did admit him, although he closed the door firmly on Thomas and the cart.

"Shall you give your name now, sir?"

"Certainly. I am Lord Philip Devalle."

The footman sniggered, until his eyes met Philip's. The smile faded from his lips and he hastened away without another word.

Philip was looking around the hall when a door to the side of him opened and he turned to see the Duchess appearing from the passage to her private closet.

"Philip?"

He bowed to her. "Your Grace!"

"So it is you! I did wonder when my man gave me your description. Whatever are you doing here?"

It was a peremptory welcome, but no more than he would have expected from the imperious Duchess.

She had been considered a beauty in her youth, with hair the colour of Theresa's. She was greying now and her features had grown heavy, yet she was not unattractive. Many found her formidable, for she was strong-willed and determined, with a violent temper, but Philip had never feared her.

"I was passing by your door and thought I should call to pay respects to one who has always held a dear place in my heart?" he suggested, flashing her what he hoped was a winning smile.

"And thought, no doubt, that you would wear your best clothes in my honour," she retorted. "What are you up to, Philip Devalle? No good, I'll be bound."

"Would I bring trouble to your door?"

"I don't believe you would. Well I am pleased to see you anyway. Shall you come to my closet or do you propose to keep me standing in this draughty hall, and me with the gout? Give me your arm."

"I would be honoured, sweetheart."

"And don't be saucy! I am twice your age. Why do you pick

now to call upon me, eh? You've stayed well clear all these months since Lauderdale's been gone. Don't answer, I will answer for you. You have been engaged in one of your nefarious little enterprises and something has gone awry, that's the truth of it. You come to me for shelter, yet you say you would not bring me trouble, therefore none are following you, am I right? Say nothing, I have not yet done."

As she talked the Duchess guided Philip to her closet and seated him opposite her. It was a pretty little room, decorated after the Eastern manner, much in vogue, with lacquered chairs and bookshelves and a gilded oriental table where the Duchess took her tea. "Now, where was I?"

"You were telling me why I came," Philip reminded her.

"Ah, yes. The reason you need my help is because you cannot travel any further. Since, as usual, you appear to be no worse for your adventures, I presume there is another with you who is in a bad way. Well?"

"Am I to talk now?" Philip said innocently.

"Yes, yes, although I dare say I am not far wrong."

"There are two servants with me, and one of them is hurt," Philip admitted.

"Then bring him in without delay. Why are you wasting time?"

Philip had not expected she would be quite so amiable about it and he felt a little guilty now at the way he was using her. "You want to know no more than that?"

"I beg you not to tell me anything. I would sooner be in ignorance. Now fetch the poor man in and I will see to it that he is cared for."

Philip found Thomas asleep in the driver's seat and shook him gently. As he lifted the covers from Morgan he noticed something which made him start.

"Thomas, look! Morgan's eyes are open."

He held the lantern he was carrying nearer to the Welshman's face and Morgan blinked before his eyelids closed again. Philip thought it was a good sign.

Morgan was put to bed in the servant's quarters and his head wound properly dressed. After Philip and Thomas had seen to the horses Philip left him in the kitchen, tucking into a hearty meal.

Later, bathed and clad in a silk robe belonging to Lord Huntingtower, the Duchess' son, Philip surveyed himself in the marquetry looking glass on the wall and thought he looked more like himself again. He thought, too, how his surroundings differed from those of the previous night!

The Duchess regarded him with approval when he joined her downstairs. "That's much better! Come here and sit beside me. The very least you can do to pay me for my hospitality is to give me an hour of your company."

"The woman with whom I spent last night made me pay her for her hospitality with more than that," Philip said wickedly.

"You dreadful man! Well I assure you I am not planning to seduce you, if that is what you think."

"I don't. I think you want to mother me."

"Do you mind?"

Philip shook his head. "No, on the contrary I would quite enjoy it, for I was never mothered as a child."

"More's the pity. You would have been a different person," the Duchess said sagely. "Your men have been taken care of but is there anything you need?"

"I'd not refuse a drink. Some brandy, if you have it."

"Dreadful stuff! Sets fire to your brain and your stomach." The Duchess rang for some all the same. "How is your injured servant?"

"I think a little better. He keeps slipping in and out of consciousness."

"I shall not ask you how it happened, but how badly is he injured?"

"His leg is broken. I have splinted it but he had a great blow to the head, which worries me more."

"When did all this occur?"

"Thursday night."

"And you have dragged him round with you since then? You should have left him, saved your own skin. There are plenty of servants to be had."

"Not like this one. Believe me he is worth saving," Philip told her.

"Worth risking your own life for?"

"Absolutely."

"There is an honourable streak in you, no matter what some say." The brandy had arrived and the Duchess watched him down a large measure. "If only you didn't drink so much and picked your friends more carefully you could go far."

"Do you not count yourself amongst my friends, your Grace?" Philip said. "I most certainly regard you as one, for the service you are doing for me tonight…"

"Is equalled only to that which I shall be called upon to perform for you tomorrow, I'm sure," she interrupted him. "You've not finished with me yet. I'll warrant."

"I did wonder if my servants could remain here whilst I ride to London tomorrow to fetch my coach," Philip admitted.

"Then where will you go?"

"To High Heatherton. It's mine now and it's all I want. Apart from Theresa," he added, a little wistfully. He was missing her a great deal. "I only hope she still wants me."

He knew how much Theresa loved Versailles and he was worried she might not want to return to England, after what had happened to her and Giles on his account. The letters she had written to him were filled with all the things she was doing and in her last one she had told him she had danced in one of the Court ballets and that Louis was making a great fuss of her.

"Oh, your wife will come back to you," the Duchess predicted. "She'd be a fool not to, now you've got your country estate."

"Is that the only thing to tempt her, do you think?" Philip said, a little put out.

"I will be honest, it would be a great temptation to me if I were nothing but the daughter of some meagre country squire who had advanced myself by becoming Shaftesbury's mistress," the Duchess said frankly. Her own breeding was as impeccable as his and Philip knew that, along with many others, she was of the opinion that he had married beneath him. "Do you really want her back?"

"Of course! I love her."

"Then, if there is any wisdom in that handsome head of yours, you will get down upon your knees and kiss her feet and beg her to remain with you. You won't do it, I know. You're laughing at me even now."

"No, I'm not," Philip assured her. "I am just imagining Theresa's face if I did any such thing, but I will make sure she knows she is important to me."

"How? By giving her a child? That's the usual way men think to make us feel important."

"Do you know, that's not a bad idea," Philip said thoughtfully. "An heir for Heatherton."

The Duchess laughed. "You're going to do it, then?"

"I most certainly am and as soon as possible. That's another debt I owe you, sweetheart! I shall never forget the kindness you have shown me," he said seriously, taking her hands in his. "If there is ever any service I can perform for you then do not hesitate, I beg you, to call upon me."

"Silly boy," the Duchess said gruffly. "As if you will have time to think of me when you are master of your own estate."

"My own estate. I like that," Philip decided. "It makes me feel as though I am a country gentleman already."

"You? You'll never make a country gentleman," she said emphatically. "You'll be residing back in London before this year is out."

"I'll wager you are wrong!"

Before he retired for the night Philip went to look in on Morgan. He found Thomas sitting by the Welshman's bed, smiling broadly.

Philip soon saw why.

Morgan was propped up on his pillows. Although he still seemed to have difficulty in focusing his eyes, he obviously recognised his master.

"My Lord, it seems I owe you a debt of thanks."

Philip sat beside him scarcely believing he had heard him speak, for he had feared he would never hear Morgan's voice again.

"Thank me when you know for certain you are not lame, for I have never fixed a broken leg before." Philip said, unable to control the emotion in his voice. "Morgan, you cannot imagine how I've felt these last few days. I really thought I had killed you this time."

"I have put you to a great deal of trouble, I'm sure."

"Indeed you have," Philip agreed. "You've slowed us up and been most inconvenient!"

"Perhaps you should have left me behind, my Lord."

Philip smiled. "After all the years it has taken me to train you? And even now you don't obey me. If you had heeded my orders and not gone back for your wretched knife you would not be in this state! Now get some rest, for we shall soon be travelling to High Heatherton." He regarded his two loyal servants happily. "I am going home!"

The Duchess agreed to keep the poor old carthorse, which had served them so well and earned his retirement, and Philip set off with Ferrion and Scarlet early the next morning. He took Scarlet to Buckingham's stables, since Giles was still out of town, and was at Cheapside by midday. Jonathon and Ned greeted him calmly, despite his strange clothes, for they were used to surprises.

"We are leaving for Sussex as soon as we can," he told the two coachmen. "Pack only what you need, you can return for the rest later, and get some things together for Thomas and Morgan."

Philip changed and was throwing some of his own clothes into a trunk when Ned informed him that he had a visitor, Lord Grey.

"Damnation! What the devil does he want here?" Philip wondered.

He found Grey looking most intrigued with all the activity.

"I came to tell you that the King is returning early from Newmarket, but it would seem you've already heard the news. Some blasted fire broke out, apparently."

"So I understand," Philip said evenly.

"Then all our careful planning was in vain?"

"I fear so. Fate was not upon our side this time. I have decided there is little point in delaying my move down to Sussex any longer."

"So I see! Shall you rally again for Monmouth?"

"Yes, when the time is right."

"You are a bloody liar, Philip! I should be surprised if you were not delighted at the way events have turned out. You've got what you wanted out of this, haven't you?"

"What do you mean?"

"Why, your estate. That's all it was really about for you, I know. Shaftesbury helped you get it and in exchange you did his bidding, as you always have. Is there nothing that man could not pay you to do? My God he even made you marry his mistress!"

Philip controlled his temper with difficulty. "Get out of here, Grey. It will alter nothing to abuse me."

"You are right, and yet it seems that matters always turn

out to your advantage. Does Monmouth realise you are leaving London?"

"Not yet. You can tell him if you wish."

"Very well, if you do not have the courage to tell him yourself."

"I have the courage but not the time. You should be pleased to have me out of the way, for now he'll rely on you again. That would suit you, wouldn't it?"

"He does have his advantages," Grey admitted. "I'll tell him for you. Is there anything in particular you'd like me to say?"

There was a great deal Philip wanted to say to Monmouth, but this was not the moment, and none of it could be confided to Grey.

He shrugged. "Tell him I am sorry."

FIFTEEN

⁓

John Bone stripped off his shirt and flexed his huge biceps. "Are you quite sure about this, Lord Philip?"

"Quite sure, thank you," Philip said.

"Well I'm not sure," Morgan muttered. "I say call it off and admit, for once, that you have been rash."

John grinned. "Don't worry, Morgan, I'll be gentle. I suspect his fancy living has softened him!"

Philip had been pleased at how quickly John and Morgan had established a rapport. Their personalities were very different but the two men shared a love of the land and a sound knowledge of rural matters.

"Surely someone must believe I'm going to win," Philip said. "Thomas?"

Thomas shook his head apologetically.

"What about the rest of you?" Philip asked his audience, made up of the estate workers and their families, who were gathered in front of the house around the circular lawn, where the two contestants stood. "Do none of you support me?"

"We support you, that we do, Lord Philip," someone cried, "for we should dearly love to see that lard bag beaten, but no-one's ever done it."

"Have any tried?"

"Well, no," the man admitted. "We don't have your courage."

Philip had endeared himself to the workers on the estate, for he had shown them that he was equal to his word. He'd worked beside them, as he'd promised he would do, and provided the wherewithal for the sowing of the late crops and the purchase of more livestock but also, most importantly of all, Philip had turned businessman. He had negotiated a good price for his timber at the Shoreham shipyard and obtained sufficient advance orders to employ his little army of dependants for the rest of the year.

All in all he felt he had done rather well and he looked forward to the day when he could boast of his not inconsiderable achievements to the friends who had scoffed at his endeavours at the outset. He would not, however, have wanted those same friends to have witnessed him hauling timber alongside his own men, or to see the austere way that one so used to comfort was having to manage in that dilapidated house.

Although he had not been in the least unhappy, Philip's new life was hard, with little relaxation and no diversions whatsoever. When John had reminded him that morning of his commitment to a contest Philip had agreed, partly to provide a little entertainment for those who had worked so well and so willingly for him and partly because, after a few weeks of almost mindless labour, he welcomed the prospect.

Some might have missed the opportunity of pitting their wits in conversation with their social equals, but Philip had never been very intellectual. Accustomed to a life of action, he felt the need of a physical challenge, but one that, unlike labouring, tested the speed of his reactions and his ingenuity.

The pair removed their boots and Philip took off his shirt, revealing his back, which was covered with the scars of Henry's repeated beatings. John had seen those scars before, when they were both youngsters, but, even so, a flicker of pity crossed the big man's face.

Philip saw it, but he did not want John's sympathy. "If you are figuring to be kind to me we shall have no contest here at all!"

Their audience applauded his audacity.

Philip was well aware of John's strength. It was far superior to his own and always had been, but he knew that if he could keep out of his friend's clutches then his guile would bring him victory. That had always been the way with them when they were boys and, since John had grown even heavier and slower whilst Philip himself had learned more cunning, he doubted things would be much different now.

John moved toward him and grasped at the space which he had been occupying a split second before. Philip had very neatly sidestepped, turning round at the same time to watch his opponent lumbering away from him.

John turned on his heel and faced him once again, not looking too dismayed. He repeated the manoeuvre somewhat faster, but with no more success.

This time he did look slightly disgruntled, for a howl of laughter went up from the onlookers.

"So you think to make a fool of your old friend, do you?" He walked steadily toward Philip, holding both hands out in front of him, inviting Philip to grasp them. "Let's see if you have the nerve to stand still long enough for me to reach you."

"I have nerve enough for you." Philip obligingly grasped his opponent's hands and interlocked fingers with him.

John looked happier now, but if he had thought to have the advantage then Philip soon changed his mind for him. He pulled John very slightly toward him, so that he pulled back more strongly. Philip then pushed him even further back until John, to prevent himself from overbalancing and falling backwards, leaned toward him once again.

This was exactly what Philip had wanted. A sudden tug caused John to fall forwards. Philip sank down to the floor, still holding his hands so that John had no choice but to follow him. Philip quickly lifted his feet and planted them firmly into the bigger man's lower trunk, throwing him backwards over his head with ease.

He released his grip as John flew through the air, landing on his back with a loud thump.

"That was a neat trick, my Lord," Thomas cried.

It was actually a trick Philip had learned in Paris from an Italian tumbling act, and the labourers were applauding it loudly.

He jumped up and, with a little studied affectation, brushed himself down as he awaited John's recovery. Their audience appreciated that immensely! John raised himself to his feet very carefully, for he had hit the ground with considerable force. He did not trouble to brush the dirt from his own clothing but only spat on his hands and rubbed them together before advancing with a determined expression on his face. This time he moved much more swiftly. He lunged forward, grabbing Philip's legs and brought him crashing down.

They rolled over two or three times until John arrived on top of him, pinning him securely to the floor. He moved up Philip's body and then bounced on his chest, almost knocking the wind out of him.

A few months ago, grown soft from London living, such an onslaught would have finished him but his recent hard work had restored Philip's vigour. Still, John was a hefty man and Philip realised that he would not be able to stand too much of this kind of treatment.

He decided the time had come to put an end to the match.

Using all his strength he managed to make his opponent roll off him so that he attained the superior position. He covered John's face with his chest and, at the same time, applied a grip to either side of his neck. After a few seconds John's body went limp He had passed out.

Philip slowly rolled away from him and the crowd gasped. They obviously had no idea what he had done. Morgan knew, of course, and was shaking his head disapprovingly.

John lay still for an instant and then his eyelids flickered and opened. "You always had the tricks, Lord Philip," he said, taking the hand which Philip held out to him to help him rise. "How the devil did you do that?"

"I will teach you one day," Philip promised, putting an affectionate arm around his shoulders. "I believe we could both use a drink. What do you say?"

"I say I want another chance to beat you some time." John gave a rude gesture to the crowd, who were taunting him good-naturedly.

"And you shall have it," Philip said, "on this very spot one year from now and every year upon this day until we grow too old for such absurdities!"

The audience cheered enthusiastically at that and John looked pleased, for in this way he left the field with honour intact.

"Now," Philip said, when they had downed the draughts of cider which stood ready for them, "it is time we were about our work, for this estate has not yet learned to run itself!"

He stayed behind with Morgan for a moment after John and the others had gone. "A good man that. Well, Morgan, did I not say I could beat him?"

The Welshman wrung out his handkerchief in some of the cider that was left in the jug and dabbed it, none too gently, on the scrapes upon Philip's back and shoulders.

"Ouch! That smarts, Morgan!"

"Serves you right! You cheated."

"For heaven's sake! He could have really hurt me. What would you rather have?"

"I would rather have you behaving in a way which befits your dignity."

Philip laughed and helped him walk to the house. Morgan was still a little unsteady but, when the splints had been removed, Philip had been relieved to see that his leg appeared to have set correctly and he would be as mobile as ever in time.

Philip had appointed him to be his steward, so that Morgan now virtually ran the estate, taking on also the roles of treasurer, receiver and clerk. A tenant farmer's son, Morgan had always been a man of the soil at heart and the arrangement suited Philip excellently. He knew nothing of these matters and had no more head for figures than he had for letters.

"You certainly seem to have won the estate workers over," Morgan said.

"You sound surprised!"

"I am," Morgan told him frankly. "They are perceptive, country folk. I had my doubts as to whether they would take to you."

"And why shouldn't they?" Philip demanded. "You did and you are from the country."

"Maybe so, my Lord, but you are not to everybody's taste."

"Infernal cheek!"

Although the entertainment of the fight had taken up nearly an hour there was still the same amount of work to get through before the day was ended. Philip allowed nothing to interfere with what he had determined to be the quota for the day's timber and those who worked with him upon the cutting of it would know that from experience.

By late afternoon the felling had been done but there remained the task of dragging it up from the woods.

Horses were needed for this heavy work and Philip had purchased a pair of strong Sussex Greys. As the last load came out the men leading the team were ankle deep in mud, for there had been a good deal more rain than was usual for May and the continual working of the area had turned the outskirts of the woods into little better than a quagmire.

The men slipped and slithered, perilously close to the horses' huge hooves.

"Call them back, Lord Philip," John cried. "They will be trampled underfoot."

"This load is promised for tomorrow," Philip reminded him. "We have to get it upon the road to Shoreham by first light."

"Shall you kill two men for that?"

Philip watched them struggling for another minute and then made a decision. "Call the men away. I have a better notion. Gather sticks, loose branches, anything to make a firmer footing for the horses' hooves."

"You still can't risk a man to lead them," John said, "and they'll not move without they're led."

"Don't argue with me. Do it!"

John organised every hand to gather kindle wood. Philip, meanwhile, whistled Ferrion.

He inspected the wooden track critically, pointing to where he wanted more wood laid. When he was quite satisfied he mounted Ferrion and urged him, rump first, gently onto it.

"You're never going to lead them with that stallion?" John said. "You will break his leg."

"You have a better idea perhaps?"

John hadn't, and admitted that he could see no other way they were going to shift the load.

Philip, all distractions put from his mind, concentrated very hard upon the task before him. He leaned low over Ferrion's neck to whisper the words that would walk him backwards along the treacherously slippery path.

He backed him to within a few feet of the two shires and then took a coil of rope from off the pommel of his saddle. He reached back and fastened it securely to the lead reins of both horses.

His onlookers were silent as he started slowly back across the uneven wooden track. Ferrion, accustomed to negotiating every kind of terrain, picked his way sure-footedly and the greys, although they tossed their heads and whinnied nervously, followed him. Encouraged by the sound of Philip's voice, they pulled their great hooves from the sucking mud onto the comparative firmness of the sticks.

The load started to move.

Philip was so absorbed in his endeavours he did not see a vehicle approaching the estate.

∽

"This is it, ladies, High Heatherton," the driver said, reining his horses to a halt outside the gates.

Theresa looked at the tall gates apprehensively. "They look so formidable, Bet."

"Don't tell me you've lost your nerve!"

Theresa denied it, but it was partly the truth. The approach to Heatherton had reminded her, as nothing else could have done, of the difference between hers and Philip's backgrounds. Despite his title, Philip had never had any money of his own since she had known him and had needed to earn his living one way or another. It was sometimes easy to forget that he came from such a distinguished family.

"I had no idea the place would be so big," she said lamely.

"I would say it was a wee bit late to have misgivings," Bet muttered, "and I, for one, can't wait to sink into a comfortable chair."

Bet detested travelling, and they had done a fair bit of it since leaving Paris. After a rough sea crossing they had come on a crowded coach from Dover to Horsham. There they had hired an open carriage, all that was to be had, for the final part of their journey. The driver had seemed to take a fiendish pleasure in bouncing them along the rough Sussex lanes but Theresa knew that, for Bet, it would all be worthwhile once she was back with Morgan. Theresa was suddenly far less sure of what kind of reception she would receive. She couldn't help wondering whether Philip might have changed now that he was the master of his family's estate and a man of means.

"I wonder if we have to open the gates ourselves?" she said.

Bet looked about. "Well I don't see any servants rushing to help us. In fact I don't see any signs of life at all, except amongst those trees over yonder."

"They must be Philip's woods." Theresa craned her neck to see the activity. "Do you know I'd swear that was Ferrion over there with them."

"Ferrion a working horse? The master would never allow that. Wait, though," Bet stood up in the carriage to get a better view, "that is Ferrion, and with his Lordship on his back."

"That's never Philip!"

"But it is. Who else rides Ferrion, except for Thomas, and it certainly isn't him."

"It must be someone he's engaged to work for him," Theresa said, for the rider looked like a stranger to her. "What do you suppose they're doing?"

"How should I know? Am I a country girl?" Bet asked. "I suppose I'd better be the one to tell the driver to open these gates, or we'll be sat here all day!"

He opened them and they were about to drive through when a cheer went up from the woods. As Theresa turned to look she saw that the rider had noticed them and was heading in their direction.

She stepped out of the carriage as he approached at a fast gallop. "It can't be Philip, can it? He looks…different."

And so he did from the last time Theresa had seen him. He was wearing a plain linen shirt, open to the waist, with mud-stained trousers and boots, and he had a black bandana knotted around his neck.

As he drew nearer, though, she was no longer in any doubt. "It *is* him, Bet," she said incredulously.

"Told you!"

❧

Philip was halfway to the gates before he realised who was in the carriage. It had been weeks since he had written to say he was at Heatherton and he had begun to think that Theresa would not return to him. But she had.

He brought Ferrion to a spectacular halt in front of them and leapt down from the saddle.

For a moment no-one spoke.

It was Bet who broke the silence. "You did want us to come, didn't you, my Lord?"

Philip smiled. "I most certainly did, Bet." She could have had no idea how much!

"How's my Morgan?"

"Recovering from a slight mishap," Philip admitted, "but I'm sure he will positively flourish under your care. Why don't you drive up to the house and see him, sweetheart? We will follow on."

Bet needed no second telling and the carriage was soon out of sight amongst the trees that lined the drive. Philip and Theresa were left alone.

There were tears in her eyes when he looked at her. "What's the matter, Tess?" he asked her softly.

"I've missed you so much."

She put her arms around him and pressed her face into his bare chest, clinging to him as though she never wanted to let him go.

Philip held her there for a few moments, enjoying the feel of her again.

"I've missed you too, more than you can know. Come, don't cry. I want my little wife to greet her new home with a smile. I'll take you up to the house, but don't be too discouraged at what you see. There is still a great deal of work to be done."

Leading Ferrion, Philip walked with his arm around Theresa's tiny waist.

Men had already been hard at work upon the orchard,

pruning back the tangled trees, and Philip stopped to introduce her to Sam Bone, who was in charge of the work there.

The formal gardens were still overgrown, for their restoration was a luxury that Philip could not yet afford although, with the sale of the timber, he had managed to begin work inside parts of the house.

When Theresa entered the building she looked as awed as Thomas had done. Although she had been brought up in the country, her father's house had been nothing like this.

"It's like a palace, Philip!"

"Unfortunately my brother managed to cause considerable damage to several rooms and he left parts of the house exposed to the elements after the fire," he explained. "I'm afraid High Heatherton is but a shabby shadow now of what it used to be, though it will soon be plenty grand enough for all the entertaining we are likely to do."

He led the way up the magnificent carved staircase, on which some workman were repairing the decorative scrollwork of the banisters. Theresa stopped to admire their skill but Philip hastened her on.

"Please don't encourage them to waste time talking! I'm paying each of them a full two shillings a day for what they are doing. It is a pity that my grandfather did not retain the original staircase, which was stone. Although stone staircases are no longer fashionable at least it would not have needed repairing."

"But this one will be so pretty," Theresa said.

"Certainly it will, when I have paid out another twenty pounds to have the mouldings gilded, and that's before I pay the joiners five pounds for each door they make. This place is going to drain me of every penny that I earn for many years to come, and I haven't yet begun the reconstruction of the burnt-out wing. I ask you – five pounds for a door!"

Theresa giggled. "Oh, Philip, I have known you to pay more

than five pounds for a coat, and wear it only twice before you tired of it."

Philip ignored that. The loss of his magnificent collection of clothes was still a tender subject to him, although Theresa would be unaware of his sacrifice.

High above them, the painted ceiling was being lovingly restored by a craftsman that Philip had found in Chichester. "This was badly damaged by water," he explained.

The man perched perilously on a scaffold reminded them both of the finishing touches being made to Le Brun's masterpieces in the Hall of Mirrors at Versailles. The scene above may not have been quite up to that great artist's standard but it was, nonetheless, very beautiful. It showed the goddess Ceres sitting before a fountain, where cherubs offered her flowers, fruit and corn. Upon her knee was a naked, golden-haired baby, with startlingly blue eyes.

"The goddess is a likeness of my mother," Philip said, following Theresa's gaze. "She was lovely, don't you think?"

"Indeed she was." Theresa looked from Philip to the baby. "And is that you?"

"Of course not!" Philip said, attempting to sound dismissive, but she caught his eye and started laughing.

"It is, isn't it?"

"It might be," he allowed, hastening her on.

There was a door at the top of the stairs. Philip opened it and made a mock bow. "Your suite, my Lady, prepared in readiness for you. You are to have my mother's rooms, one of the few Henry could not bring himself to defile."

Theresa looked around the bedroom in obvious delight. The bed was hung with rich, red velvet, the tester domed and topped with a spray of feathers and a jewelled cascade, like an exotic eastern tent. Behind the gold tassels of the bed curtains she could see a carved gilt headboard, set with still more jewels around the Countess' cipher.

On the wall above the fireplace Philip had placed a portrait of his mother, which had hung in his own room when he was a boy. "She was a famous beauty," he told Theresa proudly. "What induced her to marry my father I shall never know."

On the mantelshelf beneath the painting stood a dainty gold clock, a parting present from Louis X111, as Philip explained, for Madeleine Pasquier had been a favourite at his Court. In the hearth there were some fire tongs which were made of solid silver.

"Those are about the only things of value I still have," Philip told her, "but they were my mother's and I could never sell them. Here's your dressing room."

He led her through to a smaller but still elegantly decorated room, this time in a pale shade of pink. There was a closet too, in which was an ornate ebony cabinet, inlaid with tortoiseshell and brass. It had the appearance of a house, with miniature marble porticos framing two tiny doors. Philip watched as she discovered the cabinet's ingenious little drawers, as excited as a child with a new toy.

"I thought you'd enjoy that! I'll send Thomas up with your things, for I am sure he's longing to see you. I think Morgan and Bet deserve to spend a few hours in each other's company after we have separated them for so long but, if you need help, a couple of girls from the estate are being trained as house servants and they are very willing."

"I'm sure I shall manage very well by myself."

"Then I will leave you now. Come downstairs at eight o'clock and we will dine together."

"I'd like that very much." Theresa looked out of the window, which overlooked the formal gardens. They were overgrown and wild but still showed the faint outlines of the once neat squares and diamonds that had been the frames for flowers, shrubs and firmly pruned yews. "Oh, Philip, this place will be so beautiful one day."

She turned to him, aglow with happiness, and Philip thought that she was never lovelier.

He smiled. "I'd say it's looking considerably better right now!"

When Theresa came down to the hall at eight o'clock, Philip was waiting for her. He had selected for the occasion one of the only two elegant outfits he had left. The brocade coat, in a shade of blue that exactly matched his eyes, was his favourite. It was trimmed with a great deal of silver lace, which matched well with the cloth of silver waistcoat that he wore and with the silver buckles on his high heeled shoes.

"I had forgotten you were so handsome," Theresa said admiringly.

"I had forgotten too! I haven't dressed for weeks."

"You don't mix with your neighbours?" she said in surprise. "You always liked to be around people."

He shrugged. "My sorts of people live in town."

"Do you miss London?"

"Sometimes," he said truthfully, "but not tonight. Are you hungry? I expect you are, you always were!"

Theresa laughed at that. "I'm ravenous!"

He led her through to the downstairs parlour, where they were to eat, for a great many of the grander rooms were still closed off. Philip had not exaggerated when he said that his mother's rooms were the only ones which still had items of real value in them. The little parlour no longer even had a rug upon the floor, for it had been so mildewed Philip had thrown it out. The only furniture the room contained was a table and two chairs, whilst the only decoration it could boast was one of Philip's gilded mirrors, which he had hung upon the faded landscape-painted panelling of the walls.

The meal was simple, consisting of a shoulder of mutton, freshly caught trout, a boiled salad and some local cheese. Philip apologised for the fact that there were no desserts, for he knew Theresa, like her brother, loved sweetmeats.

She shook her head. "I'm rather glad of it. I've been eating so much marzipan and preserved fruit at Versailles that I had a toothache and Bet made me take spirit of vitriol! That reminds me, King Louis gave me a package to bring to you."

Philip stiffened. He guessed that Louis had sent him money and he did not want Theresa to know anything about his secret dealings with the King of France. "Did he tell you what it contained?"

"Why no. I'll give it to you tomorrow. He still thinks highly of you," Theresa said, "and he bade me tell you that he has forgiven you now for leaving France."

Philip could see why, since he was being useful to Louis in England by reporting the plans being made by the supporters of William of Orange!

"I have not quite forgiven him," he said honestly. "He took away my army, Tess. They were my men; I recruited them and they wore my colours. They marched with me for three years and at the end of it I was not even given the opportunity to say goodbye to them."

"He regrets it now. He says they are rebellious and nothing can be done with them."

"Of course. Even Louis cannot command men to forget their loyalty. When soldiers have served with me they want no other commander."

Philip spoke without conceit, but only stating a fact, for if he had any talent in the world he knew it was that of leading fighting men. His own disregard for danger inspired them and they wore his uniform with pride.

"He still hopes you will return to Versailles one day."

"Why would I want to be at Versailles when I am living in such luxury here?" Philip wryly indicated the bareness all around them. He had almost dreaded her seeing his house for the first time, for he had not explained in his letters quite how much needed doing. He was still not sure whether she would be happy to live in such basic surroundings after growing accustomed to life at the Court of the King of France, with all its opulence and gaiety. "Come with me, if you have finished eating, and I will show you what it is that I do want."

He took her hand to help her rise and they walked together up the staircase to the first floor, where a gallery ran the length of the central part of the house.

"The gallery was used for taking exercise in bad weather," Philip told her, "and also for recreation. I recall that my father had a billiard table set up at one end. It has even been used for the staging of masques, though not in my memory. There was never much furniture in here, for it was essentially a place to move about, so you can see this room just as it was."

"It's very impressive," she said

It was. The dark oak panelling seemed to stretch the length of a small street. Portraits were hung between some of the panels.

"Something to look at to break the monotony of the walk," Philip told her. "Henry would never have harmed these paintings. He always considered himself to be the embodiment of all his ancestors, so perhaps he thought that to destroy their images would be to destroy himself! Would you like to meet my family before I show you what I brought you here to see?"

"Indeed I would." Theresa took his arm and they slowly walked the length of the gallery, pausing before each portrait while Philip spoke briefly about the subject.

"They are all handsome," she decided as they walked along, "but they look so fierce. There is not a kind face amongst them." She paused before the painting of Philip's grandfather, who seemed to positively glare out of the canvas at them.

Philip shuddered. "I scarcely remember him, thank God, but I was told he grew so violent at the end they used to chain him to his bed."

In his darker moments Philip often wondered whether the demons that had driven so many of his ancestors insane would ever manifest itself in him, but so far he appeared unaffected by what the locals called the 'Devalle sickness'.

The next portrait was of Philip's father, Sidney. "He looks nicer," Theresa decided, "and he is the only one who smiles."

Philip snorted. "He was weak."

"Do you despise him for that?"

"Yes, I suppose I do although, according to King Charles, he gave a good account of himself after Worcester. He even helped Charles to escape."

"You never told me that," Theresa exclaimed.

"Did I not? My family's history is so rich in noble deeds that such a small event does tend to slip my mind!"

"Why must you always belittle your father?" Theresa said.

"Because he might have had the courage to risk Cromwell's wrath in order to save his future monarch but not to face my brother in order to defend me," Philip said bitterly, "still, I will tell you of it if you wish. He accompanied Charles, together with Wilmot, Buckingham, Derby and Lauderdale, through Somerset, down to your county of Dorset and then on to Bramber, only to find that the Roundheads had taken the bridge and overrun the place. The castle had already fallen and it seemed that Charles would never make it to the coast but my father managed to find him sanctuary at the Old Monk's House, which was owned by a friend of his, called Gough. Charles passed the night there in safety and in the morning left for Shoreham, right under the noses of the soldiers."

"How exciting," Theresa cried.

"Yes. My father, having seen him escape aboard a coal-brig, returned to Heatherton to find that the house had been confiscated and his older brothers lay dead. Cromwell had discovered his part in it and wreaked retribution on the rest of the family, who had taken refuge under one roof, as was common during the Civil War. Such are the rewards of heroism, my dear."

"That is the reason Charles has forgiven you so often,"

Theresa guessed. "I can't understand how you can treat with Major Wildman and his kind, for they were the very people who were responsible for the slaughter of your family."

"Does that include Shaftesbury too? He supported Cromwell's cause at times, when it suited him," Philip reminded her. "Don't try to fathom it, sweetheart, for even fewer principles apply in times of war than they do in peace. Besides, have you stopped to think that but for their deaths," he indicated the portraits of his two uncles, "I would not inherit High Heatherton now!"

Theresa gave a little cry of delight when they came to the portrait of Philip's mother. It was a particular favourite of Philip's too, for it showed him as a small boy standing by her knee and was the only formal one ever painted of them together.

"Do you think me like her?" he asked. "I'm supposed to be."

"You are very like her," Theresa said, studying them side by side.

Philip's own portrait was in the next space. It was a life-size study, painted some years before, in his full military regalia and mounted upon Ferrion. He was rather proud of it and deemed the painting a worthy representation of the new master of Heatherton.

The next frame was covered by a cloth. Philip smiled wickedly. "I said I would show you what it was I wanted, Tess. Well here it is."

He pulled aside the sheet and Theresa gasped, for it was a portrait of herself, represented as Boudicca. Shaftesbury had commissioned it when she had first come to London, for it had been fashionable at the time for ladies of the Court to have themselves painted as some historical or mythological figure. Theresa, on a whim, had posed as the warrior queen, a leather tunic round her waist, her breasts bare and her long red hair streaming out behind her as she drove her chariot into battle.

Theresa laughed to see that irreverent canvas hung in the

stately gallery alongside so many generations of austere earls and their dignified wives.

"You are too terrible to hang that foolish thing in here," she said. "Now I know why they all look down so disapprovingly at me!"

"They'll have to grow accustomed to it and to you too. That is if you are going to stay," he added more seriously.

A strange expression crossed her face. Theresa had never been able to hide her feelings and Philip feared she might wish to return to Versailles but was unsure of how to tell him.

"Do you really want me to stay, Philip?"..

"That depends."

"On what?"

"On why you came," he said, remembering the Duchess of Lauderdale's opinion on that.

His answer seemed to surprise her. "Because I love you, and I want to be with you," she said simply.

Philip was relieved. He took her in his arms and kissed her tenderly. "I was afraid you would prefer to stay in France."

"And I was afraid that now you had your big house you would feel I wasn't ...," she hesitated, searching for the words.

"Well-bred enough to be the lady of High Heatherton?" he finished for her, smiling. "Well you're not, of course, but you are all I want, you silly girl!"

"And you are all I want," she assured him, snuggling closer.

"I am not expecting you to devote yourself entirely to me," he told her, for he had given thought to some of the Duchess of Lauderdale's views. "There is a matter which I feel is appropriate to raise here, before my ancestors. I think it is time our union became a fruitful one."

"You mean have a child, you and me?" Theresa said in astonishment. "I always thought you did not want a family."

"Well now I do, unless you are afraid to bear my children, of course. There appears to be no trace of insanity in any of my illegitimate offspring but there will be a risk, you must know that."

"I'll take that risk," Theresa said decidedly, "provided you agree to place your hat upon my abdomen whilst I am in labour, for it dulls the pain, so Bet says!"

"It is the very least I can do!" He walked her back to her room. "You have had a long day, Tess, and you must be very tired. I think it time we said goodnight."

She looked a little put out as he turned to leave her at the door. "Won't you come in and stay with me for a while?"

"You will see enough of me tomorrow and in the days ahead," he told her. "Sleep well, sweetheart."

He kissed her goodnight and went resolutely down the corridor to his own room. It was over half a year since they had been together and, much as he desired her now, he thought it would be considerate to give her a little time to herself, to recover from her journey.

He flung himself, fully dressed, upon the bed and lay there for a while, lost in his thoughts, until he heard a tap upon the door. "Come in Morgan. I did not expect you to attend upon me tonight."

"Will I do instead?" asked a small voice as the door opened.

Philip sat up in surprise. "Tess?"

"I was concerned at the thought of you having to shift for yourself," she said archly. "Stand up and let me help you off with your coat."

A smile played on Philip's lips but he did as he was bid. "Are you annoyed with me, Tess?"

"Now why ever should you think that?" she demanded. "Perhaps because you left me at my bedroom door, and after telling me only a few minutes before that you wished to give me a baby?"

"Well I wasn't going to give you one tonight."

"Evidently!"

"So you thought to come here and seduce me, did you?"

She laughed. "Do you mind?"

"Not at all, but you might be so good as to hang my coat up first," he suggested as she took it from him.

She disappeared into his closet with the coat and then gave a little cry of surprise.

"What is it, sweetheart?"

"Where are all your clothes? Are they still in London?"

"No. I fear that what you see is all I have left," he said sadly. "I sold the rest."

When Theresa emerged from the closet she was no longer laughing. "What, for Heatherton?"

"For Heatherton."

"Oh, Philip," she murmured, "how I love you."

"Because I sold my clothes?"

"Because to me you are the noblest, dearest person in the world. I've missed you so much and I never want to be without you again."

Philip held her close. He could no longer hide the passion that he felt for her. Nor did he want to.

"Nothing shall ever part us again. I swear it."

SIXTEEN

༄

The end of June saw Bet and Morgan married at long last.

As the bells rang from the steeple of the little village church there was much rejoicing at High Heatherton. Morgan had gained the respect of every man on the estate whilst Bet, with her sharp London tongue and her sound knowledge of the old remedies, had become a popular figure with the women of their little community. She could rarely be seen about the grounds without a crowd of children hanging round her, not caring if she scolded them, for they had quickly discovered the soft heart which was shielded by her prickly nature.

Great changes had been wrought upon High Heatherton, for everyone had been busy, contributing in effort and enthusiasm. Herds of livestock now grazed in the meadows and the downs beyond, whilst good crops had sprouted from the neatly hedged fields behind the row of freshly whitewashed cottages.

Beside the largest of these, which belonged to John Bone, barns had been erected for the new implements and to house animals in winter. Nearer to the house, the stables that Thomas had been refurbishing were at last ready to receive their inmates.

Philip walked the length and breadth of the shining building, examining the repaired and freshly painted wood, testing the fit of every door and sliding each bolt home. He checked that there was not one gleam of daylight showing through the newly timbered roof, that the stalls were firm and strong and free from draughts, and even that there were no dangerous crevices left unfilled on the spotless floor.

When he had done his inspection he turned to Thomas, who was watching him with an anxious expression.

"You have worked hard at a task which was quite new to you, Thomas, and I know you have suffered setbacks and discouragements which you never talked about. I'm proud of you, both for your skill and your tenacity. You have done well."

Thomas positively glowed at the praise. "So can we keep the blacks now, my Lord? You said we might if I did all the work myself."

Which he had, for Philip had found other work around the place for Jonathon and Ned, leaving Thomas not only responsible for the restoration of the stables but also with all the care of the horses.

"I did say that, didn't I?" Philip looked into his earnest face. "If we keep them it means more work for you to do, for they take more grooming than all the rest."

"You think I mind that? Please, my Lord."

"We'll keep them for a while," Philip promised, "perhaps forever, since my fortunes seem to be improving."

Thomas cheered. "This is the happiest day of my life."

"If it is so, Thomas, I am glad," Philip said, "for you deserve your happiness." He looked round as Theresa rode up on the little Palomino mare he had given her for her birthday earlier that month. "She truly is a beauty, isn't she?"

"Indeed she is a fine animal, my Lord," Thomas agreed, studying the golden mare with an expert eye.

"Actually it was not the horse I was talking about," Philip said, smiling. "Should you ride so much now?" he asked Theresa. "Won't it do you harm?"

"Of course not!" Theresa dismounted gracefully and stroked the cream mane of the dainty horse, which she had named Barleycorn. "I am a sturdy country girl, not one of your delicate ladies of the Court," she linked her arm through his, "but fuss over me if you like, for I enjoy it!"

"You have seven months to wait before my baby is born," Philip reminded her sternly. "You will not cavort about like some mad thing for all of them, I can assure you."

"No. I'll soon be fat and slow and fit for nothing save embroidery," she laughed, "but tell me, Thomas, have you good news?"

"Extremely good, my Lady." Thomas beamed as he led Barleycorn into the smart stables. "We're to keep the blacks!"

"Thank you, Philip, for his sake."

"He's earned it," Philip said simply. "He has done a most magnificent job."

"Yes he has," Theresa said. "Everyone has. As I look around me I can scarcely believe the way Heatherton is taking shape, and do you know why? Because of you, my love. It is your example which inspires us all."

Theresa looked gloriously happy herself these days, and not only on account of the knowledge that she was carrying Philip's child. With Bet's help she had rallied the women of the estate and organised them into an efficient and industrious force. The vegetable gardens were tended and the fishpond restocked. They kept poultry, picked and stored their produce and bottled fruit for the winter months. There was much to do, for an estate the size of High Heatherton should be completely self-sufficient and Theresa, brought up to the country life, was no stranger to this satisfying work.

They walked together, arm in arm, down the gravel path that led through to the still wild formal gardens, as yet untouched. Their restoration would be time-consuming and, to Philip's mind, a far less vital project than the tending of the fields and the orchard.

"Whatever is going through that funny little head now?" Philip asked her, for Theresa had a faraway look on her face.

"I was just picturing these gardens as they once must have been and will be again one day, planted with the Dutch tulips you've described to me and with the little glass banqueting house repaired and laid out with a feast of sweetmeats. Can we have some guests from town, please, when all the work is done? I want Giles and Buckingham and the all the rest who advised against your coming here to see how beautiful High Heatherton really is."

"You shall do exactly as you please," he said. "You are the mistress now, my darling, and there is nothing I would refuse you if you truly wanted it. Speaking of Buckingham, I have to go to London soon to see him."

Philip had only had time to return to London once since his move down to Sussex. On that occasion Buckingham had been out of town, which was annoying as he stilled owed Philip money for information he had gleaned some while ago for Prince William.

Theresa still knew nothing of any of this. Her loyalties were simple and sincere, quite untainted by practical considerations. Philip was certain she would regard his own far-sightedness in safeguarding their future by working for both France and Holland as nothing short of plain deceit!

"Must you go?" Theresa sounded disappointed.

"I fear so, for I have a little business to settle with him. Don't question me, sweetheart," Philip begged. "Just accept that my life is still linked with Buckingham's."

"All the same I wish you would not go," Theresa said. "You'll laugh at me I know, and I probably deserve it, but fear that if you go to London this time you won't come back."

Philip did not laugh, but took her in his arms instead. "I can assure you that the delights of the city no longer tempt me."

"I believe you, but I have a dreadful feeling of misgiving."

Philip frowned. She was trembling like a leaf. "This is not like you, Tess. Do you feel faint?"

"No, just a little cold." Theresa clung to him, shivering despite the hot sun. "What if you are in some sort of danger?"

"From Buckingham? What nonsense! I shall go and you are not to worry. I'm certain I've faced greater dangers in my life than any which await me now." He seated her upon the grass, beneath the shade of a chestnut tree, and lay down beside her with his head upon her knee. "Do you think I want to leave you?"

Theresa stroked his hair where it fell across her skirt. "I hope not, for I dread the thought of being separated from you again, even for a little while. I have never been so happy in all my life."

"Thomas told me that too," he said. "Even Bet and Morgan smile these days! It seems that everyone has found their heart's desire at Heatherton."

He felt a little wistful as he said it, for there was a slight shadow over Philip's own happiness. He had foiled the plot against the King's life and none but a few had even been aware of its existence yet, in his quiet moments, he felt anxious. He had gone too far this time and he feared he might still have to pay the penalty.

Theresa looked down at him sharply. "You see, you feel it too."

"Feel what?"

"That our contentment will soon be at an end."

He forced himself to smile. The last thing he wanted was to worry her. "My dear girl, we have only just begun! Oh, I am not such a dreamer that I can close my eyes completely to reality. Life has a few dirty tricks to play upon me yet, I'm sure, and I have not forgotten the horoscope I had cast in Paris which predicted I would end my days in prison, but that does not mean I shall spend my life in dread of the next move fate might make against me. I will travel tomorrow and I'll only be away a week, less if I can manage it. I am sure you'll find plenty to occupy you whilst I am gone."

"Even so, a week without you seems a long time," she said dismally.

"You did not take on so when I went off for months upon campaigns for Louis," Philip pointed out.

"But I love you even more now. Oh, Philip, if anything should happen to you I don't know what I'd do."

Philip sat up, suddenly serious. "If anything happened to me, Tess, you would stay here and fight for Heatherton and our child. You have the spirit and you'd find the strength. You have to promise, for it is important to me."

Theresa looked surprised at the vehemence of his tone, but she nodded. "Very well, I promise."

"Good girl!" He pulled her to her feet. "Now don't look so sad. I'll be home before you know it."

Theresa managed a cheerful wave as the carriage started down the drive early the following day. Philip was taking Thomas with him, partly for company and partly because he wanted help in packing up some more of their possessions to bring back with him.

She still felt uneasy and, try as she might to dispel her gloomy thoughts, the feeling did not leave her all morning. Once it so took possession of her that she decided she would follow him and went to tell Bet of her plan but when she came upon her maid Theresa changed her mind. Bet was working in the physic garden she had planted and she was surrounded by her usual little crowd of children, who she was instructing with their alphabet as she picked the herbs which she would later dry and use for medicines. Everything seemed so normal that Theresa felt ashamed of her own stupidity and went, instead, to the orchard to see Sam Bone.

Sam's labours had begun to show rewards and the blossom

had left behind it a plentiful show of apples and pears to ripen in the summer sun. He had told her that Philip's mother had often walked there and Theresa liked to imagine her wandering amongst the trees, perhaps with her little golden-haired baby cradled in her arms.

Theresa liked Sam for the kindness he had shown when Philip was a boy. She talked with him for a while and then went to sit inside the tower.

High Heatherton's tower, like that of many other great houses, was designed as a completely self-contained unit, like a house within a house. It had been used in olden times when the servants were sent away once a year and the family shifted for themselves, keeping 'secret house' as it was called, whilst they prepared their annual accounts.

The little furniture which had survived from the tower's rooms had lately been redistributed to other, more used, parts of the house and the only item left was a heavy octagonal table made of stone. It was situated in the highest room and Theresa would sometimes sit upon it and gaze out around her, never tiring of the view, for the windows faced the four points of the compass and had a commanding view of all the surrounding countryside.

The sun was casting patterns of the lattice windows onto the table top and Theresa traced over them with her finger, deep in thought. She was remembering her conversation with Philip the previous day and it still puzzled her that he had made her promise to remain at Heatherton. She wondered now whether she would really want to stay there without him.

Theresa was not a part of the place, as Philip was, and it still seemed a little daunting to her at times, rather like his disapproving family in the gallery!

She wandered over to the window and threw it open, taking in the glorious view. Spread out before her were the downs, the woods and the sparkling river and, closer, Heatherton's boundaries. She could see the orchard and the labourers working in the fields, the timber horses straining with their load and, accompanying it all, the sound of children's voices as they sang the songs Bet had taught them. They were the voices of children who, but months ago, were sad and hungry and whose parents had forgotten how to sing, just as they had forgotten how to laugh.

This was Philip's Heatherton. Suddenly she knew that he was right. It was worth fighting for.

"This has not always been a happy home," she said out loud, her voice echoing slightly in the bare-walled, empty room. "That is not to say it cannot be so in the future." She patted her abdomen which, though still flat, seemed charged with life. "I carry in me your heir, lords of Southwick. He has your blood and you cannot resent me if I fight for his inheritance."

Theresa knew that she was powerless to protect the husband she loved. The best thing she could do for Philip was to devote her life to his vision and his aspirations.

"You will live on forever here, my darling, in the stones of Heatherton and in the blood of those generations who will follow and bear your name. None shall take High Heatherton from me or from your child." Theresa clenched her fists determinedly. "I swear it."

SEVENTEEN

⌘

"The Duke of Buckingham looks forward to dining with you at Pontack's tonight, my Lord," Thomas said when he returned from the Duke's house near St. James' Park. "He says he has something for you."

"Excellent! In that case I can see no reason why we should not be upon our way back to Sussex tomorrow," Philip said.

Thomas looked surprised. "So soon?"

"I promised your mistress I would not stay away too long." Philip smiled as he thought of Theresa and the child she was carrying. There was little to keep him in London now. Everything he wanted was at Heatherton and he had a warm feeling just thinking of his life there.

Even when he heard a sharp rap on the front door he never thought the sound could be the herald of misfortune.

"Evidently the word is around town that you are here, my Lord. There will be a string of callers all the afternoon," Thomas predicted.

"I do hope not. All I want to do today is to visit Giles and then look for a present to take Theresa," Philip said, little realising how long it would be before he was allowed the luxury of passing so simple and private an afternoon. "Bring them up, whoever it is. I'll try to make it brief."

As Thomas ran downstairs Philip listened for the sound of a familiar voice below, perhaps the Duke of Monmouth or Lord Grey. The sound he did hear was Thomas' shout of alarm. "My Lord, it is Sergeant Ramsey."

"Out of my way." Ramsey pushed him aside. "Upstairs, men. Search the whole place. You're to find his Lordship if you have to tear it down."

"There is no need for that." Philip went to the top of the stairs. Although his thoughts were in turmoil he looked down upon the Sergeant coolly. "Ramsey, so we meet again. What is it you want, other than to destroy my property?"

"Don't trust him," Ramsey warned his men. "He is a dangerous man."

"I assure you, Sergeant, I am not even armed." Philip pulled aside his coat to show that it was so. "It is not my custom to go about my house in a state of readiness for combat, although, in view of this intrusion upon my privacy, perhaps I should."

"This is no mere intrusion, my Lord. We are come here to arrest you, and this time it is not a charge you will wriggle out of, as you did before."

"What is the charge?" Philip said, although he feared he knew.

"Why, that of treason, my Lord. You and all your rebel friends are being rounded up, all those who were party to your plot to kill the King and the Duke of York."

Philip's head swam, but he managed to stand steady. "All, you say?"

"Aye. Lord Grey and Sir Thomas Armstrong should be in custody by now, and your brother-in-law, Giles Fairfield."

At the mention of Giles' name Philip gave Thomas a look more eloquent than any words he could risk uttering at that moment.

Thomas was still standing by the door. He gave the briefest of nods before darting out into the street.

"Do you have a warrant for me to see?" Philip asked Ramsey, hoping to distract him whilst Thomas made good his escape.

"I have it here, my Lord. Make no false move, I beg you,"

he said as Philip slowly descended the stairs. "Our orders are to bring you into custody, whether alive or dead. You'll not escape us."

Philip looked at the ten men who surrounded him, their muskets raised. "I'd be a fool to try. I am astonished, and not a little flattered, that the Secretary of State considered it would need so many men to take me."

"Your reputation is well known, my Lord," Ramsey said, handing him the warrant.

Philip glanced at it. He was in no state to read the document but he had succeeded in delaying the soldiers long enough for Thomas to be well on his way.

"Wait!" Ramsey cried suddenly. "Where is your servant? I know why you are doing this, my Lord. It is in order that he may have a chance to warn the others, No matter, there are none that he can reach in time."

"Perhaps and perhaps not." There was a bottle of brandy on the table next to where he stood. Philip poured himself a large measure and drank it straight down. "Lead on, Ramsey, I am ready to accompany you now."

Giles lived just off Cornhill, near the Royal Exchange. Thomas had less than half a mile to cover and he made good time. Even if a troop had set off from Whitehall at the same moment as those who had arrested his master, he reckoned he would still be able to outrun them.

All was quiet as he came into Poultry. Thomas breathed a sigh of relief, although he knew there was no time to lose.

He approached Giles' lodgings by an alley, which led to the rear of the building, and hammered urgently upon back door, praying that Giles was at home.

He was. Thomas burst in as soon as he opened the door. "You

have to get away, Giles, now," he panted. "There is a warrant out for your arrest."

Giles stared at him. "Why? What have I done?"

"God only knows, but they've got his Lordship already."

"Philip has been taken?" Giles said, stunned.

"There was nothing I could do to help him, but I can help you. Come with me now and I'll try to get you out of the city."

Giles did not hesitate. Throwing on his coat, he buckled a sword around his waist and thrust two pistols into his belt. Before he followed Thomas into the alley he opened a drawer in his bureau and pressed a hidden catch to reveal a mother-of pearl box.

"What's in there?" Thomas wondered as Giles lifted out the box.

"All that I own," Giles said for, indeed, it was. Jewellery, money, everything of value he had accrued in the years since he'd left home.

"You can't take that," Thomas said. "It's too cumbersome."

"I can assure you I do not intend arriving wherever I'm going empty-handed."

"Be quick, then," Thomas urged him, "or you'll go nowhere save the Tower."

Giles tipped the contents into two leather bags, one of which he shoved into each pocket. "I'm ready."

Just then they heard the heavy sound of a Sergeant's staff upon the front door.

Giles froze. "It's too late."

"Not quite. They may not think of the alley." Thomas grabbed his arm. "Come on!"

Thomas had guessed right. The soldiers, less familiar with the area, had not yet discovered the alternative exit to the premises. Before they did so Giles and Thomas were safely at the crossroads, where Cornhill met with Bishopsgate Street.

"We must cross the bridge." Thomas said. "It is your only

chance. I've got friends upon the other side who'll help us get a boat. Here comes our opportunity."

A cart loaded high with vegetables was rumbling along Bishopsgate Street in the direction of the bridge. Before it had quite passed them Thomas ran and jumped on the back, with Giles close at his heels. Being both small, they had soon concealed themselves amongst lettuces and cabbages, burrowing down as far as they could.

The driver, unaware of the existence of his uninvited passengers, slowly made his way down Bishopsgate Street and into Gracechurch Street before passing the junction with East Cheap and turning into Fish Street.

"Supposing he's not making for the bridge?" Giles whispered.

"Of course he is." But he wasn't. Even as Thomas spoke the driver turned his cart left into Thames Street, heading towards the Tower! "On second thoughts we'll run it to the bridge from here!"

A woman shrieked as the two figures materialised from amongst the vegetables right before her eyes. The driver glanced round, cursing as the pair leapt from his cart and sped toward the bridge, scattering his load upon the cobbles. Thomas feared he might give chase but his produce was disappearing into the pockets of the onlookers as swiftly as it fell and he evidently decided he'd do better to stay and protect what remained in the cart.

Once upon the bridge Thomas and Giles were quickly lost to view amongst the crowds that pushed and jostled their way beneath the tall shops and houses which lined both sides. At one point they were forced to stand aside with everyone else and wait impatiently as a man drove ten fat sheep across, but they were soon over the bridge and safe, for the moment, upon the other side of the river.

Thomas made straight for the church of St. Mary Overy nearby and, bidding Giles to wait there for him, disappeared into the huddle of narrow streets that lined the river on the east side of the bridge.

Giles slipped inside the church and knelt down in a dark pew, his head bowed as if he was praying, although his thoughts, as he felt for the comforting bulges in his pockets, were more secular than divine!

He had a long while to wait, nearly three hours, during which he pondered now and again upon Philip's fate, a fate Giles had predicted many times. He was in no doubt that his own attempted arrest was in connection with Philip's plot and he cursed himself for allowing his brother-in-law to land him in such a mess.

The church doors opened and he ducked down, his pistol ready in his hand before he saw who was there. "Thomas! I feared they had captured you."

"It's not me they want yet, but we must go carefully. The streets are crawling with soldiers."

"In search of me?"

"Not only you. I've heard that Ferguson and Sir Thomas Armstrong also escaped them but the word upon the streets is that they have taken Hampden, Sydney, Lord Grey, West, Rumsey and the Earl of Essex."

"All of whom attended Philip's meetings," Giles said, his worst fears confirmed. "But I understood from Monmouth that the plot was abandoned after there was a fire at Newmarket."

"So it was." Thomas could say no more than that for, to protect Giles, Philip had wanted him to know nothing of their part in the fire. "About a mile from here is a bend in the river that the watermen call the Pool," he said instead. "At eight o'clock a cargo boat, sailing from Wapping, will pull in at a place I know beside the bank. It will take us to Gravesend. From there, with the help of a Searcher, Mr. Cresswell, who knows Lord Devalle, it should be an easy matter to obtain a passage across the Channel. Do you fancy going to France?"

"France will do very well," Giles said. "What is in that bundle you have there?"

Thomas threw the bundle to him. "I thought you should be disguised."

"As a girl?" Giles asked, horrified, as he discovered a skirt, an apron and a woman's cloak inside the bundle.

"Why not?" Thomas grinned. "Doesn't King Louis' brother do it, just for fun! Besides," he added, as tactfully as he could, "you have a scar which makes you easily recognisable. I thought you could pull the hood well down to hide your face."

"That might work," Giles agreed. "Where did you get them?"

"The skirt and apron from a washing line. The cloak I saw upon a lady in the street."

"You took it off her back?" Despite his troubles, Giles began to laugh. "Thomas, how could you?"

"Stop complaining!" Thomas tied the skirt, which was much too large, around Giles' waist with the apron strings. When he had fastened on the cloak he put Giles' coat and waistcoat into the bundle and admired his handiwork. "You look quite fetching with your hood held so," he decided. "I don't believe the soldiers will suspect you one bit. I think we should leave right away, for it is half past six already and the boat cannot wait long at the Pool without alerting suspicion."

Giles had cause to be glad of his disguise almost immediately. A few yards from the church they encountered three soldiers, who barred their way.

Thomas took Giles' arm protectively. "Excuse me, sirs, would you let us pass, for we are in great haste."

One of them stepped forward. "Are you indeed, young man? And who is this who covers up her pretty face, your sister?"

"Not at all." Thomas beckoned him closer. "Can you be discreet?"

The soldier guffawed at that. "You may trust the secrets of your soul to me!"

"Then listen to this." Thomas whispered into the soldier's ear and what he said brought forth more raucous laughter.

"Pass on, young friend. You perform an honest task, for it is right that even gentlemen of the cloth should have their pleasures! Tell me something, though, before you go. We are searching for two men. Have you seen anyone who looks suspicious?"

"No, sir." With the minutes to their rendezvous with the boat ticking by Thomas was growing impatient. The soldiers had stood aside, so that the way was now clear for them to leave and he contemplated making a run for it but he thought that Giles, hampered as he now was by a skirt, would be too slow. "What men do you seek?"

"Two rebels, gentlemen both. Sir Thomas Armstrong and Captain Fairfield."

"I would not know them if I saw them, sir. I am but a humble servant."

"Keep alert, they're dangerous," the soldier warned.

Thomas thanked him for his advice and they went on swiftly.

"What was all the whispering about?" Giles asked when they were out of earshot of the soldiers.

"Oh, I told them my master was a minister of the church and that you were his bedding piece, who I was charged with seeing safely home!"

"You are an agile liar, Thomas, for which I'm grateful."

Thomas shuddered. "So you should be! Even after all these years I cannot stand close to an officer of the law and not tremble. Come, we must be quick. This city is no longer safe for you."

"I wonder how Armstrong is making out."

"Thank God I am not helping him as well," Thomas said with feeling.

The Pool at Rotherhithe was little more than a mile away but, although they had no more encounters, it still took them an hour to reach it, for they dare not use the main roads.

"We are ahead of him by fifteen minutes," Thomas

said, pulling out a silver watch. It was the one Philip had loaned him during their escape from Newmarket and he had later made him a gift of it in gratitude for his courage and resourcefulness.

Giles looked at it curiously but made no comment as they concealed themselves in the bushes near the bank to await the boatman.

"Supposing he lets us down?"

"He won't."

Sure enough, shortly after eight o'clock, the little sloop came into view around the bend.

The pair got closer to the water's edge. At a place the water folk dubbed Toper's Landing a broken jetty stood before what had once been a brewery. It was now an empty, derelict place, used occasionally as a shelter by the tramps that traversed the highways to the city. The spot was totally deserted as Giles and Thomas mounted the creaking pier.

The boat pulled over to the side and kissed the bank as its two passengers hurled themselves onto its deck, disappearing swiftly down the stairway to the hold.

The hold had a fusty smell, which made Giles turn up his fastidious nose.

"I'm sorry, Giles, it was the only passage I could book for you at such short notice," Thomas said solemnly, although his lips were twitching.

"It will suit me well enough," Giles told him with a sigh as he changed back into his own clothes. "This whole thing has been rather a shock, that's all. I was due to go to the theatre this afternoon," he said wistfully. "The King's House are playing 'Philaster'. Still I'm better off than poor Philip at this moment, thanks to you."

"What will happen to him, do you think?" It was the first time Thomas had really had time to give thought to his master's fate.

"If he is accused of treason they may execute him," Giles said quietly.

"But first he must stand trial. What if there is insufficient evidence against him?"

"Thomas, Philip devised a plan to murder the King and the Duke of York," Giles reminded him. "We both know that he never intended to go through with it but you can be sure they will find someone willing to give evidence against him to save their own skin. This is just the opportunity Charles needed to be rid of him."

"Surely something can be done." Thomas sat dejectedly upon one of the empty crates. "I owe him so much. To thieve was all I knew until he took me in. Can you imagine what my life would be now? The shadow of the gallows hanging over me probably or transported, to spend my life in bondage. He has protected me and treated me with nothing but kindness. Can you wonder that I would do anything to save him?"

"He has certainly been good to you," Giles agreed.

"And so have you, Giles. You've always been my friend and I shall see you safely away, no matter what," Thomas vowed.

"Why don't you come with me?" Giles said. "I could take care of you."

It was a tempting prospect, but Thomas put it resolutely from his mind. "I can't do that. There is still your sister to consider. I couldn't desert her, or Bet and Morgan. Besides, there may be something I can do to help."

It didn't seem very likely, but Giles said no more on the subject and for the remainder of the journey they slept as best they could upon the bare floor, for they were both exhausted.

The boat's captain awakened them just before midnight.

"You must leave the boat now, for it is certain the authorities will be searching every craft that anchors in the port tonight."

"My thanks, sir, for your transport and your vigilance," Giles said, taking some coins from his pocket.

The man shook his head. "You'll need them more than I. This is a favour that I do for Thomas. Good luck, Captain Fairfield. I hope you find a ship to take you safely away."

"Incredible," Giles said as they crouched on the deck awaiting their opportunity to leave the vessel in the same way as they had boarded it. "Why would he not take any payment?"

Thomas smiled sadly. "You would never understand, Giles. Jump now!"

The boat's owner had brought his vessel as close to the river bank as he dared and they leapt together, landing in the soft mud.

"That's the first part over." Thomas tossed the bundle of female clothing into the river and they watched it sink into the black depths. "Now to find Searcher Cresswell."

The river bank appeared to be deserted as they walked, in single file, toward the town. The moon was high, illuminating the bank well, and the only sounds to be heard were the warbling of the frogs near the water's edge and the rustling of the creatures of the night.

Suddenly Thomas stiffened. He had seen a movement in the bushes by the side of Giles, who was walking some ten yards ahead of him. Without slackening his pace, Thomas bent down and picked up a large, round stone. Even as he straightened up a figure in soldier's uniform materialised behind Giles.

Before Giles could even turn Thomas had aimed the stone. It caught the man on the back of the head and he dropped with a moan.

Giles spun round, drawing his pistol as he did so. He was in time to see a second soldier leap out, and this one brought Thomas crashing to the ground.

Thomas was agile but not as hefty as his assailant, and it did not take long before the soldier had the better of him. Giles pointed his weapon at the struggling pair, who were rolling over and over on the muddy path, making it difficult for him to aim safely.

Difficult, but not impossible. He fired.

Thomas scrambled to his feet with an oath and looked down at the soldier, who lay dead with a bullet hole in his back.

"What a shot! Small wonder Lord Devalle says you are the best marksman he has ever known!"

"Is that what he says?" Giles smiled faintly. "Be that as it may, I should have been more alert. We might have guessed that soldiers would be patrolling the river banks this close to the port. We'd better press on quickly before anyone investigates the gunfire and sees us."

But they had already been seen.

There was considerable movement in the area of the port, indicating that the officials had been alerted, but the streets of the town were quiet at that hour and they reached Searcher Cresswell's house without more incident.

Cresswell answered the door himself, clad in his nightgown, and stared out at the two figures that remained in the shadows beside the door.

"We need your help," Thomas whispered.

"Who has sent you?"

"I am Lord Devalle's man and I have Captain Fairfield with me."

"Dear God! They are searching for him everywhere!"

"How soon can I be bound for France?" Giles asked as Cresswell hastened to get them inside.

"You can't. There's no chance," the frightened man protested. "All the ports are being watched."

"Pull yourself together, man," Giles snapped. "You know my brother-in-law would want you to help me."

"I curse the day I ever heard of Philip Devalle!" Cresswell said with feeling.

"And you are probably not alone in that, but shall you risk his displeasure by refusing to give me aid?"

"What can he do to me now? I hear they've got him good and proper this time."

"What if he manages to get out of trouble, as he has so many times in the past? He's a resourceful man, and a dangerous one to cross," Giles reminded him.

"I know that," Cresswell said grimly, "but once before I helped him get a friend away, Colonel Scott it was, and it transpired the man was wanted for murder. The authorities were suspicious of me then and they're most likely watching me now."

Giles shrugged. "You'll have to take that chance, and so will I, for you are all I've got. You must be able to find someone who will take me to France."

Cresswell still looked worried but he sighed resignedly. "Very well, I'll try, but there is nothing I can do until the morning."

He brought them some cold food and then went upstairs to dress.

The knowledge that they were about to be separated, perhaps forever, drew Thomas and Giles even closer for these last few hours. Good companions they had always been but, as they talked over old times, both realised how fond they were of one another and Thomas began to dread the question he knew Giles would ask him again before he sailed.

Cresswell appeared to have donned his courage with his uniform and, before he left the house, he studied his lists and selected a suitable vessel, one which, with luck, he could clear before the morning tide.

Thomas watched the Searcher go off about his business in the early dawn. "Are we to trust him, do you think?"

"We've little option, for without him I should never get away by sea," Giles said. "Anyway, I suspect he's too afraid of Philip to be dishonest with us."

It seemed that he was right for Cresswell was back before an hour was up and bade them follow him. A brig bound for Calais was ready to cast off anchor with the tide. Its cargo had been cleared and, in lieu of payment of excise, its captain had been pleased to accept a mysterious passenger.

The harbour, even at that time of the morning, was a bustle of activity. Great ships were anchored as far as the eye could see, from huge merchantmen, bound for the Indies, to trading vessels of every shape and size, awaiting their final clearance from the Customs men. Cresswell led them to the one he had selected.

"Get aboard and quickly or they'll miss the tide. This place will be alive with soldiers before the day is out," he warned Giles, before disappearing swiftly.

Giles looked up at the square rigging lifting from the two main masts as the breeze rose up around them, and then he looked at Thomas.

"He's right, you must be going. " Thomas swallowed, trying in vain to rid himself of the lump which was filling his throat.

"I beg you, change your mind." Giles took him by the shoulders. "I don't want to leave you here."

"No." Thomas closed his eyes as if, that way, he could shut out temptation. "I must go back."

"I pray God you do not regret it. Wish me luck."

"With all my heart. May fortune shine upon you, Giles."

"On you too. If you should ever wish to take up my offer then seek me out." Giles felt inside one of his pockets and produced a bracelet made of solid gold and encrusted with precious gems. "Here is your fare to wherever I am."

"I can't take that," Thomas gasped.

"I insist you do." Giles pressed it into Thomas' palm. You may be glad of it, for you do not know what awaits you, and it will fetch a good price. I'd like you to have this as well." Giles removed a strangely-shaped silver band from his finger and twisted it so that the ring split into two parts. He handed one part to Thomas. "This is a bond between us. Should you ever have need of me you have only to send me your half of the ring."

"And the same goes for you," Thomas said, greatly touched by the gesture. "I will always wear it proudly."

"Take care of Scarlet for me." With that Giles boarded the

ship, turning once to wave before disappearing from Thomas' view.

They set sail immediately and Thomas was left alone on the dock. He slipped the silver ring onto his finger, wondering whether he and Giles would ever meet again, for Thomas suspected some trouble may lie ahead for him as well.

He was no stranger to it. Brought up amongst the thieves and cut-throats of London's dingiest back streets, life had always been an uncertain matter before he had joined the Devalle household. From earliest childhood he had become accustomed to the perilous existence of those who live outside the law, always knowing that one day his luck might desert him.

But Thomas was no coward. Whatever lay ahead of him now, he would face it without flinching.

He watched the ship sail nearly out of sight before turning back toward the town, his hands thrust into his pockets as he walked dejectedly along the quay.

He had successfully accomplished the last task his master had given him and he felt a strange emptiness inside as it properly dawned upon him how savagely his happy life had been disrupted by the events of the last few hours.

By eight o'clock the town had properly come to life and he mingled with the townsfolk, attempting to look as purposeful as the others going about their business. He had to find a way to get back to London and he was looking out for a cart leaving the town, on which he might beg a ride.

He saw some soldiers in the street and thanked his stars that Giles was not still with him. Thomas was quite sure that he would be in no danger himself in Gravesend, where no-one knew him.

He was wrong.

"That's him!" a voice cried. "The small one, there!"

Thomas looked about him, scarcely believing anyone could be talking about him. Across the street a man was pointing squarely in his direction. "That's the one who stoned the soldier. It was his companion shot the other one dead."

Thomas cursed and backed into the crowd as the four soldiers made a dash for him. He turned and began to run, keeping ahead of them for several yards, but he was hampered by the traffic on the road.

He dodged into the first side street he came upon. Alas, this was not London, which Thomas knew so well. He found himself in a blind alley, trapped like a fly inside a bottle as the soldiers cornered him.

"You were seen with Captain Fairfield on the river bank this morning," one challenged him.

"No, not I, sir." Thomas frantically eyed the wall above him. It was all of eight feet high, but there was a tree close by from whose branches he could easily mount the wall. The only problem was that the soldiers advancing on him were between him and the tree.

"You were spotted by a fisherman collecting whitebait in the shallows," the soldier insisted. "He saw Fairfield clearly in the moonlight and described him, even to the scar on his face, and you too. Give yourself up now, or we will have to take you by whatever means we can."

"I am not armed, sir. Would you hurt me when you don't even know whether I am the one you want?" Thomas asked, keeping them talking as he swiftly judged the distance between the two men nearest to him.

"You're the one, you've been identified," the soldier said, "and I'll warrant you are Lord Devalle's servant, that escaped when he was arrested. You warned Captain Fairfield, and you shall pay with your own life for harbouring a traitor."

Thomas mouthed a certain word that had always brought him luck and then charged between the soldiers. Reaching the tree before any of them could draw their weapons, he jumped up, managing to grab a lower branch. Kicking his feet forward, he propelled himself upwards into the body of the tree, so that he was all but hidden from view amongst the leaves. Sitting astride the branch that overhung the wall, Thomas swiftly edged his way along until he was directly over it. Before the soldiers could react he dropped down to land, sure-footed as a cat, upon the narrow top of the wall and leapt down upon the other side.

Behind the wall were the gardens of the houses on the main street. The soldiers' shouts filled Thomas' head as he sped across a lawn and flowerbeds before diving through a passageway which divided two of the houses.

He was back on the street now and he knew he had only bought himself a little time before his pursuers caught up with him again. He sought desperately for some means of escape.

Across the road was an inn and tied to a post outside was a brown mare. Thomas had been many things but never a horse-thief. He balked at the prospect but his instincts of self-preservation were stronger than his principles. Drawing his knife as he ran, he reached the horse before the soldiers emerged from the passageway.

He mounted, cutting the mare loose as he did so. The startled animal shied but Thomas quickly had control and urged her forward with a sharp word.

By the time he reached the outskirts of the town there was no sign of any following him and he took the Dartford road at a fast gallop.

All was different now. Thomas would have no chance to find his mistress, for he was a wanted criminal himself and, to add to his other crimes, he had stolen a horse.

There was but one place left for him to go, the one place where the authorities would not find him and where he would be protected by his own kind; the lawless district around Whitefriars that was a safe hide-out for the most villainous characters in London and where even the soldiers never ventured in.

Alsatia.

EIGHTEEN

❦

"Lord Grey has escaped us," Sir Leoline Jenkins, the Secretary of State, told King Charles.

"How could that be?" Charles said irritably. "I heard he had been arrested."

"It happened as Deerham, the Sergeant-at-Arms, was conveying him to the Tower, your Majesty." Jenkins said. "Apparently his Lordship had the coach stop at the Rumner Tavern, in Charing Cross, where he ordered some bottles of claret for Deerham. The Sergeant was inebriated by the time the coach arrived at the Bulwark Gate and Lord Grey was nowhere to be seen! We later learned that he had taken a boat across the river, landing at the Pickled Herring Inn, beside the Customs House Stairs, and from there he hired a horse. That was the last we heard of him."

"Bring Deerham to the Tower in his stead," Charles ordered as he scanned the list of prisoners. "Despite Grey's escape you have done well. I little thought you would take so many, and especially not the resourceful Devalle. I trust he, at least, arrived at the Tower without mishap."

"He did, your Majesty. He is being held for questioning in the Queen's House."

"Good. What reason did he give for being in town?"

"He was here to visit the Duke of Buckingham, he claims. His Grace has verified it but I am still far from happy with Lord Devalle's explanation. I hope to learn more when we question him this afternoon."

"Ask him what you will, but don't expect too many answers," Charles warned. "Was he difficult to take?"

"No. He apparently surrendered himself without a fight, your Majesty."

"Really? I never would have thought it."

"Even so I do not trust him," Jenkins said. "I have made sure he can do no harm either to those who guard him or himself."

"You think he would attempt to take his own life?"

"He might, to save himself from the disgrace of a traitor's death."

"Nonsense," Charles said. "If I know Philip at all he still presumes he will escape the penalty of the law, just as he has so many times before."

"I don't believe he does. What your Majesty will see this time is resignation, not defiance from Lord Devalle."

"That should be interesting," Charles decided.

Philip looked up as Charles and Jenkins entered, ready to meet the King's hard eyes. His wrists were manacled, and it was that which first drew Charles' attention.

"I never ordered this," Charles said angrily to Jenkins. "Have them removed now."

"But he may be troublesome, your Majesty," Jenkins protested.

"Then double his guard. Lord Devalle is a peer and, no matter what he might have done, he will be treated with the respect due to his rank."

The guard unlocked the iron bands and Philip gently rubbed his wrists. The manacles had already left red sores from which a little blood had stained his lace cuffs.

"I must apologise for the way in which you have been treated," Charles said stiffly.

"It is of no consequence, your Majesty," Philip said, thinking how ironic it was, under the circumstances, that the King's first words to him were by way of an apology. "I've suffered worse discomfort in my life and I have no doubt there is more to come."

"That will depend upon how much you cooperate with us," Charles said. "You know the charges that are to be brought against you?"

"Yes, your Majesty."

"And how do you propose to answer them?"

Philip tossed his head. "Your Majesty knows as well as I that I do not have to answer any charges until I stand trial in a court of law. You do propose to try me, I presume? "

"Oh yes, my Lord, you will be tried, but there are certain questions I would have you answer for us now. You are acquainted with an Anabaptist merchant called Josiah Keeling?"

"I don't believe I am, your Majesty," Philip said truthfully.

"Well he knows you or, at least, of you," Charles said. "Sir Leoline, would you please tell Lord Devalle what Keeling had to say?"

"The man came to me and told me of a plot against the lives of the King and the Duke of York, a plot led by you, my Lord. He mentioned several other influential men who were conspiring with you."

"I am constantly the target for fanatics, scandalmongers and the like," Philip said. "Why do you give credence to this Keeling?"

"I did not, at the start, but he returned the next day with a brewer who is known as a substantial man. He verified his tale. Upon their joint information we arrested Thomas Sheppard."

Philip bit his lip but made no comment.

"I assume you'll not deny you know him," Jenkins said.

"No. I know Sheppard," Philip admitted.

"Certainly you do, for it was at his house in Abchurch Street that you called a meeting in which you discussed plans to waylay the King and his brother upon their return from Newmarket."

Philip's worse fears had been realised. The only slight chance he thought he might have now was if every person who had been involved denied the charges, but that didn't seem too likely.

"Did Sheppard tell you I had held a meeting at his house?" he asked cagily.

"He has confessed to everything."

"In that case there seems little point in this," Philip said heavily. "What can I tell you that he has not?"

"There may be others, not then present, who were nonetheless a part of this."

"You want their names?" Philip could hardly believe what he was hearing. "Do you honestly think I would tell you that?"

"Affairs may go much better for you if you do," Jenkins said.

"Go to blazes!"

Jenkins turned to Charles. "Perhaps Lord Devalle will reconsider his position when he has had a little time to reflect upon his sins in the Beauchamp Tower."

"Perhaps." Charles came closer. "Did you really want to kill me, Philip?"

"No, your Majesty. That was never my intent."

"Then why did you do all this?"

Philip decided he could hardly tell him the truth, that he had done it solely to gain Heatherton. "Because it was expected of me, I suppose," he said instead.

"No! That will not do. Shaftesbury is dead. You are not answerable to any now, unless it is my son. I know that he was at the meeting."

Philip saw the torment in the King's face and could almost have pitied him. "Have you arrested Monmouth too, your Majesty?"

"No, not yet, but I shall not hesitate to do so if I have sufficient evidence to convince me that he was involved in this plot. Will you swear positively that he wanted his own father and his uncle dead?"

"I shall not speak out against your son in any way," Philip said quietly. "Nor shall you persuade me to give any information to incriminate anyone else."

"It makes no difference whether you do or not," Jenkins said crossly. "There will be others far less reticent, I'm sure, who will gladly tell us all we wish to know."

Philip had no doubt of that; indeed he could have confidently named those sources from which the Secretary could elicit information. He also guessed, from Jenkins' tone, that the King's refusal to arrest Monmouth was a tender point with him.

Charles sighed. "Very well. There seems little purpose in continuing this. You have conspired against me and incited others to plot against my life. For that, my Lord, you'll die, for there are none left who can save you. Think on that, you will have time enough, and ponder, too, if such a cause was worthy of your talents, or if such as you now defend by your silence are worthy of your loyalty."

Philip wondered that too as he walked between two guards past Tower Green, where so many famous heads had fallen.

The Bastille, where he had previously been a prisoner, was far more formidable but this time he suspected that his only release might come on the execution block, after the distasteful prospect of being tried for treason.

A squawking roused him from his dark reverie.

"What's that?"

"Only the ravens, my Lord, see?" The guard on his right pointed to the great black, shiny bird that hopped along quite close beside them. It opened its beak and cawed again.

"Of course, I had forgotten the ravens," Philip said. "For a moment I thought it was Lord Shaftesbury's laughter that I heard!"

The two guards exchanged looks.

Philip caught their expressions and smiled. "I am not suffering from the 'Devalle sickness', if that is what you fear, but I may well lose my sanity if they keep me long in here."

The guards handed him over to his warder, a brutish-looking man named Haggerty, square of body and grim of visage.

"I alone shall be in charge of you, my Lord."

"That's nice for you," Philip said, with a lightness that his heart did not share, for there was nothing about the man to indicate that he would make a pleasing companion. "Did you draw lots for me?"

"Indeed not. Most were afraid of you, my Lord."

"But not you?"

"Not I." Haggerty flexed his broad hands and cracked each knuckle in turn, a habit Philip never could abide in anyone. "You'll not escape from me, Lord Devalle, and do not think to charm me either. I've heard how persuasive you can be but, I warn you, I am immune to all your ways, and nor can I be bribed."

Philip raised an eyebrow. "I see this is going to be an entertaining visit! Do you have no pleasing qualities whatsoever?"

"I have no humour either," Haggerty warned him.

"Well I have very little myself at the moment," Philip said ruefully. "Are you to be with me all the time?"

"Aye, every day. You are my responsibility and I have been promised that I shall be considered for the post of Chief Warder if I deliver you safely to court for your trial. If I fail, which I shall not, then I'm to lose my head. So says Sir Leoline Jenkins himself."

Haggerty seemed to be absurdly proud of this.

"It seems hard that, as well as all my other miseries, I must endure you too," Philip said, looking out of the tiny window in his cell onto the less than cheerful sight of Tower Green. He thought of Heatherton, with its rolling acres, and of Theresa, so fresh and lovely, riding Barleycorn. She had been right to worry that he would not return. He put the pleasant picture from his mind. It was too painful now. "Am I to be allowed visitors or a servant?"

"Neither," Haggerty said emphatically. "You are to have no privileges."

"That is preposterous," Philip said. "Lord Shaftesbury not only brought his own cook into prison but he was allowed out every afternoon to drive with his wife."

Haggerty looked unimpressed. "I suggest you take up your grievances with Sir Leoline Jenkins when he comes to question you, my Lord."

"Much good that will do me, I am sure," Philip muttered.

Philip did take his grievances up with Jenkins when the Secretary of State came to visit him a week later, but Jenkins looked upon him coldly. "It is as your warder says, my Lord. You are to have no privileges until you show you are ready to cooperate with us."

"I am entitled to a servant," Philip complained, for so he was, but Jenkins was as adamant on that point as he was concerning the brandy Philip had requested. A week within the confines of his cell without even that solace had been hard on his nerves, especially with only the surly Haggerty for company.

Nevertheless he faced Secretary Jenkins defiantly. He might be suffering but he had no intention of giving Jenkins the satisfaction of knowing it.

"I am sure you will be delighted to learn that Captain Fairfield has escaped us, my Lord," Jenkins said. "He is believed to be in France."

"That is, indeed, good news," Philip said, smiling at the plain annoyance on Jenkins' face.

"He was aided by a lad believed to be your servant, who we are now seeking. Fairfield shot a soldier dead during his escape, which means that he is a murderer on top of all his other crimes, and he shall pay if I ever get him back in England."

"What are his other crimes?" Philip asked. "He was not involved in any plot."

"Come, come, my Lord, it will be an easy matter to prove in court that such is not the case," Jenkins said sneeringly.

"How?"

"I shall merely establish that you and he are on intimate terms."

"He is my brother-in-law," Philip said. "Of course we are on intimate terms, but Captain Fairfield has done nothing wrong, for he had no part in this."

"It is to be expected that you will try to protect him, my Lord, but he was known to have attended a meeting of the Green Ribbon Club, at which you talked of a plot against the King and the Duke."

"Exactly! When Captain Fairfield came to the meeting he had no notion of what I was about to say. That was the only one he ever attended."

"No, my Lord, that was not the only one," Jenkins insisted. "I have here an excellent report from a barrister of your acquaintance, Robert West. He says that on more than one occasion meetings were held at the Nonsuch Tavern and that those present included yourself, Sir Thomas Armstrong, John Hampden, Lord Russell and Captain Giles Fairfield. What do you say to that?"

"Fairfield and I were merely drinking in a tavern with some friends," Philip said, although he hardly expected Jenkins to believe him.

"Friends who, coincidentally, happen to be amongst those at the Abchurch Street meeting," Jenkins said scornfully. "Do you claim that the company did not assemble for seditious purposes?"

Philip knew it would be extremely difficult to claim any such thing. "Have it as you will. None of this proves that Captain Fairfield was party to the plot."

"He was there, my Lord. What more proof do we need? Are we to suppose that he heard nothing of the conversation?"

"Fairfield knew as well as I did that, no matter what was said on this or any other occasion, nothing would ever come of it."

"What?" Jenkins cried disbelievingly. "You worked the plan out to the last detail, so I understand, my Lord."

"So I did, but still I had no wish to put it into operation."

"You told Captain Fairfield this?"

"Of course."

"And he believed you?" Jenkins scoffed. "Why do you persist in this ridiculous attempt to protect his name?"

"For one thing I care what might happen to my servant," Philip said. "It would appear to me that if a case cannot be found against Fairfield then it can hardly be found against the man who helped him flee the country."

"I don't suppose you would care to furnish us with any information to facilitate our search for your servant?" Jenkins said. "Even such a small degree of cooperation might look well for you."

"Don't be ridiculous!"

"Very well, my Lord. I wonder, though, if you would at least give me the answer to a question which has been intriguing me greatly. Robert West has told me that he was amongst those picked to lead the assault upon the King's guard and that you planned it as a military operation."

"I was a Colonel in the French army," Philip reminded him. "What would you expect?"

"I would expect to have seen you at the head of your troops, my Lord. Instead it was to have been Colonel Walcot who led them. What was your part in the plan?"

"I had no part. I was not even planning to be there," Philip told him.

Jenkins looked unconvinced. "A somewhat curious decision, is it not, for one acknowledged as a man of courage?"

"But not for one accredited as a man of some intelligence, which I believe even the King concedes that I am. I've told you, Jenkins, this plan was never intended to be put into action."

"And how did you propose to stop it? Come, my Lord, enough of this," Jenkins said crisply. "Would you not prefer to die with a light heart and an easy conscience?"

"Do you mean confess my sins so that I might cause my friends to suffer similarly?" Philip's voice was scathing. "I care not particularly how I die, Jenkins. Oh, I would have hoped that it might be with honour, fighting on some battlefield perhaps, but it seems that is not to be. I am, however, adamant that when I do die everything that I have done dies with me. I shall not confess a thing to you. I die as I have lived, quite unrepentant."

"Then my Lord, your soul will go to hell," Jenkins said pompously.

"Very probably, but I have the consolation of knowing it will be in most illustrious company!"

Philip pointed to some carvings on the wall. The five Dudley brothers had all been kept in that same cell and each had carved his device. Haggerty, in a rare conversational moment, had told him that Guildford Dudley had been beheaded on Tower Hill on the same day that his wife, Lady Jane Grey, had been led to the scaffold on the Green.

Philip had come to know the sight of that only too well!

He had meant every defiant word he had said to Jenkins, but Philip desperately did not want to die, especially not now, just when he had finally found contentment after a life time of searching for it.

Giles was beginning to have misgivings as he waited in the antechamber of the Palais Royale. He had no idea whether

Monsieur would even agree to receive him, let alone offer him sanctuary now that he was a fugitive from justice.

There was also the matter of his scar. Monsieur liked to surround himself with attractive people, and Giles knew that his own good looks were gone forever.

These unhappy thoughts raced around Giles' overwrought brain as he waited, weary from travelling and the strain of the past few days.

Monsieur bustled in on his high heels. "Giles! What a delightful treat. Have you come to stay with me?"

"If you will allow it, Monsieur." Giles kept the left side of his face turned away from him. "I did not know if I would still be welcome. There is a warrant out for my arrest in England."

"I know." Monsieur laughed his own affected little laugh. "Did you think I would send you away because you have annoyed my cousin, Charles?"

"Not only because of that, Monsieur." Giles slowly turned his damaged cheek toward him, steeling himself for the reaction he had come to expect. Most people, upon seeing his scar for the first time, gasped with horror or cried out in pity, and Giles was not sure which was worse.

In fact Monsieur did neither of those things. The First Gentleman of France may have been shallow and self-centred but he was not entirely insensitive.

He barely glanced at the livid mark which had blighted Giles' life. "To me you are still handsome," he said simply. "You are my friend and you will always be that, no matter what you have done or what has been done to you."

"Thank you, Monsieur," Giles said quietly, touched by Monsieur's words, and relieved too. "In that case I would be delighted to stay here with you."

"Good! We'll have such fun," Monsieur promised. "I've been worried about Philip, though," he added seriously. "Is it true that he's been taken?"

"I fear so."

"But he will be able to talk himself out of trouble, won't he? He always has before."

"I expect so," Giles comforted him, but he was more concerned for Philip than he wanted to admit, either to Monsieur or himself. He feared that, this time, his brother-in-law was in too deep for mere words to extricate him.

⁂

"I have some news that you may find distressing, my Lord," Jenkins said.

"That will make a pleasant change!"

Philip's spirit was in no way daunted after three weeks imprisonment, even though Jenkins had informed him the previous day that true bills had been found against all twenty two conspirators, including Monmouth.

"Lord Russell stood trial today and was found guilty."

That came as a shock, but Philip was determined not to lose his composure in front of Jenkins. "Is the King to let him die?" was all he said.

"Indeed he is. His Majesty refuses every offer made for his pardon, for he says that if he does not take Lord Russell's life then Russell will soon have his."

Philip knew that if Charles would not intervene to save Russell, who he liked, then there was little hope of a pardon for himself. "And how is he to die?" he wondered, for hanging, drawing and quartering was the usual penalty for treason.

"Since he is a peer of the realm the sentence has been commuted to beheading though for myself I see not why it should be so, for did not Lord Russell himself endeavour to withhold that courtesy from Stafford when you sent him, innocent, to his death?" Jenkins said.

"I did not send Stafford anywhere. I was in France at the time," Philip reminded him.

"It was you who put him in the Tower, you and your lying confederate, Titus Oates. There is another thing I have to tell you. It concerns Lord Essex.

"Have they tried him too?"

"Lord Essex will never stand trial, my Lord, for he has cut his own throat."

"What a fool," Philip said bitterly. "Charles would certainly have spared him."

"'It is likely that he would," Jenkins said. "The King is much distressed. It happened today, whilst his Majesty was in the Tower."

"What was Charles doing here today?" Philip said.

"He was inspecting some repairs."

Philip frowned. He detected an evasive tone in Jenkins' voice. "You lie. Were there new prisoners brought in?"

"Do you interrogate me now, my Lord?" Jenkins said.

"Were there?"

"Only one."

"Who? Lord Grey? Or is it Ferguson or Thomas Armstrong?"

"None of those, my Lord. We've heard they are all three in Flushing, and the Earl of Argyle too. I am to tell you nothing more."

"When is my trial to be?" Philip said. "Can you tell me that?"

"No, for I do not know. I think the King may save you to the end."

Philip smiled wryly. "A glorious finale? If I am to be incarcerated here much longer then I would request some favours of you."

"What are they?"

"First, a fire."

"It is not usual in July, my Lord."

"I want one, nonetheless." Philip was finding it difficult to disguise the discomfort he was feeling, for the cold and dampness of the Tower were beginning to affect the old wound in his side. "I'll pay for it."

"Very well. I'll have logs sent up. What else?"

"My servant."

"No, my Lord, you may not have your servant, nor may you have brandy. Is there anything more?"

"Not unless I may have visitors."

"Who is it that you want?"

"Who do you think? My wife."

"I fear that is not possible, my Lord." Jenkins turned away, but not before his expression had aroused Philip's suspicions.

"Don't tell me it is Tess that Charles came here to interview?" he said, as the dreadful thought occurred to him. "She is your latest prisoner?"

"I did not mean for you to know, but yes, we have arrested Lady Devalle."

"Theresa can tell you nothing," Philip cried angrily.

"She must have been aware of your plans even if, as you claim, her brother was not. At the very least she must be guilty of misprision of treason. She could stand trial for that if she will not cooperate."

Philip hit his fist into his hand. He was not used to being in situations he could not control, and he found it most frustrating.

"Have your men harmed her? She's pregnant."

"She is still carrying your child," Jenkins assured him. "All care will be taken that no mishap befalls her, even if it may mean that your heir is born in prison."

"But I tell you she had nothing to do with this."

"No more did any of you, if you are to be believed, my Lord," Jenkins retorted. "You cannot save yourself, but you could prevent your wife from further suffering by answering my questions."

"You would like that, wouldn't you? Damn you, Jenkins! Do you believe I would divulge anything to you under such circumstances?"

"You would let your pregnant wife languish in captivity rather than betray your friends? She would not be pleased to learn that, I am sure."

"Because Theresa *is* my wife she would expect me to behave no differently," Philip said, "and nor would she respect me if I did."

After Jenkins had gone Philip called for Haggerty.

"Did you know my wife was imprisoned here?"

"I heard today, my Lord."

"Then why the devil did you not inform me?"

Haggerty jutted out his chin. "I do what I am told, and I was not told to do that."

"Have you no human feelings whatsoever?" Philip asked him incredulously.

"You are a traitor and my prisoner, my Lord. I have no feelings for you but repugnance."

"Haggerty," Philip recommenced, when he had fought back the words he longed to say to this man he had so quickly learned to hate, "do you know where she is?"

"Aye, in the Lieutenant's Lodgings."

"Just across the Green?" Philip's window looked the other way and yet it seemed that even being able to see Tower Green made Theresa feel closer. "Could you smuggle her into me?"

"That I could not, my Lord, even if I would, for she is heavily guarded.

"Are you not acquainted with her guards? I want to see her."

"You cannot, my Lord. It is not allowed."

"But it would be most advantageous to you if, just on this one occasion, you were less rigid in your duty," Philip said, in as pleasing a voice as he could manage under the circumstances.

His gaoler in the Bastille had been a vile man, but even he had responded to the bribes Morgan had given him to make Philip's imprisonment more bearable.

The inexorable Haggerty, however, shook his head. "It

makes no difference what you offer me, my Lord, the answer still is no."

"A warder who is totally incorruptible?" Philip rolled his eyes to heaven as Haggerty stomped off. "What trick of fate is this?"

He lay for a long while on his bed, looking up at the grey stone walls which, at times, seemed to close around him. He was upset about Lord Essex, and Russell too, but mostly his thoughts were with Theresa. He felt enraged at his own impotence to protect the woman he loved so much.

"She is still carrying my child," he reminded himself. "That, at least, is something to be thankful for and, if I know my Tess, it will take more than the Secretary of State, or even the King, to break her spirit."

༝

Theresa was a great disappointment to Secretary Jenkins. Although she looked frail he quickly learned that she was not easily intimidated. After two weeks imprisonment Theresa still defied him.

He decided to ask the King's advice.

"I was wondering what to do about Lady Devalle, your Majesty."

"I am beginning to fear there is little point in holding her any longer," Charles said. "It appears that nothing can be proved against her save concealment of treason."

"Even that is punishable by law, your Majesty," Jenkins protested.

"But can I exact that punishment from a pregnant woman?" Charles said. "She would fast become a martyr with the mob, and I daren't risk that. Even the Queen, who she once wronged, has interceded for her. Her Majesty asks very little of me, Jenkins, but she did beg for this and I believe she would have begged for

Devalle's life also if she thought it would do any good, for she always liked him."

"Perhaps if you were to talk with Lady Devalle again yourself," Jenkins said, but Charles shook his head.

"I want no more to do with her. The last time I saw her she not only had the impudence to complain of her husband's treatment but she swore my brother had her kidnapped and, what is more, she told the tale as though it really happened. She is dangerous, Jenkins, and always will be as long as there are those who still glorify the likes of Shaftesbury and Devalle. I want her out of England. See to it."

"And has your Majesty made any decision regarding the Duke of Monmouth?" Jenkins asked, whilst he had Charles' ear. He had informed the King a month ago that Monmouth was at Henrietta Wentworth's house at Toddington, but still no action had been taken to arrest him.

The truth was that, despite the five hundred pounds Charles had offered as a reward for Monmouth's capture, Jenkins knew the King had no wish to see his son arrested. He would not believe Monmouth capable of cold-bloodedly planning to kill him and he would have liked it best if the charges against him could be quietly forgotten.

Of course this was not possible, not whilst Philip and the rest of Monmouth's friends were being brought to justice.

"I will consider what is best to be done regarding my son," he told Jenkins coldly.

Jenkins knew well enough what that meant.

Nothing.

NINETEEN

✑

Philip was asleep. He was sleeping a good deal of the time lately. The fire Jenkins had allowed him had helped his stiffness and he was trying to exercise as best as he could within the confines of his cell, but the idleness enforced upon one who normally led so busy a life was causing lethargy to overtake him. His energy and powers of concentration deserted him after very short periods, leaving him both mentally and physically drained.

In an effort to win his cooperation Jenkins had sent him some books to ease the boredom, but it was a struggle for Philip to read at the best of times so these were not much of a comfort and the time passed slowly.

He did not hear a soft footfall on the bare stone floor, but he did feel a gentle hand stroke his cheek.

Philip stirred and opened his eyes. "Tess?" he said disbelievingly.

He stared at her for a second, fearing she was a figment of his dream and then he smiled as the sweet reality dawned upon him.

"Jenkins said I could see you, just for a short while."

He pulled her to him and held her so close that he could feel the beating of her heart.

"My little sweetheart! Have they hurt you?"

"No, I am not hurt and I am free to go," Theresa said shakily. "That's splendid!"

"No, it isn't, for I have been exiled." She bit her lip. "I cannot keep my promise to you now, Philip, and I did so want to keep it."

"Promise?" He kissed her forehead and her damp eyelids. "What promise can't you keep, my pet?"

"To fight for Heatherton."

"Oh, that. Don't worry, you'll be back."

"I can't come back, not ever. The King has told me so."

Philip stood up and led her over to the window, where the light was better, for he wanted very much to look at her.

The girlish innocence was gone from her elfin features and there were lines of grief etched there which might never be quite erased but, to him, Theresa had never looked lovelier. In place of the idealistic young girl he had once been forced to marry he saw a woman, proud and strong, able to face what lay ahead and bear her sorrow with dignity but, most of all, he saw a woman who cared for him honestly and devotedly.

"Listen, my darling, High Heatherton is yours by right upon my death and none can take it away from you. Go to France and have our child. Giles will watch over you and you can stay in our Paris house. Even Charles can't live forever and when he dies, no matter whether it is the Duke of York or the Orangeman who takes the throne, you may return and live in safety."

"How can you be so sure?" Theresa said.

"Never mind that, just accept that it is so because I have taken steps to make sure of it."

Theresa laid her head upon his chest. "You are a clever man, Philip."

"Not quite clever enough this time," he said ruefully. "I gambled once too often and I lost, but at least your future, and that of our child, is secure."

She raised sad grey eyes to his. "I am grateful, believe me, but I would sacrifice everything to have you beside me for the rest of my life."

"I fear there is but little chance of that," he said softly.

⌘

Monmouth bowed low before his father. "It was gracious of you to grant me this interview."

"Why should I not see you, James?" Charles said "Why would any father not wish to see his son, even if that son has erred against him."

"Have you not read the letter I sent you?" Monmouth asked.

"Read it? Yes, a dozen times I've read it, and it still makes no sense to me. Neither can I fathom what you're doing here in London when you know there is a reward of five hundred pounds offered for your capture."

"I could not bear to have you angry with me any longer." Monmouth, who was an affectionate person, took both his father's hands in his and kissed them. "Do you not believe the things I wrote?"

"That you never plotted against me and your uncle? How can I believe that?" Charles asked. "You were present at the meetings Devalle held. You heard his plan to waylay us."

"But Philip never planned to kill you," Monmouth said. "On the contrary, he promised me that he would not."

"And you believed him? Am I to accept that my son is a villain or that he is a fool, taken in by one he knows to be corrupt?"

"But Philip would not lie to me," Monmouth protested. "He has been my companion ever since he came to Court and he has shown me nothing but loyalty. He is a good friend, the best that I have ever had."

"If you believe that then you are indeed a fool. Devalle has used you for his own ends, just as Shaftesbury did." Charles still smarted at the memory of his son standing bail for Shaftesbury two years before when it had been the Earl who was accused of treason. "Why will you not see it? If you truly wish to please me then you must denounce him for the traitor that he is."

"Speak out against Philip?" Monmouth looked appalled. "I could not do it."

"Then do not ever hope for my forgiveness if you side with those who plot against me."

"Don't say that, Father," Monmouth pleaded. "You know I love you very much. May I die as I stand here if it is not so."

Charles regarded him despairingly. For all his elegant bearing and the military command he had once held, Monmouth was still a spoilt and impulsive child, so immature as to imagine that a declaration of his love could undo any wrongs he might have done to his father. Charles found it an endearing trait, nonetheless, and few fathers had ever forgiven their sons so much.

"It is not only I who you have offended," he pointed out. "There is your uncle too, and you will not win him over easily."

"I told you in my letter that I would be prepared to leave England if it would show my good intentions toward him."

"You did say that," Charles agreed, "but he is not impressed with extravagancies of speech."

"What will impress him then?" Monmouth said sulkily.

"The only way to demonstrate your good intent to your uncle would be to do what I ask and condemn Philip."

"That is the only way?"

"Yes. The choice is yours. Remain a fugitive or confess everything you know," Charles insisted.

Monmouth sought the advice of the Marquis of Halifax, who was the Lord Privy Seal. Halifax was a born mediator; it was he who had set up the meeting between Monmouth and his father in the first place. He was not too successful as a politician because he tended to take the side of whoever he thought was right, regardless of their political allegiance, but as a man of independent judgement Halifax was the ideal person to act as a go-between.

"I fail to see quite where the problem lies, your Grace," he said when Monmouth had related the outcome of his interview with Charles. "His Majesty has made it plain that, should you but confess, he and the Duke of York will pardon you. What more can you ask?"

"I never thought that I would be expected to inform against my friend," Monmouth said unhappily.

"What difference does it make? Lord Howard turned King's Evidence after he was arrested so your father already knows of Devalle's guilt."

"I still won't accuse him. What Philip did he did for me."

"Whatever Philip Devalle did he did for himself," Halifax said in an exasperated tone. Not even the knowledge that Philip, like himself, was now supporting William of Orange could endear him to Halifax.

"My father says that too, but if you only knew him as I do you would think much better of him."

Halifax considered the situation, weighing up the characters of those involved. There was York, stubborn and implacable, the King, desiring most of all reassurance of his son's affections and Monmouth, bewitched by Philip. Monmouth could be stubborn too, and he might throw away his own chance of salvation if Halifax did not handle him very carefully.

"Maybe you are right about Lord Devalle and I am wrong," he said smoothly.

Monmouth looked surprised. "Then you allow that there is good in him?"

"You see it, and who am I to doubt your judgement?" asked the urbane Halifax. "I wonder only how you may best aid him in his plight."

"There is no way," Monmouth said sadly. "If there were then I would gladly do it, even if it meant that I offered myself to die in his stead."

"I don't believe your father would consider such a sacrifice,"

Halifax said hastily. "In my view you could best help Devalle by pleasing his Majesty and his Grace the Duke."

"But to please them I would need to condemn Philip as a traitor," Monmouth said. "How would that help him?"

"I don't think he will be tried this year. You will have the opportunity to first endear yourself to your father and then beg a favour of him, say, that Lord Devalle might suffer a term of imprisonment instead, or even exile with his wife."

Monmouth was no match for the wiles of such as Halifax. Guided for so long by Shaftesbury and inspired by Philip, he was a person lost without a mentor.

"What do you think I should do?" he said.

"Why, what the King desires. Tell him you will write a full confession. You can first ask for his undertaking that it will not be made public, that way none need ever know that you have spoken out against your friends. I will help you write it, if you like."

"Then, when the time is right, will you assist me when I beg for Philip's life?"

"Have I not said so?"

Monmouth could not recall that he had, but he thought it better not to pursue the matter, for he did not want to alienate the influential Privy Seal. His heart felt lighter as he left Halifax's office.

It was not so light, however, as his carriage passed Philip and Theresa's house in Cheapside and he was reminded of what he had actually promised to do.

"What will Philip think of me if he gets to hear of it?" Monmouth asked himself. "He'll deem me no better than Howard. I must let him know, somehow, that my sole intention is to save him. I'll tell Theresa," he decided. "She will understand."

Theresa was a little taken aback to see Monmouth on her doorstep. "Whatever are you doing in London?" she said, ushering him inside quickly. "They will take you."

"Do not fear for me, Theresa, I am safe enough," Monmouth assured her. "I was glad to hear that my father has pardoned you."

"He has not pardoned me," Theresa said bitterly. "He's exiled me. I have until the end of the year to sort out my affairs in England and spend some time with my family in Dorset before I must leave."

"But surely that is not so bad," Monmouth said. "At least your baby won't be born in prison."

"Neither will it be born at Heatherton. " Theresa patted her slightly swollen abdomen. "I suppose I should be grateful for the King's mercy and to the Queen, who, I understand, begged it of him, but I dread the thought of returning to France alone. If you truly love your Lady Wentworth you will understand me when I say that I don't know how I shall face life without Philip."

Monmouth pressed her hand. "It may be that you won't have to," he said mysteriously. "How is he?"

"They have only let me see him once, and it was an experience that will haunt me forever. He was so resigned to everything. I believe he accepts that he is to die in the Tower, for a fortune-teller once predicted he would end his days a prisoner."

Monmouth, who was a devout believer in astrological predictions, looked alarmed. "Then perhaps there is nothing I can do for him after all."

"What were you planning to do?" Theresa said, without too much enthusiasm. Although she liked Monmouth, she had no faith in him whatsoever.

"Lord Halifax and I have discussed a plan which may yet save him," Monmouth told her proudly.

"Lord Halifax, you say?" Theresa turned her eyes despairingly toward Morgan, who had just entered with some refreshment for the Duke. "You have discussed a plan to save my husband with Lord Halifax?"

"That's right."

"But Halifax hates him."

"You are wrong, Theresa, for he said that he would trust my judgement in the matter and if I can see good in Philip then there must be good. I think those were his words." He nodded. "Yes, I'm sure they were. He said I should endear myself once more to both my father and my uncle and then, when I am back in favour, I can crave a pardon for Philip as a personal reward."

"How will you endear yourself?" Theresa said.

"Why, I'll make a full confession, tell them everything I know about the Rye House Plot."

Theresa stared at him, thinking for a moment that he was making some sick jest, but then she sighed as she realised he wasn't.

"What do you think?" Monmouth said.

"What do I think?" Theresa stood up angrily, but Morgan put a finger to his lips and she sank down weakly in her chair again. "I think it makes no difference what you do, your Grace. I pray that matters turn out well for you, for there are still those who see you as the Protestant salvation. For that reason you should save yourself at all costs."

"But you will make sure that Philip knows the reason I have confessed?" Monmouth said worriedly.

"I'll tell him, if they let me see him again," Theresa promised. "You should go now for, until you make your peace with Whitehall, there is still a reward upon your head and you may find some who are not too particular as to how they collect it."

When Monmouth had left her Theresa could not hold back her tears. "That is the dunderhead for who we have all risked our lives, Morgan. Monmouth will leave this as free as air, fawned on by his besotted father, who has not even had him arrested, whilst Philip and the others face death. It can't be fair."

Morgan agreed. Later, without a word to anyone, he quietly left the house.

⌒

Morgan walked to Strand Bridge. He had an hour to wait before a certain boat pulled in beneath the bridge and he approached it silently.

The waterman looked up. "Do you want oars, sir?"

"No. I want to talk with you."

"My boat's for hire, sir, not my tongue."

"I wish to contact Thomas."

The burly fellow glanced around him. "Who is Thomas?"

"Your nephew, I believe, or so you told us on the night you took us in your boat to Rotherhithe. I am Lord Devalle's man."

The boatman scrutinised him closely. "Yes, you could be. What is it you want with Thomas?"

"To talk with him, that is all. Lord Devalle is in trouble."

"So I've heard, and I am sorry for his Lordship, but Thomas has some trouble of his own."

"I know, and I shall not endanger him. I only want to ask him something. I'll meet him anywhere he cares to name and with whomsoever he pleases, if you do not trust me. Tell him it is Morgan."

"He has taken risks enough for your master," the waterman said. "He's back amongst his own kind now. Leave him be."

Morgan knew he was in no position to argue. "The choice must be his," he said. "I'll come back tomorrow night at ten o'clock to learn from you whether he will meet me. If he decides he'd rather not then I will understand and bear him no ill feeling."

Morgan returned the following night and the waterman was there to meet him.

"You're to come with me."

Morgan climbed into the boat, though not without

misgivings. He knew Thomas would never wish him harm but he had no way of knowing if his message had even been delivered, or whether the boatman had decided to take matters into his own hands and dispose of someone he thought to be endangering Thomas' life. They travelled in silence over to Bankside and stopped before the Bear Garden.

"He will find you," the boatman said. "Come here when you're done and I will row you back."

Morgan had only walked a few yards before he heard his name called softly. Looking around he could just make out Thomas in the darkness, beckoning to him from amongst the trees.

Morgan smiled. Thomas had not let him down.

He was ragged and dirty, for he had no clothes save those he had been wearing on the day of Philip's arrest, and he was considerably thinner.

Morgan told him how matters gone for Theresa and of Philip's situation.

Thomas' face was sombre when he'd finished. "Is there nothing to be done for him? No hope at all?"

"The mistress was trusting in some intervention from the King of France, but last month the news came that his Queen had died suddenly and that King Louis had broken his arm whilst riding and has practically no contact with the world at present. It was her last hope gone. There are few left now who would help him or, in truth, who could."

"Then he is really going to die?" Thomas could barely say the dreadful words.

"They executed Russell," Morgan said grimly.

Thomas shuddered. "I heard about that. They say it took three cuts before Lord Russell's head came off. I can't bear to think about it, Morgan. Is there no way we can save him?"

"But one way that's occurred to me, and that depends on you, my friend."

"Ask anything of me and I will do it, anything at all," Thomas vowed. "I would give myself up willingly if I thought I could help him by doing so."

"That will not be necessary," Morgan said, "but you are obviously better acquainted than I as to what happened after Newmarket. It seems to me that if we could prove the master foiled the plot against King Charles' life then, no matter what else he might have done, he would be shown to be the King's saviour rather than a traitor."

"Prove it? You mean with witnesses?"

"There must be some we met who would remember us. The keeper at the inn we went to in Newmarket, for a start, and any others you and he encountered along the way whilst I was unconscious."

Thomas frowned thoughtfully. "There was a girl he spent the night with at St. Albans, and then there was the farmhouse which I robbed and Buckingham's bay, it's possible that has been found. But how do you propose to seek these people out, Morgan? They were spread from Newmarket to Richmond!"

"I shall find them, with the help of the mistress. If I offer myself upon the witness stand and tell my part in it perhaps the jury may go softer with him."

"They may charge you both with murder," Thomas warned. "The groom in the stable was killed and the owner of the cart which his Lordship stole. He shot a soldier too."

"The King may show mercy if it was all on his account."

"He may not."

Morgan shrugged. "I'll take that chance, for I doubt it can much worsen the master's situation. I'd like you to think back to everything that happened and list down all the details as plain as you remember them. Ask your waterman friend to meet me at the bridge with it tomorrow night. I'll do the rest."

"He'll be there," Thomas said.

"Good. Get back now to the safety of your hiding place, for I would never want to be the cause of your undoing."

Thomas sighed. "I wish I could come home with you."

"You are safe in Alsatia, aren't you?" Morgan asked anxiously.

"At present, though I can't stay there much longer, for my credit's nearly gone."

"Your credit?"

"Yes. You must give something for your keep and your protection. I had to offer them a bracelet which Giles gave me on the day he sailed, but I must soon go back to thieving and it is risky now, with a warrant out for me. I may well try to get to France when things have quietened down a little here. Giles will look after me."

"What will you use to pay your fare?"

"I still have the watch his Lordship gave me." Thomas patted his pocket. "I can sell that if I truly need to, though it would break my heart to part with it."

"I'll bring some money for you when I meet with the waterman tomorrow," Morgan promised.

Thomas looked moved and turned aside to hide a tear. He had not shed many tears during his short life but parting from Morgan, who had been like a father to him, was hard.

Even Morgan, who was not much given to emotion, was finding the moment poignant.

"I beg you, Thomas, to be wary," he said gruffly. "If we should hear that anything had befallen you then Bet and the mistress would be beside themselves with grief."

It was the closest Morgan could come to saying how much he cared, but Thomas understood and gave him a brief hug before blending like a shadow into the dark night.

Morgan took the boat to St. Paul's Wharf and slowly walked the short distance to their house, behind the Cathedral. The decision to contact Thomas was one he had made alone. Theresa still knew nothing of their Newmarket adventure, nor had Philip planned to tell her of it but, in view of the desperate nature of the situation, Morgan felt justified in betraying his master's confidence.

❧

Theresa sat silently whilst Morgan related to her everything that had happened at Newmarket. Bet, to whom the tale was also new, dabbed her eyes upon her apron when she heard the true story of how Morgan came to break his leg and of all that her master had done to keep him safe.

Theresa also found the story touching, although she was not surprised to learn that Philip had risked his life for Morgan. Nor was she surprised that the Welshman was prepared to risk his now.

"I trust I acted right, my Lady," Morgan finished. "In truth I cannot think of any other way that we might save him now."

Before Theresa could answer him there was an urgent knocking on the front door.

Bet went to the door cautiously. Since the dreadful night when the soldiers had come to Heatherton to take Theresa they had all been on edge. As she opened it she cried out in surprise and pleasure.

It was Thomas.

Bet pulled him inside, crushing him to her ample bosom so that it was all he could do to breathe!

Theresa, hearing the commotion, ran to the door and embraced him too. "Oh, Thomas, we've been so worried about you. You should not have risked coming here, but it is so good to see you."

"It was a foolish thing to do," Morgan agreed worriedly.

"Well foolish or not, I have done it," Thomas said. "I'm going to help you find the witnesses and, what is more, I intend to surrender myself when the time is right."

"Thomas, no!" Theresa protested. "You must do no such a thing."

"If you find these witnesses, my Lady, you have still to bring them to a court of law. They were mostly country people; they will be nervous and they may be incoherent. The gentlemen of the bench will make mincemeat out of them and Morgan, though I know he'll do his best, can't tell the story the way I can. If I appear as a witness then all the others will have to do is to corroborate what I say."

"But Thomas, you are already a wanted criminal. They may hang you."

"I have come to the conclusion that life as I have lived it these last few weeks is not worth living anyway," Thomas said. "I can't go back to hiding in corners, waiting always for the sound of the sergeant's boots when I dare to show my face. The master rescued me from that. I'll wager the existence I have now for the chance of his freedom and my pardon."

Theresa looked at him with real admiration. "Thomas, go to France and join my brother. We will get you away somehow."

Thomas only smiled. "You'll not refuse my help because you love his Lordship, as do all of us."

"What am I to do with him?" Theresa asked Bet and Morgan. "We cannot let him sacrifice himself upon so slender a chance."

"It may be our best chance though," Morgan admitted reluctantly.

"You're a good lad, Thomas." Bet kissed him on both cheeks. "I'm proud of you. Now go and change out of those filthy clothes. You smell worse than you did the day we first took you in!"

Thomas winked at Theresa as Bet bustled off with him. "It would seem you are outvoted, my Lady!"

TWENTY

❧

As the carriage entered St. Albans Theresa tapped upon the panel that divided her from Jonathon and Ned.

"Stop here, please, there is a stable. Thomas, do you think that might be where Philip left Ferrion?"

"It has to be the place, for I can see the inn a little further down the street," Thomas said.

"Then you and Morgan go and see the ostler. It's for certain he'll remember the horse, if not the rider. Bet and I will find the girl."

Heads turned as the two women entered the inn alone and seated themselves at a table.

Theresa nudged Bet. "That's her for sure."

Audrey, unaware of their scrutiny, chatted perkily to two young men, wiggling her hips provocatively as she turned away.

"She's pretty," Theresa allowed reluctantly, "and well made."

Bet looked at her doubtfully, but Theresa read her thoughts.

"Don't worry, Bet, I'll not cause any trouble. Why should I? Has this girl done worse than any of the many others he has bedded in his time?"

"Why no, in fact she's done much better, for at least she provided him with a night's rest when he needed it!"

Theresa laughed. Bet's matter-of-factness always brought her round if her thoughts became unruly and, just for a second, they had.

Audrey approached their table. "What do you require, good ladies?"

"A little of your time, Miss Audrey, that is all," Bet said.

"Who are you and how do you know my name?" Audrey said warily.

"We've been told about you. Sit down beside us if you please."

"Why? I've done nothing wrong," Audrey protested, her voice rising.

Bet grabbed her firmly by the wrist. "I said sit down."

Audrey sat.

"In answer to your first question," Bet continued, "this is Lady Devalle."

Audrey gasped at the mention of that famous name. "You are the wife of Lord Philip Devalle, my Lady?"

"I have that honour, although it is a dubious one at present," Theresa said, all remnants of hostility fading away when she saw how terrified Audrey was of her. "My husband is in a great deal of trouble, you see, and I have come to you for help."

"Me?" Audrey frowned. "Are you playing tricks on me? How can I help him?"

"Do you recall a gentleman named Thomas, who spent the night with you when the fair was here in March?"

Audrey's brow cleared. "Thomas? Oh yes, I remember him alright. He was a handsome man was Thomas." She spoke wistfully, her eyes taking on a faraway look. "Wait, though," she regarded them both suspiciously, "What has Thomas got to do with Lord Devalle?"

"The man you knew as Thomas *is* Lord Devalle."

That news obviously came as a considerable shock. Audrey blanched and clutched onto the table. "Do you mean that I actually made love to...," she looked elated for a second and then the smile quickly faded from her lips, "... your husband?"

"Yes, that's right, but don't be troubled by it. I'm not," Theresa lied.

"You're not angry with me?"

"Not at all. He is a most attractive man and you are not the first to fall for him, but I meant it when I said you could help him."

"What have I to do?" Audrey said cautiously.

"You must appear in a court of law and tell the jury exactly what you just told me."

Audrey gasped. "In court? What has he done?"

"He has done a great many things, but now he stands accused of something he has not done. Do you know what is meant by an alibi, Audrey?"

"No, my Lady."

"An alibi is when a person can prove he was elsewhere when a crime was committed. I, on the contrary, need to establish that my husband was at the scene of a crime, and it would help me to do that if I could prove he spent that particular night with you. Do you understand?"

Audrey plainly didn't, but she seemed eager to assist, for all that, and Theresa arranged that the carriage would be sent to bring her to London when the time came.

"There, that wasn't too bad was it?" Theresa asked Bet when Audrey had left them. "Did I not behave myself?"

"You did better than I would have done," Bet said darkly. "If it had been Morgan she had lain with I would likely have slapped her."

"Much use that would be in persuading her to help us," Theresa laughed. "I thought you were the practical one!"

Whilst they waited for Morgan and Thomas to join them Theresa listened idly to the conversation of the four gentlemen at the next table. She paid it no particular attention until the name of Monmouth was mentioned. She looked over toward them and her glance fell on a copy of the 'London Gazette', lying on the table.

"Excuse me, may I see that please?" They looked at her in surprise, but passed the paper over. She scanned it quickly and gasped.

"What is it?" Bet said, seeing the colour drain from her face.

"He's done it,"Theresa said weakly. "Monmouth's made a full confession and they've published it. He's named them all, even his followers in Cheshire and the West. Oh, Bet, how could he, after all we've done for him? "

Bet took the paper from her. "Lord Devalle misled me from my duty to the King," she read out in a trembling voice. "He filled my head with thoughts of rebellion against my father and my uncle, though I was unaware of the evil designs he had upon the lives of those two noble persons."

They looked at one another in despair.

"We won't give up, Bet,"Theresa vowed.

"No, that we won't," Bet agreed. "I hope his Grace feels well pleased with himself when he reads this."

⁓

Monmouth was far from pleased.

He waved a copy of the 'London Gazette' angrily at Halifax. "I have been duped. Everything I have confessed is printed here, and I was promised it would not be made public. This is my uncle's doing, I'll be bound. He cannot stand me being back in favour with my father."

"It very likely is the Duke of York's doing," Halifax said, "but I see no reason the article will harm you."

"What? It would appear from this that I have turned King's Evidence and betrayed my friends, as Howard did. I have a good mind to retract it, yes that is what I'll do. I will deny it all."

"You can't do that, your Grace. The King has pardoned you on account of this confession," Halifax reminded him. "Not only that, he's given you six thousand pounds in gratitude for your admissions. If you retract now you will have the devil's own job to win him over again."

"I'm going to do it all the same," Monmouth said, "for he made me a promise which he did not keep. The world must know that I am not a man of so little honour that I would inform against my friends."

"But if the King rescinds your pardon then you yourself may have to stand trial," Halifax pointed out patiently. "Surely the best way to save your friends, Lord Devalle in particular, is for you to be free and with influence again."

Monmouth considered that. "I suppose so. When do you think I should approach my father on Philip's behalf?" he wondered, already forgetting the delicacy of his own situation.

"Not yet, not for a long while yet," Halifax said hastily.

"But Sydney is soon to be tried and Philip will surely be next. It is nearly November and they have held him now for four months without a trial. I'll warrant we shall hear any day when it is to be."

But November came and went.

Algernon Sydney was found guilty in a trial made discreditable by the interruptions and harassment of Judge Jeffries, and he was executed early in December.

Of Philip's future or, indeed, of his condition, there was no word.

There was even some speculation on the streets that he was already dead. A broadsheet was circulated entitled 'A History of the New Plot' and it showed not only Lord Russell's execution and the suicide of Lord Essex but also Philip dying of sickness in prison.

Although that winter was a bitter one, the coldest the Londoners ever remembered, Philip, within the icy stone walls of the Tower, survived it.

"Lord Devalle is a strong man," Sir Leoline Jenkins said to Charles, soon after Sydney's death. "He suffers agonies from the cold and yet he still does not break. There is nothing to be done with him. He had more spirit than the lot of them."

"Are you surprised?" Charles said. "Philip Devalle has many faults but he has never been short of either courage or resolve. To class him with such as Lord Howard is to insult him."

"Yet he is as guilty," Jenkins put in quickly.

"He is more guilty, damn him. Such scum as we have arrested could never have formed so bold a plan without his leadership, any more than my son could have been persuaded to plot against the government."

Charles no longer spoke of Monmouth plotting against himself.

"Am I to continue with the visits to Lord Devalle?" Jenkins asked.

Charles shook his head. "We will learn nothing from him. I could have told you so at the beginning. Let him stand trial. At least then we shall have his life and I shall not be troubled by any more wretched petitions. I have even received some from France, including one from Monsieur, if you please. My own cousin!"

"He has the ability to draw men to him, it would seem," Jenkins said sourly.

"Indeed he has, and I much regret that a man who can beguile so many into following him was not better harnessed than by Shaftesbury. Has he asked for anything?"

"Only that his manservant may be permitted to attend upon him. He has requested that each time we speak."

"Let him have his servant, and anything else he wants. He has but little time left. Make no mistake Sir Leoline, I spare no pity for him," Charles said, seeing Jenkins' expression of disapproval, "and I shall not intervene to save him, but you must allow me to respect the memory of his late father and a Philip I knew long ago. Besides, he is still a peer of the realm and he has rights which I should not deny him any longer."

℘

Morgan was not to be found, either in London or at Heatherton, and that news had a profound effect upon Philip.

Morgan had been his mainstay through a good many difficult periods of his life and he had become quite dependent on him. The Welshman understood him as no other person ever had, and Philip knew he could bear anything, even the horrors which lay ahead, if he only had Morgan at his side.

His spirits sank lower during the two weeks that followed than they had done during the whole of his incarceration. He knew nothing of the petitions the King was receiving on his behalf or of the efforts being made by Theresa and his loyal servants. Philip felt deserted by one and all.

Christmas Eve brought a letter from Monmouth, although that was more of a pain than a pleasure, since Philip found the Duke's flowery handwriting even harder to read than he had the books Jenkins had sent him. He was sitting on his bed, vainly attempting to decipher the missive, when he heard Haggerty speaking to someone outside his cell.

Philip was cold, despite the fire burning in the grate and the blanket he had draped over his shoulders, and he was not in a good mood.

"What is it now?" he asked tetchily, as his door was unlocked. "Have you brought Jenkins back to annoy me with more gleeful tales of the demise of my friends? Whatever it is, tell me quickly and be gone, for there is nothing more obnoxious to me than the sight of your ugly face."

"I see the Tower has not improved your disposition my Lord!"

Philip started at the sound of the wonderfully familiar Welsh accent. Just to hear that voice made him feel as though he were home again. "Morgan!"

They clasped each other in a tight embrace, both overcome with emotion. "Where the hell have you been?" Philip demanded, when he could trust himself to speak again. "I have been asking for you ever since they brought me to this damned place and when Charles finally agrees to my request you are nowhere to be found."

"I was upon your business, my Lord."

"My business? I have no business now, and you have no duties save to care for me," Philip said. "Is that so onerous? It is only for a few more weeks."

"I shall not leave your side again," Morgan promised.

"I should hope not. Now, tell me, how is your mistress?"

"She is well, my Lord, and your child kicks and turns inside her. He'll be strong."

Philip felt wistful. This was the one child of the many he had sired that he would dearly love to have been able to see. "When does she leave for France? The year is almost ended."

"Yes, my Lord."

Philip frowned. There was something in Morgan's tone which aroused his suspicions. "Surely she intends to visit me before she goes, or has she left already? Is that it?"

"She has not left," Morgan said uneasily.

"Come, out with it, Morgan. From you I would expect the truth. Grant me that courtesy, or do you think me grown so feeble-minded in captivity that I can no longer face reality?" Philip asked. "If she has gone just tell me so."

"She has not gone, but I fear you will not like what I am going to tell you all the same, for she has decided not to go."

"Not go?" Philip's brain was not so dulled by inactivity that he was unable to comprehend the consequences of such an action. "But she must go or she will lose Heatherton. Charles could take it from her if she openly she defies him. What has induced her to act so foolishly, and why have you not stopped her?"

Morgan took a deep breath, as though not relishing what he was about to say. "We're going to try to save you. That is the reason I was out of town and also why the mistress will not leave until you are tried."

Philip stared at him. "What are you talking about, man? I have no salvation. They are going to kill me, can you not accept that?"

"No, I can't," Morgan said flatly, "and nor can Thomas."

"You've seen Thomas? How is he?" Philip asked eagerly, for he had been worried to distraction over the fate of his young servant.

"Thomas is back with us now, and as determined as the mistress and I to see you freed. He intends to surrender himself to the authorities in order to give evidence on your behalf."

"No, he must not," Philip said, appalled. "What is this nonsense anyway? If Charles let Russell die, and Sydney too, he'll not spare my life."

"Not even if he learns the truth, that you saved his?"

Philip listened, stunned, as Morgan related everything they had done on his behalf.

"You and Thomas are a pair of sentimental fools," he said when Morgan had finished. "They'll hang you both for this. You will not testify."

"But it may clear your name of treason."

"To hell with my name! I used to think it mattered, but it doesn't. All that matters is Theresa, High Heatherton and my child. Defend them and you will serve me in the best way that you can."

"Do you think I will let you die if there's but half a chance that I can save you?" Morgan said.

"But you can't. It was even prophesied that I would die in a prison." Philip had been thinking a good deal about that lately.

"You did not die in the Bastille, my Lord, despite that prophesy," Morgan reminded him.

Philip dismissed that with a wave of his hand. "The time had not come then. Now it has. You're not to do this, do you hear me? I forbid it. Think of Bet, if not about yourself."

"Bet will manage very well without me if she must. She's as determined on this as the rest of us, and she knows full well where my duty lies."

"Morgan, your duty to me is nearly ended," Philip said sadly.

Morgan shook his head. "Never, not whilst I draw breath."

"Is this why I saved your life after Newmarket? To sacrifice it for my ambition?" Philip cried. "I had no noble motives, you know. I did what they say; I plotted against the King, and I did it in order that I might have Shaftesbury's help to gain High Heatherton. You cannot give your life for that, and as for Thomas, thanks to me he's already wanted by the law for helping Giles to escape."

"We have both pledged our lives to you already, my Lord, and, as we see it, it makes little difference whether we lay them down this way or in some skirmish."

"There is every difference, my friend, for in a skirmish at least you would have a chance." Philip had not allowed himself to hope for a reprieve but now, despite his protestations, he was starting to consider the prospect. Even so he made one last attempt to dissuade his devoted servants from an action which he still feared might be futile. "I entreat you not to do this rash thing, for I am not worth it."

"You," Morgan said quietly, "are worthy of all a man can give." He picked up the letter which Philip had been struggling to decipher when he came in. "Shall I read this to you?" he asked, changing the subject.

Philip knew when he was beaten. "Yes, please. It's from Monmouth."

"My dearest Philip," Morgan read, "it is with deep regret I must inform you that the reconciliation with my father, upon which I had set such store, has been thwarted by the evil intent of the Duke of York. That which they ask of me I cannot do, for they would force me to give evidence against you at your trial, and such was never my intent, but only to save you. May I die as I am writing this if such is not the case. I have told my father I shall never be the instrument he uses to condemn my friends, especially you. During the next few days I shall be taking leave of this country, even though my father has begged me to stay. My thoughts are ever with you and, should affairs go well for you, I heartily pray that we shall be together again one day. Your loving friend, James."

"Exit Monmouth," Philip said with a sigh.

Morgan screwed up the letter and threw it on the fire disgustedly, muttering something in his native tongue.

"At least he has refused to appear at my trial, which is something, I suppose." Philip had not truly expected any help from Monmouth but the ease with which the Duke had abandoned him was hurtful nonetheless.

Morgan crossly added more logs to the blaze in the hearth. "Perhaps you'll have the sense to turn away from him the next time he comes to you for aid."

Philip smiled wryly at that. "The next time?"

"Yes, my Lord."

"Do you honestly think to save me, Morgan?"

Morgan looked up from his task and their eyes locked for a moment.

"Yes, my Lord, I do."

TWENTY ONE

❧

"Must I remind you, my good man, of who I am?" Titus Oates asked the Captain of the Guard stationed at the Bulwark Gate of the Tower.

"No, Doctor Oates, I know who you are well enough. What I need to know is the nature of your business here?"

"I wish to see Lord Devalle, naturally. I understand he can be visited now."

"But not by everybody. You need a permit signed by the Secretary of State."

"Well I haven't got one," Titus said dismissively. "I demand that you admit me."

"If I let enter all who came to see him I'd have a line of them from here to his cell," the Captain said. "I can't allow just anyone in."

"I'm not just anyone. I am Doctor Titus Oates," Titus squeaked, growing ruddier by the minute, "and I want to see Lord Devalle."

"I've told you, half of London wants to see him. What makes you think he will want to see you?"

Titus folded his hands in a pious pose. "I am his Lordship's chaplain. It may be that I can offer him some spiritual comfort."

"Very well," the Captain said heavily, "but he has a visitor already, his tailor, and I fancy Lord Devalle will find more comfort in his wares than in any of your prayers and sermons, Doctor Oates!"

Titus passed through, looking disgruntled. He gave his name airily to Haggerty, who grimaced. He obviously needed no prompting to recognise the infamous Doctor Oates either!

"Shall you see Titus Oates?" he asked Philip, entering his cell unceremoniously.

"But of course, with pleasure."

"No accounting for taste," Haggerty muttered as Titus swept past him.

"Don't mind my warder, he's a pig," Philip said, smiling as Haggerty slammed the door shut after him. "Titus, this is good of you. Oh God, don't cry or I shall make you leave. I don't look that bad, surely!"

"You look wonderful," Titus sniffed, seizing his hand and kissing it, "but I cannot bear to think of what they're going to do to you."

"*Might* do to me," Philip corrected him. "You are supposed to speak as though you have an element of doubt. It is only I who am allowed to say outright that I am going to die!"

Philip's tailor, Monsieur Robertin, tutted to himself. "It would be a wicked waste of one so handsome, my Lord."

"Now there I do agree with you, although I suspect you grieve my passing mostly on account of all my business you will lose."

"Not so, not so at all," the little Frenchman protested, "besides I shall still use your name to my advantage. I have already ordered a sign to be written which says, 'Pierre Robertin, tailor to the late Lord Philip Devalle'."

This caused Titus to sob out loud. "How can the wretch be so callous?"

"Hush, hush." Philip managed to find a handkerchief about his person and tossed it to him. "He is not callous, but only a businessman. Anyway I think he's joking." He looked over his shoulder at the tailor, who concentrated very hard upon the pleat he was pinning. "Well perhaps not, but he has served me well over the years, so why should my name not serve him?"

"I don't see what you want a tailor here for anyway," Titus said, pocketing the handkerchief.

"I want him here because I want to look my very, very best on the sixteenth of this month." The sixteenth of January was the date set for Philip's trial. "Call it my final vanity, if you will. It is probably my last appearance on this worldly stage, other than my execution, and I fancy this attire will do for both occasions!"

The outfit Philip had chosen was of black brocade, trimmed with shining gold lace. Upon his right shoulder there was cloth of gold knot, and long gold tassels hung from the black satin sash fastened around his slender waist. He had lost some weight during his imprisonment, a fact much bemoaned by Robertin, who had cut his cloth to the familiar measurements he had come to know so well, but Philip was a delicate eater at the best of times and the food brought to him here was seldom to his liking. He had lost his colour too, but he fancied his pallor was not unflattering in contrast with the black brocade.

"Do you like it?" he asked Titus.

"Yes, yes," Titus said impatiently. "I like it. Can you not get rid of him? I've something private to discuss."

"Your pardon, Monsieur Robertin. It would appear that Doctor Oates wishes to be alone with me," Philip said to the Frenchman.

Robertin shrugged expressively. He had grown accustomed, over the years, to working upon Philip amidst the comings and goings of some of the most famous names in London. "It is up to you, my Lord. Do you or do you not want perfection?"

"Everything you make is perfect, and I really think you've pulled me about enough today."

The tailor sighed and carefully removed the garment. "I have all but done in any case. I shall return tomorrow."

"Are the buttons ready?"

"Yes, my Lord. They are safely locked up in my chest," Robertin assured him as he left.

"I have had them made in solid gold," Philip told Titus, "with my initials engraved on every one."

"A trifle extravagant, aren't we?" Titus cried.

"Why should I not be now?" Philip's 'final vanity' had cost him all the money he could lay his hands upon. "Tess can always sell them afterwards. I will ask her to give one to you, if you would like it," he offered, for he guessed that Titus was still impecunious.

"That would be most generous of you, my Lord," Titus said delightedly. "I would always treasure it in memory of you."

"Nonsense! You'd sell it before they had me buried! Now what is it you want to tell me that requires such privacy? If you are fearful of your own position then let me assure you I have positively sworn you had no part in the plot."

"I know, and I am grateful, but this is a different matter. I received a visit from Mrs. Matthews, Sir Thomas Armstrong's sister. Apparently the Duke of Monmouth is in Antwerp with Sir Thomas and he wished you to know that he is safe."

"I'm very glad to hear it," Philip said, although it was difficult to prevent his voice from betraying the bitterness he felt. "I should have known all would turn out well for the Duke, no matter what happens to the rest of us."

"Don't brood upon it," Titus advised, watching him worriedly.

"I'm not." Philip winked at him. "I was merely worrying about whether my new coat is going to fit!"

On the morning of the sixteenth Philip viewed himself in the mirror Morgan had brought in for him. The coat fitted superbly and Philip knew he looked his best.

"Will I make a good impression, do you think?" he said,

turning to the Welshman, who looked oddly tidy with his wild, black hair combed down, for once.

"I pray you do, my Lord."

"My prayers are all for you and Thomas," Philip said sincerely, "although I do not promise they'll avail you much, for they are made to a God I've long neglected. Is it nearly time for you to leave?"

"I fear so, my Lord."

Morgan, being a witness, needed to report early to the courtroom.

Apart from short absences to run errands, Morgan had been with Philip constantly since Christmas Eve and the moment of parting, now that it had finally come, was difficult for both of them.

"If they find me guilty you are to return and stay with me until the end," Philip said quietly.

"If I can," Morgan pledged.

Neither wished to dwell on the likelihood that Morgan, after giving his evidence, might not be a free man himself, but it was a possibility they had to face.

"In case you cannot and we never get to meet again I must say something which I have not said often enough. It was a fortunate day when you persuaded me to take you as my servant. You have been my counsel and my strength, but most of all you have been my friend, the best I could ever have wished for. Thank you, Morgan."

Morgan clasped the hand which Philip offered him. "You honour me by your friendship, my Lord. If matters should go ill for us all today I beg you not to reproach yourself on Thomas' or my account. We do what we do willingly and for love of you who has enriched both our lives beyond measure."

"Bon chance to you, my Morgan," Philip said, in a voice taut with emotion.

"And to you, my Lord."

Philip swallowed hard as he heard Morgan's steady footsteps fading down the corridor. He had been dreading his farewell from the faithful Welshman, but he was composed again before Haggerty, in his best uniform, came to escort him.

"Ready, my Lord?"

Philip looked around his cell. It would be the first time he had left it for seven months and he wondered whether he would be back in it again before the day was out.

"I am not ready to die," he said emphatically.

The air outside was raw and chill, but it still felt good to Philip after being confined for so long and he enjoyed the short walk to the Wakefield Tower, where a coach was waiting for him

The vehicle, heavily guarded, passed along Thames Street and Philip viewed with interest the unfamiliar sight of the river covered with ice so thick that there were booths erected on it around the arches of the bridge. People, both on foot and in their carriages, swarmed unconcernedly over its frozen surface, so that it would have been difficult to remember there was water there at all had it not been for the occasional rigging showing from boats, stranded in the ice.

What is it, a market?" Philip said.

"Folk are calling it the Frost Fair," Haggerty told him. "An ox was roasted on the ice on front of Whitehall, so they say, and a pack of dogs pursued a fox upon the river from Lambeth Marsh to Wapping."

After that he lapsed into his usual sullen silence and did not speak again until they turned from Thames Street towards the site where Christopher Wren had begun the rebuilding of St. Paul's cathedral. A great crowd was gathered in front of it.

"What the devil is this?" Haggerty signalled the guards flanking the coach. "Clear those people out of the way. It could be trouble."

"You'll have trouble if you try to move them," Philip

predicted, as several rounded upon the guards. "Unless I'm much mistaken they have turned out to see me."

He was right. An enormous cheer went up as they drew level with the crowd.

Philip was pleased to see that the Londoners were still for him. He guessed that many of those gathered there today must have waited hours to glimpse him passing and it was evident they were not about to be shifted as soon as he came by.

"You see, Haggerty, the people still love me!"

"They will hate you by the time this is over, my Lord."

Philip raised his hand in salute to those who called his name. "Would you like to place a wager on that, Haggerty?"

"I am not a gambler."

"I might have guessed at that! You are without doubt the most uninteresting person I have ever been forced to endure. In all this time I have not found in you one quality I like."

"That is because I am a loyal subject of the King and a law-abiding man," Haggerty sneered.

"You may be that, but you are also a very foolish man," Philip said evenly.

"What do you mean by that?"

"Since I have been in your custody you have not made the slightest effort to be pleasing to me."

"Why should I? You are a foul traitor who will shortly be beheaded."

"What if I am not?" Philip said. "What if they acquit me? I'll not forget you, Haggerty, or your manners, for no-one has ever been as rude to me as you."

Haggerty spun round to face him. "Is that a threat, my Lord?"

Philip nodded, smiling.

He had the satisfaction of seeing a sudden expression of fear pass across Haggerty's face before the gaoler turned away. Philip did not think it likely he would ever be in a position to implement his threat, but the knowledge that he had managed to chill Haggerty's blood was of some small comfort to him.

Haggerty looked relieved when they reached the end of their journey. Ludgate Hill had been lined with cheering well-wishers and the crowd converged upon them as soon as the coach stopped. Despite the efforts of the guards to hold them back, several broke through, trying to get a better view of Philip.

Haggerty got out of the coach first and indicated with a gesture that Philip was to follow him.

Philip, incensed at this final affront, did not budge. "Help me down."

"I will not."

"Then I shall not stir."

"I'll drag you out," Haggerty said warningly.

Philip looked about him. They were plainly surrounded by his friends. "Do that, Haggerty, and they will set upon you. Who knows, I might even be able to escape in the confusion. Would it not be a pity to lose me now, so close to the end of your assignment?"

Haggerty looked thunderous but he offered his arm and Philip stepped down, his lips twitching, for he was enjoying the opportunity of taking a little revenge upon him.

"Have a care, Haggerty, or they might think you have grown attached to me and will presume you to be no better than myself," he taunted the surly gaoler, who looked most embarrassed at having to act the part of a servant to his prisoner.

"They'll change their minds when they see me cheering at your execution."

"There you go again." Philip shook his head. "My one consolation is that, no matter what the verdict is today, I shall be relieved of the necessity to see your ugly face much more, since I'll be either dead or free."

"You will be dead, my Lord," Haggerty said grimly, as they

went inside and Philip was handed over into the charge of the Sergeant-at-Arms.

"Who knows?" Philip gave a last wave to his admirers, who had waited so long in the cold to see him. "I am feeling exceedingly lucky today!"

His flippancy was but an act, for he thought, along with Haggerty, that there was not a chance of his acquittal, no matter what surprises Theresa and his servants had prepared for the entertainment of the jury. Still, he was not yet on Tower Hill and for the next few hours all attention would be focused on him, so he resolved that his performance would be one that London would remember.

Another great cheer sounded outside and Philip stopped. "What's that?"

"It would appear that someone else has arrived, my Lord," his escort said.

"Someone also popular with the crowd, it seems." Philip turned to the guard. "Find out who it is."

"At once, my Lord."

Philip was used to command and he had an authority about his manner which, even now, made him difficult to disregard.

"Wait!" bawled the Sergeant-at-Arms. The young soldier stopped in his tracks, flushed with confusion. "May I remind your Lordship that you are our prisoner and in no position at all to give your orders to my men?"

Philip laughed as he was led away to the cells.

He would have been surprised to learn for whom the people cried out with such warmth, and even more surprised if he could have witnessed the little scene taking place outside.

What had first caused the crowd to cheer had been the sight of Philip's own distinctive carriage, pulled by the matching pair of beautifully groomed black trace-horses. Jonathon, in gleaming black and gold livery, jumped down and threw open the coach door with a flourish.

Theresa stepped out slowly, savouring the drama of the moment.

She had been at Heatherton since Christmas, not even daring to visit Philip for fear of drawing attention to herself, but now she was openly defying the King's order for her exile.

Theresa never normally attempted to make herself too conspicuous, for such was not truly her nature. She had always remained contentedly in the background whilst Philip had basked in the adulation of the people but today was different; today she was transporting herself with all the blatant showmanship that had come to be expected of members of the Green Ribbon Club.

She was dressed as a widow, totally in black, a veil before her face and jet combs in her upswept auburn hair. The crowd was for her right away, for she looked tiny and alone, a brave, sad heroine, and the citizens of London loved a heroine, provided she was Protestant.

Bet, clad also in deep mourning, came behind her, distributing leaflets amongst the throng. A true Londoner, Bet had no fear of the mob that pressed around them.

"Read the truth, good people," she cried. "Read how they would murder the man who saved the King's life."

"Stop that!" A guard rushed toward Bet but the crowd, incensed, closed round her and jostled him aside. Bet threw the rest of the pamphlets over the heads of the mob, so that they fluttered down, soon grabbed by eager hands.

"Seize that woman," the Sergeant-at Arms ordered.

"No!" Theresa lifted up her veil and confronted him. "She has done nothing wrong save let these people learn the truth."

"The distribution of pamphlets is illegal, my Lady. You know that."

"Tell it to those who litter the streets with their filth to smear my husband's good name, or do you condone only literature which is defamatory to the reputation of a man who has dedicated his life to the Protestant Cause?" she cried, playing her part to the full.

The atmosphere was growing ugly. The Papist threat was not forgotten by the populace, who, likewise, did not forget their champions. Every soldier in the city had been prepared for trouble on this, the most significant trial of all, and every one of them had been charged with the task of preventing riots at all cost, by order of the King.

Theresa was the one person who could still easily inflame the mob, and she knew it. "Stand aside, Sergeant, unless you would threaten physical harm to one who carries a Protestant child." She patted her swollen belly. "A child who may never see its noble father. Come, Bet."

There was no way the Sergeant could properly prevent her from entering the court, so he got them inside quickly and with a minimum of fuss.

One of the guards picked up a pamphlet from the ground after Theresa and Bet had passed through. For the benefit of those who could not read there were drawings illustrating the words, so that none could doubt the message of the broadsheet.

"The Protestant Innocent or the Unlawful Murder of the Saviour of the King," the guard read out. "What do you reckon, Sergeant?"

"What do I reckon?" The Sergeant looked gloomily at the crowd, already chanting for Philip's freedom. "I reckon that we should not count Lord Devalle finished until his head is in the basket. And even then I, for one, shall not be sure!"

TWENTY TWO

⟡

Philip's entrance into the courtroom was dramatic, as he had intended it to be, and he bowed to the Bench with all the flamboyance of an actor acknowledging his audience.

This earned him some cheers from the Public Gallery, and a scowl from Lord Chief Justice Jeffreys.

"Lord Devalle draws a crowd still," he remarked loudly, to no-one in particular, glaring round at the full-packed courtroom.

Philip scanned the Gallery anxiously until he spotted Theresa, seated with Bet. Their eyes met and he blew her a kiss.

The Clerk of the Court approached him and the procedures began.

"My Lord, you stand accused of High Treason, in that you did plot to overthrow the government of this land. How do you plead?"

"Not guilty," Philip said slowly and clearly.

"You are also accused of conspiring against the life of his Royal Majesty, King Charles, and his Grace the Duke of York. How do you plead to that charge?"

"Not guilty," Philip said again.

"How will you be tried, my Lord?"

"By God and my country."

"God send you a good deliverance."

The formalities completed, the Clerk of the Court stepped down and Roger North, the Attorney General, opened for the Prosecution, calling Lord Howard to the witness stand.

Howard took the oath, studiously avoiding Philip's piercing gaze.

"My Lord Howard, please describe to this court the events which took place at the King's Head tavern on the night of the twenty ninth of July last year."

"There was a meeting of the Green Ribbon Club."

"A meeting called by whom?"

"Lord Philip Devalle."

"And what was the purpose of this meeting?"

"He told us that he wished to lead the Whigs once more to victory."

"Did he say how he intended to achieve this aim?"

"Indeed he did. There would be an uprising, so he said, and the Duke of Monmouth would be placed upon the throne."

North paused just long enough for this choice morsel to be digested by the Jury. "Was he alone?" he asked.

"No. Doctor Oates was with him. Lord Devalle had brought him, so he claimed, to remind those present of all that was achieved by the Popish Plot and he said the time was right to organise another, bolder than the first, those were his words, and one which would end with victory, complete and absolute."

"He called you, then, to tell you of a plot he had formed?"

"No. He mentioned nothing of a plot that night. He called us together that we might elect him as our leader."

"Did you do so?"

"Yes. He had Lord Shaftesbury's support, as usual, but even without it Lord Devalle is not a person one should lightly cross."

"Are you saying that the members of his own club feared him?"

"Many did. Others, such as Lord Sydney and Lord Russell, found no fault with him."

"Even so, it seems he easily persuaded you all to join him in rebellion, Lord Howard. What information did he give you that would have induced you all to blindly follow him?"

"He told us Lord Shaftesbury had persuaded the Earl of Argyle to gather up his forces and await our word."

North turned to Philip. "Do you wish to speak, my Lord? You may address Lord Howard through the Bench if you would cross-examine him."

"I have no questions of Lord Howard yet," Philip said.

"Very well. Lord Howard, please tell this court of the next meeting that you had with Lord Devalle."

Howard then described the meeting at Abchurch Street in detail, and this time Philip did cross-examine.

"Lord Howard states he heard me speak against the Duke of York's succession to the throne, and that he also heard me say that King Charles should be removed from his position. Ask him whether, at any time, he heard me say that I wished either of them dead."

"Not in so many words," Howard was forced to admit, "but..."

"Gentlemen of the Bench," Philip interrupted him, "would you also ask Lord Howard to confirm that when his Grace the Duke of Monmouth said he would never suffer his father to be killed my reply was that he should only be captured and that every care was to be taken that no harm befell him."

"He did say that then," Howard agreed, "but he told a different tale when I met him at a later date."

"What tale was that?" North asked.

"Why, that he had pretended the King should not be harmed only in order that the Duke of Monmouth should be satisfied. The real plot, which he had hatched with Major Wildman and the republicans, was that both the King and the Duke of York be killed."

"There were, in fact, two plots?"

"Aye, that is truth of it, as Devalle knows."

"Who else says I knew there were two plots?" Philip asked of the Bench.

"We have only Lord Howard's word for that," the Solicitor General admitted.

"There were only a few of us he told," Howard said. "Sir Thomas Armstrong, Robert Ferguson and myself."

"How convenient for Lord Howard that neither of those gentlemen can be present to substantiate his preposterous story," Philip said, "particularly since I understand he has received a pardon for fabricating this so-called evidence against me."

"You will not undermine the credibility of the witness for the Crown, my Lord," North said sternly. "It takes a man of courage to come forward and speak the truth."

"Was he a man of courage when the soldiers who arrested him discovered him hiding in his own chimney?" Philip asked.

Loud laughter from the spectators followed this remark.

"Silence or I shall clear this courtroom," Jeffreys shouted angrily. "Have you any further questions of Lord Howard?" he asked the Attorney General.

North had not and Howard stepped down, looking displeased.

Colonel Rumsey was called next and then Robert West and, finally, Thomas Sheppard. They all repeated everything Lord Howard had already said but when questioned similarly by Philip were forced to admit that, far from openly planning to kill the King and York, Philip had categorically stated that they should not be harmed.

Philip turned to the Bench again. "It would appear that there are no other witnesses to prove my intent to commit murder, therefore I would suggest that the charge be dropped."

"Do you presume to teach this court its business?" Jeffreys cried. "Lord Shaftesbury no longer has control of the judicial machinery of this city, my Lord. The days are long passed when his own selected men of the jury could declare an Ignoramus verdict."

If such a verdict was declared then the accused went free, since it meant there was no charge to answer. Philip knew that these verdicts still remained a very sore point with Jeffreys, for many of Shaftesbury's associates had escaped justice in such a fashion.

Philip also knew that, no matter what Jeffreys might say, there was insufficient evidence to charge him with murder. There was plenty to convict him of treason, however, and the testimony of only two prosecution witnesses would be enough for that.

North now began his cross-examination of Philip himself.

"My Lord, do you admit that you called a meeting at the house of Thomas Sheppard?"

"I was invited there to taste some sherry."

"So Lord Russell claimed, my Lord," North said dryly, "and had you done no more than that you would not be facing these grave charges now. You discussed a plan of your own making in which the King and the Duke who, I understand, were referred to in your later meetings as the Blackbird and the Goldfinch, would be waylaid in their coach as they travelled home from Newmarket. Four witnesses have testified to this under oath. Do you deny it?"

"I do not deny it," Philip said steadily.

"Then you are plainly guilty of High Treason, my Lord," North cried, above the murmurs which had begun in the Public Gallery.

Jeffreys had to bang his gavel a dozen times before he could be heard once again threatening to clear the courtroom.

North continued when the noise had subsided. "I repeat, my Lord, you are plainly guilty of High Treason, although you claim, no doubt, that you were acting as an instrument of the Protestant faith."

"Not at all."

North looked put out at this answer and Philip guessed he had planned a pretty speech around such a claim! "If you were not working for the Protestants then who, pray, did you serve, my Lord? The Duke of Monmouth?"

"The Duke of Monmouth had no servants." Philip would never have implicated Monmouth, even though he did feel the Duke had deserted him. "We all served the Earl of Shaftesbury."

"Do you tell this court that Monmouth hatched no plans against the Duke of York?"

"Monmouth did nothing without he turned to Shaftesbury for advice," Philip said firmly.

"You were close to Shaftesbury, perhaps the closest, do you not agree, my Lord?"

"Not latterly. I was living in France, if you recall, and came back only a year and a half ago."

"And why did you return to England, my Lord?"

"To try to take my family estate, from my brother."

"Do you expect us to believe that you gave up a promising career in the French army to return home for the sole purpose of dispossessing your brother of his inheritance?" North sneered.

"I had no promising career, as you term it, left in France. King Louis had already taken away my troops."

"Why should he do that to a Hero of France?"

"Why don't you ask him?"

"You will not ridicule the authority of this courtroom, my Lord," North said crossly. "You will answer the questions put to you in a straightforward manner or be held in contempt of court."

Philip turned to the bench. "My Lords, I fail to see how what occurred between the King of France and myself has any bearing whatsoever upon the matter for which I now stand trial."

"It has no relevance, it's true," Justice Wythens said, "although I see no reason why you should not answer the question. Presumably because you feel it may adversely affect our judgement of this case today."

Philip sighed resignedly. "It is nothing like that, but I suppose you will have it out or make things seem much darker than they are. King Louis wished me to remain with him at Versailles and I declined. The only reason I lost my command was, quite simply, because he felt I had advanced too far and caused jealousy amongst my fellow officers. It would appear I was too successful, and you may make of that exactly what you please."

"I think we have dwelt enough on it," Wythens said. "You are right, my Lord, it has no relevance whatever to this case, and I thank you for your courtesy in answering as frankly upon a subject which I'm sure must pain you."

"Let it not be said that I attempted to keep anything from the knowledge of this court," Philip said evenly.

"For whatever reason you came back, my Lord, it was not long before you were once more embroiled in plotting for the Duke of Monmouth," North said huffily, "or, if you would have it so, for Shaftesbury."

"I commenced working for him straightaway," Philip admitted.

"Even though you had been out of England for three years? Must we then assume that you had been in communication with Lord Shaftesbury during that time?"

"He wrote to me occasionally."

"And do you still have those letters?"

"No."

"What did they contain?"

"One, I remember, contained news of the Abhorrers and of the trial of 'Elephant' Smith."

Philip had chosen his words well. Jeffreys had prosecuted Smith, a Whig pamphleteer, and lost! In addition to that both Jeffreys and Sir Francis Wythens had been among the original Abhorrers, those who fought against petitions intended to put pressure on the King, and they had personally advanced on account of it.

"Did he write to you about nothing else?" North asked, passing on quickly.

"He informed me of the dissolution of the parliament."

"And did you answer those letters?"

"No. I write few letters. He expected none."

"When was the last time you heard from him prior to his recalling you to England?"

"The Earl did not recall me," Philip replied carefully, aware of North's implications. "The last I heard from him was, I would say in '81."

"And yet you sought him out directly you returned to England?"

"Yes."

"For what reason?"

"I wanted his help to gain High Heatherton. The courts seemed to have been somewhat reluctant to hear my case, even though my brother, Henry, had been committed as insane."

"And did he help you?"

"Yes he did."

"And in return you agreed to aid him in a conspiracy against his Majesty King Charles and his Grace the Duke of York."

Philip looked him in the eye. "Yes."

There were some gasps to be heard from the Public Gallery at that.

"And yet you still say you are not guilty, my Lord?" North cried.

"I am innocent," Philip said, "in fact I saved both their lives."

Abruptly the courtroom fell silent again.

"And how, pray, did you accomplish that?" North asked derisively.

Philip ignored North's tone, which he knew was intended to goad him.

"By causing them to return to London earlier than planned. I knew that by doing so I would ensure their safety, since the plotters would be taken by surprise."

"Surely these 'plotters' were your own men, my Lord."

"I had disassociated with them."

"But you were their leader."

"I had not thought they would follow me so far. I led them only that the Earl of Shaftesbury might see proof that I worked for him."

"And after the Earl's death you thought you would abandon them? Monmouth, your friend since boyhood? Lord Essex and Lord Russell? We will not believe you to be that disloyal, my Lord."

"I wished to stop them, not to turn them in," Philip said pointedly.

"Did you lose faith, then, in your own plot?" North scoffed.

"No, my plan was faultless. Had it gone ahead then the Duke of Monmouth might be on the throne even now."

"But is that not what you have schemed for all these years? Do you say that you deliberately thwarted you own plans, just when all you had worked for was within your grasp?"

"Yes, that is exactly what I did."

"Lord Devalle, you cannot surely hope to convince us of that," North said. "Why would you do such a thing?"

"Shaftesbury died," Philip said simply. "Whilst he lived I might have been content to see the Duke of Monmouth on the throne but without the Earl there was little point in any of it. Monmouth was merely Shaftesbury's puppet and, although he is my friend, I do not believe him capable of ruling England."

North had no rejoinder to that. He informed the Bench that the Prosecution's case rested.

Philip felt he had stood up well to North's questioning. The spectators seemed to be still for him, despite the shock of hearing him admit to the plot. He looked round for Theresa, who gave him an encouraging smile.

Since he was being tried for treason he was allowed no defence counsel, but the prospect of conducting his own defence did not particularly trouble him. What was of more concern to him was the position in which he was about to place Morgan and Thomas, and the apprehension he felt as he began to speak was for them rather than for himself.

"My Lords, whilst it is true that I did formulate a plan to overthrow the King and prevent the Duke of York's accession I hope to prove that myself and two of my servants did, by criminal means, prevent my erstwhile associates from carrying out that plan."

"By criminal means, my Lord?" North asked in surprise.

"I fear so, although I feel that, in view of the importance of those lives we saved, the means were justified."

"Lord Devalle is an expert at interpreting the law to his advantage," Jeffreys put in, laughing at his own snide remark.

Philip ignored him. "I would like to call my steward, Morgan Davis."

Morgan came up and took his place resolutely. Philip exchanged a brief glance with him and then began.

"Morgan, please tell the court where we found ourselves upon the night of Thursday the twenty second of March last year."

"Wait," Wythens interrupted before Morgan could reply. "Does, this man fully understand the circumstances under which he gives his evidence? Since, by Lord Devalle's own admission, the means used to foil the plot were criminal then the witness must be made aware that what he says here will be taken as a confession of his guilt and that he may be punished accordingly for any crimes he has committed, for whatever purposes."

"I am aware of all that," Morgan said patiently. "It makes no difference to what I am about to say."

"Very well, you have been warned. Answer the question, if you please."

"We were at Newmarket, my Lord."

"For what purpose were we there?"

"To start a fire at the stables, in hopes that the King would travel back earlier than expected," Morgan answered boldly.

"Please tell the court everything we did."

"We first repaired to the Wheatsheaf Tavern to wait until the streets grew quiet and then we made for the racing stables. We gained entry and I kept watch upon the door whilst Lord Devalle and the other witness, whose testimony you shall also hear, led the horses out to safety."

"Hold!" Jeffreys roared. "This man abuses our intelligence as lightly as his master tries to do. You say that, having got inside the stables and with the intent of firing them, Lord Devalle and this other man led out every horse in the place. How many were there?"

"Twelve, my Lord. It took them nearly half an hour."

"Can you believe that?" Jeffreys asked Wythens.

"You would believe it if you knew my master," Morgan said. "He would never have harmed the animals."

"He has more respect for their lives than for those of his fellow human beings, it would seem," Jeffreys sneered.

It was well known that Jeffreys considered himself quite a wag and that his witty asides often interfered with those attempting to give their evidence, but Morgan was not about to let that happen.

"Yes, my Lord. Shall I continue?"

"Oh, continue," Jeffreys said dismissively. "It is all nonsense anyway and not fit to be heard."

But it was obvious that the Public Gallery thought differently and that they were warming to the stocky little man who faced the fearsome Lord Chief Justice to tell the tale he hoped would save his master.

"When we got all the horses away we set fire to the stable."

"A groom died in that blaze. Did you realise there was anyone inside the building?" North said.

"No," Morgan lied. "How could we have known? There was no sign of him and he must have been dead drunk not to have heard us below."

"And how did you escape the town without being seen?" North asked.

"That I don't recall, sir. A beam fell down upon me," Morgan said, bending the truth a little. "It knocked me senseless and I fell, breaking my leg. Lord Devalle carried me to safety and I did not regain full consciousness for several days."

"That is an incredible story," North said.

"Incredible," Jeffreys agreed, for Morgan, although he had omitted to mention his knifing of the groom, had just confessed to arson and a share of murder. "Why have you come forward, man?"

"To clear my master's name."

Jeffreys snorted at that. "No doubt he fears that with his master dead there will be none to feed him."

"Food will be of little use to him if he is swinging from the gallows," Philip said, "and that is what this man has risked by giving the evidence he has today. I hope to prove his words, and those of my other servant, by producing witnesses unconnected with me in any way."

Thomas was called next, and he was brought in under guard. Philip shook his head despairingly, but Thomas only grinned at him.

"What is this?" North asked.

"The witness is in our custody," explained the Sheriff's man who was accompanying him. "He was recognised in Gravesend as the one who helped Captain Fairfield to escape."

"Was he indeed? When did you apprehend him?"

"He walked into court this morning, bold as brass, my Lord, and said he was to give evidence."

Their Lordships looked at one another.

"Surely you must have known that you would be arrested as soon as you set foot inside this place," North said.

Thomas shrugged. "I wanted to help my master."

"Devalle certainly inspires great loyalty," Wythens remarked to Jeffreys.

"He's bewitched them, most like," Jeffreys retorted loudly. "Let the witness speak if he wants. It's all a pack of lies."

Thomas told exactly the same tale as Morgan and then went on to tell of the events of the next few days, omitting nothing save the part the Duchess of Lauderdale had played in their escape, for Philip had been adamant about that.

"You said there were some independent witnesses who can corroborate your servants' stories," North reminded Philip when Thomas had done.

Philip first called the landlord of the Wheatsheaf, who confirmed that the three of them had been in his inn on the night of the fire.

"How can you be so sure it was them?" North asked, when his turn came to cross-examine. "I'll warrant you had many customers that night, with the King being in town."

"That is so," the landlord said, "and yet I do remember them, for I found them strange."

"In what way strange?"

"The way they talked together and the way they looked. The young man has a finger missing and one of the other gentlemen spoke in an accent unfamiliar to me."

"Very well. Those two could have been in your inn that night, for all it proves, but what about Lord Devalle? He is a person usually conspicuous."

"I did not see his face," the landlord admitted, "for he kept it hidden and he did not speak to me, but the gentleman had a lot of yellow hair and looked to be about as tall as Lord Devalle. I reckon it was him alright."

Next on the stand was the Captain of the Life Guards that had given chase to Philip. He thought that the man they had pursued was undoubtedly him, whilst the description he gave of the fast, black stallion fitted Ferrion exactly.

"Why did you pursue Lord Devalle, if it was he?" North asked.

"The town was in an uproar and the King ordered us to keep the peace, for there was looting and the like. I took five of my men on the heath to search for a thief who had stolen a horse and cart and murdered the owner. One of my men thought he had seen something and was riding back to tell me when he was shot. We saw a rider and gave chase."

"Did you discover what your man had seen?"

"Not at the time, for he had fainted, but later he was able to tell us that it was a horse and cart."

"And did you ever find the murderer you sought?"

"No, sir, nor the cart."

North swung round on Philip. "My Lord, how did you get your injured servant away?"

"I stole a cart," Philip said calmly.

"And did you kill a man to get it?"

"Really, my Lords," Philip protested to the Bench, "I see not how I can be held responsible for every murder in the vicinity! There was a great deal of panic in the streets before we left, as the Captain has just verified, and doubtless many crimes were committed in the confusion. The cart I took was standing unattended, so I simply drove it off."

North did not look satisfied. "How was the man killed?" he asked the Captain.

"With a knife, I understand."

"I rarely carry a knife," Philip said, although he knew it proved nothing.

"But you doubtless carry a pistol, my Lord, and presumably you will not deny you shot at the soldier?"

"I was hiding Morgan at the time," Philip explained. "I fired to bring the man down, not kill him, and then I led the soldiers off so that Thomas could get Morgan safely away."

Jeffreys, who had kept remarkably quiet during North's interchange with Philip, leaned forward now. "Captain, how can you be so certain that the man you chased was actually Lord Devalle? Did you see his face?"

"No, my Lord, but I did see his horse."

"A black horse is a black horse, surely."

"Oh no, my Lord, this was no ordinary stallion. It did fly like the wind, no matter how hard the terrain and the rider was no ordinary horseman. I must confess it was a joy to watch them both, for all the trouble they gave us. I would swear it was Lord Devalle, for he is a horseman of great repute."

"He may be that," Jeffreys said tartly, "but so far neither of these independent witnesses has seen his face. There must be many men of his height who can ride a horse well and can aim a pistol."

Philip chewed upon his lip. The line that Jeffreys was taking was one none of them had anticipated, and he did not like it. Morgan and Thomas had put themselves at risk for absolutely nothing if it could not be proved decidedly that the third man was himself.

The next three witnesses were quickly dealt with. One was the farmer's wife from whom Thomas had stolen the food, the next was the owner of the barn where he had spent the night, who confirmed the tracks of a horse and cart had been found there next morning, and the third was the ostler from St. Albans.

He described both horse and rider perfectly but, after being disgracefully bullied by Jeffreys, the poor man was forced to admit that the rider's face had been dirty and he had not removed his hat.

"Another did not see his face," Jeffreys crowed triumphantly.

Philip cast a desperate glance in Theresa's direction. He was relieved when Audrey mounted the witness stand next. At least this was one person who had seen his face!

She smiled at him, a little shyly, and he winked at her.

"Now, Audrey, please tell this court everything that happened on the night I came to your inn," he instructed her.

"Everything, my Lord?" she asked timidly.

"Yes, everything. You will not shock the Gentlemen of the Bench, I'm sure!"

Audrey did tell them everything. She blushed once or twice as ribald comments came from the spectators, but her soft Hertfordshire lilt, sounding very countrified in such a setting, never wavered, nor did she falter when she described how she had stolen the landlord's clothes to give to the stranger she had known as Thomas.

"So, you worthless girl, you stole from your employer to disguise a man you thought to be escaping from the law?" Jeffreys asked.

"Indeed I did, and I would do so again for Lord Devalle," she said boldly.

"You say you'd do it again for Lord Devalle, yet you did not know it was him."

"Oh no, I never for an instant thought it was. Why should I? He was dirty and his clothes were in a state," Audrey said, falling into Jeffreys' trap.

"Dirty was he?" Jeffreys looked smug. "You have said the stranger was handsome but if his face was dirty can you be sure that he and Lord Devalle are the same man?"

Audrey looked at him in amazement. "Don't be daft, sir. I know who I slept with. Besides, he washed before we went to bed."

"Young woman, curb your tongue," Jeffreys shouted above the laughter that followed her remark. "You'll answer what you're asked and say no more."

"Is there anything that you remember which could positively identify Lord Devalle as your lover?" North said. "You have told us that his hair was burned, but it will have grown back by now. His face you could describe by simply looking at Lord Devalle here. Is there some other means by which the court may know for certain that it was, in fact, he?"

"Lord Devalle, if you prompt this witness we shall disregard her testimony altogether," Jeffreys threatened.

Audrey looked alarmed for a moment, but then she

brightened. "There is something I could tell you about him that I cannot see from here. Lord Devalle's back is covered in scars. I thought he had been flogged."

The defence breathed easy again.

"Is that true?" North asked Philip.

"It is. I will show you, if it would help you to believe her." So saying, Philip removed his coat and waistcoat and, finally, his shirt.

North pulled a face. "You've made your point, my Lord."

"I little thought those scars would ever help me," Philip remarked as he dressed again.

"They have not helped you, my Lord," Jeffreys said nastily. "If your reputation as a womaniser is to be believed there are plenty who could have told the girl about your scars."

Philip did not deign to reply to that, for he knew it mattered little what Jeffreys thought of Audrey's evidence so long as the Jury was convinced and, from their faces, she appeared to have won them over.

The only witness left to appear was the farmer who had taken in Buckingham's cob. A letter was read out to the court from the Duke, confirming that he had loaned the horse to Philip and conferring ownership upon the man who had found and cared for it.

It remained only for Jeffreys to sum up the case. This was the part of the proceedings which Philip had most dreaded, for now, as at no other time, could the vengeful Justice attempt to poison the minds of the Jury.

"We live an age when every Whig feels he must cry out against the church and government so as to be thought a good Protestant," Jeffreys began, "and when every man with the wit to libel a person in office seems to think he has a right to expose that person to public knowledge. This was the way Lord Devalle came to popularity, and by pandering to the common want for such exposures he brought many innocent, good men to their deaths. Such is the service he did his country."

A loud humming noise began, quietly at first then growing steadily louder. It was how the crowd always signified their displeasure at a Justice's speech, but Jeffreys only raised his voice.

"We have heard here of a terrible conspiracy involving our King and his noble brother. This evil council, consisting of Lord Devalle, the Earl of Essex, Lord Russell, Algernon Sydney and, by his own admission, Lord Howard, plotted High Treason. Lord Russell is already brought to justice, Lord Essex is dead by his own hand, which proves his guilt in that he could not face a trial, for all he claimed he was innocent. Mr. Sydney was condemned by his own writings, vile, treasonable pages, but Lord Devalle is condemned not only by witnesses but by his very nature."

"What about his saving of the King's life?" shouted a voice from the Gallery. "That shows his nature plain enough."

"Lies, lies, all lies," Jeffreys snapped, indicating to the guards that the heckler was to be removed. "You may be wondering why so many honest people should give false evidence on his behalf or why, indeed, his own servants should risk their necks to speak out for him; because they fear him that is why." He paused to give weight to his words. "Lord Devalle is a dangerous man and I say it makes no difference whether he foiled this plot or not. He invented it and that is harm enough."

The humming had stopped and the crowd listened to him in sullen silence.

"Lord Devalle should not be tried on what you hear him say today, gentlemen of the Jury, but on what he is; a rebel who would destroy the very foundation of our way of life and plunge us into dreadful revolution; a rabble-rouser who represents that which we need to fight if England is to remain strong. Strength is unification, not insurrection, strength is loyalty, not defiance, and strength is trust; trust in the King, who God has appointed over us. A Deo Rex a Rege Lex – from God the King, from the King the law. I say we must make a firm example of every traitor, for only then will others fear to tread the path they trod."

A few cheered him, but their voices were soon silenced by the murmurings of discontent which had begun again. Philip was still regarded as a hero by the Londoners for his part in the fight against the Papist threat five years ago, whatever the Lord Chief Justice might say against him.

Philip had expected little less of Jeffreys. He attempted to appear unconcerned throughout the vicious tirade but it was hard to hear himself reviled in so unjust a manner.

The Jury filed out to discuss their verdict, although Philip feared he now had no chance of acquittal.

It was an agonising hour and a half before they returned. The entire Bench had remained to await the outcome, which was unusual, since only the Recorder generally stayed.

"Who is your spokesman?" the Recorder asked.

"A man stepped forward. "I am, Mr. Recorder."

"Have you reached your verdict upon the charge that the prisoner, Lord Philip Devalle, did conspire against the lives of His Majesty, King Charles, and his Grace the Duke of York?"

"Yes, sir. We do not feel that Lord Devalle has a charge to answer there, for we heard insufficient evidence against him and therefore," he lowered his voice, "we return an Ignoramus verdict."

"What?" Jeffreys yelled. "Speak up, man!"

The Foreman of the Jury stood his ground. "We return an Ignoramus verdict," he said, louder.

Philip could not restrain a smile at that. He thought the decision would make little difference to his fate but at least it had annoyed Jeffreys.

"Have you reached your verdict upon the charge of High Treason?" the Recorder asked, when the cheers of the crowd had subsided.

"Although the charge is High Treason, would it be permitted

for us to bring in a verdict against the charge of Misprision of Treason?" the Foreman asked.

"No," the Recorder said. "You have heard the evidence. You must either convict or acquit Lord Devalle on the charge upon which he stands indicted. Do you find him guilty or not guilty of High Treason?"

Philip looked straight ahead of him, his head held high.

"Not guilty."

Philip clutched the rail in front of him, feeling dizzy.

A deafening cheer drowned out the Recorder's next words and, almost in disbelief, he saw Theresa and Bet embracing one another joyfully.

Jeffreys was pointing to him, shouting words that could not be heard above the tumult, and the sight brought Philip to his senses.

He saluted the Foreman of the Jury and bowed to those who called to him from the Public Gallery.

He knew that his ordeal may not yet be over, for he had admitted shooting a soldier and causing the death of a groom, but he had won today and won a victory he had not expected.

Philip looked once more at the furious face of Lord Chief Justice Jeffreys.

And laughed.

TWENTY THREE

Philip felt apprehensive as he waited outside the Great Chamber in Whitehall palace to see the King. He had no idea why Charles had summoned him, or how he would be received.

He was still awaiting trial upon the lesser, but still serious, charges of injuring the soldier and killing the groom but the date of his trial had not yet been fixed and, in the meantime, he had been released upon a surety of five thousand pounds, the whole sum stood for him by his old friend Buckingham. Morgan and Thomas were to stand trial with him and Philip himself had stood bail for Morgan, but Thomas had been taken to Newgate. As well as being party to the murder of the groom he was also accused of aiding Giles' escape, and his prospects looked bleak. In view of his own situation, Philip feared there was very little he would be able do to aid his loyal servants but now, as he was ushered into the King's presence, he determined to use the opportunity to plead for them.

Charles acknowledged him with a curt nod of the head. "I am surprised to see you before me once again, Philip."

"I doubt your surprise is any greater than mine, your Majesty," Philip said truthfully.

"I am pleased to find you still in London. I had thought you might have returned to Sussex at the first opportunity."

"I would have done so, your Majesty, but Theresa is near to giving birth and I will not risk moving her."

"Your wife has turned into a formidable woman," Charles

said. "One who, it seems, will stop at nothing to save her husband's life, even to procuring one of his lovers as a witness!"

"I am not yet a free man, as I understand it, Sire," Philip said, ignoring the reference to Audrey.

"Indeed you are not, but the Jury acquitted you of treason and none of Jeffreys' abuse could make them change their minds. Now some say I owe you not only your freedom but a debt of gratitude. What do you think of that?" Charles said.

"I think I have enough experience of this world to place but little store on gratitude, your Majesty," Philip said heavily.

"Really? Some years ago I offered you an earldom if you betrayed Lord Shaftesbury and you refused. Would you refuse an earldom now, I wonder?"

"Try me!"

Charles smiled at that, but his face soon grew solemn again. "I always credited you with more sense than to work against me without Shaftesbury's protection. Evidently I was wrong. Is there any reason on this earth why I should pardon you?"

Philip could think of plenty, but he hardly thought it was serious question! He knew the answer he was expected to give it, however. "Should you decide to be lenient with me, your Majesty, you will find me to be a most loyal subject," he said dutifully.

"What are your promises worth?" Charles said. "Do you think that I could ever really trust you?"

There was nothing Philip could say to that. He did not believe, in any case, that Charles was actually considering dropping the charges against him.

Charles' next words confirmed it. "If I pardoned you I'll warrant you would hatch some plot against me before the year was out, or incite my own son to fight me for my throne."

Philip decided to humour him. "I would never again aid Monmouth, I assure you of that."

"You have finished with him?"

Philip thought back to the letter which Monmouth had written to him. "Yes, if your Majesty wishes it."

"I thought you were his friend," Charles said pointedly.

"Because I am his friend I pledge to you that, as long as your Majesty lives, I would do all in my power to dissuade him from rebellion."

"And after my death?"

"You could hardly hold me to a pledge then," Philip said reasonably.

Charles paced the room in silence for several minutes.

Philip watched him coolly. He suspected it was amusing Charles to taunt him and he had no intention of betraying any emotion for the King's benefit.

At last Charles stopped in front of him. "Are you not afraid to die, my Lord?"

Philip raised an eyebrow at the question. "My life has been a full one, your Majesty. I would reckon I have lived more in four and thirty years than some do in sixty, but I think I have only lately discovered true contentment, so I certainly have no wish to die."

"Yet you have not begged me for your life."

Philip could no longer doubt that Charles was merely playing with him.

He sighed resignedly. "There seems little point, your Majesty. You'll never let me go."

"Little point, eh?" Charles picked up a sheaf of papers from his desk. "Do you know what these are?"

"I have no idea."

"Then I will tell you. These are supplications made on your behalf by those who, unlike yourself, are not too proud to beg in order to save your skin. There's one from my misguided son, one from Buckingham, of course, and another here from my cousin, King Louis, and that would make you blush if I should let you read it, so much does he praise all those virtues I have never seen! There are many more, and they signify to me that there are those who think most highly of you."

"So it seems, your Majesty."

"But why? What qualities have you shown them that you could not show me, your own King? I asked you for loyalty and you have given me nothing but deception."

"I was loyal to you when I saved your life, your Majesty," Philip said. "Not that I would expect to be treated with any leniency on account of that, for justice is a thing in which I have but little faith."

"Why so?"

"Because my servants, who had no part in any plotting but who were, nonetheless, instrumental in your own salvation, must stand trial for murder with me."

Charles shook his head. "You really are an amazing man, Philip Devalle. After all you have endured I would have thought to find you weeping at my feet, yet you regard me sullenly and complain that your accomplices have been charged with a crime to which they were a party."

"I have accepted that I am to die, no matter what farce is played out before my time comes," Philip said irritably, for he was growing tired of Charles' game now. "My reprieve has bought me nothing but the prospect of another trial before I lose my head, but this time two men that I care about will likely die with me."

"Your servants sacrificed themselves to clear your name of treason."

"They should not have done so," Philip said.

"There I agree with you, but it is your fate, not theirs which is my concern today." Charles took another turn about the room. "You saved my life," he said at length, "and that of York, for reasons I do not pretend to understand, but I shall judge your motives pure on this occasion." He sat down at his desk and put his name to a piece of paper in front of him. "On account of that I am giving you your freedom."

Philip stared at him. "Your Majesty is granting me a pardon?" he asked, certain he must have misunderstood.

"Perhaps now you can believe that there is such a thing as gratitude – and justice too," Charles said.

Philip found his hand was shaking as he took the document. "Thank you, your Majesty."

"There will be conditions, though," Charles warned, "so listen, Philip, and listen well. Firstly, you will not plot against the throne as long as I do live, or associate with any of your rebel friends, and that includes the Duke of Monmouth. If he contacts you, as I am sure he will, you are to tell him what I have just told you and then have no further correspondence with him, or meet him here or anywhere abroad. If you do you will be arrested under suspicion of inciting a rebellion and there will be no pardon for you then, no matter who petitions it. Do I make myself clear?"

"Abundantly clear, your Majesty."

"The other condition concerns High Heatherton."

Philip swallowed nervously, dreading what might be coming next.

"Oh, I shall not take it from you," Charles reassured him. "It is yours by right of birth and you have waited long enough for it, but you shall not reside there. On that point I am adamant. I have decided you are one of those best kept at Court, where I can see you every day and know exactly what you're up to."

"You mean live here again? At Whitehall?" Philip said in dismay.

"I'm afraid I do. You may occasionally visit High Heatherton of course, but as for becoming a country gentleman, no, I cannot allow it. That dream is for others, Philip, those I can trust out of my sight! You, on the other hand, will attend upon me daily in my bedchamber, accompany me whenever I take a walk and, when I go upon a visit, you will be amongst my entourage."

This sounded to Philip uncannily like the proposition Louis had offered him at Versailles, only now he was in no position to refuse!

"What slavery is this your Majesty offers me?"

"By some it is accounted as an honour," Charles said, with a slight smile. "Anyway it's either that or exile for life. Make your choice."

"My choice? What choice?" Philip said, although he realised, if he was honest, that the terms Charles was offering him were more than fair under the circumstances.

"I shall still not receive your wife at Court," Charles stressed. "In fact I would prefer it if she resided in Sussex, well out of my way."

"You mean to separate us?" Philip cried. That made the prospect worse than ever. "But I love her."

"Well you should have thought of that before," Charles said. "You'll find diversions here again, I'm sure. I doubt you've changed that much and, for all you say, you're more suited to Court life than any other. You practically grew up here. It is the only life you truly know."

"The only life your Majesty will let me know, it seems!"

"Perhaps the title of Earl of Southwick might make your bondage easier to bear," Charles suggested.

Philip had certainly not expected that! "Perhaps it would," he admitted, when he had sufficiently recovered from the surprise Charles' words had given him. This was more than he had dared hope for, but there was still the fate of Morgan and Thomas to consider. He knew that, whatever the cost to himself, he could not agree to anything whilst their futures remained uncertain.

"What about Morgan Davis and Thomas Sullivan?" he asked.

"That again?" Charles said in an exasperated tone. "Very well, a pardon for Davis." He wrote a few lines on a sheet of paper, which he handed to Philip.

Philip was glad, for Morgan's sake, but he knew he could not leave the matter there.

"What about Thomas?" he persisted.

"That is a different matter," Charles said. "Sullivan is a wanted criminal who, by the by, it transpires your wife had been harbouring. Be thankful I see fit to be lenient concerning that, although I suppose she could hardly be expected to turn away the man who helped her treacherous brother to escape."

"Giles is innocent," Philip insisted. "Not a scrap of real evidence has been found against him, so I do not see how Thomas can be convicted of aiding and abetting a fugitive from justice."

"Giles Fairfield is certainly guilty of murder, if nothing else," Charles reminded him tartly. "There was a witness to that. Your servant, as well as being a party to that crime, stole a horse to make good his escape when the soldiers tried to arrest him. I think it better you abandon him to his fate."

"Abandon him?" Philip was incensed. "What is to happen to him, for heaven's sake?"

"If the court finds him guilty he will hang."

"No!"

"That is all, Philip," Charles said in a firm voice. "This audience is at an end. I would exhort you to accept what I have offered and to leave me now, lest you say hasty words you may regret."

Philip knew he should take Charles' advice, and yet he had to risk pushing him further.

"It is unjust," he said determinedly. "Thomas should not hang for helping Giles, for it was I who ordered it."

"The matter is no longer in my hands."

"Of course it is," Philip cried. "What was it Jeffreys said at my trial? From God the King, from the King the law? If your

Majesty truly claims to represent God than spare the life of this young man who risked his for your sake."

"Are you forgetting that I still hold *your* life in my hands?"

Charles' voice was dangerously cold, but Philip was beyond caution now.

"Then you had better take that too, your Majesty. If you allow this to happen I fear I cannot undertake to keep a single promise to you, not even for an earldom."

"What did you say? " Charles looked at him incredulously. "Are you such a fool as to risk everything for the sake of this young gallows-bird?"

Philip considered this and smiled wryly. "It would appear I am, your Majesty."

"How can one who remains so indifferent to his own fate care so fervently about that of another?" Charles asked him, in a tone of disbelief. "Oh, I have misjudged you, Philip Devalle, that I have."

Philip's heart sank as he saw Charles take another sheet of paper from his drawer and commence to write. He had gone too far, he realised that, but he had always been a gambler and he could never have lived with himself if he had not wagered his own freedom against Thomas' life. Even now, when it had cost him so dearly, Philip did not regret it on his own account, but he was praying that Morgan's pardon had not also been rescinded.

Charles was watching him again. "I had deemed you a clever man, Philip, clever and far-sighted, a man no longer governed by passions, loyalties or ideals but by self-interest." He signed the paper with a flourish. "I am pleased to discover that I was wrong! You have proved to me, by your irrational outburst, that you still have qualities which I'd presumed long dead." He held the document out. "Here is the pardon for your wretched servant. I expect you will wish to deliver him yourself from Newgate."

It was Philip's turn to be surprised now. And he was.

༄

Newgate prison was a vastly different place to the Tower. Gaol fever was rampant in its cramped and overcrowded quarters and Philip carried a bunch of rosemary and rue to ward off the disease.

"Sullivan, eh?" The Governor, Captain Richardson, looked surprised as he read the pardon Philip handed him.

"Yes, Sullivan. And he had better be unharmed," Philip warned.

"That he is, my Lord. Secretary Jenkins said I was to take all care that he was fit enough to stand trial."

He summoned a gaoler, who Philip followed down what seemed an endless maze of dark, damp corridors. The fetid stench given off by the prisoners and the filthy straw on which they lived was overpowering, and even the scent of the herbs that Philip held up to his nose could not block it out.

"Is this the first time you have been in here, my Lord?" the gaoler said.

"It is, and I sincerely hope that it will be my last. How do you stand this stinking air?"

"I'm used to it."

They stopped before a blackened door and the gaoler took out his keys. "I'll fetch him out to you, my Lord. You may not like what you see in there."

"Captain Richardson told me he was unharmed."

"He is, but he's in irons, by order of the Secretary of State."

"Damn Jenkins and damn you!" Philip seized the gaoler's lantern and went into the cell.

Thomas was fettered to the wall. He blinked in the sudden glare of the light, unable to make out who stood there.

"Get up, Thomas," Philip said softly. "We are going to undo your chains."

"My Lord?" Thomas struggled to his feet. "Is it really you?"

"Yes, Thomas," Philip assured him as the fetters were removed. "It is your master, the man who has caused you all this suffering."

"Have you come to set me free, my Lord?"

"It is the very least I can do, my little hero."

Thomas staggered, for his legs were stiff from inactivity, but Philip caught him and held on to him protectively as Thomas walked to freedom. He was weak from lack of exercise and good food but otherwise seemed unharmed.

Outside the prison walls the air smelt clean and good. They both inhaled it deeply for several minutes.

"How did you do it?" Thomas asked him. "They said I would hang."

"Oh, I still have a little influence, you know," Philip said modestly. He had no intention of telling Thomas how much he had risked for his sake. "Well, are you coming with me, or have you grown so attached to this infested place that you do not want to leave it?"

Jonathon and Ned, waiting by Philip's carriage, grinned broadly when they saw their young friend.

"I just knew you'd get me out of this, my Lord," Thomas said as they started off.

"Of course you did! You always had this most unnerving faith in me."

"But what is going to happen to you and Morgan?" Thomas asked anxiously.

"Morgan has been pardoned and I'm free too, if you can call it that." Philip told him of the King's conditions and of the earldom that had been so unexpectedly offered him by way of a sweetener.

"I think you got off lightly, my Lord, all things considered," Thomas said.

"Oh you do, do you? Once again, it seems, I have a master."

"That may not be such a bad thing for you," Thomas said wisely. "And the King is right; this city is your true home, as it is mine."

"You will not mind it, then, when the others are all at Heatherton and you and I live here?" Philip asked him.

Thomas looked puzzled. "You and I, my Lord?"

"Well I can hardly ask Morgan to stay in London with me. He will have an estate to run in my stead. I thought you might like to take on his duties. Do you think you can cope with being the personal servant of the Earl of Southwick?"

"I'll do my best, my Lord," Thomas said excitedly.

"I know you will!" Philip grew suddenly serious. "I would quite understand, though, if you said that would rather go to join Giles or seek your fortune with another master."

"What? I'd never leave you," Thomas cried. "How could you think such a thing?"

"I nearly led us all to disaster this time. If you would stay with me then know the risks you take," Philip said as they passed the building works of St. Paul's Cathedral. At that very spot the people had shouted for him as he went to face his trial. He shuddered. "That was the closest I have ever come to losing, Thomas."

"But you didn't lose, my Lord, you won. You always win."

Philip shook his head. "I pray you do not think of me as utterly infallible, for I am not. But for you and Morgan I'd be dead now. I owe you both such a debt as I can never in my life repay, although I will try." He meant that sincerely.

"I need no other reward than that which you have just offered me, that of being your manservant," Thomas assured him, "although I realise I shall never be able to replace Morgan."

"Don't try," Philip advised him. "Be yourself and you will suit me very well. In fact," he added thoughtfully, "you might even suit me better."

"Better?"

"Yes, especially now. Oh, Morgan and I will always be close. There is nothing he does not know about me and I prize him more highly than any man alive, but he does have his disadvantages, you know! He is a man of solid values, is my Morgan; principled and unimaginative. He is better suited to the country folk that he manages so well, for he is everything that they admire, and rightly so. You now, Thomas, are a creature of this city. You know its ways and you know its people, and you have a mind that is not only quick but devious. What is more you are not burdened by too many tiresome scruples." Philip winked at him. "Together who knows what we may achieve?"

∽

"How long do these things take?" Philip asked Bet, as she ushered him from Theresa's bedroom.

"It is her first child, there's no telling. Maybe two hours, maybe twenty."

"Twenty?" Philip looked at her aghast.

"Yes, that is what I said, and not even for you, my Lord, will Mother Nature change her course, so you may as well resign yourself to being patient. Go away please."

"But is there not something I should be doing?"

"You did your bit nine months ago," Bet said crisply, brushing him aside. "It's up to her now and to me, so take yourself off and let me get this child of yours delivered."

Morgan coughed tactfully. "Best do as she says, my Lord."

"And you as well!" Bet rounded on her husband. "Sit the master down somewhere and give him brandy. That will keep you both out of my way."

Philip laughed as Morgan, somewhat sheepishly, did as he was bid. "We used to vow we'd never marry, Morgan."

"Well it wasn't my idea, any more than it was yours," Morgan said, "but I dare say neither of us would change things now."

"You're right." Philip downed his glass and poured himself another, and one for Morgan. "You don't think she will die, do you?" he said suddenly, as the dreadful thought occurred to him.

"Of course not!"

"Woman do die having babies," Philip reminded him.

"She won't die. She is strong and healthy," Morgan said firmly.

"But supposing she did?" Philip gripped his arm, filled with a sudden, irrational fear. "It would be my fault, wouldn't it? Why are you looking at me that way?"

Morgan was regarding him almost paternally. "I was thinking about the many situations I have seen you through, my Lord. You have endured even the worst of them magnificently."

"So?"

Morgan sighed. "I have a feeling I'm about to have more trouble with you now than I have ever had before!"

Fortunately for Morgan they did not have twenty hours to wait, although they did have six, which seemed like an eternity to Philip.

It was nearly midnight before Bet came out wearily. In her arms was a tiny bundle wrapped up snugly in a sheet.

"They are both well, my Lord, the mistress and your daughter."

"Daughter?" Philip stared at her quite blankly. He had always assumed, for some reason, that the baby would be a son.

"Yes, look. Is she not beautiful?"

"If you say so." Philip looked in amazement at the tiny red-faced creature, for he had never seen a newborn baby in his life.

"Would you like to hold her?"

"Good God, no!" Philip drew away in positive horror at the very suggestion. "She is far too small."

"Do you mean to tell me that a Hero of France, who has faced a thousand foes, is afraid of a little baby?" Bet mocked him.

"Yes, that is exactly it, and don't you laugh at me," he warned Morgan, "I shall remind you of this on the day you see your first offspring!"

He entered the bedroom quietly and Theresa smiled up at him as he bent to kiss her damp cheek.

"You have done well, my love," he told her.

"Are you disappointed she is not a boy?"

"Why, no," he said, for it had not occurred to him that one was less desirable than the other. "She is beautiful. Bet says so. Shall we call her Madeleine, after my mother?"

"Whatever you wish." Theresa took his hand. "Have you been worried about me?"

"Of course not. You are strong and healthy."

"He's been worried," Bet retorted as she laid baby Madeleine in her crib. "Poor Morgan has had a dreadful time with him. He feared you were going to die."

"Oh, Philip, did you really?" Theresa kissed the hand she was holding. "You are so sweet."

"I'm not sweet at all, and your maid has always had too big a mouth." Philip glared at Bet, who merely pulled a face at him. "I was, quite naturally, a little concerned. This is your first child, after all."

Theresa smiled. "It will not be the last, I hope. Perhaps next time I will give you a son."

"Next time?" Philip blanched at the thought. "I beg you, sweetheart, spare some small consideration for my feelings. It will be a long while, I assure you, before I feel inclined to go through six more hours like that!"

TWENTY FOUR

It was March before the roads to Sussex were negotiable again.

As they drew near to High Heatherton Philip wondered what awaited them, but he need not have feared. The timber had been cut, the fields ploughed and the livestock tended. All around was order and there was an evidence of industry that did credit to John Bone and all those who had been labouring under his direction.

When they arrived Philip found the hearty welcome he received from everyone very touching. He had become accustomed to the adulation of the Londoners, who cheered his carriage louder than ever since his release, but he was unprepared for such an enthusiastic reception on his own estate. It was a far, far different one than he had received the first time he had come, with Giles, on a cold November day which seemed a lifetime ago now, for so much had happened since.

John Bone spoke for all of them. "My Lord, you have been ever on our minds and in our hearts, and we have waited with impatience for the day when you'd come back to us."

"Why, thank you, John, but how did you know that I'd be coming back?"

"We knew the charges must be false, and the courts can't find you guilty if you're innocent, can they?"

"Of course they can, you great lummox," Philip said fondly.

John grinned. "I may be that, but I have always been loyal to you."

"I know you have."

Overcome by his feelings, John seized Philip's hand and kissed it enthusiastically. It was a clumsy action, for he had never done a thing like that in all his life.

"I'll make a courtier of you yet, John Bone," Philip said, laughing. "Now see who we have brought you." He stood aside as everyone crowded round the baby sleeping peacefully in Bet's arms.

"What do you make of that?" he asked Thomas, who was near to him, as usual. "Upstaged by my own child. So that is what it means to be a parent!"

Theresa, Bet and Morgan were soon surrounded by the estate workers and their families, talking to this one and that and looking very much at home again.

"They belong here, don't they?" Thomas said quietly.

Philip nodded. He felt, suddenly, almost an outsider.

It was a feeling that, if anything, grew stronger with him as the days went by, and he was strangely restless.

Heatherton was thriving; all around was progress that it gladdened him to see. The first stage of the house repairs were completed, the timber programme he had set down was up to date and men had even, during the winter months, begun tidying up the formal gardens. Every person had a job to do, including Thomas, who soon lost himself in caring for his beloved horses. Every person, that is, except Philip himself.

To be superfluous was a sensation he had never known before, and it was not one he particularly liked. King Charles had ordered him to be absent from Court for no more than a month, but it was quite long enough and one fine, spring morning he decided the time had come for him to embark upon some new, more challenging, undertaking.

Bet was sitting on a bench in the garden, singing as she rocked little Madeleine in her cradle, and Philip thought she made a pleasant picture amongst the daffodils. She would allow no other servant near the baby and it seemed as though the role of nursemaid suited her, for her expression was soft and tender as she looked into the crib.

"Should she be outside?" Philip asked. "It's none too warm."

"A little air will do her good," Bet said huffily. "You tend to your concerns, my Lord, and I will tend to mine."

"I might just do that if I had any to attend to! Anyway, you saucy jade, Madeleine *is* my concern." Philip held a finger near his daughter's hand and smiled as she grasped it, looking up at him with clear blue eyes, so like his own.

Bet was watching him knowingly. "Do you still say she is not beautiful?"

Philip gently touched a little golden curl. "She will be, Bet, and she will be fair, just like me. There will be none to rival her at Court. We shall have suitors by the dozen fighting for the tiny hand which now holds mine so tightly."

"Is that what you want for her?" Bet cried. "A life at Court? I would have thought you'd learned more sense by now."

"She will want it too, Bet, it is in her blood. You will be proud of her when she's a famous lady of society and as handsome as her father!"

"As long as she's not as vain as him, or as obstinate," Bet muttered, just loud enough for him to hear.

"Have I not even one redeeming quality in your eyes, Bet?" Philip teased her, for he knew she was devoted to him, however much she always tried to hide it.

"Aye, you have some, but there's not one of them that I would wish upon this innocent here," Bet said cheekily. "Her mother's ways and your looks would be the best."

"At least you would give her that of me!"

"Oh yes." Bet looked him over with an approving eye. Philip had got his colour back and regained some of the weight he had lost in prison. "I've always reckoned you to be the comeliest sight in all the world. It would have been a sin to cut your head off."

"You would not have shed one tear for me, I'll warrant, Mistress Bet!"

Bet jumped up indignantly. "That I would! I'll have you know, my Lord, that I was worried to distraction over what was going to happen to you. If they had killed you I would have been beside myself with grief."

Philip laughed. "Hush, sweetheart! You'll disturb the baby. I shall try to remember how you really feel about me the next time you are rating me for some fault or another! I came out here to look for Morgan. Have you seen him anywhere about?"

"The last I saw of him he was with John. And there's another thing," she said, as he turned to go, "young Thomas is not strong enough to govern you."

"What?"

"Heaven only knows what harm you will get up to back in London when you don't have Morgan by your side."

"Listen, woman, I don't need your husband to look after me, and even less do I need to be governed," Philip protested.

"Yes you do," Bet said emphatically, "and I'm surprised Morgan has agreed to let you go without him."

"He has not agreed entirely, if you must know. He is to visit me upon the first of every month, ostensibly to keep me informed of how affairs stand here, but if I know him it is I who will be scrutinised, not his reports!"

Philip located Morgan and John in the orchard, where the Welshman was examining the new buds on the trees.

"We shall have a good crop this year," Morgan predicted, "providing we don't have late frosts."

"Really?" Philip tried to look enthusiastic but, in truth, he was not too much inspired by fruit trees.

"Several trees were so diseased that my father had to cut them down," John said. "We were just discussing the planting of the new stock."

"Don't we have enough left?" Philip looked about him

at the acres of apples, pears and plums that old Sam Bone had pruned.

"Of course we have enough," Morgan said patiently, "but certain strains need other varieties near them if they are to produce their best. If you cut down trees then you disturb the balance."

"That is fascinating, Morgan."

"Yes, I thought you'd think so," Morgan said dryly. "John and I were just identifying what was missing from this plan, which I discovered in the library. It was made when the orchard was first planted. Would you like to see it?"

"More than anything," Philip said solemnly.

He leaned upon Morgan's shoulder but his eyes were on the Welshman's face, not the plan they were discussing.

After a few minutes Morgan abandoned the attempt. "You haven't listened to a word, have you, my Lord?"

"Well what do you expect? You're talking like a rustic. I had no idea you were so knowledgeable."

"There are more things to be learned in life than how to dress and behave in company," Morgan said.

"You never even learned that properly! Why is it you can feel so cordially toward some blasted apple trees and yet you never once tried to be obliging to my friends?"

"Some of your friends, my Lord, do not inspire a man to be obliging."

"What about being obliging to me, then? You can't manage that half the time either," Philip reminded him.

"One should not give in to you too much," Morgan maintained. "Thomas will spoil you dreadfully, no doubt, and you will love it, but it is not good for you to be indulged too often."

"What nonsense!"

John smiled. "I reckon you two are going to miss each other sorely."

Philip's eyes caught Morgan's for a moment. "More than you can know, John."

"I could still come with you."

Philip shook his head. "Your place is here. You will be happier and, besides, of far more use to me. It will be better for you when I've gone. I'm only in the way these days."

"No, my Lord," John protested. "That is not so. Why, without your leadership we would never have even started."

"That may be true, but I have served my purpose now. My part is done and you have proved it, John. Heatherton has run without me all these months, and run efficiently from what I can see. I am certain you and Morgan will easily cope with the place between you." He looked with affection at his Steward and his Farm Manager; Morgan, small and stocky with a taciturn manner and John, a noisy giant of a man. Philip thought the pair could not have been more different, except for the fact that they shared a common love of the land. "Whether you cope with each other is different matter, of course!"

John guffawed at that. "Everyone on the estate will do their best for you, my Lord, depend on that, but we are disappointed you are not to stay with us. This is your home."

"A man may have more than one home if he chooses," Philip said. "There is a nobleman in France called Monsieur le Prince who has four, and a dinner of chicken, bread and soup prepared in each one every day, lest he should call!"

"That's different, he's a foreigner," John said dismissively. "Your place is here at High Heatherton."

"My place is wherever it is advantageous for me to be, John, and right now it is very advantageous for me to be at the King's side, since the plain alternative is exile," Philip told him frankly. "Please believe me when I say that my earldom is not a prize but more of a bribe. I am not free to do exactly as I choose."

"It's all a mite too deep for me," John said, "but I dare say you know what you're doing."

Morgan snorted. "Don't be quite so sure of that!"

Philip was saved from a reply by the approach of Thomas, who was leading Ferrion.

"The mistress requests the pleasure of your company across the downs, my Lord." He held out Ferrion's bridle and indicated where Theresa waited on the hill, a slim, dainty figure, mounted upon the cream horse that Philip had bought for her.

"Does she now? Would you excuse me, Morgan?"

"My Lord?" Morgan barely glanced up from the plan which he was studying again with John.

"I'm going for ride, if you can spare me, that is!"

"Yes, of course, my Lord. Go where you please. There's nothing here for you to do."

"You see the way he sends me off about my pleasure, as one dispatches a tiresome child?" Philip asked Thomas. "I have just had the answer to my question."

"Question?" Thomas said.

"Yes, the one that I was about to put to Morgan. I was wondering how soon we could be gone."

"I do believe you're looking forward to it after all, my Lord."

"I am, I confess it, Thomas. Oh, I love this place and more than anything I want to see it thrive, but Buckingham and Giles were right, loath as I am to admit it; I was not cut out to be a country gentleman."

"I never thought you were, for all you seemed to be enjoying it."

"When I had a part to play it was a little different but, hell's teeth, I do not intend to spend my whole life cutting timber, any more than I intend to spend it idling or paying calls upon my country neighbours." He looked at Thomas and frowned. "Are you laughing at me, wretch?"

Thomas was, and Philip didn't really mind.

"I understand the way you feel, my Lord, for I enjoyed restoring the stables, but I would not want to do the job again."

"Exactly. You and I are city folk, Thomas. Bet is too, but she appears to have come to terms with life here. Morgan's in his element and he will stay, despite the fact that he's reluctant to turn me over to your care! As for your mistress," Philip looked wistfully toward Theresa, sitting gracefully on Barleycorn, "I think she will be content for a while."

He mounted Ferrion. "So, Thomas, do you still wish to come to London with me?"

"I love London, my Lord, but my only real desire is to be by your side, wherever that might be," Thomas said sincerely.

"Thank you. And are you going to spoil me dreadfully, as Morgan says? I do hope so!"

Theresa turned around and smiled as he approached her. He pulled Ferrion in beside the mare and for a while they sat in comfortable silence, the Earl and Countess surveying their estate.

The wind blew fresh and strong in their faces, seeming to purify them of the horrors they had endured.

"When?" Theresa asked at length. She had obviously guessed the topic of his conversation with Thomas.

"Tomorrow."

"I'm going to miss you," she told him.

He kissed her tenderly, for he did love her very much, and he would never forget how she had fought to save him. "I'll miss you too, but I shall come back here as often as I can."

"Will you, Philip? At the start, perhaps, but London is your true home, I know that, and you will soon be a part of it again, with all its temptations."

Philip laughed. "What are you suggesting, Tess, that I will be unfaithful to you?"

She gave him a sideways glance. "Actually I was thinking more about you taking up with your rebel friends again."

"You need have no fear of that, my love," he said emphatically. "Rebels are out of fashion for the moment. Shaftesbury went too far, as usual, and we have scared the people nearly out of their wits."

"But they supported you all the same."

"They did so only on account of what we did for them five years ago. Those were the days, my little pet, when panic gripped the city and we were all considered heroes!" Philip sighed nostalgically. "They were loyal to that memory, but it does not signify they are ready to be led into rebellion. I am not as blind as Shaftesbury was. The Whigs have no powers left. It's over; I knew that before I ever came back to England. The only thing that did surprise me was the ease with which the others let themselves be led. The high-minded Russell, Essex, Sydney – I still can't believe they're all gone."

"You must not blame yourself."

"I don't. I blame their own stupidity. If I knew then why did they not know it too?"

"I think they did really. You were persuasive."

"Howard said they were afraid of me, but that is not the truth," Philip said. "They just could not accept there was no Cause without Lord Shaftesbury. It was only ever his dream that we dreamed, Tess."

"Are you attempting to convince me that your days of plotting and contriving are behind you?" Theresa said sceptically.

"Now is not the time for change, for bold new plans and promises, my sweet. This is an apprehensive time, the last years of a nervous reign, the time to show one's loyalty to the King and one's compliance with the elected government of the people."

Theresa was looking at him in amazement.

"It is unfortunate," he said, "but there it is. No matter, hopefully things will soon be back to normal again." He winked at her. "I do believe, for a moment there, I had convinced you that I had reformed!"

"What game do you play now?" she asked him sternly.

"It's called a waiting game, Tess."

"You do intend to keep your promise to the King, I hope."

"What choice has he given me? I'll keep it."

"Truly?"

"All that he has asked is that I do not plot against the throne during his lifetime or associate with Monmouth and the others. Such was never my intention in any case."

"I suppose it's no use asking what your intention is."

"No use at all." He pushed her windblown curls back from her face. He still had not revealed to her the arrangements he had made with both King Louis and the Prince of Orange. She would discover everything in good time. "You'll just have to trust me."

"Where have I heard that before? I don't believe you with your talk of loyalty and compliance. They're fine words, Philip, but no more than words with you."

"You'll see. Come on, Ferrion; let's put these fillies through their paces!"

The great black warhorse was soon galloping down the hill and Philip glanced back over his shoulder, laughing to see Theresa, her red hair flying out behind her in the wind, urging Barleycorn on as she tried to catch up with them.

Life felt good; life was precious. Philip was more aware of that now than he had ever been.

And life was full of possibilities!

EPILOGUE

For the remainder of Charles' reign, some eleven months, Philip was to play the part of the exemplary courtier, resisting all of Monmouth's attempts to embroil him in another plot.

Monmouth remained in Holland with his mistress, Henrietta Wentworth, where his supporters made plans for a Protestant rebellion.

Ferguson, Lord Grey and the Duke of Argyle also stayed at liberty abroad, but Sir Thomas Armstrong was not so fortunate. He was arrested in Leyden that summer and brought back to England, where Jeffreys, claiming him to be an outlaw, had him executed without trial.

Lord Howard sank into obscurity and lived the remainder of his life in fear of Philip's retribution.

The warder, Haggerty, received a mortal knife wound from an unknown assassin outside the Bulwark Gate of the Tower.

Giles prospered in France, using Monsieur's friendship to advantage, but he grew restless and, much against Philip's advice, he went to join Monmouth and the rebels in Rotterdam.

Philip's faithful servants were bound to him with an even deeper loyalty than before whilst he, for his part, was never to forget the debt he owed them.

Theresa had learned many things during the trying months since the discovery of the Rye House Plot, things which she had more sense than to ever let herself forget. Shaftesbury's ambition had very nearly brought about Philip's demise and Theresa vowed she would never again engage in any fight save to defend her husband, their family and their home.

The only person apparently unaffected by the events was Philip himself.

The prophesy concerning his death remained unfulfilled, and it could have been that he saw little purpose in reforming his ways since, ultimately, his end would be the same, but the more likely reason was simply that he could not change.

The experiences which had helped form his character, with all its strengths and weaknesses, had scarred him much too deeply. Until the day his fate finally overtook him Philip would stay exactly as he was – scheming, stubborn, cynical and brave.

It was the only way that he knew how to be.

ABOUT THE AUTHOR

Brought up in Lincolnshire, Judith Thomson studied Art in Leicester before moving to Sussex, where she still lives. She is passionate about the seventeenth century and has gained much inspiration from visits to Paris and Versailles. In her spare time she enjoys painting, scuba diving and boating. She is the author of the two 'Designs of a Gentleman' novels – 'The Early Years' and 'The Darker Years'.

Follow her on Judiththomsonblog.wordpress.com
and on Twitter @JudithThomson14

ALSO BY THE AUTHOR

Designs of a Gentleman: The Early Years

Designs of a Gentleman: The Darker Years